BORN TO BE KILLED

LOOK FOR THESE EXCITING WESTERN SERIES FROM BESTSELLING AUTHORS WILLIAM W. JOHNSTONE AND J.A. JOHNSTONE

The Mountain Man
Luke Jensen: Bounty Hunter
Brannigan's Land
The Jensen Brand
Smoke Jensen: The Early Years
Preacher and MacCallister
Fort Misery
The Fighting O'Neils
Perley Gates
MacCoole and Boone
Guns of the Vigilantes
Shotgun Johnny
The Chuckwagon Trail
The Jackals
The Slash and Pecos Westerns
The Texas Moonshiners
Stoneface Finnegan Westerns
Ben Savage: Saloon Ranger
The Buck Trammel Westerns
The Death and Texas Westerns
The Hunter Buchanon Westerns
Will Tanner: Deputy U.S. Marshal
Old Cowboys Never Die
Go West, Young Man

Published by Kensington Publishing Corp.

BORN TO BE KILLED

WILLIAM W. JOHNSTONE
and J.A. JOHNSTONE

PINNACLE BOOKS
Kensington Publishing Corp.
kensingtonbooks.com

PINNACLE BOOKS are published by

Kensington Publishing Corp.
900 Third Avenue
New York, NY 10022

PUBLISHER'S NOTE: Following the death of William W. Johnstone, the Johnstone family is working with a carefully selected writer to organize and complete Mr. Johnstone's outlines and many unfinished manuscripts to create additional novels in all of his series, like The Last Gunfighter, Mountain Man, and Eagles, among others. This novel was inspired by Mr. Johnstone's superb storytelling.

All Kensington titles, imprints, and distributed lines are available at special quantity discounts for bulk purchases for sales promotion, premiums, fundraising, and educational or institutional use.

Special book excerpts or customized printings can also be created to fit specific needs. For details, write or phone the office of the Kensington Sales Manager: Kensington Publishing Corp., 900 Third Avenue, New York, NY 10022. Attn. Sales Department. Phone: 1-800-221-2647.

First Kensington Books Hardcover Printing: January 2026
First Pinnacle Books Trade Paperback Printing: May 2026

ISBN: 978-0-7860-5173-1

ISBN: 978-1-4967-5280-2 (ebook)

10 9 8 7 6 5 4 3 2 1

Printed in the United States of America

The authorized representative in the EU for product safety and compliance
is eucomply OU, Parnu mnt 139b-14, Apt 123
Tallinn, Berlin 11317, hello@eucompliancepartner.com.

BORN TO BE KILLED

Chapter 1

The wagon train rolled into Big Rock a little before noon.

The vehicles, with their arched canvas covers over the beds, drew a considerable amount of attention as they entered the settlement from the south and turned onto the main street. Once, wagon trains had been a fairly common sight in these parts, but since the arrival of the railroad a year or so earlier, not many came through here anymore.

This group was unusual, too, in its size: only four wagons, each drawn by a team of six sturdy horses. In previous years, before the completion of the transcontinental railroad, when wagons had carried hundreds of thousands of immigrants on their westward trek, a typical wagon train had forty or fifty or even more wagons in it.

"Would you look at that?" Sally Jensen said as she stood on the front porch of the Big Rock Mercantile with her husband, "Smoke," who thumbed his hat back on his head and smiled.

"Yeah, it's been a while since we've seen a wagon train around here," he said. "I wonder where those pilgrims are headed."

"Maybe they plan to settle around here," Sally suggested.

"The valley is pretty big," Smoke said. "Still plenty of room for new folks."

That was true. Smoke and Sally's ranch, the Sugarloaf, was the largest in the area, and there were several other good-sized spreads in the region, too. Even so, good, unclaimed land was still there for the taking. Land with thick grass and good water, which would provide plenty of grazing for cattle.

However, the folks in this wagon train didn't appear to be cattlemen, Smoke noted.

In fact, with one exception, they weren't men at all.

This was a wagon train full of women.

The driver handling the reins of the first vehicle was in her midthirties, Smoke estimated. Even though she was sitting on the driver's bench, he could tell she was tall and had a splendid figure in a square-necked blue dress. Thick honey-colored hair was pulled together and tied at the back of her head.

The lone male in the group sat beside her, swaying back and forth slightly as the wagon rocked along. With his snowy hair and bushy white eyebrows, he appeared to be an older man. He wore a brown suit and a flat-crowned cream-colored hat, and even sported a vest and a cravat over his white shirt, not typical garb for somebody in a wagon train. A walking stick rested on the floorboards between his knees, and his knobby-knuckled hands were clasped on the stick's silver head.

"She's a very attractive woman, isn't she?" Sally asked.

"Who, the lady on the lead wagon?"

"Yes. The one you're looking at so intently."

Smoke chuckled. "I don't think I was looking any more intently at her than I was at the old fella riding beside her. I always pay attention to newcomers. Seems to me there's a resemblance between those two. Father and daughter, I'd say."

"Yes, I can see that," Sally agreed. "And I can't blame you for keeping up with strangers. You feel a certain responsibility to look after Big Rock, since it wouldn't be here without you."

Smoke's forehead creased a little in a frown at Sally's comment. She wasn't the first one to give him credit for Big Rock's existence, but such things didn't sit all that well with Smoke's natural modesty.

It was true that he'd played a major part in the founding of the town a couple of years earlier, but so had a lot of other people. Plenty of folks had risen up against the tyranny of Tilden Franklin and his army of gunmen when Franklin tried to take over the area, operating from the stronghold of the town he had established and called Fontana.

At the urging of Smoke and others, Big Rock had been founded as an alternative to Fontana. The honest citizens had abandoned Tilden's town, and Big Rock had flourished. Fontana was nothing but a memory now—a bad memory for most of those who had lived through that turbulent time.

Smoke's recollections of those days were bittersweet. Quite a few good people had died or been injured in the violence, and he had been forced to buckle on his gunbelts again after several years of having set his Colts aside. But he had new friends in men such as Wes "Pearlie" Fontaine, currently the foreman of the Sugarloaf, and Monte Carson, the sheriff of Big Rock. Both men had been brought to the valley by Tilden Franklin as hired guns, but they had seen the evil of what was going on and switched sides, becoming staunch allies of Smoke and the other good people of the valley.

All that was in the past. Big Rock had continued to grow, especially after the arrival of the railroad. Maybe these newcomers would add to the town's expansion, mused Smoke as he looked over the rest of the vehicles.

A plump blonde in her twenties was on the driver's seat of the second wagon. Her short hair framed a round, friendly face. A woman with dark brown hair handled the reins of the third wagon's team. The driver of the fourth and final wagon in the string was the youngest in the bunch, probably no more than eighteen, a coltish girl with long, wavy chestnut hair. All were dressed in plain, simple outfits intended to stand up to the rigors of long days on the trail.

Smoke saw a few more women looking out from the openings at the front and rear of the canvas covers on the wagons, but no men. The elderly gentleman on the lead wagon appeared to be the only man in the group. That was just downright odd.

So was the way he held his head aimed straight forward, never glancing to the left or right, even though his female companions all seemed interested in gazing about at their new surroundings. Smoke suddenly wondered if the man was blind. That would explain his apparent lack of interest.

"Where do you think they're going?" Sally asked.

"Probably out to that open area on the west side of town with the trees around it," Smoke said. "That's a mighty good place for wagons to camp. Pilgrims have stopped there before."

Sally nodded and said, "I'm sure you're right. I'll go on in and see if Mr. Baker has my order ready."

She had a standing order with Don Baker, the owner and proprietor of the mercantile, for the supplies they needed out at the ranch. Earlier this morning, she had driven the buckboard into town to pick up the provisions, while Smoke rode alongside on his big black stallion, Drifter.

She added, "I'll meet you at Louis's in a little while. We can have some coffee and a bit of lunch before we start back out to the ranch."

"Sounds good to me," Smoke said. He bent and brushed a quick, affectionate kiss across her forehead, under her thick dark hair. They smiled at each other and then parted, Sally turning to go into the store, while Smoke moved along the boardwalk at a deceptively lazy pace.

He might look like he was just loafing along, but in reality every sense was on alert and his instincts would let him know if there was even the slightest sign of potential trouble. His hands were never far from the walnut grips of the twin Colt .45 Peacemakers holstered on his hips. He had carried two guns for many years, switched to just one for a while, but recently had gone back to packing two irons in crossed gunbelts. He just felt more balanced out that way.

Smoke was a man of medium height, but incredible strength, and unusually wide shoulders. He had a ruggedly attractive face and a shock of ash-blond hair under his broad-brimmed brown hat. With the friendly, open grin he usually wore, he didn't really look like a dangerous man, but in reality he was, perhaps, the fastest man on the draw and the most deadly accurate with his guns west of the Mississippi—and east of the "Father of Waters," too, if you wanted to throw in the rest of the country.

He had been a lot of things in his short life: gunfighter, outlaw—although the charges laid against him by some of his enemies were false, lawman, gold miner, scout, horse trader, and rancher. In recent years, he had concentrated on establishing the Sugarloaf and building it up into a successful spread, and, most importantly, he had been married to the former Sally Reynolds and was building a life with her, too. It would be perfectly fine with Smoke if he never had to use his guns again.

But trouble seemed to have a way of finding him, and those instincts had stirred faintly inside him, in fact, as he watched that little wagon train roll past—although for the life of him, he didn't see how there could be any threat in a bunch of women and an old man traveling together.

CHAPTER 2

Annabelle Wilkinson was used to people staring at her and her companions. She knew they were an unusual sight, especially in these frontier towns where folks were desperate for anything unusual to break up the humdrum existence of day-to-day life.

Even so, she felt a prickling of annoyance go through her. It wasn't like they were a traveling circus or a blasted freak show. There was nothing out of the ordinary about them—at least, not on the surface.

"What did you say this place is called again?"

"Big Rock, Colonel. Big Rock, Colorado."

Beside her on the driver's seat, the old man grunted. "Named that because there's some outsized boulder somewhere in the area, I'll wager."

"More than likely," Annabelle agreed.

"Not very imaginative, these small-town folks."

She heard the tone of disdain in her father's voice. It was easy for him to look down on the simple farmers and ranchers, storekeepers and blacksmiths, saddlemakers and dressmakers, who were pushing ever westward and bringing civilization to this part of the country. He still remembered what it had been like to be the richest man in the country, back in Mississippi, the lord of all he surveyed and the man the common folks bowed and scraped to when he drove by in his fancy carriage.

Annabelle remembered those days, too. Remembered them well. But they were all blown to hell and gone now.

Now each day was a matter of survival, although with any luck things might not be that way forever.

"We're going to stop here, aren't we?"

"That's right, Colonel. We need supplies, and it probably wouldn't hurt to let the horses rest for a few days, either. We've been on the trail for a good long while and have been moving pretty steadily."

"Now, I don't know if that's a good idea or not." The old man's voice held a petulant tone. "We don't ever know if trouble could be coming up behind us."

"We've traveled a long way from home," Annabelle said. "If trouble was going to catch up with us, don't you think it would have by now?"

"You never know, child. You just never know."

Annabelle felt her face warming with anger. She was far from a child. Hadn't been one for a long, long time, in fact. But she supposed that to a parent, a child never completely grew up. In some ways, the colonel still felt responsible for her, even though, in truth, she had been the one taking care of him for quite some time.

"We'll get the supplies, stop overnight, and then figure out what to do in the morning," she told him. "Just resting for half a day might be enough to help the horses."

"I hope so, I truly do."

Annabelle suppressed the sigh of exasperation that tried to escape from her. It wouldn't do any good.

"I can see a place up ahead at the edge of town," she went on. "It looks like it would make a decent campsite for us."

"I trust your judgment, Annabelle. You always were a mighty smart little thing for a girl."

She laughed and shook her head. That was better than getting angry at him, which wouldn't accomplish anything. He'd just sull up like a possum and act like she was being unfair.

A group of riders was coming toward them in the street up ahead, she noted. Seven men on horseback. She had trained herself to pay attention to details and be a good judge of character, especially when it came to men.

She didn't have to look at these riders for very long to get the feeling that they might be trouble.

They were dressed roughly, like cowhands or prospectors, but most men in those lines of work weren't as heavily armed as this bunch. Each man wore at least one holstered revolver, and most of them had sheathed knives, too. Rifle butts stuck up from three or four saddle scabbards. A couple of the men had full beards, and the faces of the others hadn't felt the touch of a razor in several days. Their saddles had known a lot of hard use, and their horses looked tired, as if they had been on the trail for quite a while.

Most of the men rode with shoulders slumped and their eyes downcast. They looked as weary as their mounts.

Annabelle suddenly wondered if they were tired because someone had been chasing them.

The man riding in the lead, slightly ahead of the others, wasn't like that, though. His head was up and he was alert. Clearly, he had noticed the wagons full of women because he straightened in the saddle and watched them intently as the two groups approached each other.

The man was stocky and barrel-chested, with a beefy face that reminded Annabelle of a bulldog. Black stubble covered his cheeks and chin, and his hair was dark under a hat that looked like it might have belonged to a cavalryman at one time, before it got so battered and stained.

The hat was the only thing about his garb that was even vaguely military. He wore a dark brown vest over a faded gray shirt with the sleeves rolled up to reveal brawny forearms thickly covered with dark hair.

His face split in a grin as the two groups passed in the street. The man's front teeth had a noticeable gap between them, which didn't improve his looks. He reached up and ticked a finger against the sagging brim of his hat as he nodded to Annabelle.

She didn't acknowledge the gesture, just continued staring straight ahead as she flicked the reins of the team.

The other riders had noticed the wagons by now. The rough-looking men perked up considerably at the sight of the women. Several of them grinned and rode straighter. A few low-voiced comments were exchanged. Annabelle couldn't make out what they were saying, but she didn't have to understand the words to know that they were probably lewd and suggestive. At least, the men didn't call out any crude comments to her or her companions as they went by.

She was glad when the men were past, plodding on along the street to wherever they were bound. They were trouble, she was sure of that.

The kind of trouble that she, her father, and her friends absolutely didn't need right now.

Gus Gerhardt reined his horse toward one of the hitch rails in front of the first saloon he came to after he and his friends rode into Big Rock. The front window was a little grimy and the paint was already starting to peel from the sign on the awning over the boardwalk. The sign proclaimed THE EMPIRE SALOON, even though the building probably wasn't more than a year or two old.

Gerhardt didn't need anything fancy, just somewhere that served beer and whiskey. If poker games and loose women were available, too, then so much the better.

Now that he thought about it, he didn't care that much

about the poker. After taking a good long look at that high-toned blonde on the wagon, his appetite for female companionship was whetted.

"Did you see that, Gus?" Danny Murphy asked excitedly as he brought his horse alongside Gerhardt's at the hitch rail.

"See what?" Gerhardt responded, even though he knew perfectly well what Murphy was talking about.

"Those women! A whole wagon train full of pretty women!"

Gerhardt swung down from the saddle and looped his horse's reins around the railing. He chuckled as he said, "Say, I must'a missed that."

"No, you didn't," Murphy said as he followed suit and dismounted. "I saw the way you was lookin' at that gal handlin' the lead wagon. She was sure a looker. A mite old, maybe, but still fine, sure enough."

Murphy was a kid, a pugnacious redheaded Irish sprout, otherwise he wouldn't have considered that blonde old. Gerhardt was pushing forty, and she'd seemed like just the right age to him. He supposed Murphy was more interested in the girl driving the final wagon in line, who'd looked like little more than a kid herself.

Lean, dark-faced J.D. Styles and rawboned Abner Farnum dismounted and tied their horses at the same hitch rail. Stan Hamilton, Al Townsend, and "Concho" Warren put their mounts at the other rail in front of the saloon.

Styles looked like what he was, a former gambler who had given it up because his hands, while fine for pulling a gun, weren't quite deft enough to manipulate the pasteboards with the skill necessary to make a living that way.

Farnum, on the other hand, looked like he was right off the farm, but, in truth, he had never spent even a minute behind a plow. He liked to boast that he'd been on the wrong side of the law ever since he'd learned to walk.

Hamilton and Townsend were both the sort of fellows that

you could look at, and five minutes later you wouldn't remember enough about them to describe them. In their line of work, being forgettable didn't hurt a thing.

Warren was a Texan, dubbed Concho because he came from around the river of the same name. He looked like a 'breed, but none of the others knew for sure, one way or the other, because he was touchy about that and they didn't see any reason to get him on the prod.

The seven of them together were a pretty salty bunch. They had been over in Utah recently and had gotten crossways with some Danite hard cases. Those Mormons were tough as nails, and since you couldn't go much of anywhere in Utah without running into more of them, Gerhardt decided it would be a smart move to light a shuck out of there.

They had headed east into Colorado, and now they had come to this good-looking settlement. Gerhardt didn't know the name of the place, but it looked big and prosperous enough to have a bank, so that was promising, anyway.

"Are you thinking about pulling a job here, Gus?" Styles asked quietly as the men stepped up onto the boardwalk in front of the saloon.

"I don't know yet," Gerhardt answered honestly. "It's something to think about, but there's no need for us to get into any hurry."

"I want a drink before we do anything else," Warren said.

"My thoughts exactly," Styles agreed.

Gerhardt entered the saloon first, pushing through the batwings and advancing a couple of steps so the other men would have room to come in behind him.

Then he stopped to take a gander around the place and size it up for any possible threats.

The Empire Saloon looked like hundreds of other such drinking establishments scattered across the frontier, from the Rio Grande to the Milk River. A thin layer of sawdust was spread on the floor to soak up anything that was spilled on it, from beer to blood and everything in between. The bar was on the left-hand side of the room, running from near the front window most of the way to the back wall. At its far end was a door that probably led into an office. Wooden tables and chairs were laid out in rough rows in the center of the room, along with a couple of slightly larger, baize-covered tables toward the back for poker games. A roulette wheel and a keno layout, neither in use at the moment, stood on the right side of the room. Near the front window on that side was a piano, also not being used.

Only one of the regular tables was occupied. Three men in town clothes sat around it, discussing something and sipping whiskey from glasses they had filled from a bottle in the center of the table.

A man in a gray tweed suit sat alone at a poker table, dealing himself a hand of solitaire. A fancy stickpin glittered in his cravat. He was lean to the point of gauntness. His drooping mustache and a short spike beard gave his face a satanic cast. He looked up with interest when Gerhardt and the others entered the saloon.

Four younger men, cowhands by the look of them and their outfits, stood at the bar nursing mugs of beer, while a bald-headed bartender ambled back and forth, aimlessly polishing a glass with a rag. They glanced around at the newcomers, but didn't seem all that interested in them.

The Devil-looking gent looked down at the cards on the table and studied the hand he'd dealt. Then he made a face and swept the cards back into the deck, which he tapped square and left lying on the table as he stood up.

"Welcome to the Empire, gentlemen," he greeted Gerhardt and the others. "Come on in and have a drink."

Chapter 3

Longmont's was several different things: saloon, restaurant, gambling hall, and the home of another of Smoke's best friends, the former hired gunman Louis Longmont. Snake-fast and almost as deadly as Smoke, he had put those dangerous, adventurous, drifting days behind him and settled down here in Big Rock.

Lean and dapper, he spent most of his time sitting at his personal table in the back of the room, sipping endless cups of coffee, reading, and occasionally venturing to one of the other tables to play a low-stakes game of poker with friends. His real profession these days, he had been known to say, was avoiding trouble.

That was the reason for the slight creasing of his forehead when he spied Smoke Jensen coming across the room toward him.

Smoke grinned and said, "Why, Louis, you look like you aren't happy to see me."

"It's not that, Smoke. You're always welcome here, and you know it. But when you walked in just now, I realized that it's been quite a while since any trouble broke out around you."

Smoke pulled out an empty chair at the table and sat down. He signaled to the bartender for a cup of coffee, like the one Louis was drinking, and then went on, "You make it sound like I'm some kind of lodestone for ruckuses."

"Well, when you consider your history . . ." Louis lifted his cup toward Smoke in a small salute.

"You've burned quite a bit of powder in your time, too, you know." Smoke nodded to the aproned man who set a cup in front of him. "Thanks, Barney."

"I've never denied my colorful past," Louis said. "And yet most of my days and nights pass peacefully now."

"Mine did, too, for a while. You know, before Tilden Franklin showed up in the valley, I'd gone three years without ever touching a gun in anger."

"And yet since that trouble and the founding of Big Rock, violence has erupted on several occasions. Not only that, but any time circumstances have taken you elsewhere, you've run into one calamity after another in those places, so it's not just Big Rock."

"Well, shoot," Smoke said as he leaned back in his chair. "Put that way, you make it sound like I'm nothing but a blasted jinx."

Louis smiled over his coffee cup. "You said it, my friend, not me."

Smoke scowled and sat forward again. He wrapped his hands around his cup and asked, "What do you reckon I can do about it?"

"Honestly, at this point it seems that the universe is in the habit of dumping trouble in your lap. I'm not sure you can do anything about it other than deal with the problems as they arise." Louis took another sip of his coffee and went on, "Let's move on to a more pleasant subject. What brings you to Big Rock today?"

"Sally."

"See? A much more pleasant subject. I assume you accompanied her on her weekly trip into town to pick up supplies?"

"That's right. She said she'd meet me here later, once she'd taken care of business over at the mercantile."

"I'll be pleased to see her, as always." Louis put his hand on a book that was sitting on the table and pushed it toward Smoke. "Have you seen this? The new novel by Henry James."

A dubious look appeared on Smoke's face. He didn't reach for the volume. Instead, he said, "I remember that other book of his you recommended to me. It was kind of like a herd of buffalo."

Louis looked puzzled and said, "Henry James is like what?"

"Here's what I mean. You've been out on the plains hunting buffalo, right?"

"I have."

"When you come on a herd that's on the move, you can sit on a hill and watch them go past, and the herd stretches all the way as far as you can see in all directions, and it can be like that all day without ever stopping, just so many buffalo the mind can't really grasp how many there are."

Louis nodded. "Yes, I understand what you're talking about, but I still don't see how it has anything to do with Henry James."

Smoke grinned and said, "He's got as many words as there are buffalo in one of those herds, and they just keep on streaming past you until you're just overwhelmed by all of them."

Louis just stared at him for a moment and then laughed. "I suppose that's a valid criticism," he said. "James can be a bit verbose. But I admire his skill at characterization. You don't want to borrow this volume, I take it?"

"I'll pass," Smoke said, "but I'm obliged to you for thinking of me."

The two of them continued to chat and sip their coffee. Smoke wasn't really aware of how much time had passed until he realized that Sally should have finished her chore at the mercantile and joined them by now.

The same thought must have occurred to Louis. "I believe you said Sally was coming by here when she was done at the general store?"

"That's right," Smoke said. "I hope she hasn't run into any

problems." He drank the bit of coffee that was left in his cup and then set it on the table as he pushed back his chair. "I suppose I ought to go and take a look. I'll probably see her on the street heading in this direction."

"No doubt," Louis said.

As Smoke started toward the door, though, Louis's earlier comments came back to him. Trouble did seem to have a way of finding him, no matter how peaceable he tried to be—and sometimes he worried about that tendency spreading to those around him, including Sally. *Especially* Sally.

It was a good thing she knew how to take care of herself.

Sally had stayed inside the Big Rock Mercantile longer than she had intended. Several of her friends from church and social circles were also in the store, and after dealing with Don Baker, the owner, and being assured that her order would be ready to pick up in an hour or so, she got to talking with the other ladies and catching up on all the news in town. That was not gossiping, Sally told herself firmly; it was staying informed about her friends and acquaintances and other things that were important to her.

Eventually, she realized that Smoke might be wondering where she was, so she said friendly goodbyes to the ladies and stepped out the store's front door onto the high porch, which also served as its loading dock.

She almost ran smack-dab into a woman who was coming in. Both women stopped short just outside the door, facing each other at close range.

Instantly, Sally recognized the woman with whom she'd almost collided. She was the attractive blonde who had been driving the lead wagon in the group of vehicles that had rolled past earlier.

"Oh, I'm sorry," Sally said. "I should have been watching where I was going."

The woman smiled. "No need to apologize. I was equally at fault. Anyway, there's no harm done, is there?"

"None at all," Sally replied with a shake of her head. "And by the way, welcome to Big Rock. I saw you and your friends drive in earlier. My name is Sally Jensen."

"Annabelle Wilkinson," the blonde introduced herself.

"It's a pleasure to meet you, Mrs. Wilkinson. Or is it Miss?"

"I'm not married," Annabelle said, still smiling. Sally thought her lips tightened just a bit as she responded, though.

"The older gentleman on the wagon with you . . . ?"

"My father," Annabelle explained. "Colonel Jasper Wilkinson."

"He's very distinguished-looking. The name suits him."

That brought what sounded like a genuine chuckle from Annabelle. "The colonel would be very pleased to hear that an attractive young woman found him distinguished. I don't believe I'll tell him, though. He might get a swelled head. Do you live here in Big Rock, Mrs. Jensen?" She paused, then asked the same question Sally had. "Or is it Miss?"

Sally held up her left hand with the wedding band on the third finger. "Definitely Mrs. And no, I don't live here in town. My husband and I have a ranch several miles west of here. We came into town this morning to pick up some supplies."

"I was just on my way to see about doing the same thing. I walked down here to place an order we can pick up later. It was nice to meet you, Mrs. Jensen."

Annabelle was about to step around Sally to go inside the store, but impulse, along with curiosity, prompted Sally to continue the conversation.

"Did you and your friends camp just west of town? Smoke said that's a good place for wagon trains to stop."

"Smoke is your husband?"

"That's right."

"Interesting name," Annabelle commented, but she didn't

seem to recognize it. Many people out here on the frontier had heard of Smoke Jensen, of course, but not all. And since Annabelle and the others were newcomers, it was no surprise that Smoke's name meant nothing to her.

"Yes, that's where we camped," she went on. "It looked like other wagon trains have stopped there before."

"Yes, quite a few of them came through here before the railroad arrived. Your wagons are the first we've seen in a while, though."

"We have our reasons for traveling by wagon," Annabelle said, even though Sally hadn't asked that question.

"Of course," Sally replied quickly. She didn't want the other woman to think she was prying, so she added, "I hope you enjoy your stay in Big Rock."

"We're not settling here, if that's what you're wondering. We'll just stop for the night, maybe a few more, depending on how the horses are doing."

"Well, that's fine." Sally smiled. "Good luck on your journey."

Annabelle frowned and shook her head. "I sounded a little sharp there, didn't I? I'm sorry, Mrs. Jensen. I meant no offense." She summoned up a return smile. "I suppose I'm a little more wary than I should be. When you're a group of women traveling alone, you learn to be very careful and watch out for trouble."

"I understand," Sally assured her. "What with your father being the only man in the group—"

"And he's not any real help, bless his heart," the blonde interrupted her. "He's blind. He lost his sight when he was wounded during the war. He's very stubborn and proud—that's why he insists on still being called Colonel—but he can't do much anymore."

"Oh, I'm sorry to hear that. But he's lucky to have a devoted daughter to take care of him. Are the other ladies in your party related to you?"

Annabelle shook her head again. “No, as far as family goes, it’s just the colonel and me. The others are all good friends.”

“I didn’t mean to be so nosy. I’ll let you get on with your business now.”

“It’s all right, Mrs. Jensen, really. Honestly, receiving such a friendly welcome means a great deal to me. Not everyone has been so happy to see us whenever we roll into a new town.”

“Well, I don’t see why anybody would feel like that!”

Annabelle shrugged. “I guess some folks just aren’t very friendly to outsiders.”

“Big Rock isn’t a very old town. It wasn’t so long ago that everybody here was an outsider.”

Sally didn’t go into the history of the settlement, but she yielded to an impulse and linked her arm with Annabelle’s. The other woman looked surprised, but didn’t pull away.

“I’ll come with you and introduce you to Mr. Baker, the owner of the mercantile,” Sally went on. “He’ll make sure that you and your friends get fixed up with whatever you need.”

CHAPTER 4

The man who had greeted Gus Gerhardt and his companions seemed friendly enough. As he waved them toward the bar, he went on in a deep, cultured voice, "My name is Andrew Rickett. This is my establishment."

Gerhardt looked over his shoulder at his companions and then leaned his head toward the bar. They followed as he started in that direction.

The four young cowboys were lined up about midway along the bar. Because of that, there wasn't room for the newcomers to stand together. As he approached the punchers, Gerhardt said, "You boys, move one way or the other."

The closest of the youngsters turned with a scowl on his face and snapped, "We're just standin' here mindin' our own business, mister. No reason for us to go anywhere."

"You got the best reason in the world, kid. I told you to move. You'd damned well better do it."

The cowboy's face flushed with anger. He didn't appear to have had that much to drink, so liquor couldn't be blamed for his reaction. It was just the pure, cussed, hot temper of youth. His hand started to move toward the gun holstered on his hip.

His friend on the other side of him moved faster. He threw his arms around the cowboy, stopping the draw before the youngster could reach his gun. As he pulled the angry cowboy back a step, the man who had intervened said, "Hold on there, Chuck! You don't want to do that."

"Lemme go, Fred! This old fella's runnin' his mouth, and I'm gonna shut it!"

Gerhardt's open hand came up and cracked across Chuck's face, jerking his head to the side.

"You're the one whose mouth is too loose, kid," he grated. "Maybe that'll tighten it up a mite."

For a moment, the slightly older cowboy called Fred looked like he was about to let go of his friend and start a ruckus himself. The other two cowboys stiffened and stepped away from the bar, readying themselves for trouble.

Gerhardt's companions tensed as well. The odds were on their side, and they had a lot more experience with trouble, too. Anybody could tell that just by looking at them. If gunplay broke out, some of them might be hit, but all four of the young punchers would die.

"Gentlemen, gentlemen!" That exhortation came from Andrew Rickett, who stepped closer to the confrontation with his hands raised in a conciliatory gesture. "Please, there's no need for trouble. Fred, take Chuck and your friends and get out of here."

"We ain't the ones who started it," Fred protested.

"Perhaps not, but you're the ones who are getting a couple of bottles of free whiskey the next time you come in, provided you leave now."

The punchers hesitated. They were mad and were being treated unfairly and knew it, but free whiskey was nothing to sneeze at on forty-a-month-and-found wages.

Tightening his grip on Chuck again, Fred started steering the young cowboy toward the batwings. He called over his shoulder to the other two, "Come on, boys."

Clearly, Chuck wanted to struggle to get loose, but awareness of his close call was beginning to penetrate the red haze over his brain. He could have gotten killed. Now he put up a little fight to save face, but allowed Fred to maneuver him out of the saloon. The others followed.

The feeling of violence about to erupt eased in the room. It evaporated completely as Andrew Rickett called, "Delia, Susie, you two girls, get out here!"

A grin stretched across Danny Murphy's young freckled face.

"Hear that, fellas?" he said. "Girls!"

The door at the end of the bar opened. Two young women, both yawning, came out into the barroom. The one in the lead had long, straight red hair and wore a green dress with a tight, low-cut bosom and a ruffled skirt. The second girl was a little shorter, but just as lithe and well-curved in a similarly styled dark blue dress. Her hair was midnight black, framing her olive-skinned face and brushing her shoulders.

Their sleepy attitudes vanished instantly as they spotted the strangers standing at the bar. Bright smiles that almost seemed genuine appeared on their faces. As they moved toward Gerhardt and his men, the redhead said, "Well, hello there, boys. New in town, aren't you?"

Danny Murphy snatched off his hat, held it over his heart, and looked a little abashed as he said, "We sure are, ma'am. It's a mighty big pleasure to meet you."

"Ladies, keep our guests company," Rickett told them. "We want them to feel welcome in the Empire Saloon."

"We'd be happy to, Mr. Rickett," the brunette said. As if she had realized that Gerhardt was the leader of the group, she moved straight to his side, gave him an even more dazzling smile, and said, "My name's Delia."

Gerhardt grunted. "They call me Gus." He was too old to be overly impressed by some saloon floozie, although he had to admit Delia was mighty pretty. But he wasn't taken in by her friendly attitude. This was just business to both of these girls.

Which didn't mean he was immune to their charms. He went on, "Let me buy you a drink."

"Why, of course," she responded. "I'd be flattered."

The redhead linked arms with Murphy and turned him toward the bar. "I'm Susie," she told him. "What's your name?"

"Uh, Danny. Danny Murphy."

"We make a fine Irish pair, don't we, Danny?"

"I'll say we do! Let's get some drinks!"

The other men wore tolerant expressions on their faces. Seven men and two girls made for numbers that didn't match up very well, but if they were patient, their time would come. That was the way these things worked.

Within minutes, Gerhardt had bought a bottle and suggested that they all adjourn to one of the tables. The three townies who had been drinking and talking earlier had left, so Gerhardt and his companions were the only customers now. They passed around the bottle and filled glasses, but Delia and Susie had drinks they brought from the bar. Tea, more than likely, Gerhardt knew, even though he had paid for whiskey.

Andrew Rickett ambled over to the table and said, "If any of you gentlemen would be interested in a few hands of cards, I assure you I run a clean game here at the Empire. You can be certain of a fair, even break."

"Maybe later," Gerhardt said. He wanted to sit for a spell, sip some whiskey, and talk to these girls.

Bartenders and barbers generally knew more than anyone else about what was really going on in a town, but saloon girls heard plenty, too. Gerhardt wanted to get an idea just how prosperous Big Rock was, because that would give him an idea of how much money might be down the street in that bank vault.

He wanted to know, too, what sort of law they had around here.

By the time Sally helped Annabelle Wilkinson finish her shopping in the Big Rock Mercantile, the two women were friends. Sally sensed that Annabelle had a streak of loneliness inside her, probably a result of the responsibility she carried on her shoulders. From comments Annabelle had made, Sally gathered that to start with, she had organized the wagon train, taken over the leadership of it, and had her blind father to care for as well. It was a lot of weight to carry, Sally thought.

That put her in mind of something else. She said to the store's proprietor, "You've already had my supplies loaded on the buckboard, haven't you, Mr. Baker?"

"That's right," Baker replied.

"Would you say there's room for Miss Wilkinson's supplies in there as well?"

"Wait a minute, Sally," Annabelle said. They had progressed to the use of first names fairly quickly. "You don't have to do that."

"It's no trouble," Sally assured her. "And if I don't take those things out to your campsite, you'll have to fetch one of the wagons back for them, won't you? It'll be much easier for you this way."

Baker said, "That's a fine idea, Mrs. Jensen, and yeah, there ought to be plenty of room in your buckboard. I'll have a couple of clerks load the boxes and bags in there in just a few more minutes, as soon as we've got everything gathered up."

Sally smiled and thanked him, then said to Annabelle, "We can go wait by the buckboard. It's a nice day."

"That sounds fine to me," Annabelle agreed.

They left the store and went down the steps at the end of the porch. Sally led the way to the buckboard, which was parked in front of the store. Before they could climb to the seat, a man walked up to them and greeted them by saying, "Hello, Sally. Where's Smoke today?"

Sally turned and smiled at the ruggedly handsome, well-built man with a lawman's star pinned to his vest. "He's around town somewhere," she said. "Probably still shooting the breeze with Louis."

Sheriff Monte Carson grinned. "I haven't heard any gunfire this morning, so I reckon it's safe to assume he's not shooting anything else. Leastways, I sure hope so." He chuckled. "The peace does have a way of getting disturbed sometimes when Smoke is around. Not that it's his fault, mind you. He goes out of his way to avoid trouble."

"But it can be persistent," Sally said.

Monte laughed again. "It sure can." He looked at Annabelle, nodded, and reached up to pinch the brim of his hat. "Howdy, ma'am. Don't believe I've seen you around Big Rock before."

"My friends and I just got here, Sheriff," she said. Sally could have been wrong, but she thought she saw a brief flare of something in Annabelle's eyes as the blonde spoke to Monte. Nervousness, maybe, as if she didn't like talking to a lawman.

Then Sally remembered Annabelle's earlier comment about not being greeted in a very friendly fashion in some of the other towns they had passed through. That still didn't make a lot of sense to Sally, but if it was true, that would account for a certain wariness on Annabelle's part where the law was concerned.

Hoping to put her at ease, Sally said, "Monte, this is Miss Annabelle Wilkinson. She's with the wagon train that just came through town. Annabelle, meet Sheriff Monte Carson."

"Hello, Sheriff," Annabelle said with a nod.

Monte reached up again and actually took his hat off this time. "It's a pleasure to meet you, ma'am," he said. "Do you plan to settle here in Big Rock?"

"No, my friends and I are just passing through."

She didn't offer any details about where the wagons were bound for. That was a little odd, thought Sally, but really none of her business.

"Well, for however long you're here, I hope you enjoy your stay. If there's anything I can help you with, please don't hesitate to let me know." Monte half turned and pointed along the street. "The sheriff's office is right down yonder. If I'm not around, one of my deputies ought to know where to find me."

"Thank you, Sheriff. I'll keep that in mind."

Monte put his hat back on, nodded, and smiled again, then said, "Good morning, ladies," before walking on along the street.

"He seems like a nice man," Annabelle commented once the sheriff was out of earshot. She seemed less uneasy about the situation now, probably figuring that Monte wouldn't cause any trouble for her and her companions, as long as they didn't break any laws.

"One of the best," Sally agreed. "He does a fine job of keeping the peace here in town. He and Smoke are good friends."

She didn't mention that Monte had once been a hired gun. He had put that part of his life behind him.

Two clerks from the mercantile emerged from the store and loaded several small crates and bags of flour, sugar, and salt into the back of the buckboard. Don Baker followed them and called to Annabelle, "Obliged to you for the business, ma'am."

"Thank you for your help, Mr. Baker," she said.

After Sally untied the reins attached to the horses, the two women climbed onto the buckboard's seat. Annabelle had no trouble pulling herself onto the vehicle, Sally noted. She was used to climbing up and down from the wagon, which was taller and more of a challenge.

Sally took up the reins and got the team moving. She turned them in the street so that the buckboard was rolling toward the settlement's west side. Even from here, she could see the wagons parked under the distant trees.

She was looking toward them as the buckboard rolled past the Empire Saloon and didn't even glance toward the place.

CHAPTER 5

When Gus Gerhardt had taken a seat at the table in the Empire Saloon, he had made sure the only thing behind him was a blank wall, no doors where a would-be killer could sneak in or windows through which a bushwhacker could target him. Such precautions were just common sense for a man who lived on the edge of trouble.

He had also made sure that Delia was sitting on his left, where she wouldn't interfere with his draw if he had to pull his iron. She had pushed her chair so close to his that her hip nudged warmly against him. When she leaned toward him, he felt the soft pressure of her right breast.

The Empire had a false front, he recalled, and no second story, but Gerhardt figured that the door at the end of the bar didn't lead to an office, as he had first supposed, but rather to rooms where the girls plied their real business. Delia was rubbing against him enough that she was having a considerable effect on him. He considered taking her back there to ease some of the tension from a long ride on a lonely trail.

Then movement caught his eye through the grimy glass of the front window, and he sat up straighter in his chair as a buckboard rolled past in the street outside.

The woman handling the reins was mighty pretty, with thick

waves of dark hair around a strikingly attractive face. But the woman beside her on the driver's seat was the one who really caught Gerhardt's attention. She was the blonde he had seen earlier, handling the lead wagon in that little caravan headed in the other direction on the main street.

Gerhardt had gotten a good look at her as they passed, and the impact she'd had on him felt almost like a punch in his ample gut.

Sometimes a woman had that effect on a man. One look at her was enough to tell him that he wanted her. Wanted her bad, and would do whatever it took to get her. Gerhardt had experienced that sensation only a few times in his life, but today had been one of them.

He had looked at that blonde and known that he had to have her.

And now there she was again, going by outside. That had to be a sign, Gerhardt told himself.

"Gus, honey, why don't we—" Delia was saying.

Gerhardt interrupted her by shoving his chair back. Delia had been leaning enough weight against him that his sudden motion unbalanced her and almost made her fall off her chair. She caught herself and stared at him as he stood up.

"What the hell?" she said. "Gus, what are you—"

He ignored her and started around the table.

Danny Murphy had been giggling and talking with the redhead called Susie. More than likely, some playing around had been going on under the table. But he looked up at Gerhardt, too, and said, "Gus, is something wrong?"

"Nothing wrong," Gerhardt said. "Just something I've got to do."

Murphy looked puzzled. So did the other men, who had been sitting around the table nursing glasses of whiskey and talking quietly. None of them moved as Gerhardt walked to the door, shoved through the batwings, and disappeared outside.

"Well, I never!" Delia said, clearly offended by Gerhardt's abrupt, unfeeling dismissal.

Murphy looked at the others and said, "Fellas, you reckon we ought to go after him?"

"He didn't ask us to come with him," Styles said. He shrugged. "I don't know what's going on, but it's Gus's business, not ours."

Abner Farnum frowned and leaned forward. "You think that's true?" he asked. "What if Gus decided to pull a job without us?"

"I think you'd better be careful what you say," Styles snapped.

Farnum snorted. "I ain't worried about these tramps."

Susie sniffed and said, "Well, you're certainly no gentleman, mister."

Since she had taken offense, Murphy felt like he had to stand up for her. "That's right, Abner. There's no call to start insulting these ladies."

"You can call 'em ladies all you want," Farnum responded with a sneer. "That don't change the fact they're soiled doves."

Murphy's jaw tightened belligerently. "You take that back," he demanded.

Farnum ignored him and pushed back his own chair. "I'm gonna see what Gus is up to," he said as he stood up.

Concho Warren got to his feet as well. "That might not be a bad idea."

Hamilton and Townsend stood up, too. Murphy glanced at Styles, who shrugged again.

"He might need our help," Styles said simply.

Murphy could see there was no point in arguing. As Styles got up, so did he. He put a hand under Susie's chin, tilted her head back, and leaned down to kiss her. When he straightened, he said, "You stay right there, sweetheart, and don't go off with any cowpuncher who happens to wander in. I'll be back."

He followed the others through the batwings onto the saloon's porch. They were looking around, searching for Gerhardt. Warren lifted a hand to point and said, "There."

Gerhardt was walking west along the street, back in the direction they had come from. He'd reached the edge of town and appeared to be heading for the covered wagons that had parked underneath some trees a short distance farther on.

Murphy, Styles, and the others went after him, having no idea what Gerhardt had in mind, but figuring it might be a good idea to be on hand if anything happened.

The women had unhitched and picketed the wagon teams by the time Sally and Annabelle drove up in the buckboard. The ones who weren't busy with other chores looked curiously at the vehicle. Annabelle's father, Colonel Wilkinson, sat on a crate and aimed his sightless eyes straight ahead.

He turned his head slightly at the sound of footsteps as Annabelle and Sally approached him after climbing down from the buckboard. Annabelle said, "Colonel, I've brought a new friend with me."

Wilkinson had both hands resting on the head of his walking stick. He leaned on it as he got to his feet.

"This is Mrs. Sally Jensen," Annabelle went on. "We met at the store, and she kindly offered to bring our supplies out here on her buckboard."

"I thought I heard another team come up," the colonel said. His left hand remained on the walking stick, but he extended his right in Sally's general direction. "Mrs. Jensen, it's a great pleasure to meet you, and I very much appreciate you coming to my daughter's aid that way."

Sally clasped his hand in both of hers and said, "I'm pleased to meet you as well, Colonel Wilkinson. On behalf of everyone here in Big Rock and in the Sugarloaf valley, let me welcome you and your daughter and the other members of your party. I hope your stay here in the area is a good one."

"Oh, I'm sure it will be," the colonel murmured. "We won't be staying long, however. We must be getting on to Wyoming."

"That's your destination?" Sally asked. Annabelle hadn't said anything about where they were going. Perhaps she had waited to see how much her father wanted to reveal about their plans.

"Indeed," he replied. "A place called Brimstone Butte. I gather that's both a settlement and the nearby geographic feature for which it was named. Have you heard of it?"

Without thinking, Sally shook her head. She could see Wilkinson's eyes; unlike some blind men, he didn't wear smoked glasses. They were pale blue and appeared normal, except that they never focused on anything. She wondered what had happened to cause him to lose his sight, but she wasn't going to be rude enough to ask that question.

"No, I'm afraid I haven't heard of it," she said. "I've been to Wyoming several times, but not there, I suppose."

She waited to see if Wilkinson would explain why the wagon train was headed for Wyoming, but no more details were forthcoming from the man. Then there was an interruption as Annabelle said, "Who is that, and what in the world could he want?"

Sally turned her head and saw a man approaching the clearing where the wagons were parked. He strode along with a firm resolve in his step that said this was his destination and nothing would turn him aside from it. He was a stranger to Sally, a stocky, beard-stubbled man with dark hair, well-worn range clothes, and a gun on his hip.

Having been married to Smoke for a while, she had learned how to spot trouble. This was a good example of it marching straight toward them.

The other women had seen the stranger, too, and clustered together nervously. Sally studied them briefly. They were all younger than Annabelle. With one exception, they appeared to be in their twenties. The one who wasn't that age was probably eighteen or nineteen, Sally estimated, a very pretty young woman with long chestnut hair.

All of them, in fact, were attractive, which was a bit unusual, but Sally didn't have time to think about that. The stranger had reached them. He nodded curtly and said, "Howdy."

Then, belatedly, as if he'd just realized he ought to be more polite, he took his hat off, nodded again, and said, "I mean, hello, ma'am."

It was clear he was speaking directly to Annabelle and equally clear that he had eyes only for her. He had glanced at the other women as he approached and looked at Sally and the colonel as well, but now all his attention was focused on Annabelle.

Stiffly, with a cool edge in her voice, Annabelle asked, "What can I do for you, sir?"

The man didn't answer her directly. He said, "My name is Gus Gerhardt."

"What exactly do you want, Mr. Gerhardt?"

"Well, ma'am . . . I want you."

Annabelle stared at him in disbelief. Sally was surprised, but not shocked, at the blunt nature of the man's response. Gerhardt had the look of a hard case about him. Sally could tell he was a crude, rough man by nature who had a habit of taking whatever he wanted—or at least trying to, anyway.

Colonel Wilkinson's face flushed with anger, which made his white mustache and eyebrows stand out even more. "Sir, how dare you speak that way to my daughter!" he berated. "You'll apologize to her right this instant, and then you'll go away and leave us alone."

"I'm not going anywhere," Gerhardt said. "Not until I've got what I'm after." He addressed Annabelle again. "Ma'am, as soon as I laid eyes on you, I felt like somebody had walloped me over the head with a fence pole. I even tipped my hat to you. You didn't seem to notice, but I knew in my gut that the two of us were meant to be together."

"Your gut is wrong," Annabelle snapped. "You should leave, Mr. Gerhardt. I'm not interested in anything else you have to say."

"Come with me," Gerhardt insisted. "Let me buy you a meal. You'll see what I'm really like. I may be a mite rough around the edges, but I mean what I say, and I'm sure taken with you."

Annabelle shook her head. "I'm not going anywhere with you."

The other women had been edging closer so they could hear what was being said. When Sally glanced toward them, she looked beyond them, too, back along the street.

Six other men were now headed this way. They looked as rough and dangerous as Gerhardt. A drifting band of ruffians, Sally thought. They might even be a gang of outlaws.

She wished Smoke had been here, but at the same time, she had always had a great deal of confidence in her own ability to take care of herself and anyone else who needed standing up for. She said in a calm, level voice, "Mr. Gerhardt, I really do believe you should leave now and stop annoying this lady."

"I'm not talking to you." Gerhardt switched his gaze to her briefly. "Who are you, anyway?"

"I'm Miss Wilkinson's friend. My name is Sally Jensen." She paused for a second. "My husband is Smoke Jensen."

She saw a flicker of recognition in Gerhardt's eyes. A mention that she was married to Smoke was usually enough to make anyone who was bothering her think twice about it and back off. But although Gerhardt evidently had heard of Smoke, he wasn't impressed enough to take that as a warning.

"I don't care if you're married to Wyatt Earp," Gerhardt said. "The lady's coming with me."

And as if he intended to drag her along the street, he reached out quickly and took hold of Annabelle's upper left arm in a tight, painful grip.

Chapter 6

Annabelle gasped. She looked more shocked than hurt, even though Gerhardt's cruel grasp had to be uncomfortable. She tried to pull away from him and said, "Let go of me."

Instead of releasing her, Gerhardt's fingers just dug in more tightly as he said, "Look, the last thing I want to do is hurt you—"

"Then let me go!"

Gerhardt continued to speak, as if he hadn't heard her. "But I know the two of us are meant to be together, and until I make you understand that, I'll have to hang on to you. I can't have you getting away from me."

Furiously, Colonel Wilkinson shook his walking stick at Gerhardt and said, "Leave my daughter alone, you . . . you animal! I don't have to be able to see you to know what kind of man you are. I can hear it in your voice!"

"Back away, old man. I don't want to hurt anybody."

Wilkinson lifted the stick higher and looked like he was about to start flailing away with it. That had to be his first impulse, to strike out in defense of his loved one.

But he hesitated, clearly not wanting to hit Annabelle and hurt her.

The other women started toward the confrontation, their

expressions a mixture of fear and anger. They didn't want trouble, Sally knew, but they weren't going to stand by and let this stranger drag their friend away, either. They outnumbered Gerhardt by a lot.

But as Sally watched, Gerhardt's companions began trotting toward them. Their arrival would change the odds completely.

This had gone on long enough, she decided. Too long, in fact. She slipped a hand into a pocket on her dress and closed her fingers around the inlaid ivory grips of the over-and-under .41 caliber derringer she carried there. She was seldom without the little gun. It wasn't very accurate beyond a few feet, but up close like this, it packed a pretty potent punch.

She figured Gus Gerhardt would back off if he found himself staring down the derringer's barrels.

Before Sally could pull the gun, Annabelle took action of her own. She produced a knife from somewhere—the movement was so swift and smooth, Sally was unable to see where Annabelle got the weapon—and raked the blade's point across the back of the hand holding her arm. Gerhardt yelled in pain and jerked his hand back.

"What did you do that for?" he shouted. "I wasn't trying to hurt you!"

"I won't be manhandled!" Annabelle snapped back at him. She raised the knife and brandished it in front of her. "Now get out of here or I'll cut you again!"

Gerhardt stared for a second at the thin line of crimson across the back of his hand. The wound wasn't bleeding much, but it must have hurt. His already-beefy face turned an even darker red with rage.

"Annabelle!" Colonel Wilkinson exclaimed worriedly. "Annabelle, are you all right?"

Before Annabelle had a chance to answer, the two groups converging on the scene came together. One of the men, a big, rawboned individual who looked like a farmer in overalls and a floppy-brimmed hat, blocked the path of the women, held up his arms, and said, "You gals, just stay back. This is between our pard and that stuck-up she-devil."

The short, chubby blonde who was in the forefront of the women pushed herself up against him and yelled, "Get out of our way, mister, or we'll trample right over you!"

Cursing, the man in overalls grabbed her by the shoulders and shoved her away. As he did that, one of the other women leaped forward and swung a piece of firewood from the stack they had gathered earlier. It cracked against the man's head, knocked off his hat, and sent him staggering backward.

Before she could press her attack and strike again with the branch, a man dressed like a gambler sprang forward, grabbed it, and wrenched it out of her hand. As he started to toss it aside, she punched him in the face.

With that, the melee was on. The rest of the women attacked—clawing, scratching, and punching. The men, somewhat to their credit, didn't respond in kind, but reacted more by trying to defend themselves, warding off the blows and attempting to grab the women and subdue them. The knot of struggling figures lurched from side to side.

"What's going on? Annabelle? What's going on?" Colonel Wilkinson shouted as he twisted back and forth in agitation. As Gus Gerhardt, ignoring the threat of the knife, lunged at Annabelle again in another effort to grab her, Wilkinson's wildly flailing walking stick went between his shins and tripped him. Gerhardt waved his arms and tried to catch his balance, but he toppled forward, with a yell, onto the ground.

Unfortunately, on the way down one of his blindly grasping hands latched on to Annabelle's left arm, and he pulled her down with him. She hit the ground hard enough that she lost her hold on the knife. It slid away from her in the dirt.

She tried to retrieve the blade, but as Gerhardt saw what she was doing, he threw himself on her and held her back. They rolled over, struggling. Annabelle got a hand on his face and raked her fingernails over it, leaving bloody scratches on his cheeks. He bellowed curses, pushed himself up on one hand, and slapped her with the other.

Sally had drawn the derringer from her pocket, but hadn't tried to use it, because with the way everybody was mixed up together, the risk of hitting Annabelle or one of the other women was too great.

But in the process of striking Annabelle, Gerhardt had put a little separation between them, and Sally thought she might be able to wing him now. She drew a bead on his left shoulder, but hesitated, still unwilling to trust the little gun's accuracy.

The next instant, a shot crashed, but it didn't come from Sally's derringer.

An angry shout caught Smoke's attention just as he stepped out of Longmont's. He looked west along the street, toward the trees at the edge of town, where the wagons that had rolled into Big Rock earlier were now parked.

Another vehicle was parked there, too, Smoke saw, and he recognized it instantly. It was the Sugarloaf Ranch buckboard that Sally had driven to the settlement earlier. Smoke had no idea what it was doing with those covered wagons, but if it was there, Sally likely was, too; and sure enough, as his legs carried him in that direction, he spotted her a second later, standing with the blonde who'd been driving the lead wagon.

They were confronting a man who looked angry—Smoke judged from his tense stance—and a group of other men and the women from the wagon train were coming together nearby. Smoke knew trouble brewing when he saw it. He broke into a run toward the wagons.

The situation deteriorated rapidly as Smoke approached. The men and women began fighting, an out-of-control ruckus with a lot of lurching around and yelling.

The blonde and the stocky man who had accosted her were on the ground now, rolling around and wrestling. Sally stood nearby; she held the derringer she often carried. She raised the little gun, but didn't fire.

One of the men involved in the brawl shoved the woman he was tangled up with off her feet. He must have spotted Sally holding the derringer and believed she was about to shoot the man on the ground, because he grabbed a revolver from the holster on his hip and started to raise it.

That potential threat to Sally was more than enough to make Smoke take action. He skidded to an abrupt halt, and by the time he'd stopped moving, his Colt was in his hand. The draw was a blur of flashing movement. He didn't seem to take aim, but rather just snapped a shot at the man about fifty feet in front of him.

In reality, the shot wasn't rushed at all. Smoke's eyesight was so keen, his muscles so well-trained, his nerves so swift, that his bullet was as accurate as if he'd stood there drawing a bead for a full minute before he squeezed the trigger. As the Colt blasted, the slug tore through the flesh on the outside of the man's left thigh and spun him off his feet. The gun in his hand exploded as he fell, but the shot sailed off harmlessly into the sky.

The roar of Smoke's Colt made everyone freeze. Some of the other men looked over their shoulders and seemed like they wanted to turn and slap leather themselves, but Smoke's gun was already leveled and the hammer was eared back under his thumb, ready to fall again. None of them moved.

Sally stepped closer to the man and woman on the ground and aimed the derringer at the man's face. "Get away from her," she ordered in a clear, steady voice, which Smoke had no trouble hearing in the sudden quiet that had fallen.

"The rest of you men step back," Smoke said. The barrel of his Colt moved slightly to indicate the direction he wanted them to go. With obvious reluctance and resentment, they complied, although one of them, a young man with a freckled face and red hair, said, "You shot J.D.!"

"He looked like he was about to shoot my wife," Smoke replied coolly. "If any of the rest of you make any threatening moves, I'll drill you, too." He added, "You, Red, you can check on him."

The young man hurried to the side of the one Smoke had wounded and knelt to see how badly he was hurt.

A familiar voice called, "Coming up behind you, Smoke." Sheriff Monte Carson knew better than to startle his old friend, especially when Smoke was holding a gun. Monte had his own Colt in his hand as he moved up alongside Smoke and asked, "What's going on here?"

"I'm not sure," Smoke replied, "but I'd appreciate it if you'd keep an eye on those hombres, Monte, so I can make sure Sally's all right."

Monte covered the strangers as he said, "Go ahead. I've got these boys."

Smoke didn't pouch his iron as he circled around the wounded man and the redhead, who had helped him sit up. He saw the look of relief on Sally's face as he walked up to her.

"Are you all right?" he asked quietly.

"I'm fine," she answered. "Was that man about to shoot me, Smoke?"

"He looked like he might have it in mind. I didn't want to take a chance on him going through with it."

"Thank you." She smiled. "I should have known you'd show up just in time."

She slipped the derringer back into her pocket, clearly confident that she no longer needed it, now that Smoke was here. Stepping forward, she reached down to help the blonde—disheveled and dirty, but no less attractive for it—to her feet.

"Are you all right, Annabelle?" Sally asked.

Before Annabelle could answer, the white-mustached old-timer asked pathetically, "Won't somebody please tell me what's going on? Is my daughter hurt?"

Annabelle put her hand on his shoulder, causing him to jump slightly. "I'm not hurt, Colonel," she told him. "Not really. Just shaken up a little."

"That . . . that scoundrel! What did he call himself? Gerhardt? Is he still here? I heard a shot. Did somebody shoot him down? He had it coming!"

The stocky man picked up the hat that had fallen off his head and climbed to his feet. The back of his hand was bloody from what looked like a minor knife wound. Slapping the hat against his thigh, he said to Annabelle, "You shouldn't have treated me like that. I never meant you any harm."

"You didn't have a right to come in here and bother us," she said. "You should have left when we asked."

He glared and shook his head. "You made a mistake," he said. He turned to Smoke and added, "And so did you, mister. You had no call to shoot one of my friends."

"He looked like he was about to shoot my wife," Smoke said coldly. "He's lucky I just winged him and didn't kill him."

"Mighty lucky," Monte Carson put in. "In case you didn't know it, that's Smoke Jensen you're talking to."

"I know it," the man called Gerhardt snapped. "I just don't give a damn."

He put his hat on and turned away.

"Am I under arrest, Sheriff?" he asked Monte.

"I reckon not, as long as you and your pards get out of town and don't bother these folks anymore."

"My man's wounded."

The redheaded youngster put in, "J.D. needs to have a doc look at him, Gus."

Monte said, "I'll show you where the doctor's office is. When you're finished there, you can all mount up and get out of Big Rock."

"What law did we break?" Gerhardt demanded.

"Disturbing the peace, for one thing. Assaulting these ladies, for another. I can guarantee that if you hang around here, you're going to wind up behind bars, maybe for a good long while."

"We'll go," Gerhardt responded sullenly. "Danny, you and Concho help J.D. up. Come on, let's get him to that sawbones."

With a lot of scowls and muttered curses, the hard cases took their leave. Monte followed them, still with his gun drawn.

Smoke figured it was safe to holster his Colt. When he had done that, Sally said, "Smoke, meet Miss Annabelle Wilkinson, and this is her father, Colonel Jasper Wilkinson."

Smoke pinched the brim of his hat as he nodded to Annabelle and said, "It's a pleasure, ma'am. Wish we'd met under less hectic circumstances."

Annabelle had been straightening her clothes, brushing some of the dust off, and patting her honey-colored hair back into place. She smiled at Smoke and said, "I'm pleased to meet you as well, Mr. Jensen. Thank you for your help."

"If I'd gotten here a little sooner, maybe the trouble wouldn't have broken out, to start with. Although that Gerhardt fella seemed mighty determined to stir up a ruckus."

Colonel Wilkinson put out his hand and said, "I'm obliged to you, too, son. I regret to say I can no longer take care of my little girl the way I wish I could."

Wilkinson was blind, just as Smoke had speculated while looking at him on the wagon. He clasped the colonel's hand in a firm grip and said, "Don't mention it, sir. Around here, folks help each other out anytime we can. That's just the way we do things in these parts."

"Did you serve in the Late Unpleasantness, Mr. Jensen, if I may ask?"

"No, sir, I was just a tad young for that. My father and brother both served the Confederacy."

And Emmett and Luke Jensen had both given their lives for

it, too: Emmett indirectly when he set out to track down some traitors after the war, but Smoke didn't see any need to go into that.

"It's nearing midday, isn't it, Annabelle?" Wilkinson asked.

"That's right, Colonel."

The old man smiled. "Well, then, I have a splendid idea. Mr. and Mrs. Jensen, why don't the two of you eat dinner with us? I'd enjoy talking more with you."

Annabelle said, "Now, Colonel, Sally and Smoke may have plans of their own. Sally told me they own a ranch west of here, and I'm sure there are things that need tending to."

"And we have an excellent foreman to tend to them," Sally said as she smiled. She linked arms with Smoke. "We don't want to intrude, but if it wouldn't be too much trouble, we'd be happy to stay for dinner. Wouldn't we, Smoke?"

"As long as it's not too much trouble, like Sally said." Generally, he was willing to go along with whatever she wanted, as long as it didn't put her in danger.

"In fact, I'd be happy to help prepare the meal," Sally added. "I'm not a bad cook, if I do say so myself."

Annabelle chuckled and shook her head. "You brought the supplies out here in your buckboard," she said. "It's only fair that you get to share in them. But don't worry about helping with the preparations. We have a couple of excellent cooks traveling with us. I'll just tell them to make enough for some guests, too."

"It's settled, then," Colonel Wilkinson enthused. "Splendid!"

CHAPTER 7

What Annabelle said about having good cooks in the group proved to be true. Within the hour, Smoke and Sally were enjoying some surprisingly tender steaks, potatoes, vegetables, and biscuits—light and fluffy enough to have come from a fine restaurant—all washed down with cups of excellent coffee.

Furniture was loaded in some of the wagons, but since the travelers didn't know how long they would be staying in Big Rock, they and their guests made do with crates for seats around the campfire.

As they ate, Colonel Wilkinson said, "I'm sure you're curious about our little expedition, Mr. and Mrs. Jensen."

"Call me Smoke."

"And I'm Sally," she added.

"I reckon we're curious, all right," Smoke allowed, "but we're not in the habit of sticking our noses in other folks' business, either."

Annabelle said, "I'm not sure you need to be boring our guests with a bunch of talk about the past, Colonel."

"Nonsense," Wilkinson replied. "Smoke just said they're curious. As you've undoubtedly already gathered, my friends, we're from the South."

Smoke chuckled and said, "Yeah, we figured that, Colonel, from how you talk."

"I would never deny my Mississippi heritage. The Wilkinson family settled along the Tombigbee River, long before we threw out the blasted British redcoats. Of course, little did we know then that someday we'd have to deal with the accursed Yankee bluecoats, too, but that's an entirely different story."

"One that it might be best not to go into," Annabelle warned. "You know what we said when we decided to come out here, Colonel. We would put the war and all its unpleasant memories behind us."

Wilkinson sighed. "Easy to say, my dear, but sometimes not so easy to do." He nodded. "But you're right, of course. There's no point in dwelling on the past." He turned his head toward Smoke again. "You've probably also guessed, Smoke, that I served in the Confederate forces. Rose to the rank of colonel. In those days, I still had my sight. I didn't lose it until I was wounded in battle. A Yankee rifle ball struck me in the head."

He raised his hand in a vague gesture, as if about to touch his temple where the rifle ball struck him, but he stopped before he did so.

"The wound bled so much that my men believed at first I was dead," Wilkinson continued. "However, they carried me to a field hospital, where our gallant doctors attended to my injury. In time, I recovered, but when I finally regained consciousness, I could no longer see. My sight never returned to me."

"I'm sorry, Colonel. That's a mighty rough thing to happen to a man."

Wilkinson waved a hand and said, "Indeed, it is, but still a definite improvement over dying!"

"I imagine so."

"The war ended that day for me, of course, and as a matter of fact, the hostilities were soon over for everyone else when General Lee surrendered at Appomattox. I returned home to the family plantation to discover that my dear wife had passed on while I was away."

Annabelle stood up, apparently distraught at having to hear her father rehash this terrible period of her life. She walked off. Sally looked at Smoke, who nodded in agreement with what he could tell his wife was feeling. Sally went after Annabelle, caught up to her near the wagon, and the two women stood there talking quietly to each other.

"Annabelle just walked off, didn't she?" Wilkinson asked quietly.

"I'm afraid so."

"I didn't mean to upset the poor girl. Naturally, she took everything that happened in those days very hard. It was a difficult time."

"I know it was," Smoke said. "You really don't have to talk about it, Colonel."

"I know, but somehow I sense a certain kinship between us, Smoke. You said that you lost loved ones to the war?"

"I said that my father and brother served. My father came back."

"But your brother didn't?"

"No," Smoke said. "Luke didn't. Sometimes I think that maybe something happened, that he's still out there alive somewhere, but it's been so long without a single word that I can't summon up any hope for him."

Wilkinson reached out, fumbled a bit, but managed to pat Smoke's knee. "Never give up hope, son. Even if it never comes true, it gives us something to cling to, and that can be mighty important sometimes." The colonel cleared his throat. "What about your father?"

"He's passed on, too. It was after the war was over, but still connected to it, if that makes any sense."

"Of course, it does. The impacts of that terrible war were far-reaching. They still echo today."

The two men sat in silence for a moment, then Wilkinson

went on, "I sense that you've suffered other losses, too, not just in the war."

Smoke thought about Nicole, his first wife, and their infant son, Arthur, both brutally murdered by hired killers working for his enemies. He nodded, remembered that Wilkinson couldn't see him, and said, "That's true, Colonel. But I'd just as soon not speak of them."

"Of course, of course." Wilkinson paused and a solemn moment passed between the two men before he went on, "To be honest with you, my boy, it's a real pleasure to speak with another gentleman. I love my daughter, of course—and the other ladies in our little group are splendid people, just splendid—but I spent most of my life in the company of other men and I miss that. Along with that kinship I mentioned, it's the main reason I'm enjoying talking to you. But if you get bored by an old man's ramblings, don't hesitate to say so."

Smoke took a sip from the coffee cup he held and said, "I'm fine, Colonel, and more than happy to listen to anything you want to tell me."

"I appreciate that. You and your wife came to our aid today, and I'd like for you to know who you were helping out." The colonel clasped both hands on the head of his walking stick, which was planted on the ground between his knees. "I'm sure I don't have to tell you what the South was like after the war."

"Pretty bad, from everything I've heard."

"The damned Yankees came in and took almost everything," Wilkinson said with bitter anger in his voice. "If it wasn't the soldiers, it was the politicians, and if it wasn't the politicians, it was the carpetbaggers. They wound up taking our family home away from us. Cast us out like rootless vagabonds, they did. In my condition, I could do nothing to help us make ends meet. Fortunately, Annabelle is the enterprising sort and a tireless worker. She took in washing, did sewing, made fancy dresses for those high-toned carpetbaggers' wives who came down from the North and bulled their way into our homes and tried to live with the same genteel elegance we true Southerners have always possessed. It was a sham, of course, a mere sham. Those Yankees, men and women alike, were crude and crass and could never be anything other than that way. It was their nature."

Smoke sipped his coffee again and kept his mouth shut. He didn't have any more use for carpetbaggers than the colonel did, but there had been no "genteel elegance" to be found on the hardscrabble Jensen farm in the Missouri Ozarks. Only hard work and not much reward. He and the colonel might both be Southerners, but in all but the most basic ways, they came from two different worlds.

Wilkinson lowered his voice more and said, "The ladies you see around you have their own tragic stories, Smoke. They are all widows and orphans, cast adrift by the misfortunes of war. That's why they became friends and banded together, helping each other whenever they could. And then at last, after those long, terrible years of hardship, a stroke of good luck came along for a change."

"What was that, Colonel?" Smoke asked.

"A man in Wyoming died."

Smoke said, "I think you're going to have to explain that one to me, sir."

"Years ago, a distant cousin of mine named Albert Lowe left Mississippi and went west to seek his fortune. He claimed the climate in the South never suited him. In all truthfulness, the air can be rather oppressive along the Tombigbee at certain times of the year. At any rate, Cousin Albert wound up in Wyoming and established a ranch there in an area recently opened up for settlement. Evidently, his efforts were quite successful and the ranch is now a lucrative operation."

Smoke's keen mind made the next leap in Wilkinson's story. "And this cousin of yours is the fella who died?"

"That's right. He had no other relatives, so a lawyer in the nearby town of Brimstone Butte tracked me down and sent me a letter informing me that I had inherited Albert's ranch. It's called the Three Cross, I believe, although I'm not sure why he chose that as his brand."

"So you and Annabelle are on your way up there to claim that inheritance?"

"Precisely." A smile appeared on the colonel's weathered face. "The Three Cross is going to be our salvation, Smoke. A fresh start for all of us, not only Annabelle and myself, but for our friends as well."

"You mean the ladies are going to help you run the ranch?"

"That's right." Wilkinson frowned. "Do I hear a certain dubious tone in your voice?"

"Well, Colonel, running a ranch is a lot of work, especially if you don't have any experience doing that."

"Naturally, but these ladies are very determined. Also, I'm sure Albert had men working for him, and when Annabelle read the lawyer's letter to me, I gathered that they were going to stay on and help keep things going, at least for a while."

"Most cowboys will ride for the brand as long as they don't have a good reason not to," Smoke agreed. "If the spread has a good crew, that'll be a big help to you."

"We'll make the effort succeed," Wilkinson said with firm resolve in his voice. "At this point, none of us can afford not to." He chuckled. "Any bridges that lay behind us are long since burned, I'm afraid."

"Sometimes that's all you can do," Smoke said.

Sally and Annabelle walked back over to them. Annabelle asked, "Have you talked Mr. Jensen's ear off enough with all your old war stories, Colonel?"

Wilkinson lifted his chin and said, "We didn't really talk that much about the war. Instead, I explained our pilgrimage to Smoke and told him about the ranch in Wyoming."

Annabelle's lips tightened. "I thought we agreed not to go around talking about that until we got there."

"Smoke has proven that he's trustworthy," Wilkinson insisted. "Didn't both he and his lovely wife come to our aid in a time of need? Besides, I can hear it in the man's voice. Are you going to tell me that I'm not a good judge of character, my dear? After the leadership I demonstrated during the war?"

Annabelle looked at him for a moment, and it was almost as if they were trading stares. Maybe the connection between them was so strong that it didn't matter if Wilkinson couldn't actually see her. Then Annabelle smiled.

"All right, Colonel, I suppose I can't fuss at you too much," she said. "After all, I did the same thing. I told Sally where we're going, and what we're doing, because I trust her."

"And I think it's admirable, Colonel Wilkinson," Sally said. "You had some terrible luck, but you're doing everything you can to improve your lot in life."

"We've had our share of good fortune as well, Mrs. Jensen. The surgeon in that battlefield hospital said I would have died, had that rifle ball been a fraction of an inch more accurate. And today, of course, it was a stroke of luck indeed when you and Annabelle met, to say nothing of the moment when Smoke arrived to run off those troublemakers."

"We were glad to help, weren't we, Smoke?"

"Sure," he said. "If there's anything else we can do for you while you're in these parts, Colonel, I hope you'll let us know. The same goes for you, Miss Wilkinson, and all the other ladies as well."

"Thank you, Mr. Jensen," Annabelle said. "I'm sure we'll be fine. After everything that happened a little while ago, I don't believe that man Gerhardt and those other ruffians will bother us anymore."

Smoke nodded and smiled, but he wasn't as convinced as Annabelle claimed to be. Gus Gerhardt had seemed like the kind of man to hold a grudge. The whole bunch struck Smoke as being disgruntled and angry, and their hostility would be even worse, since he had wounded one of them. It would be easier for them to take out their resentment on these pilgrims than it would be to come after him.

If he could manage it, before he and Sally left Big Rock, he would have a word with Monte Carson and ask the lawman to keep an eye on the Wilkinson party. Monte wouldn't let anything happen while they were here.

But once they left the settlement, they would be on their own again, Smoke thought, and that was a troubling prospect.

CHAPTER 8

With Danny Murphy helping him, and a couple of the other men holding the batwing doors open, J.D. Styles thumped into the Empire Saloon on a pair of crutches.

The doctor had cleaned and bandaged the wound in Styles's leg and advised that he stay there to recuperate for a few days in one of the spare rooms he used for patients who required continuing care. According to the sawbones, Styles needed, at the very least, to get a hotel room and hole up for a few days, staying in bed as much of the time as possible. It was imperative that he didn't try to ride for at least a week.

Hearing that, Gus Gerhardt had said harshly, "You can forget about that, Doc. We're not going to be around this backwater town for that long. Can't he get around with some crutches?"

"I suppose," the doctor admitted, "if you want to risk that leg not healing properly."

"That'll have to do."

Styles hadn't put up any argument. The idea of being flat on his back in bed for an extended period of time didn't appeal to him, either—unless maybe one of those girls from the saloon was around to keep him company.

So he had borrowed the pair of crutches from the sawbones

and then he and the others had come back here to the saloon. Gerhardt was the last member of the group to enter the barroom. His florid face was set in an angry scowl as he followed the others to the same table where they had been sitting before.

The saturnine Andrew Rickett came over from the bar and greeted them.

"I heard gunshots earlier, not long after you left," the saloon owner said. "I assume you gentlemen were involved in that altercation?"

"Mighty observant of you," Styles responded with an edge in his voice. "I got a bullet through the leg from a man named Jensen. That's why I'm on crutches, if you didn't happen to notice."

Rickett ignored the angry sarcasm and said, "Smoke Jensen is the one who shot you?"

"Yeah, the famous Smoke Jensen. Isn't he supposed to be some sort of notorious gunman?"

"From everything I've heard about Jensen since I've been here in Big Rock, you're lucky he didn't kill you. If he wounded you in the leg, that's exactly what he intended to do." Rickett glanced at Gerhardt's hand, which had a bandage and some plaster tape on the back of it. The doctor had tended to that wound as well. "What happened to you?"

Gerhardt grunted. "Hellcat got me with her claw. But she's going to be sorry she didn't give me a chance."

"Too bad," Rickett said with a shrug. "Do you want another bottle?"

Danny Murphy asked, "Can you get those two gals to bring it over and sit with us again?"

Rickett smiled. "I think I can manage that."

Susie Beale and Delia Tracy were in Susie's room, sitting on the bed while playing cards. The room was narrow and furnished only with the bed, a single chair, and a washstand. The floor was bare; no rug graced the planks. Since a wardrobe would have taken up too much room, the few dresses and other garments Susie owned hung from nails driven into the wall. Delia's room next door was identical.

Across the hall were the rooms where the other two girls who worked at the Empire lived. Mattie and Cora were their names, although they called themselves "Fancy" and "Desiree."

Susie and Delia were a little unusual among saloon girls in that they used their real names. Delia was exotic enough that it sounded good. The other two had tried to talk Susie into calling herself "Flame," on account of her red hair, but she had refused. If Susie was good enough for her mama to call her, it was good enough for her to stick with, she insisted.

Besides, she was young and pretty and fresh enough that it didn't really matter what name she used. The customers flocked to her, anyway. Mattie and Cora resented both of the other women because they were younger and better-looking.

The older women spent most of their time during the day sleeping. They would wake up around dusk. The saloon's owner, Mr. Rickett, had started talking about replacing them and letting Susie and Delia work at night, which was more profitable. He didn't say anything while Mattie and Cora were around to hear it, though. He didn't want a mutiny on his hands before he was ready to make the move.

The little room's door was partially open. They dimly heard male voices coming from the saloon's main room. Delia gathered up the cards and squared them into the deck.

"Sounds like customers," she commented. "We'd better get out there. If we don't, Rickett will be calling us soon enough."

Susie stood up, smoothed her dress, and took a deep breath, steeling herself to go out into the barroom, play up to the men, and earn her living.

It wasn't that she hated it so much. Mr. Rickett wasn't a bad boss, and most of the customers were at least tolerable. That young man she'd been talking to earlier—Danny was his name, she recalled—had actually been nice in a boisterous way.

It was just that Susie hadn't been at this profession for all that long. Even though she and Delia were the same age, within a few months, the dark-haired girl had been on her own a lot longer and that had toughened her up. Susie was glad she'd had Delia around to show her the ropes.

They walked into the main room a moment later and Susie felt a little thrill go through her as she saw that the group of men who'd been here before had returned. Danny looked up from the table, where they were sitting, and grinned when he spotted her.

Mr. Rickett said, "Get a bottle and glasses and bring them over here, girls."

Delia got the bottle from the bartender and picked up some of the glasses he placed on the hardwood. Susie gathered up the rest of them. They joined the men at the table.

Delia headed for the man she had picked out as the leader of the group, but he pointed to the one in a dark suit who had a pair of crutches leaning against the table beside his chair.

"J.D.'s the one who's hurt," the leader said. "He can use your attention more now than I can. Besides, I'm not in the mood to be fussed over."

"Well, I am," Danny said. He turned on his chair and patted his knee. "Come over here and sit down and keep me company, Susie."

"Oh, pshaw," she told him with a smile as she leaned over to place the glasses on the table. "I can't do that. It would be uncomfortable, not to mention indecent. You get me a chair if you want me to sit with you, honey."

Danny didn't argue. He just sprang to his feet and dragged over a chair from one of the empty tables. One of the other men placed a chair next to the wounded man for Delia. She poured drinks for all the men.

"Aren't you drinking?" the man called J.D. asked as Delia sat down beside him.

"No, there'll be more for you and your friends if Susie and I don't drink," Delia said. "Besides, just visiting with you gentlemen is enough to keep us entertained." She put a hand on his shoulder and went on, "What in the world happened to you, honey?"

"I got shot by Smoke Jensen."

"Oh! I've heard of him. He's famous around here."

"He's a damn bully if you ask me," the leader said. "Stuck his nose in where it wasn't needed. All I wanted to do was talk to that woman with the wagon train."

"There's a wagon train in town?" Susie asked.

"They made camp just west of the settlement," Danny said. "From what I saw, the lady Gus was talking about is the wagon boss."

"Wait a minute," Delia said. "A woman is in charge of a wagon train?"

"As far as I could tell, they're all women," Danny said, "except for that old blind Colonel Wilkinson. I think the blond woman is his daughter Annabelle."

Delia leaned forward to look past J.D. at Danny. "There's an old blind man with them?"

"Yeah. He's got white hair and a mustache and bushy eyebrows." Danny gestured vaguely toward his forehead. "I heard somebody call him Colonel, but he wasn't wearing a uniform or anything. He was dressed more like plantation owners I've seen in New Orleans."

Susie asked, "How do you know he's blind?"

"Well, I don't reckon I know for sure," Danny admitted, "but he sure was acting like he couldn't see anything. And he had a walking stick that he kind of felt his way around with."

"A blind colonel," Delia said slowly. "What did the woman look like?"

"What business is it of yours?" Gus asked.

Delia shrugged and shook her head in apparent unconcern. "No business. I'm just curious, that's all. It's not every day you run into a woman who's the boss of a wagon train."

"She has hair the color of honey," Gus said. "And she's the prettiest woman I've ever laid eyes on."

"Probably in her thirties?"

"That's right." Gus frowned at Delia. "How'd you know that?"

"I didn't," she replied. "It was just a guess. I mean, if she's in charge of an entire wagon train, she couldn't be all that young."

One of the other men, the one who looked like a farmer, said, "It's not that much of a wagon train. Only four wagons." He scowled. "Women got no right to take off on their own like that, actin' like they're just as good as men."

"Did they say where they're going?" Delia asked.

"Not that I heard," Danny told her, and a few of the other men shook their heads to indicate that they didn't know, either. "What does it matter?"

"It doesn't," Delia said.

Susie wasn't sure her friend was telling the truth, though. Delia seemed awfully interested in this whole affair.

But if there was something more to it, she could find out later, Susie told herself. For now, she squeezed Danny's arm and smiled at him and hoped she could stay with him for a while instead of being forced to go with any of the other men.

Susie didn't get a chance to satisfy her curiosity until late that evening.

Several of the men in the group had drunk themselves into stupors, including J.D. Styles, the wounded man. With that fresh bullet hole in his leg, he had declared that he was in no shape to fully appreciate Delia's charms. Gus Gerhardt was still mooning over the woman with the wagon train, so that left Abner Farnum, the one who looked like a farmer; Concho Warren, who, to Susie's eyes, resembled some of the Indians she had seen over in Kansas; and the other two, who, she thought, were called Townsend and Hamilton, although she had no idea which was which. Delia played up to Concho Warren, and the other men respected her choice with grudging acceptance. Apparently, none of them wanted to cross Warren.

As for Susie, she stayed as close to Danny Murphy as she could.

The residual tension eased when Mattie and Cora appeared late in the afternoon and soon paired off with Farnum and one of the others, either Hamilton or Townsend. Over the course of the evening, a few more bottles of rotgut were consumed, and all the men—except for Gerhardt and Styles—got to take one of the women to the back rooms.

Susie went only with Danny, and it was nice enough, as she had hoped it would be, if nothing special. But at least he was gentle and appreciative, which most men weren't.

Finally, the men left the saloon in search of a late supper and a place to spend the night. A few of the regular customers had drifted in by then, but Mattie and Cora were able to take care of them.

Delia, who seemed to have something on her mind, caught Susie's eye and beckoned for her to follow. They went to Susie's room, as they usually did because Susie habitually kept it a little neater.

As soon as the door was closed behind them, Susie said, "Is there something wrong, Delia? You've seemed preoccupied all evening. Ever since this afternoon, in fact, when those men started talking about that wagon train."

Instead of answering her directly, Delia asked a question of her own. "Susie, how would you like to get out of here?"

"You mean go somewhere else? I don't know where it would be. Besides, I'm tired. I figured I'd go to bed and get some sleep."

"I'm not talking about going somewhere tonight. I mean getting out of Big Rock permanently."

"I don't know," Susie said. She was really confused now. "It's not such a bad town, and Mr. Rickett is a good boss."

"You say that because you don't know him. You've never really crossed him. I've known men like him before. If you ever get on their bad side, they're mean as hell. You've heard the way he talks about Mattie and Cora just because they're getting old."

"He pays them. He's got a right to expect them to work."

"And they don't bring in as much money for him to take a cut of as they used to." Delia put her hands on Susie's shoulders. "That's us someday, honey. And in this line of work, you can't really say how long it's going to be before that day comes along. You don't want to stay a doxie your whole life, do you?"

Susie made a face and pulled away. "I don't like that word."

"The truth doesn't care if you like it or not. It's still the truth."

"Well, then, no, I never figured I'd keep on doing this the rest of my life. But it really hasn't been that long—"

"Not for you."

Susie knew her friend was right. Delia had had a rougher time of it. If she believed there was a chance they could leave it all behind, Susie ought to at least hear her out.

"What do you think we should do?"

"I don't know where that wagon train is going," Delia said, "but when it leaves Big Rock, I think you and I should be with it."

CHAPTER 9

On their way back out to the Sugarloaf, Sally carried on an animated conversation with Smoke about the events that had occurred in town.

"I never heard of a woman being in charge of a wagon train, did you?" Sally asked.

Smoke shook his head as he rocked along easily on Drifter beside the buckboard.

"I've met a few wagon masters in my time," he said, "but never one who wore skirts."

"Or one as pretty as Annabelle."

Smoke grinned. "You said that, not me. I'm an old married man. I'm not allowed to talk about how pretty other women are—or even think about it."

"Nonsense," Sally said. "It's just a statement of fact. And while you are definitely a married man, you're not old, and I know good and well you have the same sort of thoughts that every other man in the world does."

He laughed. "I won't argue with you."

"What do you think about their plan to start a ranch?"

Smoke grew more serious as he said, "I think there's a good chance they're going to run into trouble."

"You don't believe they can do it because they're women?"

"I believe it's going to be rough for them because they're inexperienced. From the sound of the story they told, Annabelle grew up on a plantation, so she at least knows something about how a spread operates, but to be honest, a cotton plantation in Mississippi is mighty different from a cattle ranch in Wyoming. The problems they'll face aren't the same at all. But, if we're being honest, the fact that they're female won't help any, that's for sure. Some men just don't cotton to taking orders from a woman. What kind of foreman she has, assuming that there still is one on the spread, will make a big difference."

"A foreman who's willing to work with Annabelle, in other words."

"That's right. If he respects her and doesn't have a problem carrying out her orders, that attitude will go a long way toward spreading out among the rest of the crew. At the same time, she has to be able to trust him and feel confident that he's acting in her best interests. The group's best interests, I should say, since they're all supposed to be in this deal together."

"You make it sound like it's going to be quite a challenge," Sally said.

"I don't see how it could be anything else," Smoke told her.

They drove and rode in silence for a few moments, when Sally said, "They've made it this far, but I have a feeling that the hardest part of the journey may still be ahead of them."

"Could be," Smoke allowed. "Lots of rugged country between here and Wyoming Territory. I don't know where Brimstone Butte is. They may still have a long way to go once they cross the line out of Colorado. At least, the Indians have been fairly peaceful lately. Plenty of other potential problems they might run into, though."

"That's what I thought," Sally said.

She sounded to Smoke as if something else was on her mind, but he didn't press her about it. When she wanted to talk about it, she would.

And he would listen to what she had to say and give it fair consideration, as he always did.

The next morning at breakfast, Sally announced, "I'm going back to Big Rock today."

"Forget something at the mercantile?" Smoke asked as he picked up his coffee cup.

"No, but there's something I need to do."

Smoke sipped the strong black brew and nodded. "All right. I'll come with you."

"That's not necessary. I'll be all right."

"I'm sure you would be, but I'm not going to pass up the opportunity to spend another day with my beautiful wife."

"What about the ranch?"

Smoke grinned. "We have the best foreman in the state, in Pearlie. Whatever work needs doing will get done just fine with him in charge."

Besides, although he didn't say as much to Sally, his instincts were telling him that his presence might be needed on this trip into town. Smoke didn't know why he felt that way, but he had learned over the years to have plenty of faith in what his gut was telling him.

It had kept him alive this long after all.

After meeting briefly with Pearlie and discussing the work that needed to be done on the ranch that day, Smoke hitched a pair of horses to the buckboard and saddled a mount for himself. Since he had ridden Drifter the day before, he chose another horse from his string: a dun gelding that wasn't much for looks, but had all the sand in the world.

Sally came out of the house wearing a long brown skirt, a brown jacket over a white shirt, and a black hat with the chin strap snugged tightly. She had put her dark hair up under the hat. She carried a Henry carbine in her left hand.

Smoke smiled and commented, “You look like you’re ready to go to war.”

“I just believe in being prepared, as you do.”

“It never hurts,” Smoke agreed. Sally set the carbine on the floorboards of the driver’s box, and then Smoke helped her up to the seat.

He swung up into the saddle as she took the reins and got the team moving. The dun trotted alongside the vehicle.

It was a pleasant morning, with high clouds and a welcome hint of crisp coolness in the air. Smoke enjoyed the ride as he and Sally moved along the trail in companionable silence. They were about halfway to Big Rock when he gave in to an impulse and said, “I have a pretty good idea why you wanted to go to town today, you know.”

Sally looked over at him. “Is that so?”

“You want to talk to Annabelle again and get to know her better, maybe find out more about this journey they’re on. The ladies in town, who are your friends, are plenty nice, but sometimes you feel like they’re a mite tame for you.”

“Is that so?” Sally asked as she arched an eyebrow at him. “Are you saying that I’m a wild woman, Smoke Jensen?”

“I’m saying you have an adventurous streak,” Smoke replied. “Let’s call it that.”

“Yes, that does sound a little better,” Sally said in a dry tone.

“Mind you, it’s not a bad thing,” Smoke went on. “Right from the start, ever since you’ve known me, you’ve been well aware that trouble has a habit of following me around. You knew all hell was going to break loose up there in Idaho, where we got together. Most women would have run the other way as hard as they could, once they figured that out. You never did, though. You were willing to stay at my side, no matter what happened.”

“I loved you,” Sally said simply. “I still do.”

“And I love you,” Smoke said. “That doesn’t mean I haven’t worried about you plenty of times and wished you were somewhere safe when the shooting started.”

"I suppose I have taken some chances now and then. But as you said, I knew what I was getting into when I married you." She laughed. "Just like you should have known what you were getting into!"

"I know you want to find out more about this trip to Wyoming they're making."

Sally looked over at him in surprise. "You figured that out?"

"Wasn't very hard to," Smoke said with a smile. "You seemed mighty interested in the whole thing when you were talking to her yesterday."

"I admire her, the way she took charge and got her friends together and set out on such a long journey like that. And she has to take care of her father as well. She seems like a very strong woman. I certainly hope they make it to where they're going without too much more trouble."

Smoke didn't say anything else, and Sally fell silent again as well, but he had a pretty good idea what was going through her mind.

He figured he would find out for sure once they got to Big Rock.

"I don't know about this," Susie Beale said as she and Delia walked along the boardwalk. Susie tried not to pay any attention to the disapproving looks they got from some of the other women on the street, but it was difficult not to notice them.

She and Delia were wearing respectable dresses today, not the gaudy, revealing outfits they sported when they were working in the saloon, but even so, the ladies of Big Rock knew who—and what—they were. It was also a bit scandalous that their heads were bare and their hair was loose around their shoulders. They hadn't put on hats or bonnets before leaving the Empire.

This early in the day, Andrew Rickett had been in his quarters, probably asleep. The bartender on duty hadn't paid any attention to the two young women as they left. No customers were in the saloon, and it was entirely possible there would be little or no business for a couple of hours yet.

So they probably wouldn't be missed, Susie knew, but even so, she felt nervous being out here in public like this. The shame she tried unsuccessfully to banish just added to her unease.

As did the plan that Delia had come up with. If she was being honest, Susie had to agree that it might be a good idea to leave Big Rock. But it meant taking a risk—a lot of risks, more than likely—and she wasn't sure she was up to that anymore. It would be easier just to sink deeper and deeper into the routine of what she was doing, even though it was unpleasant at times.

"Are you sure we're doing the right thing?" she went on as she and Delia walked toward the wagons parked under the trees.

"You can't be sure of anything in this world," Delia replied. "No matter how clever you are or how carefully you plan, something can always go wrong. So you're better off not worrying too much about it. Just do what seems right at the time and see what happens. You admitted you thought it was a good idea for us to get out of town."

"Mr. Rickett might not like us leaving the saloon. You know that he plans on us taking the place of Mattie and Cora as his top girls."

Delia waved a hand dismissively. "He can't do a thing to stop us. And being the top girls in a place like the Empire isn't anything to brag about, Susie."

"I'd never brag about it."

"Maybe somewhere else we'd do something we could brag about."

The idea of being proud of something she'd accomplished was so foreign to Susie that she couldn't grasp it. But it sounded good, she couldn't deny that.

A well-dressed old man, with white hair and a walking stick, was sitting on the lowered tailgate of one of the wagons as the women in the group bustled around, cleaning up after breakfast, tending to the picketed horses, and taking care of other chores. The tall, attractive blond woman, who had to be the one named Annabelle Wilkinson, set something over the tailgate of another wagon and then came over to the old man to speak quietly to him.

She looked curiously at Susie and Delia as they walked up. "Good morning, ladies," she said. "Is there something I can do for you?"

That was the first time they'd been called ladies in a long while, Susie thought. The first time since they'd come to Big Rock, in fact, except by Andrew Rickett, who used the term occasionally. But Susie always felt that when he called them that, it was in a mocking way.

This blond woman appeared to mean it, though.

"You're Miss Wilkinson, aren't you?" Delia asked.

"That's right." She tipped her head a little to the side. "Have we met?"

Delia didn't answer that. She nodded toward the covered vehicles and said, "I believe you're the leader of this wagon train."

"We're all friends and equal partners in this venture, but I suppose you could say I'm in charge. Someone has to be."

"Are you taking on any new members in your party?" Delia asked bluntly.

Annabelle looked surprised by the question. "Oh, I don't know. We haven't added anyone since we left Mississippi—"

"We're hard workers, ma'am," Susie interrupted her. "We can cook and clean and feed and water horses, and I lived on a farm one time and can handle a team. I can even chop firewood. You won't be sorry if you take us on."

The words bubbled out of her unexpectedly, surprising her as much as they appeared to surprise Delia. But Delia had said that she should go along with what felt right at the time, and as

Susie looked at Annabelle Wilkinson, she had felt a sudden urge to join forces with the woman. Annabelle looked like she knew what she was doing and was determined to accomplish her goals. There wasn't enough difference in their ages for Susie to regard her as a substitute mother, but more like an older, wiser sister.

So it made Susie feel as if somebody had kicked the feet out from under her when Annabelle shook her head and said, "I don't think that would be a good idea. There are plenty of us to handle everything that has to be done, so we really don't need anybody else joining our group."

The old man spoke up for the first time, saying, "Now, Annabelle, these two young ladies sound mighty sincere. I know we weren't looking to add to our numbers, but I'm not sure it would do any harm."

"Two more mouths to feed, Colonel," Annabelle said.

"And we'd earn every bite," Delia insisted. "Like Susie said, we'll work hard. You have our word on that." She drew in a breath. "It's important that we leave Big Rock and go somewhere else."

That statement prompted a quick, intent glance from Annabelle. "Why do you say that? Is the law after you?"

"What?" Susie said as her eyes widened. "No, ma'am! We haven't broken any laws."

Technically, that might not be true. Susie had no idea what the local ordinances were. But if the things that went on at the Empire were against the law, none of the star packers around here were bothering to enforce it. Susie had a pretty good idea that the local authorities, like those in nearly every other town on the frontier, looked the other way when it came to vice, as long as the lid stayed on and the pot didn't boil over.

"It really doesn't matter," Annabelle said. "We still don't need you two to come along with us. What are your names, anyway?"

"She's Susie Beale," Delia said. "I'm Delia Tracy. And if I

could have just a word with you in private, Miss Wilkinson, I think I can change your mind about us."

Annabelle shook her head. "That's not very likely."

"Please. Just a moment."

Annabelle considered the request and then surprised Susie by nodding.

"All right," she said. "Come along."

The two women walked off under the trees. Susie could still see them as Delia spoke earnestly to the older woman. Annabelle appeared to be listening carefully as she stood with her arms folded across her bosom. At one point, she stiffened and frowned.

Then she nodded and said something and a big smile broke out on Delia's face. Susie was shocked, but it appeared that Delia's plea had changed Annabelle's mind.

"What's going on, Miss Beale?" the old man asked.

"They're coming back over. I . . . I think Delia and I are going to join your group after all."

The man smiled. "That's excellent! I can tell from listening to you that you're fine young women. I wish I could see what you look like, but I lost my sight some time ago."

"We're nothing special," Susie said.

"Oh, I doubt that. I can tell a pretty girl when I hear one! I'm Colonel Jasper Wilkinson, by the way, Annabelle's father."

"I'm pleased to meet you, Colonel, and I'm, uh, sorry about your eyes."

"As I said, it was quite some time ago. And I still have my other senses. I've found that when you lose one thing, something else makes up for it, if you're fortunate. That doesn't apply just to your senses, either, but to everything else in life."

"I'd sure like to believe that's right," Susie said.

As Delia and Annabelle walked up, the older woman said, "Colonel, I've decided that Miss Tracy and Miss Beale can join us, as long as the others go along with that decision."

"I'm sure they will, my dear," the colonel said. "Our friends all have a great deal of faith in you." He smiled. "And now we have two new friends in these fine young ladies!"

"How soon can you be ready to leave?" Annabelle asked.

"As soon as you need us to be," Delia said confidently. "It won't take us long to pack, will it, Susie?"

"No, not at all," Susie replied.

But they hadn't told Andrew Rickett that they were leaving, she reminded herself.

And that could change everything.

CHAPTER 10

Danny Murphy was disappointed when he pushed through the batwings into the barroom of the Empire Saloon and didn't see Susie.

In fact, the only person in the saloon was the bald-headed bartender, and he looked to be half-asleep as he leaned an elbow on the hardwood and rested his chin in his cupped hand.

When he saw Danny, the apron straightened, yawned, and said, "Mornin', kid. Want a drink?"

"I'm looking for Susie."

The bartender shook his head. "Not here. Her and Delia left a while ago. Leastways, I think they did. I wasn't paying too close attention. It's too damn early to notice much. How about that drink?"

"I don't want a drink," Danny said, struggling to contain the irritation he felt. "Unless maybe you've got a cup of coffee."

"Sorry. Pot's empty right now. If you want coffee, you ought to go on down the street to Longmont's. Best coffee in town, and they serve up some mighty fine grub, too."

Danny shook his head without bothering to explain that he'd already had breakfast at a hash house, not far from the cheap hotel where he and his friends had spent the night. Instead, he asked, "Do you know where Susie and Delia were going?"

"How in blazes would I know? Those floozies don't talk much to me. Reckon they think they're too good for me, especially those two."

Danny's temper flared up. He wanted to reach across the bar, grab the stained front of the man's dingy white shirt, and slap him a couple of times for talking about Susie that way. Sure, there was no point in denying what she was, but this hombre didn't have to be so disrespectful about it.

He managed to suppress the violent urge and said, "When they come back in, tell Susie I was asking about her, all right?"

The bartender shrugged. "Sure, kid. If I can remember."

Danny started to tell him that he'd damned well better remember, but then he scowled and turned to walk out of the saloon. He didn't want to get in a fight this early in the day. Besides, if there was trouble, that sheriff might get involved, and he had looked like a pretty tough gent. Gus would be upset if Danny got himself tossed in the hoosegow.

Of course, Gus was upset pretty much all the time, anyway, especially after what had happened the day before. It wasn't like Gus to go hog wild over any woman.

Although, considering the way Danny felt about Susie, he could almost understand it.

The young hard case paused on the Empire's porch and looked up and down the street, searching for a flash of bright red hair.

Somewhat to his surprise, he actually spotted what he was looking for. Susie and Delia were walking in this direction, coming from the west side of the settlement, where those wagons were parked.

What in the world had they been doing out there? Danny wondered.

A terrible thought suddenly struck him.

What if they were leaving Big Rock and going with the wagon train?

He waited where he was, resting his hands on the railing that ran along the front of the porch. When the two girls saw him, they broke stride for a second, especially Susie. Did that mean she was glad to see him, or upset that he had come looking for her?

He would know in a minute or two, Danny supposed.

"Hello, Danny," Susie said, summoning a smile as they came up to him. "What are you doing here so early in the morning?"

"It's not really that early," Danny said. "I'll bet some folks have been up for hours."

"Not anybody who works in a saloon," Delia said.

Danny ignored that and went on to Susie, "I was looking for you, of course. I wanted to see you again and tell you how much I enjoyed spending time with you yesterday."

Susie blushed a little, in what had to be an uncommon reaction in her line of work. "I enjoyed your company, too," she assured him. "Actually, I was hoping I'd see you again before . . . before . . ."

"Before what?" Danny asked as her voice trailed off.

Delia answered the question. "Before we leave town."

"Dadgum it!" Danny blurted. "I was right. You two are hitting the trail with that wagon train, aren't you?"

Delia made a curt motion. "Hush! There's no reason to shout it from the rooftops. Rickett's probably not awake yet, and I'd just as soon get out of here before he finds out and gives us any trouble."

"Why would he give you trouble? He's just your boss, right? He doesn't own you or nothing like that. There's no law says you can't quit a job."

Even as Danny said that, he wished there were some way to prevent the girls from leaving town. Or Susie, anyway. He didn't really care what Delia did.

But it probably didn't matter all that much, he realized bleakly. He didn't know how long Gus intended for them to stay in Big Rock, but one thing was certain. When Gus was ready to go, they would go. Nothing would make him delay, once he'd made a decision—not J.D.'s wounded leg and, sure as hell, not Danny getting sweet on some saloon tramp.

Now he was thinking badly of her, he scolded himself. No matter what had led Susie into the life she was living, Danny was sure it wasn't her fault.

Delia said, "I just don't want to take any chances on Rickett trying to stop us. When a man like him is crossed, there's no telling what he might do."

When Danny was around the saloonkeeper the previous day, Rickett hadn't struck him as being all that dangerous, but he figured Delia knew the man better than he did. If she was worried about him, she probably had good reason to be.

Even if the idea of there ever being anything lasting between him and Susie had been foolish and doomed from the start, he ought to do anything he could to help them, Danny realized. He said, "When is that wagon train leaving?"

"I don't know, but it could be today," Delia said. "We came to get our things so we'll be ready to go with them when they pull out."

Danny nodded. "Go ahead and gather your gear. I'll hang around just in case there's any problem, and then I'll walk you back out there to throw in with them."

"You'd do that to help us, Danny?" Susie asked. She reached out and rested the fingertips of one hand lightly on his forearm.

"Well, sure," he said, trying to sound bluff and hearty about it. "Nobody's gonna give you gals any trouble while I'm around."

Delia took Susie's arm. "Come on."

"We'll just be a few minutes," Susie told Danny.

They hurried into the saloon. He followed them and paused

just inside the batwings. The girls went through the door at the end of the bar that led to their quarters.

The bartender didn't look as sleepy anymore. He asked, "What's goin' on here?"

"None of your business," Danny snapped at him. He crossed his arms and tried to look stern.

"I see you found Susie," the man said, but Danny didn't reply and his attitude discouraged any further attempts at conversation. The bartender shrugged and started aimlessly wiping the bar with a dirty rag.

The door to the back stood ajar. Danny heard another door open and then footsteps in the corridor. Andrew Rickett appeared in the doorway and paused to stretch and yawn before stepping into the room. He was fully dressed and his hair was brushed neatly, but he still looked a little bleary-eyed from sleep.

His gaze lit on Danny and he frowned. "What are you doing here?" he asked. "Where's the rest of your bunch?"

"Back at the hotel, I reckon. We're not always together, you know." Danny paused and then added, "I didn't figure you'd object to having a customer, no matter what time it is."

"You're no customer," the bartender said. "I already asked him twice if he wanted a drink, boss, and he said no. He just came around to moon over those two young chippies."

Rickett ambled toward Danny. "You're looking for Delia and Susie? I haven't seen them yet this morning—"

He fell silent as Susie came through the door from the back and gasped in surprise. She stopped short, causing Delia, who was right behind her, to bump into her.

"There you are," Rickett said. "Get on out here—" He drew in a sharp breath as he saw what the two girls were carrying. "What the deuce are you doing with those carpetbags?"

With a frightened but resolute expression on her face, Delia stepped around Susie and said, "We're leaving, Mr. Rickett. We're not going to work here anymore."

"The hell you're not! What makes you think you can just walk out on me like that?"

Danny said, "They've got a right to quit. They just work for you, Rickett. They're not your slaves."

With his upper lip curling in a snarl, Rickett glanced around at Danny and said, "Shut up, kid. I don't care how much of a hard case you think you are, you don't tell me how things are going to be in my place." Facing Delia and Susie again, he went on, "Put those bags back in your rooms. You two aren't going anywhere."

Delia's chin jutted defiantly at him. "We are. We're leaving Big Rock, and you can't stop us."

Rickett glared at them for a moment before what looked like understanding dawned on his face.

"That wagon train full of women I heard gossip about," he said. "You think you're going with them, don't you?"

"We've already talked to Miss Wilkinson," Delia said. "She's agreed that we can travel with them to Wyoming."

"What are you going to do in Wyoming? Is there a shortage of dirty hookers up there?"

Fury at that crass comment welled up inside Danny. He reached out with his right hand, grabbed Rickett's left shoulder, and jerked the man around to face him.

"Damn you!" Danny blurted out. "You can't talk to them like—"

Rickett's hand flashed inside his coat and came out holding a derringer. Danny caught a glimpse of the little weapon as it started to come up toward him; he let out a startled yelp. He knew he wouldn't have time to draw the Colt on his hip from its holster. All he could do was throw himself aside with a desperate twist.

The derringer cracked and Danny felt a fiery impact against

the side of his head. The frantic leap he'd made caused him to crash to the floor.

His ear felt hot and wet; pain swelled inside his head. The bullet from the derringer had just nicked him, he realized, but it still hurt like blazes. He tried to push himself up and claw the Colt out of leather at the same time.

Rickett's leg swung in a swift kick. The toe of his shoe dug into Danny's belly and caused a fresh surge of pain to go through him. He tried to curl up around it and shield himself, but Rickett was too fast and kicked him again.

The Colt came out of its holster. Danny tried to swing it up, but Rickett stomped down. The heel of his shoe ground Danny's wrist against the sawdust-littered planks. Danny cried out as his fingers opened involuntarily and the gun skittered away.

Rickett kicked him a third time. The brutal blow landed on Danny's jaw and jerked his head far back. The barroom spun crazily around him. Between the pain and sickness in his belly, the ache from his stomped wrist, and the agony of the bullet wound on the side of his head, he couldn't think straight, let alone summon up the energy to get to his feet. All he could do was lie there and hope that Rickett wouldn't shoot him again, fatally this time.

Vaguely, he heard yelling and screaming and forced himself to lift his head enough to see Susie and Delia struggling with Rickett. Delia had hold of the man's arm and was keeping him from using the derringer again, while Susie clawed at his eyes with her fingernails.

Rickett backhanded her and knocked her away from him. Susie lost her balance and fell. Rickett used the same hand to punch Delia in the face and cause her to collapse as well. The outrage Danny felt at seeing the girls assaulted like that energized his muscles enough that he started to rise, but that fleeting strength evaporated after only a couple of heartbeats. He slumped helplessly to the floor again.

"Clean up this mess," Rickett barked at the bartender as he flung a hand toward the sprawled figures. "I'm going to let those witches with that wagon train know they can't steal my girls away from me!"

Still holding the derringer, he stalked out of the Empire, leaving the batwings flapping behind him.

Chapter 11

Annabelle Wilkinson frowned as she noticed the tall, slender, well-dressed man hurrying along the street toward the wagon camp. Under different circumstances, she would have been happy to see someone like that approaching, but today her instincts told her that he didn't have good intentions.

"Looks like trouble coming, Colonel," she said quietly to her father.

"You think so?"

"I'm sure of it." The stranger was close enough now that Annabelle could see his angry expression. He was holding something in his right hand. She stiffened as she realized what it was. "He has a gun."

"That's not good," the colonel murmured as a frown drew his bushy white eyebrows lower over his eyes.

Annabelle reached over the tailgate into the wagon by which they stood. This situation was liable to require more than the knife she carried in a pocket on her dress. The group had rifles strategically placed within the wagons so it would be easy to grab them in times of trouble, and one of them was handy to where Annabelle was now.

She lifted out the carbine, worked the loading lever to throw a cartridge into the chamber, and held the weapon pointing toward the ground, but ready to bring up at a second's notice.

"Lucy," she called. "Helen."

Two of the women working around the camp turned toward her in response. When they saw Annabelle holding a rifle, they quickly retrieved similar carbines from nearby wagons and came over to join her.

At eighteen, Lucy Dunning was the youngest member of the group. With her slim, fresh, seemingly innocent prettiness and long chestnut hair, she could pass for even younger than she actually was.

Helen Pryor was almost a decade older than Lucy, shorter and heavier, with a round, friendly face and fairly short blond hair. If there had been an official second-in-command in the group, it would have been Helen, who had known Annabelle and the colonel longer than any of the others. Most of them looked to her for guidance whenever Annabelle wasn't around, and Annabelle valued her counsel.

"What is it, Annabelle?" Helen asked as she and Lucy hurried up. "More trouble?"

"That could well be," Annabelle replied. "Look at this fellow coming toward us."

"I think he's mad about something," Lucy said.

"And I'm guessing it's us," Helen said.

The stranger came to a stop about twenty feet away, glared at the women, and demanded to know, "Who's in charge here?"

Colonel Wilkinson took a step forward and shouted, "I don't know who you are or what you want here, sir, but you'd do well to adopt a more civil tone!"

"Shut up, old man! I'm not talking to you!"

Anger flared inside Annabelle. She didn't try to suppress it. With surprising speed, she lifted the rifle to her shoulder and aimed it at the stranger, who took a step back as his eyes widened. Annabelle could tell that he was considering opening fire on her, but he hesitated.

"I'm the one you're looking for," she snapped loudly, "and you'd better put that derringer away. A gun like that isn't accurate more than a few feet away, and this Winchester I'm holding can drill you from this distance without any trouble!"

The man sneered. "You'd have to pull the trigger first. I don't think you have the guts to do that."

"Believe me, mister, I won't have any trouble pulling the trigger," Annabelle said. "Just try something if you don't believe me."

The stranger hesitated for a few seconds longer, then reached under his coat and put the derringer away. He held out his hands to show that they were both empty now, came a little closer, and said, "All right. Why don't you lower your weapon as well?"

Annabelle let the carbine's barrel sag slightly, but didn't lower it all the way. "What is it you want?"

"I want to know why you think you have the right to damage my business."

"I don't know who you are or one blasted thing about your business, and I don't care to, either," Annabelle replied with a slight shake of her head.

"My name is Andrew Rickett. I own the Empire Saloon. And you've lured away the two best girls who work for me."

"Oh," Annabelle said. "You're the one Miss Tracy and Miss Beale were worried about. I see they had good reason to be concerned, since you don't mind going around waving a gun like a madman."

"I'm not insane, but I am angry. What kind of ridiculous promises did you make to those two girls to delude them into joining you?"

"Not that it's any of your business, but I didn't make any promises to them, and I certainly didn't try to lure them away from your saloon. That was all their own idea, and I can't say that I blame them for wanting to make something better of their lives. And for what it's worth, when they first asked me about coming along, I told them no."

"I don't believe you."

"I don't care whether you believe me or not. It's the truth. I told them they could come with us, and I stand by my word, Rickett. Now, you can just turn around and go on back to that saloon of yours."

Annabelle lifted the carbine again to reinforce the order, and Lucy and Helen did the same as they flanked her. Rickett was outnumbered and outgunned, but he didn't retreat. He just stood there glaring at them, and Annabelle began to wonder if she was going to put a bullet at the man's feet to make him leave them alone.

It was midmorning when Smoke and Sally reached Big Rock. As they started along the main street, Sally asked from the buckboard seat, "Are you going to stop at Louis's again today, Smoke?"

"No, I reckon I'll stick with you," he replied.

"I shouldn't need any help."

"Maybe I just enjoy your company," he suggested with a smile.

"And maybe you just find the idea of a wagon train full of women to be intriguing."

"I don't think that's it," Smoke said. "Handling one woman keeps me busy enough."

Sally raised an eyebrow at him. "Oh, so you believe you handle me, do you?"

Smoke winced and said, "I don't think that sounded quite the way I meant it—"

"Look up there, Smoke," Sally broke in, their bantering instantly forgotten when something more urgent reared its head. "Seems like some sort of trouble going on—again."

She was right, he thought as he rode straighter in the saddle.

They were passing the Empire Saloon, a relatively new drinking establishment in Big Rock, and they were close enough to the western edge of the settlement that Smoke had no trouble seeing the canvas-covered wagons parked under the trees.

He saw that Annabelle Wilkinson and a couple of the other women were facing down a man Smoke didn't recognize. The three women were pointing rifles at the stranger. With the man's back turned, Smoke couldn't see his face, but he struck Smoke as being vaguely familiar, as if he'd seen the fellow around town, but never actually met him.

"Stay here," Smoke told Sally as he lifted the dun's reins. "I'll find out what's going on."

He knew there was a chance she might not do what he told her, but he didn't look back to see if she was following as he nudged the horse to a faster gait. He just hoped she would stay out of the line of fire.

As Smoke rode up behind the stranger, he swung down from the saddle and landed lithely on the ground while the dun was still moving. He didn't draw either of his Colts, but his right hand was close to the gun butt on that side.

The well-dressed stranger turned to look at him. The man's lean, sardonic face looked familiar, too, as he snapped, "What do you want?"

Smoke nodded toward the women and asked, "Are you bothering these ladies, mister?"

"I'm just talking to them," the man said. His jaw was tight with anger.

"A minute ago, he was waving a gun around, Mr. Jensen," Annabelle said. She appeared relieved that Smoke had ridden up when he did.

Smoke smiled coldly at the man and said, "You ought to have more sense than that. You might spook those ladies, and those rifles they're holding might go off."

"They're stealing two of the girls who work for me! They don't have any right to do that."

Annabelle said, "Those young women are coming with us of their own free will."

"Who are you, mister?" Smoke asked the man.

"Andrew Rickett. I own the Empire Saloon."

Smoke remembered passing the saloon just a few moments earlier. He half turned and glanced in that direction now, saw that Sally had indeed stayed back and had, in fact, stopped the buckboard in front of the saloon. She was talking to a dark-haired young woman, who apparently had come out of the place.

Annabelle and the other two women had lowered their rifles when Smoke arrived. Perhaps seeing that, and noting that Smoke's attention had strayed for a moment, Andrew Rickett must have figured this would be a good time to make a move.

His hand darted under his coat and plucked a derringer from wherever he had it hidden.

He thrust the little gun toward Smoke and his finger tightened on the trigger.

Chapter 12

As soon as Rickett left the saloon, Susie and Delia rushed to Danny's side. Susie dropped to her knees next to him and took hold of his shoulders.

"Oh, Danny!" she cried. "How bad are you hurt?"

"Help him sit up," Delia urged.

She knelt on Danny's other side, and between them, they got him upright on the floor. His face was pale and drawn. He had his left arm pressed across his aching middle, and his right hand covered the bloody wound on his head.

"Let me see that," Delia said. She tugged on Danny's arm. He lowered it and his hand came away from his ear. Both his palm and the side of his head were smeared with blood.

Susie exclaimed in horror at the grisly sight. Delia said, "I don't think it's as bad as it looks." She turned her head toward the bar. "Clem, bring me a rag and a bottle of whiskey."

"If I give you any whiskey, the boss'll make me pay for it," the bartender whined.

"I'll pay for it, damn it! Now bring those things over here, like I told you."

Cora tottered through the door to the rear quarters. She clutched a dirty robe around her, and her hair was as wild as if she'd just gone through a cyclone.

"What the devil is all this racket out here? Can't a hard-working girl get a little shut-eye?"

Susie and Delia ignored her. Clem came out from behind the hardwood and brought Delia a rag and a bottle of whiskey. She clamped her teeth on the cork in the bottle's neck, pulled it out, and spat it aside. She poured whiskey on the rag and began using it to swab away some of the blood on Danny's head.

He yelled in pain and tried to jerk away. "Hang on to him," Delia told Susie and Clem, who still looked as if he wished he were anywhere else right now.

"Now be still," Delia said sternly to Danny. She went back to work, and after a few moments, she nodded in satisfaction. "I was right, it's not as bad as it looks."

"That son of a buck shot my ear off!"

"Not the whole ear. Just a little piece of it."

"The hanging-down part?"

"No, about halfway up."

Danny groaned. "That's going to look silly with a notch out of my ear like that."

"Not nearly as silly as you would have looked if that bullet had landed right smack between your eyes. It only missed that by a few inches."

"I reckon you're right," Danny replied in a surly voice. "But damn, it hurts."

"It's about to hurt even worse," Delia said. With only that for a warning, she raised the bottle and dribbled more whiskey on the wounded ear, soaking the bullet-nicked flesh thoroughly.

Danny jerked away again and howled, but it was too late. Delia had already accomplished her goal.

"You need to tie a clean bandage on there until it stops bleeding," she advised. "I really think you're going to be all right, though."

Danny looked around and asked, "Where's my gun?"

Susie spotted the Colt, picked it up, then hesitated before giving it to him. "What are you going to do, Danny?"

"Catch up to that damn tinhorn. He won't take me by surprise this time."

Susie shook her head and said, "You can't do that. Rickett almost killed you. Next time, he might do it."

"I'm not gonna let him scare off those women with the wagon train. They already said you could go with them, and they can't back out now just because Rickett don't like losin' you." He reached for the gun, but Susie drew back. "Blast it—"

"There goes Smoke Jensen," Delia said as she got to her feet. "I just saw him ride by outside."

Clem scoffed, "You don't know Smoke Jensen."

"I know him when I see him! And I know he stepped in to help those women at the wagon train yesterday. He and his wife both did. She's out there in a buckboard. I'm going to go talk to her."

As Delia hurried out of the saloon, Danny made another grab for his gun. Susie scooted out of his reach and stood up.

"I ought to bandage that wound, like Delia said—" she began.

The sudden pop of a gunshot, sounding louder than it should have at that distance, interrupted her.

Andrew Rickett was quick when he made his move, but Smoke still would have had plenty of time to beat his draw and put a bullet in him.

Instead of killing the man, Smoke lashed out with his left hand and knocked Rickett's gun arm upward. The derringer went off, but the shot sailed off harmlessly into the morning sky.

An instant later, Smoke's right fist slammed into Rickett's jaw. The punch landed cleanly, and with such power, that Rickett flew backward and crashed to the ground on his back, with both legs kicking high in the air.

He managed to hang on to the derringer. Not knowing

whether both barrels had been fired, Smoke took a quick step forward and kicked Rickett's wrist. The little gun flew out of his fingers and landed several yards away, well out of reach.

Rickett pushed himself up on an elbow, shook his head groggily, and then slumped down flat on his back again. He groaned.

Smoke took hold of the man's vest and coat in both hands and hauled him to his feet with seemingly effortless ease.

"Sorry I had to do that," he told Rickett. "When folks pull iron on me, though, I tend not to like it much."

Rickett glared at him with bleary-eyed hatred. Smoke let go of him and stepped back. Rickett swayed, but didn't fall down.

Smoke stepped over to the derringer, picked it up, and broke it open to dump both expended cartridges in his other hand. He went back to Rickett and put the derringer and shell cases in the pocket of the saloonkeeper's coat.

"Go on back to your saloon, mister," Smoke advised him. "I'm not completely clear on what your problem is with these ladies, but it's over now. You leave them alone while they're here in Big Rock, or I'll talk to the sheriff about letting you cool off behind bars."

"You can't threaten me like that," Rickett blustered. His voice was a little thick because his jaw was swelling already from Smoke's punch.

"I'm not threatening you. I'm just telling you what's going to happen." Smoke tilted his head back up the street toward the saloon. "Get moving."

Rickett didn't look happy about it, but he trudged away in sullen slowness.

Smoke looked past him and saw that Sally was back on the buckboard and had it headed in this direction. She wasn't alone, though. The dark-haired girl she'd been talking to a few minutes earlier was beside her on the seat, and two more figures rode in the back, a redheaded girl and a young man.

Rickett turned his head to glare at them as the buckboard rolled past, but he kept moving and made no move to stop the vehicle.

Still holding the carbine, Annabelle Wilkinson moved up beside Smoke and said, "Thank you, Mr. Jensen."

Her father came with her and added, "Yes, you have our deepest appreciation for your assistance, Smoke. I'm not sure exactly what happened—"

"Mr. Jensen knocked down the man who was threatening us and took his gun away from him," Annabelle said.

"Splendid!" the colonel enthused. "I wish I could have seen the scalawag get what was coming to him!"

Sally brought the buckboard to a stop. "Are you all right, Smoke?" she asked.

"Fine," he told her with a smile. "That fella got a shot off, but it didn't come anywhere close to doing any damage."

"You should have ventilated him!" Sally said fiercely. Then she laughed. "I sound a little bloodthirsty, don't I?"

The girl on the seat beside her said, "I think Rickett had it coming, just like this old gentleman said."

Colonel Wilkinson preened a little at that.

"Smoke, this is Delia Tracy," Sally said, performing the introductions. "Her friend is Susie Beale. I didn't catch the young man's name."

"Danny Murphy," he said as he slid down from the buckboard's bed. His right hand was bloody, as was the side of his head, but he used his left hand to help Susie down.

Helen Pryor came forward and said, "It looks like you could use a bandage on that ear. Come on over to the wagon and I'll fix you up."

Danny went with her, Susie following along to continue fussing over him. Smoke looked at Annabelle and asked, "Mind if I ask what all this ruckus was about?"

"Miss Tracy and Miss Beale are joining our group," Annabelle said. "They used to work for Rickett at his saloon, and he was upset about their decision to leave."

"That's no reason to try to shoot people."

"You were easier on him than I would have been," Annabelle said. "He was part of that bunch that bothered us yesterday. I was ready to put a bullet in him if he didn't leave us alone."

"And you would have been completely justified in doing so, my dear," the colonel told her.

Smoke asked, "How long are you planning to stay here in Big Rock? I can have a word with Sheriff Carson and ask him to keep an eye on you to make sure Rickett doesn't try to cause any more trouble."

A smile that held a touch of weariness appeared on Annabelle's face. "I don't blame the town, but it seems like we've had nothing but trouble since we got here. Originally, we planned to just pick up some supplies, let our teams rest overnight, and move on this morning. We didn't get an early start, like I intended, but I believe we'll still pull out this afternoon and get a few more miles closer to Wyoming before nightfall."

Smoke nodded and said, "The weather's good. You'll be able to cover some ground."

Sally had stepped down from the buckboard. She linked her arm with Smoke's and said, "My husband and I haven't really had a chance to discuss this, but I was wondering how you'd feel about the two of us coming along with you, at least part of the way." She looked up and added, "I'm sorry to spring the idea on you like this, Smoke."

"That's all right," he said, not mentioning that he'd already had a pretty good idea that was exactly what she had in mind.

"Of course," Sally went on to Annabelle, "I don't know whether you want any more company or not."

"We're used to taking care of ourselves," Annabelle began, sounding hesitant.

"But pleasant companions are always welcome," her father broke in. She turned her head sharply and gave him a frown, as if he could see the expression. The colonel continued, "However, you have a ranch to run here, I understand, and we wouldn't want you to neglect that."

"We wouldn't be," Sally said. "We have the best foreman in the state. I believe you just said that very thing, didn't you, Smoke?"

He chuckled. "As a matter of fact, I believe I did." He considered the situation quickly. He was the sort of man who thought things over thoroughly, but he didn't need all day to do it, either. "I'm confident Pearlie can handle anything that comes up, and where the crew's concerned, he's a sterner taskmaster than I am, so I don't think it would be any great hardship for us to leave the Sugarloaf in his hands for a while."

Wilkinson beamed and said, "In that case, I, for one, would welcome your companionship, sir, and that of your lovely wife as well."

Annabelle still didn't look completely convinced, but she said, "I'm not going to argue with you, Colonel, but I'd remind you that when we set out on this journey, you agreed that I would be in charge."

"With my counsel, dear, with my counsel." He gestured with the hand that wasn't holding his walking stick. "But, admittedly, the habit of command is a difficult one to break. Of course, I'll be most happy to defer to your judgment."

Annabelle shook her head and then laughed. "It's all right, Colonel," she assured him. "And you're right." She looked at Smoke and Sally. "We've already taken on two new members for our little caravan, and we'd be pleased to have you join us as well, Mr. and Mrs. Jensen."

"Smoke and Sally," Sally said.

"Smoke and Sally," Annabelle agreed.

Susie and Danny had returned from the wagon where Helen

had been bandaging the young man's bullet-nicked ear. He had a pad covering the wound, tied in place with some strips of rag that went around his head. His hat sat at a more rakish tilt than usual because of the arrangement. Overhearing the last of the conversation, Susie turned to Danny with her eyes lighting up.

"You should come with us, too," she said.

Smoke could tell from the look in the youngster's eyes that the idea held a lot of appeal for him. Or rather, it was pretty redheaded Susie who held the appeal for Danny.

But then the flash of excitement faded as he shook his head.

"I'm sorry, Susie, but I don't reckon I can do that," he said. "After that run-in Gus and the other fellas had with the ladies yesterday, I don't think I'd be very welcome here."

"You and your friends did cause a considerable amount of unpleasantness," Annabelle said coolly.

"I . . . I didn't know that," Susie said. "I mean, I heard something about it, but I wasn't sure . . ."

Danny took a deep breath. "Anyway, Gus wouldn't like it, and I don't reckon I want to be on his bad side. I wish things were different. I really do." He turned to Helen and nodded to her. "I'm much obliged to you for your help, ma'am. And I wish all of you the best of luck on your trip, wherever it is you're going."

To Delia, he added, "Thanks for cleaning up my ear, even though it hurt like a son of a gun."

"Take care of it," she told him. "I think it'll be all right."

Danny summoned up a weak smile, nodded again, and turned to walk back toward the Empire Saloon.

Delia put an arm around her friend's shoulders and said, "I'm sorry, Susie, but he's right. Now that we've gotten away from Rickett, we don't want to have anything to do with that other bunch of hard cases."

"I know," Susie said with a sigh. "Danny was different, though. He's not like the rest of them."

Smoke knew what she meant. But also, he had seen plenty of young drifters like Danny Murphy who moved back and forth from the right side of the law to the wrong side, depending on which way life's trails took them, and knew that if Susie wanted to make a new start somewhere else, she would have a better chance of doing it without Danny. He might have all the good intentions in the world, but could still be tempted to stray over into lawlessness.

Of course, Smoke reminded himself, there had been a time in his own life when folks could have said the same thing—and worse—about him.

Sally tightened her hold on his arm and said quietly, "Are you sure you're really all right with this, Smoke?"

"I wouldn't have said so if I wasn't."

"That's true," she said. "Honestly, I like these people, and I'll feel a lot better about their chances of reaching their destination safely if you're along. Besides, I've always enjoyed traveling with you, and with both of us going, it'll be a little like a holiday, won't it?"

"That's right," Smoke said. "Just like a holiday."

But remembering how trouble seemed to have a habit of riding right beside him wherever he went, he hoped he sounded a mite more convinced of that sentiment than he actually was.

CHAPTER 13

After nearly getting his ear shot off in there—nearly getting killed was more like it—Danny Murphy was going to steer clear of the Empire Saloon from now on. It would be all right with him if Gus decided not to stay in Big Rock for very long and the whole group moved on soon.

However, that might be more difficult to do, with J.D. Styles wounded the way he was. Despite Gus's single-minded, callous nature, surely even he wouldn't force J.D. to fork a saddle any time soon.

Given that Danny felt that way, he experienced some misgivings as he approached the saloon and saw Gus Gerhardt, Abner Farnum, and Concho Warren coming along the street from the other direction. He supposed Hamilton and Townsend were at the hotel with Styles.

Gerhardt and the others had seen him, too, and veered toward him, so he couldn't bypass the saloon the way he'd intended. He met the other three men in front of the building.

"Where have you been, kid?" Gerhardt asked.

Smirking, Farnum said, "I'll bet he came here hopin' to take another crack at those little tarts."

Danny swallowed the angry retort that tried to well up in his throat. Farnum was mean and brutal and quick to take offense.

Gerhardt ignored Farnum's crude comment and went on, "What happened to your head?"

"Cut yourself shavin'?" Farnum asked, still leering.

"Shut up, Abner," Gerhardt snapped. He and Warren were the only ones in the bunch who could get away with talking to Farnum like that. "You're not half as funny as you think you are."

A sullen scowl replaced Farnum's ugly grin, but he didn't say anything else.

"I ran into a little trouble in there, to be honest," Danny replied as he leaned his head toward the batwings at the Empire's entrance. "The fella who owns it, uh, took a shot at me."

"What were you doing?" Farnum asked. "You start a fight when that little redheaded tramp was with some other fella?"

Tight-lipped, Danny said, "It's a long story, Abner. I'd just as soon forget it."

Gerhardt shook his head. "The hell with that. Nobody tries to kill one of my men and gets away with it. Come on."

He turned toward the saloon and stepped up onto the shallow porch. Danny bit back a groan of dismay. He was already upset at the prospect of never seeing Susie again. Another confrontation with Andrew Rickett was just about the last thing in this world that he wanted.

But once he'd made up his mind to do something, Gus Gerhardt would never be turned aside, and Danny knew it.

"Better go on in, kid," Farnum said, smirking again at Danny's obvious reluctance. "Gus won't like it if you don't."

Gerhardt was already pushing through the batwings. Danny took a deep breath and followed him.

No customers were in the saloon, although it was getting late enough in the morning that some of the midday drinkers ought to start showing up soon. Clem was behind the hardwood, aimlessly polishing it with a rag as usual. Andrew Rickett stood in front of the bar, holding a glass with some whiskey in it.

One of the older soiled doves sat drowsily at a table. Her hands were wrapped around a coffee cup. She was staring down into the cup, as if it contained the answers to all the questions in the universe. Danny figured it had as much whiskey in it as coffee, if not more.

"You!" Rickett exclaimed when he looked past Gerhardt and saw Danny and Farnum entering the saloon. His baleful glare was directed straight at Danny.

He set the whiskey on the bar and started fumbling in his coat, as if reaching for a hidden gun. Giving up on that, he turned and barked at Clem, "Give me that sawed-off from under the bar!"

Gerhardt put his hand on the butt of his holstered gun and said, "I wouldn't do that, mister. Reach under that bar and come up with anything but empty hands, and I'll kill you."

Rickett glared furiously at him and said, "You don't have any right to come in here and start giving orders. This is my place, *not* yours."

Gerhardt ignored that. With his hand still on his gun, he said, "I hear you tried to kill a friend of mine. I don't like that very much."

"He interfered in something that wasn't any of his business," Rickett snapped. "I won't have anybody trying to tell me how to run my own saloon." He paused and then added, "Besides, I was just trying to scare him so he'd get out of my way."

That was a damned lie, and Danny was tempted to say so. He had seen the killing lust in Rickett's eyes when the man pulled the trigger on that derringer.

"Judging by that bandage on his head, I think you were trying to do more than spook him," Gerhardt said. "But I expect my men to be able to take care of themselves." He looked over his shoulder. "Danny, you want to settle any scores?"

Once again, Danny was tempted. It would feel good to smash his fist in Rickett's face a few times, not just to pay the saloonkeeper back for the pain he'd suffered, but also to square up, at least partially, any mistreatment he had handed out to Susie and Delia in the past.

But with Gerhardt and Farnum on hand to back him up, that would hardly be fair, and the streak of decency Danny still had left inside him prompted him to shrug his shoulders.

"Forget it," he said. "It's not worth it."

A spark of relief flickered in Rickett's eyes. He had lost his temper earlier and acted on impulse, but he had to be thinking it might not be wise to push things too far with Gerhardt and the other hard cases.

Gerhardt lifted his hand away from his gun to scratch his jaw, an apparently idle gesture, but it signaled that the potential for gunplay had eased a bit. He said, "A bottle might go some of the way toward making things square."

Rickett took a deep breath and then turned his head to nod to Clem. The bartender took a fresh bottle off the shelf and placed it on the hardwood. He added four glasses to it, and Rickett picked up the one he'd been holding earlier.

"I'd just as soon stay on good terms with all my customers," he said stiffly.

Gerhardt smiled. "I'm glad to hear it. Why don't the five of us sit down and have a drink together?"

Danny didn't like that idea a bit, but he didn't speak up to oppose Gerhardt's suggestion. Concho Warren picked up the glasses and carried them over to a table. Gerhardt and Rickett joined him, and after only a moment's hesitation, so did Danny.

Gerhardt pulled the cork from the bottle and poured the drinks. When everyone had downed a slug, he said, "What the hell was all this ruckus about, anyway?"

"Those two girls you saw in here yesterday are my best ones,"

Rickett said. "They up and decided they wanted to quit and join that damned wagon train full of women."

Danny saw the way the older woman at the other table shot a venomous glance at Rickett as he declared his estimation of Susie and Delia. She and the other one probably knew already that Rickett favored the younger women over them, but it wasn't pleasant for her to hear it like that.

"Naturally, I tried to talk them out of it," Rickett went on.

Danny couldn't hold his tongue any longer. "You were going to hold them like prisoners. I wouldn't put it past you to chain them up!"

"Take it easy, Danny," Gerhardt said. "Like Mr. Rickett said, he's got the right to run his own business as he sees fit."

That surprised Danny. It almost sounded now like Gerhardt was taking the saloonkeeper's side.

"He doesn't have the right to treat people like slaves," Danny blurted.

Gerhardt ignored that and turned to Rickett again. "You say those girls of yours are going off with that wagon train?"

"They're not his—" Danny began. He stopped when Concho Warren kicked his leg under the table and gave him a stern look, the sort of warning that it was best to pay attention to when it came from a Colt man, like this one from Texas.

Rickett answered Gerhardt's question as if Danny hadn't tried to interrupt. "That's right. After I dealt with this youngster trying to get in my way, I went out to where those women are camped and tried to put a stop to the whole thing."

Warren said in a dry tone, "From that bruise and the way your jaw is swollen, one of the ladies must've clouted you with a two-by-four."

"It wasn't one of them," Rickett said. "It was Smoke Jensen." He shrugged. "And it was a fist, not a two-by-four."

Gerhardt's eyes narrowed. He said, "Jensen again. You

couldn't have thrown iron on Smoke Jensen. You'd be dead if you had."

Rickett took the empty derringer from his pocket and laid it on the table next to his whiskey glass. "I tried. I realize now it was a foolish thing to do."

"Ol' Smoke must've been feeling generous today," Warren drawled. "Otherwise, you'd have a bullet hole in you and they'd be measuring you for a coffin right about now, like Gus says."

Gerhardt looked curiously at him. "You know Jensen? I'd heard of him, but we never crossed trails until yesterday."

"Neither had we," Warren replied. "I was acquainted with some of the fellas who tangled with him up in Idaho a few years ago. I might've even thrown in with them if I hadn't been involved in another little dustup just then." He picked up his glass and threw back the rest of the whiskey in it. "Just as well. Jensen went into a town and killed nineteen men who were doing their damnedest to kill him. I figure anybody who could do that could've killed twenty just as easy."

"You're saying you're scared of him?" Rickett demanded.

"I'm saying I'd be a mite nervous about facing him down." Warren picked up the bottle and splashed more whiskey in his glass. "Hard for a fella to see a rifle bullet coming at him from behind, though. Was I in a position to need to deal with Smoke Jensen, I'd had to give that some serious thought."

Danny might have taken another drink, but he already had a bad taste in his mouth. He didn't like the idea of back-shooting anybody, even as dangerous a man as Smoke Jensen was supposed to be.

But he didn't like the idea of dying, either, so he couldn't condemn Warren too much.

"So Jensen took a hand and stopped you from scaring those women off from the idea of taking your girls with them," Gerhardt mused. "I seem to remember hearing that Jensen's a rancher now."

"Yes, he has a spread called the Sugarloaf, a few miles west of here," Rickett said.

"So he's busy with that and won't be around when those wagons roll out of town, right?"

"I suppose," Rickett said slowly. He frowned. "What are you getting at, Gerhardt?"

"I have a score to settle with Jensen, one of these days. He stuck his nose into my business and shot one of my men. I'm not going to stand for that. But I'm even more interested in that wagon train. Are your girls down there now?"

"I suppose. They were headed that way the last time I saw them."

"I'm not done with that blonde who's in charge. I was thinking I might pay those wagons another visit once they're well away from here and out on the trail, where Smoke Jensen won't be around to interfere, or anybody else, either."

Warren said, "You must have a real itch for that Wilkinson woman, Gus."

"My itches are none of your business, but I'll admit that I didn't take it kindly the way that whole thing happened. You have a problem with that, Concho?"

Warren's shoulders went up and down a fraction of an inch. "No problem. You're the ramrod of this outfit. We go where you say."

"Damn right." Gerhardt looked at the saloonkeeper again. "I'll put it plain, Rickett. I'll fetch those girls back here to you—for a price."

Rickett's forehead creased even more. "I don't know if it would be worth it. There are plenty of other girls in the world."

"As young and pretty as those two?" Gerhardt jerked his head toward the other table. "Most of the ones I've seen are as ugly and worn-out as that one."

He didn't bother keeping his voice down.

The woman made a strangled sound, pushed her chair back, and stood up. She glared at the men for a second, then turned and stalked to the door at the end of the bar. It slammed behind her as she disappeared through it.

Gerhardt said, "I reckon those other two could make three, four times as much money as what the ones you have left could do in a night. It wouldn't take long for the price of getting them back to pay for itself."

Danny's mouth had tightened into a thin, hard line. He couldn't believe what he was hearing. Gerhardt was offering to take on a job for a snake like Andrew Rickett, and even worse, that job involved stealing Susie and Delia from the wagon train and bringing them back here, where they didn't want to be! Danny figured he couldn't go along with that.

But as he leaned forward and opened his mouth to protest, Concho Warren caught his eye again and gave a tiny shake of his head. The angry words froze in Danny's throat. He had been with the bunch a shorter time than any of the others. None of them would back him up if he bucked Gerhardt.

And at least two of them—Warren and Farnum—would kill him without a second thought if Gerhardt gave the word.

For a long moment, Rickett didn't say anything. Then he asked, "How much are we talking about?"

Gerhardt swallowed some whiskey, then licked his lips. "Five hundred dollars."

"Five hun—That's a fortune!"

"Not really," Gerhardt said, shaking his head. "Consider it an investment, just like your liquor supply. You have to spend money on booze in order to sell it. You can spend money on—"

Abner Farnum had been silent during the discussion, but had downed a couple of glasses of whiskey. Now he spoke up, slamming an open hand down on the table and saying in a loud voice, “By grab, I like it! We’ve rustled cattle and horses, we can rustle women!”

“Shut up, Abner,” Warren said. “You’re drunk.”

“Maybe a little, but I ain’t so drunk I don’t know I’d like to spend some more time with that dark-haired slut.” Farnum leered at Danny. “And I’m sure you’d like to see your little red-headed sweetheart again, wouldn’t you, Danny boy?”

Danny didn’t say anything. He suddenly felt as if he were being ripped apart inside. He had seen how badly Susie and Delia wanted to get away from Andrew Rickett, once Delia pushed them into taking that step. They were both smart and good-hearted and could make better lives for themselves somewhere other than the Empire Saloon.

At least, he wanted to believe that was true. What was undeniable was that he had known both of them less then twenty-four hours and hadn’t spent a lot of time exchanging deep views about anything with either of them.

Even so, his instincts rebelled at the thought of forcing them to come back here and work for Rickett.

At the same time, even though he had steeled himself to the idea of never seeing Susie again, this unexpected opportunity to be around her and get to know her better appealed a great deal to him.

And maybe, just maybe, a chance might arise where the two of them could be together away from all the others. If he helped Gerhardt and the others retrieve the two girls from the wagon, what was to say that he and Susie might not be able to go off on their own?

Gerhardt wouldn’t like it—for one thing, Rickett was bound to refuse to pay the full price for just one girl—but if Danny played it smart and moved fast enough, it might not matter.

“What do you think, kid?” Gerhardt asked with a note of impatience in his voice. “You want to come along and get your girl back, at least for a little while?”

"Sure," Danny said, his own voice sounding a little hollow in his ears. "We can do that, I guess."

Gerhardt looked at the saloon owner. "How about it, Rickett?" he prodded. "Do we have a deal or not?"

"Five hundred, you said?"

Gerhardt nodded solemnly. "Five hundred. Half now, half when we bring those girls back to you."

Rickett's nostrils flared as he drew in a deep breath.

"You have a deal," he said.

Chapter 14

It would take a while for the women to finish getting ready to depart, so Smoke and Sally headed back to the Sugarloaf while those preparations continued. The wagons would roll before they could return to Big Rock, but Smoke knew they would be taking the road north from the settlement and was confident that he and Sally could catch up easily before the afternoon was over.

While Sally headed into the ranch house to pack, Smoke switched his saddle over onto Drifter and rode out to where he knew Pearlie would be working today.

Pearlie and a couple of other hands were pushing a small bunch of cattle onto some better grass on the range. Spotting Smoke approaching, Pearlie waved for the other men to continue their work and turned his horse to lope toward Smoke.

"Howdy, boss," Pearlie said as he and Smoke reined in with their mounts next to each other. "How'd the trip to town go today?" He grinned as he thumbed his hat back. "Didn't have to shoot anybody else, did you? That seems to happen on a mighty regular basis."

Smoke shook his head. "Nope, didn't fire my gun this time." He paused and then added, "Somebody tried to take a shot at me, though."

Pearlie's eyes widened in alarm. "You ain't jokin', are you?"

"No. Fella pulled a hideout gun on me and got one shot off."

"And you didn't kill him?" Pearlie looked and sounded amazed by that.

"I gave him a good bust on the jaw and knocked him down instead."

Pearlie shook his head. "A ruckus two days in a row, and you didn't kill either of the other hombres. Smoke, if I didn't know better, I'd say bein' married must be softenin' you up a mite."

That brought a chuckle from Smoke. He told his old friend, "For what it's worth, Sally told me I should have ventilated the varmint."

"Who in blazes done it?"

"A man named Rickett. He owns the Empire Saloon. Have you been in there since he took it over a few months ago?"

"The Empire's too low-class a joint for me," Pearlie said. "The boys and me sometimes stop in at Emmett Brown's place, or Longmont's if we're in the mood for somethin' fancier. Ain't set foot in the Empire for a long time, though."

"Rickett's a gambler, by the looks of him. He has a few girls working in there, too."

"A pretty sorry lot, I expect."

"You might be surprised by a couple of them," Smoke said.

He proceeded to tell Pearlie about Susie Beale and Delia Tracy and how they had decided to leave Andrew Rickett's employ and head for Brimstone Butte, Wyoming, with the Wilkinson wagon train.

"Well, good for them," the Sugarloaf foreman said with an emphatic nod. "I believe ever'body deserves a chance to better theirselves if they want to. I mean, just take a gander at me. I was nothin' but a scraggly ol' hired gun, bound for an early grave, and now I'm the foreman of the best ranch in Colorado."

"And the spread couldn't get along without you," Smoke said. "But as long as you're here, the Sugarloaf can get along without me."

Pearlie's forehead creased in a frown under his tipped-back hat. "What do you mean by that?"

"Sally and I are going to Wyoming."

A look of understanding dawned on Pearlie's face. "You're goin' along with that wagon train!"

"Sally's gotten fond of those women, and she's interested in what they're trying to do. I have to admit, it's pretty admirable, a bunch of widows and orphans banding together that way to make a new start."

"Widows and orphans and saloon girls," Pearlie said.

"I don't know their stories, but I figure there's a good chance Miss Beale and Miss Tracy are orphans, too, or else they wouldn't be working in a saloon like the Empire for a man like Andrew Rickett."

"More'n likely you're right," Pearlie allowed. "And I know you don't want to send Sally off alone on a jaunt like that."

Smoke's face grew solemn. "From everything they said, Miss Wilkinson and the colonel haven't run into any trouble since they left Mississippi with their friends, but that may have changed now. The frontier's still pretty wild where they're headed. Not only that, but I'm a mite worried about that fella Gerhardt and his bunch, too."

"They're outlaws, you reckon?"

"They looked like the sort who ride on the wrong side of the law when it suits them."

Pearlie made a face. "Same thing could've been said about me and Monte back in the old days."

"And me as well," Smoke said. "But with the exception of that young fellow Murphy, who seems pretty smitten with Susie Beale, I wouldn't put much past any of the others. I have a hunch Murphy would go along with anything Gerhardt told him to do, too."

"You think they'll follow the wagon train and try to make trouble again?"

"I don't know," Smoke replied honestly. "It's possible. Or they might just drift on somewhere else and never look back. But since I can't rule out the chance . . ."

"You figure to make sure nothin' bad happens before those ladies get where they're goin'," Pearlie finished for him.

"That's right. Sally wants them to make it there safely, and so do I. I'm curious, too, about this ranch the colonel is supposed to have inherited. Sure, Colonel Wilkinson knows about running a plantation, but that's a far cry from keeping a cattle spread going. If we stick with the wagons all the way, I can have a look at the place and maybe give the ladies a hand taking it over."

"They'll need a good crew, less'n you think they can handle all the ropin' and ridin' their own selves."

"I doubt that," Smoke said. "The colonel's cousin had some men working for him, and I hope they stayed on to wait for the new owner."

Pearlie rested both hands on the saddle horn, leaned forward, and said, "Well, we'll sure miss you around here while you're gone, Smoke, but I'll do my durnedest to keep things runnin' good and proper." He shook his head. "It sure won't be the same without Miss Sally around, though."

Smoke grinned. "You mean you'll miss her frying up a batch of bear sign for you and the boys every week or so?" He knew how much Pearlie loved the round, sugary pastries that came from Sally's kitchen.

"Don't never underestimate the importance of bear sign in runnin' a ranch!" Pearlie said.

* * *

A short time later, after a quick midday meal, Smoke and Sally left the Sugarloaf.

Smoke rode Drifter, while Sally handled the fresh buckboard team Smoke had hitched up. An extra horse for Smoke, as well as Sally's favorite saddle mount, a chestnut mare, were tied to the back of the vehicle. Sally's saddle was stowed in the back, along with several bags and some crates of supplies they would be taking along. If they were going to travel with the wagon train, they expected to contribute to the group's provisions.

They didn't need to return to Big Rock before taking up the trail of the wagons. Smoke knew every foot of this valley intimately. He had explored it from one end to the other before he ever brought Sally here and began building the log cabin that had grown into their fine ranch house. Since they had settled on the Sugarloaf, he had learned even more about the area.

With that knowledge, Smoke was able to lead them across country, picking out a route that the buckboard wouldn't have any trouble negotiating. Sally was a skilled driver, so she didn't need a broad, smooth road to control the team.

Angling across the landscape that way, by midafternoon they had reached the road the wagons would be following. Smoke reined in and sniffed the air as Sally brought the buckboard to a halt.

"Dust," he said. "I reckon they must have passed this way not long ago."

"Your sense of smell isn't actually so keen that you can distinguish the dust raised by those wagons from dust caused by any other travelers," Sally said. She sounded confident of that, but then there was a faint note of uncertainty in her voice as she added, "Is it?"

It never paid to underestimate the abilities of Smoke Jensen.

He chuckled and said, "No, not really. That would be loco. But we know they were planning to come this way, and that dust must be pretty recent or it would have settled by now. The timing works out right."

"I suppose it does. That must mean they're not very far ahead of us."

"Not far at all. We ought to rest the horses for a few minutes, and then we can start after them again. It shouldn't take long to catch up."

"I hope they haven't run into any trouble since they left Big Rock."

"They're not likely to around here," Smoke said. "But the chances will be better—or worse, depending on how you look at it—the closer they get to Wyoming."

"Do you know anything about this place they're going?"

"Brimstone Butte?" Smoke shook his head. "Now that I've had time to think about it, I believe I've heard the name, but that's all. I don't know where it is. That's one thing I want to ask Miss Wilkinson and her father. I reckon they must have a map, or least some directions, if they're going to set out all that way from Mississippi."

"The colonel said a lawyer from the town contacted them. Maybe he sent a map with his letter."

"That would come in handy, all right," Smoke said.

After the horses rested for a few more minutes, they set off again, heading in a generally northward direction as they followed the wagon road. The trail climbed to a saddle in some hills that curved around from southeast to northwest and merged into the more impressive, snowcapped peaks of the Rockies. Grassy, rolling plains dotted by other small hills stretched to the east. It was beautiful country.

So were the Ozark Mountains back in Missouri, where Smoke had grown up, but he knew that this was truly his home and he was glad he had found it after all the hardships and perils of his earlier life.

But it was Sally who made it his home more than anything else, he reflected, and he was thankful that the tragedies he had endured had finally led him to her.

They came in sight of the wagons less than an hour later. Someone in the last wagon must have noticed Smoke and Sally coming up behind them and passed the word forward, because all four wagons slowed and then stopped to allow the Jensens to draw alongside them.

Smoke spotted Susie and Delia looking out the back of one of the covered wagon beds. Susie raised a hand and waved as he and Sally went past.

Annabelle Wilkinson dropped to the ground from the driver's seat of the lead wagon. The colonel remained where he was. As Smoke reined in, he said, "You didn't have to stop on account of us. We could have just fallen in behind you."

"Believe me, I don't mind stopping for a little while," Annabelle said. "That wagon seat gets awfully hard after so many miles."

"I know exactly what you mean," Sally told her.

Smoke swung down from the saddle and asked, "Have you run into any problems since leaving Big Rock?"

Annabelle shook her head. "We haven't even seen that many people. A few cowboys riding in the distance and one family on a wagon heading toward town."

"That's about what I expected. This isn't a heavily traveled trail. There's a road a few miles east of here that goes on up to Cheyenne. I'd like to sit down with you, Miss Wilkinson, and you, too, Colonel, to find out more about Brimstone Butte."

"I'd be happy to tell you all I know about it, Smoke," the colonel said. "We should do that when we make camp this evening."

"Sounds like a good plan. I don't reckon you happen to have a map of where you're going?"

Annabelle said, "Actually, we do, if you'd like to study it."

"I would," Smoke replied with a nod. "That can wait until this evening, too."

Susie walked up the line of wagons to join the little group at the front. She said, "Excuse me, Mr. and Mrs. Jensen, but you didn't happen to see Danny when you went back through town, did you?"

"I'm sorry, dear," Sally told her. "We didn't go through Big Rock this time."

"Oh." Susie's face fell a little. "I just wanted to make sure he was all right."

Helen Pryor called from the second wagon, "With the doctoring he got from your friend and me, he ought to be fine, honey. A little bullet nick like that might look bad, but it'll heal up without any problem." She laughed. "Although he probably will have a little notch out of that ear."

Susie lowered her voice and said, "Delia says I'm crazy, but I have a feeling I'll see Danny again someday."

"If that's what you want, I hope it comes true," Sally said.

A few minutes later, the caravan, which now numbered five vehicles, got underway again. Sally took up the last position in line after suggesting that Smoke should scout ahead.

That was exactly what he'd planned to do. He nudged Drifter into a lope that carried horse and rider a hundred yards or so in front of the slower-moving wagons and buckboard.

The group traveled at a deliberate but steady pace, and by the time the sun was almost touching the western horizon, they had put several more miles behind them. For a while, Smoke had been keeping his eyes open for a good place to camp. He found one in a clearing with a clump of boulders to one side and some trees curving around opposite them. There was no water here, but the barrels tied on the sides of the wagons had been filled before they left Big Rock.

It was easy to see that the women had a great deal of experience in unhitching the teams and setting up camp. The whole process went smoothly and efficiently. Smoke was impressed by their ability. He offered to pitch in and help, but was told that wasn't necessary.

Sally laughed at the expression on his face. "You can unhitch the horses from our buckboard, Smoke," she told him. "I don't mind."

"Thanks, I think."

He got a better count of the group now. The original party had had fifteen members—fourteen women and the colonel. The addition of Susie and Delia brought the number to seventeen, and Smoke and Sally made nineteen.

Smoke knew the names of only three of the women in the group that had arrived in Big Rock the day before: Annabelle, Helen Pryor, and young Lucy Dunning. Annabelle told him the names of some of the others and he figured he'd get to know all of them during the journey to Wyoming, which would take at least two weeks. But for now, most of the names didn't stick with Smoke.

Helen and a couple of the other women soon had a campfire going. They broke out Dutch ovens and cooking pots and set to work preparing supper as night settled down.

Annabelle and Colonel Wilkinson came over to Smoke and Sally. "You said you wanted to know more about Brimstone Butte," the colonel said as he reached inside his coat. He brought out several folded sheets of paper. "Here are the documents the lawyer sent to me after my cousin Albert passed away."

Smoke took them, unfolded them, and studied them by the light of the fire. The letter was from a lawyer named Radcliffe and informed the colonel that his cousin Albert Lowe had passed away and left his ranch, the Three Cross, to his only living relative. Another paper was the deed to the ranch.

"That deed is a copy," Annabelle explained. "The lawyer still has the original for safekeeping and said he'll turn it over to us when we get to the town of Brimstone Butte."

Smoke nodded, having taken note of that same information in the attorney's missive. He moved on to the third sheet of paper, which proved to be a neatly drawn map. He held it so that Sally could see it, too, as Annabelle leaned in and pointed with a slender finger.

"You can see that Brimstone Butte is here between these two mountain ranges, about a hundred miles west of Laramie," she said. "The actual butte itself that gave the settlement its name is a few miles north of it. There's a trail that runs northwest between the mountains and the butte that leads to the Three Cross, which is about twenty miles from town. At least, I'm guessing that's the case if the map is drawn to scale."

"You're good at reading a map," Smoke commented.

Colonel Wilkinson hooked his thumbs in his vest pockets. "Taught her everything I know about practical matters," he said proudly. "As a military man, I had to be well-versed in such things."

Smoke traced a path on the map with his fingertip. "These ranges almost close up, here along the border between Colorado and Wyoming, but there's a trail that goes all the way between them. If we turn more toward the northwest when we get closer, we shouldn't have any trouble following it all the way to Brimstone Butte. I'm pretty sure I've been through there, but it's been close to ten years. I wasn't much more than a youngster." He paused and then continued, "I do recall that it's dry and rugged terrain a lot of the way. Downright ugly, in fact. But the wagons can make it, and if we're careful with our water, I don't think we'll have any trouble."

"So you're going all the way to Brimstone Butte with us?" Annabelle asked.

Smoke smiled. "If I hear about a place I haven't seen, like this ranch of yours, I kind of want to take a look at it for myself. I'm fiddle-footed that way."

Sally laughed and hugged his arm. "And that quality has

rubbed off on me, I'm afraid. So you're going to be saddled with us the entire way, I think."

Hearing Smoke refolding the papers, Colonel Wilkinson reached out and took them from him. As he slipped them back in his coat, he said, "I, for one, couldn't be happier about that, my friends. On to Brimstone Butte!"

CHAPTER 15

Twenty miles to the north was a place known as Hidden Valley. That name conjured up an image of a peaceful, idyllic setting.

Hidden Valley was neither of those things.

A long, low, rambling log building sat in front of a bluff that rose westward in stair steps to the rugged mountains. Another stretch of rough terrain lay on the eastern side of the valley, which was about a mile wide.

The building had a haphazard appearance, because it had been added on to several times. As a result, several new rooms and sheds jutted out from it at odd angles. A low, covered porch ran along the front of the main building.

To the north was a corral, with a ramshackle barn attached to it. A blacksmith shop sat beside the barn. Not far past it, a small creek emerged from a narrow crack in the bluff and flowed erratically across the valley toward the hills a mile away. Brush and scrubby trees lined the stream's banks, but the vegetation had been cut away to allow horses and wagons through an opening that sloped down to a pebble-bottomed ford.

The name HIDDEN VALLEY had been daubed in red paint by an unsteady hand onto a large plank sign nailed to the awning over the porch. The words AUGUSTUS RASMUSSEN, PROP. were written on a smaller sign below the big one.

Six horses were in the corral. A seventh was tied at one of the hitch rails in front of the building. The young man who had just swung down from the saddle and looped his mount's reins around the rail stepped onto the porch and walked through the open door into the shadowy, smoky room beyond.

The six men who obviously went with the horses in the corral were seated around a large table to the right, ostensibly playing cards, although they seemed more interested in passing around a bottle than in studying the grubby pasteboards they'd been dealt. Occasional outbursts of raucous laughter came from them.

Straight ahead of the newcomer was a bar that ran across the back of the room. To the left, an opening in the wall led to an area of shelved merchandise. Hidden Valley, to those who knew of it, served as both a saloon and a trading post.

But it was more than that. This place offered a refuge to those who rode the lonely trails and heard the owl hoot on dark nights. The law seldom ventured into this tucked-away corner of the range.

An enormously fat man, with wispy white hair and multiple chins, stood behind the bar. His hands, with their thick, sausage-like fingers splayed out, rested on the scarred wood. He greeted the newcomer with a hearty, "Come in, come in!" that made his huge belly shake under a canvas apron.

"What can I do for you, my young friend?" Augustus Rasmussen went on.

"Beer, I reckon, if you have any."

"I ask you, what German would be caught dead without a barrel of beer somewhere nearby?" Rasmussen laughed and made his belly dance around some more. He reached under the bar, took out a metal stein with ornate designs worked into it, and filled it from a barrel. As he placed it on the bar in front of the young stranger, he said, "One of the steins from the original *Oktoberfest* in Munich, *ja*. I brought it with me when I came to this country. Drink up, my young friend, drink up."

The stranger picked up the stein, thumbed the little lever that lifted its lid, and drank. When he lowered the vessel, he licked away the foam that clung to the sandy-brown mustache on his upper lip and said, "That's pretty good."

"You are a man of the world, I see. Too many of *mein* customers"—Rasmussen rolled his eyes toward the men sitting at the table, who weren't paying any attention to what was going on at the bar—"do not understand how to drink out of anything more elaborate than a bucket."

"I don't reckon I'd call myself a man of the world, since those limits extend east of Wichita—and that's as far as I've been. Seems pretty obvious how you're supposed to work this little gadget, though."

"You would be surprised," Rasmussen said solemnly.

The stranger took another drink and then asked, "Are those fellas regular customers of yours?"

Rasmussen shrugged and lowered his voice to reply, "I have seen them in here before, now and then. That one with the red beard, he is called Pike. Billy J. Pike. If you speak to him, or about him, he insists that you use the middle initial. He is the leader."

"The leader." The stranger lowered his voice as he leaned forward. "You mean they're a gang?"

Rasmussen spread his hands. "I have said too much. I am but a simple innkeeper who asks nothing and knows nothing."

"Don't worry," the stranger assured him with a smile. "I don't intend to cause you any trouble, *Herr* Rasmussen."

The fat man's eyes widened with surprise and happiness. *"Sprechen sie Deutsch?"*

"Not really. There was a German handyman around town when I was a kid. I followed him around and picked up a few words and phrases, that's all."

"Drink up, drink up. You want something to eat? I wish I could offer you something besides buffalo steak."

With a grin, the stranger said, "Buffalo steak sounds just

fine to a man who's been on the trail eating his own cooking for a spell." He picked up the stein with his left hand. "I'm going to sit over there at that table by the door into the trading post."

That was as far as he could get from Billy J. Pike and his friends and still be in the same room.

Rasmussen's chins wobbled as he nodded. "I will bring the food to you."

The stranger carried the stein over to the table, hooked a chair with his foot, and pulled it out. He sat down with his back toward the wall, and as he sipped the beer and looked across the room at the outlaws, his right hand never strayed far from the butt of the gun on his right hip.

Despite the crude jokes and the laughter, an air of tension lurked around the table. It had been several weeks since the Pike gang had pulled a job, and the takings from that stagecoach robbery hadn't lasted very long. Funds were low, and the men didn't like it.

Billy J. Pike knew he was going to have to come up with something soon, or else the others would turn against him. They were a little scared to cross him, of course, because he could be a loco son of a buck when he got his dander up, but there were five of them and only one of him.

Hutch Dennison upended the bottle and let the last few drops of whiskey drizzle from it into his glass. Then he thumped the empty on the table and said, "Time for another, boys."

Pike turned his head and called toward the bar, "Another bottle over here, 'Dutchy'!" Then he frowned and asked the other men, "Who's that hombre sittin' over yonder? When did he get here?"

"A few minutes ago," Yancy Meehan replied. "You didn't see him when he walked in? He went up to the bar and talked to Rasmussen for a spell."

"No, I never noticed him." Pike's frown deepened. He'd had too much to drink and he knew it, but he didn't want to stop. On the other hand, his brain was a mite muddled, and that could be dangerous when the rest of the men were already getting frustrated with him.

"Where the hell's Rasmussen?" Jethro Cunningham asked.

"Ain't he behind the bar?" Pike asked. "I just told him to bring us another bottle."

"He's not there," Walt Carlisle replied. "He ducked into the back a few minutes ago. Didn't you notice that, Billy J.? I wondered who you were yellin' at."

Pike glared across. "No, I didn't notice. I reckon bein' around you boys has dulled my thinkin'. I might just have to go off on my own to sharpen my brain up."

"Go ahead, Billy J., if that's what you need," Dennison said coolly.

Well, that was a damned stupid move, Pike told himself. All he'd accomplished by berating them was to provide an opening for them to get rid of him. His brain actually was getting dull. Not even noticing that the fat German wasn't behind the bar was a good example of the mistakes he'd been making lately. Damn, if he wasn't careful, he'd forget which end of a gun the bullets came out of.

He reckoned Hutch Dennison would be happy to remind him. Hutch had always been the ambitious sort. He probably figured the gang would be better off with him bossing things.

Figuring it might be best to distract the others, Pike shoved his chair back and stood up. He was about to walk over to the bar, reach behind it, and get another bottle himself, but then he had a better idea.

"Hey, you!" he called as he pointed a finger at the stranger sitting beside the opening on the other side of the room. "Go back there and get us a bottle."

The stranger lifted one of those fancy beer jugs Rasmussen

brought out sometimes and calmly took a sip from it, then said, "I don't work here."

"I didn't ask if you work here, damn it!" Pike bellowed. "I told you to fetch us a bottle of whiskey!"

"I'm waiting on a buffalo steak," the young man replied, his voice still mild and unruffled.

Pike stomped toward him. "If you think I'm gonna let you talk back to me that way, you blasted young pup—"

The stranger set the beer jug on the table and then came up out of his chair faster than Pike expected. Pike stopped short and clawed at the gun on his hip, figuring the stranger was drawing on him.

The young man had pulled his iron, all right, his move swift and sure. But instead of leveling the gun and firing at Pike, he left it half-raised, pointing at the rough puncheon floor between them. His thumb was hooked around the hammer, holding it back.

Pike's gun was still in the holster, although he had succeeded in wrapping his fingers around the butt. He knew he wouldn't have time to finish his draw before the stranger tilted his gun barrel up and let the hammer fall.

Behind him, more chairs scraped on the floor as his men got to their feet. Unfortunately, Pike had made yet another mistake and placed his wide, barrel-chested body directly between them and the stranger. They couldn't open fire without risking hitting him.

Of course, that might be something Dennison or one of the others might do: *Poor ol' Billy J. Pike. Got hit in the back of the head by a stray bullet when that foolish stranger drew on us and we had no choice but to fill him full of lead.*

Still icy-nerved, the stranger said, "I never like to point a gun at a man unless I know I have no choice but to pull the trigger. Do I have any other choice here, Mr. Pike?"

Pike swallowed hard and said, "You know who I am?"

"I've heard of you."

"Then you know I've got the roughest bunch backin' me up that you'll find anywhere. If you kill me, you'll be full of holes a second later."

"More than likely," the stranger agreed, "but you'll have one hole in you." He squinted as if he were calculating something. "About one inch up from your right eyebrow, I'm thinking, catty-cornered a little toward the middle."

Pike just stared at him. While he was trying to think of what to say to that, Augustus Rasmussen emerged from the open door behind the bar. In his left hand, he held a big frying pan. A few sizzling sounds still came from it, audible in the tense silence, and so did the appetizing aroma of fried meat.

Rasmussen had a sawed-off shotgun in his right hand. He pointed its twin barrels at Pike and said, "You know the rules, *Herr* Pike. There will be no gunplay here at Hidden Valley. I do not like scrubbing bloodstains off the floor. I am too old and fat for such a task. So, if you please, you and your friends will leave now. Depart on friendly terms, because I would like to continue having your trade."

Pike finally found his voice again. "You crazy old man," he rasped. "You run us off now and we'll just come back and even the score with you later."

Rasmussen shook his head slowly. "I find that doubtful. I have many friends among those who ride the same trails you do. They like stopping here. Many have found it a useful and welcome respite. If they were to hear that I came to harm at your hands, they would hunt you down and have words with you."

Ben Proctor said, "He's right, Billy J. Everybody knows not to mess with Dutchy."

The stranger allowed the barrel of his Colt to sag another inch. "I'm honestly not looking for any trouble with you, Mr. Pike. As far as I'm concerned, we can chalk this up to a genuine misunderstanding and let it go at that."

Pike knew he was between a rock and a hard place here, as well as between a Colt and a sawed-off. The only way he wasn't going to die was by eating crow.

But he wasn't ready to die today, so he spat on the floor, trying to rid himself of the bitter, sour taste that had welled up under his tongue. He snarled and said, "I don't want any more of your watered-down whiskey, anyway, you big tub of lard."

He turned toward the door and added carelessly over his shoulder, "Come on, boys. I got somethin' better in mind for us. Somethin' profitable."

That was a lie. He had no idea what job they were going to pull next, let alone if it would provide a good payoff. But he knew he had to come up with something quickly if he wanted to hold the gang together under his leadership.

He felt relief go through him as he heard the footsteps of the other men following him out onto the porch. The crisis was over—for now.

And to ensure it stayed that way, the first potential payoff he saw, he was going to go after it, hard, and be damned to anybody who got in his way.

When the outlaws were gone, Rasmussen carefully uncocked the sawed-off shotgun and placed it on the bar. He forked the steak from the pan onto a plate, added a couple of biscuits to it, and carried the rough meal over to the table where the young stranger sat.

"I'm obliged to you for the food, *Herr* Rasmussen," the man said. "And for backing my play, too."

"You are very fast on the draw, my young friend, and I suspect you are accurate as well. But that will not help you if those animals ambush you later."

The stranger shrugged. "That's a chance I'll have to take, I reckon. That fella Pike had it in mind to rough me up to make a show of it for the others, and I wasn't in a mood to take it."

He grinned. "Varmint's twice my size. He could have stomped me to death if he wanted. That's why some folks call Colonel Colt's invention an equalizer."

He grew more serious as he went on, "What about you? Will they really leave you alone, like you said?"

"*Ja*, I have little to fear from the likes of them. *Mein* place is too popular among their fraternity."

"I'll have to remember that in case I ever come this way again." The stranger held out his hand. "By the way, my name is Hank Cavanaugh."

Rasmussen shook with him. "It is a pleasure to meet a gentleman such as yourself, *Herr* Cavanaugh. Do you think you will be returning to this vicinity again?"

Cavanaugh had cut off a piece of steak with a knife he drew from a sheath at his waist. He popped the morsel into his mouth, chewed slowly and appreciatively, and said, "Considering how good you can make a buffalo steak taste, I'd say there's a mighty good chance of it."

Chapter 16

The first three days on the trail passed without incident as Smoke and Sally accompanied the wagon train on its journey to Wyoming. Big Rock was more than thirty miles behind them now, the troubles they had encountered there nothing more than a memory.

Although Smoke enjoyed getting better acquainted with some of the women, he left that to Sally for the most part. He spent most of his time scouting ahead of the wagons, making sure the trail was easy enough for Annabelle and the other drivers to handle.

When he was with the wagons during rest stops and at night when the group made camp, Smoke talked more with Colonel Wilkinson than any of the others. Like most old-timers, the colonel had a fondness for the sound of his own voice, and most of his conversations tended to be about the war: the Late Unpleasantness, or the War of Northern Aggression, as he referenced it.

Smoke's own experiences during the Civil War were best forgotten. He had been a very young man in those days when the hostilities tearing apart the rest of the country had reared their bloody head in the Ozarks; as far as he was concerned, it was almost like those things had happened to an entirely different person.

As a result, when the subject of the war came up in his discussions with the colonel, Smoke brushed his own activities aside and simply said that he had spent a lot of time hoeing and plowing on the family farm.

As the colonel and Smoke were sitting by the campfire one night, Smoke was more willing to talk about his brother and father, and the things they had done, when Wilkinson asked about them.

"Both of them served as typical soldiers, at least starting out. My pa, Emmett, wound up riding with Colonel Mosby."

" 'The Gray Ghost,' " Wilkinson said. "John Singleton Mosby. I never met the man, but I heard a great deal about him. He was one of the most daring and accomplished cavalry commanders our side had. And some fine men rode with him, too. If your father was one of Mosby's Raiders, he's to be much admired."

"Yes, sir, I always thought so," Smoke said, nodding. "In the last days of the war, my brother Luke wound up being part of a plan Colonel Mosby came up with to smuggle some gold out of Richmond so that it could be taken west to continue funding the Confederacy."

"I believe I've heard some rumors about this as well." The colonel frowned. "But that attempt didn't end successfully, did it?"

"No, it sure didn't. Luke was one of the men guarding and transporting the gold. Some of the others in the group got greedy, turned traitor, and double-crossed the men who were supposed to be their comrades. They murdered the loyal soldiers and made off with the gold." Smoke paused. "One of the men they killed was my brother."

He had to wait a moment after saying that before resuming the tale. Bitter memory had tightened around his chest like a band.

"I learned all this from my pa later on, after he'd come back from the war and we headed west. My ma and sister and I had gotten word that Luke was dead, but we thought he'd been killed in the Battle of the Wilderness."

"Plenty of good men did lose their lives in that battle," the colonel said softly. "Too many."

"Yes, sir. And too many lost too much at home while the war was going on. I know you're all too familiar with that."

"Indeed, I am, my friend. Indeed, I am."

Smoke said, "By the time Pa finally got back to the Ozarks, my mother had passed away, and my sister had run off with a peddler. It was just me trying to keep the farm going, and to be honest with you, sir, it never was a very good farm, even when the whole family was there to work it. Those mountains just aren't made for such things."

As he sat on a crate, Wilkinson smiled as he rested both hands on the head of the cane planted between his feet. "I haven't been there, but from everything I've heard about the Ozarks, you're right, son."

"So with nothing really to hold us there, Pa thought we should head west." Smoke shrugged. "I thought we were just making a fresh start, sort of like you and your daughter plan to do. I didn't know that Pa was actually on the trail of those double-crossing thieves who killed Luke."

By now, Sally had come and sat down by Smoke, and Annabelle took a seat on her father's other side. Several of the other women had drawn closer, too, to listen to the story, their attractive faces attentive in the firelight.

"Did you ever catch up to those scoundrels?" the colonel asked.

Smoke nodded and said, "Pa did. He had left me with a friend we'd made on the trip, an old mountain man called 'Preacher,' while he searched for them. He found them, all right . . . and they killed him."

"Oh, no," Annabelle said. "That's terrible."

Colonel Wilkinson seemed to be staring at Smoke, even though his eyes didn't quite focus. "I suspect you took up that unfinished task, didn't you, Smoke?" he said.

"Yes, sir, I did. And I finished it."

He left it at that.

Earlier that day, head throbbing and in a surly mood because he was sober for a change, Billy J. Pike had spotted dust rising in the distance. His eyesight was keener when he wasn't drunk, so he supposed the trade, miserable though it might be, was worth it.

Ever since getting run off from Hidden Valley a few days earlier, Pike had felt a growing sense of desperation. His control of the gang was slipping away from him with every day that passed, and if their fortunes didn't improve soon, he knew he couldn't stop the revolt that was building.

He reined his horse to a stop and the others followed suit. Lifting a thick arm, he pointed to the west and said, "Look over yonder."

"Are you talking about that dust, Billy J.?" Dennison asked. "I saw it a few minutes ago."

Pike glared at him. "How come you didn't say somethin' about it then?"

Dennison shrugged and said, "I figured you'd get around to mentioning it whenever you were good and ready." He added in a mildly mocking tone, "I know how you don't like being rushed."

Damn that Hutch, always trying to undermine him and get his goat, Pike seethed. But he didn't allow the reaction to show on his face. Instead, he said, "Let's go take a look. Might be something worth checkin' out. Stagecoach, maybe."

"The stage line doesn't run over there," Yancy Meehan said. "There's a trail that wanders up toward Wyoming just east of the Park Range, but that's all."

Meehan was the most educated member of the bunch, and

the one who was most likely to back Hutch Dennison's play, if and when Dennison got around to making a move. Pike didn't like him, not even a little bit.

"Well, maybe it's a wagon train, then."

Dennison shook his head dubiously. "Not many wagon trains come through these parts anymore. And I'm not sure there's enough dust for that."

"Well, we won't ever know if we don't go take a look, will we?" Pike snapped. He turned his horse. "Come on."

Again, he didn't look to see if they were following when he gave the order. To do so would have been to demonstrate too much uncertainty. Like a hurt animal being trailed by a pack of wolves, he didn't dare show any sign of weakness. If he did, that would just encourage them to move in and take him down.

They were in an area of mostly rolling plains, with some low hills back to the east, that were just a slightly darker line on the horizon. In the far distance to the west loomed the Rocky Mountains. When the sun was right, the glistening reflection from the snowcapped peaks was visible. Other mountains, not quite as tall and impressive, but still rugged and majestic, could be seen to the northwest. That was the Park Range Yancy Meehan had mentioned.

Billy J. Pike was only somewhat familiar with this area. He had ridden through the Parks once with a posse not too far behind him, so he hadn't really had time to look around much. He'd been concentrating on getting away and had taken any promising trail that looked like it might offer sanctuary.

That was several years earlier and he was still alive and kicking, so he supposed it had worked. He had been riding alone in those days. The crew had accumulated gradually around him since then.

As they rode a little north of west, the small column of dust rising into the sky remained visible. Pike could tell they were getting closer to it. But Dennison was right—if a wagon train was causing the dust, it couldn't be a very big one.

But maybe some cowboys were pushing a small herd of cattle. Didn't seem like there was enough dust for that, either, Pike mused, but it was possible.

He and his companions hadn't engaged in much rustling. It was too blasted much work. Once you had the stolen cattle, you had to turn right around and sell them to get anything out of the deal. You couldn't spend beef on the hoof. That was why they stuck mostly to banks, stagecoaches, and trains. Those put money in your pocket right away.

Dennison pushed his horse up alongside Pike's and said, "Whatever it is, we're not going to get there before dark."

Pike squinted at the sun, which wasn't far above the mountains. "No, but we know which direction they're going. We'll close in and take a look."

"And ride right into trouble, maybe."

"I never said we wouldn't have to be careful," Pike replied testily. "Trust me, Hutch. I know what I'm doin'."

Dennison grunted and managed to pack a lot of eloquent disdain into the simple sound.

"I haven't steered us wrong yet, have I?" Pike demanded, hating that he sounded defensive.

"No, I reckon you haven't. We're not buried in some forgotten hole, and I suppose that counts for something." Dennison's voice hardened. "But there's no telling how many good opportunities we might have missed in the past because you didn't think something was a good idea."

Pike struggled to rein in the anger that bubbled up inside him. Part of him wanted to pull iron and blow that mouthy son of a buck right out of the saddle. But if he did, Yancy Meehan would kill him, more than likely. And to be honest about his own capabilities, which Pike hated doing on general principles, he wasn't even sure he could take Dennison off guard—enough to ventilate him successfully, that is.

Pike blew out a breath and said, "We're gonna have to get some things straight between us one of these days, Hutch. But not today or tonight. We've maybe got one of those opportunities you were just talkin' about. We'd better see about that before we do anything else."

Dennison shrugged. "Can't really argue with you about that, Billy J."

Night fell quickly across the plains, as it always did, once the sun dropped behind the mountains. The outlaws reined in to rest their horses for a short time and to allow the darkness to deepen even more.

Finally, a faint orange glow appeared, low to the horizon.

"That's a campfire," Pike said with triumph in his voice. "We can follow it straight to whoever that is. We'll just have to take it slow and easy when we get close so they don't hear horses comin'."

They rode at an easy pace and slowed even more, as Pike had said, when they drew within a mile of the campfire, which was visible now as a distinct light.

Pike reined in and swung down from his saddle, calling softly for the other men to do so as well. As he stood there holding the reins, he said, "We'll go on foot from here. Keep your horses as quiet as you can."

"The wind's changeable," Dennison pointed out. "The horses in that camp are liable to catch the scent of our mounts."

"We won't get close enough with the horses to stir them up too much," Pike said confidently. "Once we're within a quarter of a mile, you and me will go ahead on foot and leave the other boys and the horses to wait for us."

Even without being able to see him that well in the darkness, Pike could make out the stiff stance of Dennison's body and knew he was skeptical. But it was a reasonable plan, and Dennison couldn't refuse to go along with it.

"Sure," he said after a moment. "Sounds good."

They pushed ahead, on foot and leading their horses, and a short time later, Pike called a halt by announcing softly, "That's close enough."

He handed his horse's reins to Walt Carlisle and told him to hang on to them. Dennison turned his mount over to Meehan.

Then Pike and Dennison stole forward, moving carefully so that they didn't trip over anything, fall in a hole, or blunder into some brush that might make a noise and warn the people in the camp up ahead that someone was skulking around in the darkness.

They were still too far back in the shadows to be seen when Pike stopped again. He didn't want to get close enough for the firelight to reflect off anything metal he and Dennison were carrying or wearing. Both men dropped to their knees and from there stretched out on their bellies. Pike took his hat off so it wouldn't obstruct his view. Dennison did the same.

From where the men were, it was impossible to miss the four covered wagons parked between two and three hundred yards away. A smaller vehicle, probably a buckboard, sat near the wagons, at the edge of the light spilling from the campfire. A dark mass off to one side had to be the animals from the wagon teams, picketed out so they could graze, and several other horses by the looks of it.

"I told you it was a wagon train," Pike whispered.

"Just barely," Dennison replied. "Four wagons isn't hardly enough to call it a train."

"What would you call it, then?"

"Never mind," Dennison said with impatience in his voice. "You notice anything odd about that bunch, Pike?"

Dennison hadn't called him Billy J., which annoyed Pike, but he let it go. He stared at the camp for a long moment, and after several heartbeats had gone by, he said, "I don't see anything strange, Hutch."

"Where are the men?"

Pike peered harder through the darkness. "I see a couple of fellas sittin' by the fire. Looks like an old-timer and a younger gent. They're talkin' about something."

"Where are the other men?"

Pike looked again. He saw several women sitting by the fire, and a few people were moving around the camp . . . and all wore dresses. . . .

"Wait," he said. "Are those two men the only hombres in the whole camp?"

"As far as I can see, they are," Dennison said. "I've been watching close ever since we stopped, and I haven't seen a single one besides them."

"There could be some men in the wagons."

"I suppose that's possible. But what are the odds they'd all be inside the wagons, while their women are out moving around and taking care of the camp chores? A couple of the women just carried water buckets out to the horses."

"That's a good job for a woman," Pike insisted.

"Let's just keep watching. Maybe some other fellas will put in an appearance."

But as the minutes dragged past, that didn't happen. Pike and Dennison lay there on the ground for at least half an hour, never taking their eyes off the distant camp, and in all that time, they didn't see a single man other than the two who had been sitting by the campfire. The older one of that pair got up after a while and went to a wagon. A fair-haired woman helped him climb in and then entered the wagon herself.

The man left by the fire put his arm around the waist of a dark-haired woman and they strolled off to bedrolls at the edge of camp. They were clearly a couple and bedded down next to each other.

The fire was dying down. More of the women retreated into the wagons. Finally, only one was left in sight: a short, stocky blonde who sat on a crate with a rifle across her knees, back at the edge of the light. She had to be a sentry. More than likely, she would remain on guard duty for a while and then switch out with one of the other women.

"By grab, Harry," Pike breathed. "That's a wagon train full

of women! They don't have any men with them except the two we saw earlier."

"That's what I told you," Dennison said.

"And you were right, Hutch, damned if you weren't." Pike took a deep breath. "You know what this means, don't you?"

"You tell me," Dennison drawled. "What does it mean?"

"It means they won't be able to put up much of a fight when we raid that wagon train tomorrow and take everything they got!"

CHAPTER 17

As the wagons rolled onward the next morning, the trail began bending in a more northwesterly direction. By midday, foothills were cropping up to the left. Mountains rose on that side another twenty miles farther north, easily visible in the clear high-country air. As Smoke rode out in front of the group, he recalled that the trail would hug the base of those peaks as it led up into Wyoming.

The rataplan of hoofbeats behind him prompted a glance over his shoulder. He saw Sally trotting toward him on her chestnut mare and slowed so that she could catch up to him.

When she did, she rode alongside him and said, "I hope you don't mind that I joined you, Smoke."

"Have I ever objected to your company?" he asked with a smile.

"Only when you thought I was sticking my nose into something too dangerous."

"Well, you do have a tendency to do that, now and then," he allowed. "There have been a few times I was frustrated enough I felt like paddling your bottom."

She smiled sweetly at him and said, "Maybe I wouldn't have minded."

He rolled his eyes and then laughed. "Anyway, I'm happy

that you're riding with me today," he said. "I imagine that buckboard seat was getting a mite uncomfortable after so many days in a row on it."

"A saddle is a lot better. And I thought it might be a good idea for this mare of mine to stretch her legs a little more than she has been. I asked Charlotte McPherson if she'd mind driving the buckboard for a while. She was happy to."

"That's good," Smoke said, nodding, glad that things had worked out so she could join him.

Sally looked mighty fetching as she rode alongside. She wore a pair of men's trousers and shirt, but they weren't borrowed from Smoke's extra clothing. They were garments she had bought special for riding, and as such, they fit her well—well enough to hug the supple curves of her body in ample testimony that she was a beautifully made woman. Her thick dark hair spilled out from under a gray hat.

She wasn't wearing a gunbelt and holstered Colt today—although, more than once, Smoke had seen her pack iron like that—but the stock of a Winchester carbine stuck up from a sheath strapped under the fender of her saddle.

Smoke thought the same thing he often did when he looked at her: He was a damned lucky man.

"You seem to know where we're going," Sally commented. "But you said you'd never been to Brimstone Butte before."

"I haven't been to the settlement," Smoke said, "but I think I recall having seen the butte itself. It just didn't have a name then or a town nearby. Of course, that was nigh on to ten years ago, when I was running wild all over this country with Preacher, so I can't be certain I'm remembering it right. We saw a lot of different buttes."

"I think I trust your memory. You're one of the smartest men I've ever met."

Smoke laughed. "A fella can be smart as all get-out and still have a plumb terrible memory."

"I suppose. But I'd still rely on you to know where you're going, anywhere, any time."

"I'll try to live up to that."

"Smoke . . ."

The tone of her voice made him look over at her. She was frowning about something.

"What's wrong?"

"I'm not sure anything is wrong," Sally said. "But something odd happened this morning, and I've been thinking about it ever since."

Smoke trusted Sally's instincts completely. He knew that if something was bothering her, it was worth investigating. He said, "Tell me about it."

"It was while Annabelle was cleaning up after breakfast. She picked up the coffeepot and was turning toward their wagon when she stumbled and dropped it. Colonel Wilkinson was sitting there beside her. He reached out and caught the pot before it could hit the ground."

"You mean he reacted like he could see what he was doing?"

"That's exactly right."

Smoke thought it over for a few seconds and then asked, "Did Annabelle say anything when she dropped the pot?"

"She exclaimed the way a person does when they're startled. She said, 'Oh!' or something like that."

"So the colonel could have known something was wrong."

"You mean he just reached out instinctively in response to her cry and happened to catch it?"

"Well, you can't rule that out," Smoke said.

Sally considered and said, "I suppose not. But it's a bit of a stretch of the imagination, isn't it?"

"Sure. But we've both been around the colonel quite a bit now. Has it ever seemed to you like he's not really blind?"

"Not until today," Sally said.

"What reason would he have for faking such a thing?"

"I can't think of any," she admitted. "But it still seems strange to me."

"What happened after he caught the coffeepot?" Smoke asked.

"He held it out to Annabelle and she took it and put it away, as if nothing had happened."

"Did they notice that you were watching them?"

"I don't think so. I was on the other side of the buckboard and just happened to be glancing that way right then."

"I'll admit, the whole thing does seem a mite odd," Smoke said. "But if the colonel's been putting on an act all this time, he's mighty good at it. It doesn't make sense that he would be faking blindness. Even if he is, I don't figure it makes any difference. They're still headed for Brimstone Butte, and we're still going to do our best to get them there safely."

"Of course," Sally agreed without hesitation. "It's a mystery, but it doesn't really change anything."

Smoke nodded, but concern lurked in his eyes. He didn't care for mysteries. They had a way of nagging at his brain. During this conversation with Sally, he had been playing the devil's advocate to a certain extent. Maybe what the colonel had done was just a fluke. Maybe it didn't make any difference, one way or the other.

But he was still going to keep his eyes open and see if he could spot any strange behavior on the colonel's part.

That wasn't the only thing causing him a certain degree of unease. All day, he had experienced a funny tingling on the back of his neck. Smoke recognized that for what it was—the feeling of being watched.

That might not amount to anything, either. Could be some Indians, most likely peaceful, had spotted them in the distance and were keeping an eye on them. Maybe some other pilgrims, or a drifting cowhand riding the grub line. That wary sensation didn't have to mean a thing.

But if it did, Smoke intended to be ready.

* * *

Billy J. Pike and his men had ridden hard most of the night to get well ahead of the small wagon train. Some of them had wanted to go ahead and hit the wagons during the night so they could take the pilgrims by surprise. Pike had insisted that it would be better to get ahead of them and set up an ambush.

To his surprise, Hutch Dennison had agreed with him. "That will give us a better chance to study them," Dennison had said. "Billy J. and I only saw two men, but that's not an absolute guarantee there couldn't be others. We don't want to go riding in there tonight and find twenty well-armed men inside the wagons waiting for us."

That was pretty smart thinking. Pike was angry with himself for not presenting that same argument, but it hadn't occurred to him. He'd just been going by his instincts. It was always better to ambush somebody and cut down on the opposition with a ruthless first strike.

That was why they always gunned down the driver and shotgun guard right away whenever they held up a stagecoach, without giving those hombres a chance to surrender. A man who gave up could still turn around and cause trouble for you. A dead man couldn't.

Now Pike, Dennison, and Cunningham were hidden in some trees. The trail the wagons were following ran about fifty yards in front of their position. A hundred yards away was a gully where Meehan, Carlisle, and Proctor were hunkered down out of sight, a little farther to the south. All the horses were picketed in the trees behind where Pike and his two companions waited.

Two riders came into view before the wagons did. One of them was the man they had seen talking to the old-timer the night before. The other one wasn't that same white-haired old man, though.

Pike leaned forward and squinted. "There was another hombre

somewhere in them wagons after all," he said. "Blast it, Hutch, how'd we miss that fella?"

"I suppose he never showed himself while we were watching," Dennison said. "He doesn't look very big. A kid, maybe?"

"Kid or not, he's packin' a rifle in his saddle boot, so he's dangerous," Cunningham put in. "If there's any more where he came from, this job ain't gonna be the sure thing you claimed it'd be, Billy J."

"One man won't make any difference," Pike insisted. "We don't even know that there's more of them with the wagons."

Dennison leaned forward and peered intently at the riders as they came closer. After a moment, he laughed.

"Hold on a minute, boys," he said. "Take a better look at that second rider. You notice anything?"

Pike frowned and shook his head. "I don't know what you're talkin' about."

"I never saw a man who filled out a shirt front as well as that so-called hombre does."

Pike looked again and let out a low whistle of surprise and admiration. "By grab!" he exclaimed. "That's a woman."

"And a good-looking one, I'd guess," Dennison said. "I wonder if she's the one that fella bedded down with last night."

Cunningham chuckled. "Maybe he's takin' turns with all those fillies. Bein' the only young gent in a wagon train full o' gals who need satisfyin' would sure wear a man out, but what a way to travel!"

"Damn it, get your mind back on what we're doin' here," Pike said. "Women who'd set out across country in wagons like that aren't gonna throw up their hands and surrender. Chances are, we're gonna have to kill most of 'em right off. Any that are left, we can figure out what we're gonna do with them later on, but until then, just think about the loot we're fixin' to get our hands on."

"Sure, Billy J., sure," Cunningham said. "But you can't blame a fella for bein' interested when good-lookin' women are involved."

They let it go at that and continued watching as the two riders moved past them. It was easy to see now that one of them was female, even though she was dressed like a man.

The wagons were in sight a hundred yards back. They rolled forward slowly, rocking a little from side to side. The terrain was fairly level where the trail ran, but there were always little humps and depressions in the ground and those irregularities were magnified by the big wheels.

The outlaws had worked out their plan before they took their positions. Pike, Dennison, and Cunningham would shoot the leaders in the first two teams. Meehan, Carlisle, and Proctor would disable the second two teams by killing the leaders in them, as well as the pair of horses pulling the buckboard.

As soon as that was done, then whoever had a good shot would drill the two men. The old-timer, who was riding on the driver's seat of the lead wagon next to a blond woman handling the reins, might be dangerous despite his age, so he had to die, too.

What happened after that would depend on how the women reacted. If they fought back, Pike and his bunch would shoot to kill, until all the defenders were either wiped out or had surrendered.

Pike hoped a few of the women would give up. Having some female company around would go a long way toward improving the bunch's morale and postpone any uprising against him for a while.

The first wagon had drawn even with the spot where Pike, Dennison, and Cunningham were hidden in the trees. Pike leaned against a trunk to steady himself and raised his Winchester to his shoulder. He had already levered a round into the chamber so there would be no chance of that distinctive noise alerting the intended victims. He settled his sights on the lead horse on this side and began tightening his finger on the trigger.

Hank Cavanaugh was ambling along on horseback, not feeling any real urgency. Sure, he had places to be, and things to do, but despite his youth, he knew that some things had to play out at their own pace. If you tried to rush them too much, you ran the risk of messing things up and not being able to accomplish your goals at all.

And despite appearing to be an unambitious drifter, he had goals he wanted to attain in this life. Yes, sir, he did.

But he also knew that when the chance to seize an opportunity came along unexpectedly, you sometimes had to move fast to seize it.

As he reined in sharply and leaned forward in the saddle, he realized this was one of those chances.

He had just topped a little knoll that gave him a good view of the terrain for several hundred yards. Directly ahead of him, a gully ran north and south. Off to the left, toward the foothills and the mountains, a thick stand of trees sloped gradually upward.

In the center of the landscape spread out before him, four wagons and a buckboard rocked along, following the rough trail.

In the gully, which was about five feet deep, three men crouched, holding rifles. They were hidden from the people on the wagons, but Cavanaugh could see them just fine from where he was.

As the wagons passed the men, they straightened and lifted the rifles to their shoulders. They drew beads on the wagon teams, or on the drivers, Cavanaugh had no way of knowing which.

The travelers clearly weren't aware that those bushwhackers were there. That meant the would-be killers had plenty of time to aim.

Cavanaugh didn't have that luxury. He yanked his Winchester out of its saddle sheath, levered the rifle as he threw it to his shoulder, and opened fire, sending a sizzling volley of bullets at the men in the gully as fast as he could work the repeater's lever.

CHAPTER 18

As the shots crashed out behind Smoke and Sally, four or five of them in a matter of heartbeats, Smoke whirled Drifter around and called to Sally, "Keep going! Get out of the line of fire!"

He dug his bootheels into the big stallion's flanks, causing Drifter to leap ahead into a pounding gallop. More gunfire blasted from both sides of the trail. One of the horses in the lead wagon's team screamed and leaped against its harness, then stumbled, obviously hit.

Powdersmoke gushed from rifle muzzles in some trees to the west of the trail. Seeing that, Smoke pulled his right-hand Colt and emptied it in that direction. The range was too long for much accuracy with a handgun, but all Smoke was trying to do at the moment was spook the bushwhackers hidden in the trees and maybe disrupt their ambush.

He pouched the empty iron and leaned forward in the saddle to urge the stallion to greater speed. A glance over his shoulder showed him that Sally had ignored what he told her and was galloping after him, right back toward the thick of the battle. She was about twenty yards behind him and had drawn her carbine from the saddle boot, clutching it in her right hand, while her left held the chestnut's reins.

Maybe he really ought to paddle her bottom good and hard instead of just joking about it, he thought fleetingly. But he could ponder that later on, assuming they both survived this little dustup.

All the wagons had come to an abrupt halt, and so had the buckboard at the tail end of the column. Smoke was a little surprised to see that all the driver's seats were empty. The women handling the teams must have dived into the wagon beds at the sound of the first gunshot ringing out. He didn't see Colonel Wilkinson, either, and hoped the old-timer was keeping his head down. The sideboards of the wagon beds were thick enough to stop most bullets.

Rifle barrels thrust out from under the canvas covers, as well as from the openings at the front and back of each wagon. The weapons cracked swiftly as a haze of powdersmoke began to form in the air. The women were fighting back and not wasting any time about doing it.

Movement in the distance caught Smoke's eye. A man on horseback charged down from a knoll, firing a rifle as he rode hard toward the scene of the ambush. He didn't appear to be aiming at the wagons, however; instead, his shots were directed at something off to Smoke's left.

It looked like the stranger was trying to help them, so Smoke veered his horse toward the trees on the other side. The bushwhackers hidden there saw him coming in their direction and tried to discourage him. He felt the hot breath of a slug passing close by his face.

Drifter was moving too fast for the concealed riflemen to draw a bead on him or Smoke. The big stallion reached the trees and dashed between a couple of them.

Smoke was ready. He had kicked his feet free of the stirrups already, so all he had to do was reach up and grab a sturdy-looking branch as Drifter passed under it. His hands slapped against the branch and closed in an iron grip. The horse's momentum pulled Smoke cleanly out of the saddle. He swung back and forth for a second before dropping lithely to the ground.

Spinning around, Smoke pressed his back against a tree trunk and, taking cartridges from the loops on his shell belt, swiftly reloaded the Colt he had emptied a few moments earlier. He drew the left-hand revolver, as well, and had both hands filled with iron as he crouched and twisted toward the spot where he thought the bushwhackers had been lurking, waiting for the wagons to come along.

Somebody had spotted them and set up this ambush, he thought, probably figuring that the little caravan would be easy pickings.

They were about to find out different.

A shadow flickered in front of him. An instant later, a man holding a rifle darted into view, frantically twisting his head from side to side searching for Smoke. They knew he was somewhere in the trees with them now, and they were trying to bring the fight to him.

The problem was, this hombre wasn't anywhere near quick enough. He spotted Smoke and tried to swing the rifle toward him. The man's eyes widened in alarm as he realized he wasn't going to be able to do it in time.

Smoke's Colts crashed in unison. Both slugs pounded into the man's chest. One bullet shredded a lung, while the other pulped his heart. The double impact lifted him off his feet and dumped him on his back. His left leg kicked a couple of times and then the unmistakable stillness of death settled over him.

As the echoes of the gun-thunder died away, a man shouted, "Jethro! Did you get him, Jethro?"

Jethro wasn't going to be answering, Smoke thought as he eased forward through the shadows of the thick growth.

Jethro's friend should have known that he hadn't been successful. The booming of Smoke's Colts was much different from the crack of a rifle.

Instinct warned Smoke and caused him to press against a tree trunk again. A fraction of a second later, a gun roared in front of him and a slug chewed splinters from the trunk only inches from his face. He fired back at the muzzle flash, felt as much as heard the wind-rip of another bullet whipping past his ear. His other Colt bucked against his palm as he fired again.

The undergrowth thrashed wildly ahead of him. A lean, dark-faced man reeling into view, crashing through the branches as he pawed futilely at the blood-leaking hole in his chest. He snapped off one final shot from the gun he held as he twisted off his feet and sank to the ground. He didn't move again as he lay there in a huddled heap.

Smoke didn't know how many bushwhackers there were, so he stayed put for a minute to see if any more of them would come to him and save him the trouble of looking for them.

No one showed up, but the same voice Smoke had heard earlier called nervously, "Hutch? You hear me, Hutch? What happened? Did you get that son of a gun? Hutch?"

The voice had turned into more of a plaintive wail by the time the ambusher finished wasting his time by asking questions of a dead man. Smoke wasn't surprised when a sudden crashing in the brush told him the man's nerve had broken and he was trying to get away. Smoke triggered a couple of rounds toward the racket, but he couldn't tell if his shots found their target.

A moment later, he heard the rapid drum of hoofbeats. The third bushwhacker—probably the last one—had reached his horse and was lighting a shuck away from here as fast as he could.

Smoke didn't have any interest in pursuing him. Let the varmint run, he thought as he thumbed fresh cartridges into the Colts' cylinders, replacing the ones he had fired. He didn't figure the bushwhacker would stop for a long time.

Right now, the gunfire coming from the wagons had stopped, and Smoke was more interested in checking on the colonel, Annabelle, the other women—and Sally.

Hank Cavanaugh was enough of a skilled rider to guide his horse with his knees as he used both hands to aim and fire the Winchester as fast as he could work the lever. He gripped the reins tightly between his teeth to keep them from trailing. The rifle kicked hard against his shoulder as he poured lead into the gully where the three bushwhackers had lurked, only to have their ambush turned around on them.

Now they were the ones under attack from an unexpected threat.

One of the men must have panicked as bullets flew around him. Instead of hunkering down lower in the gully, he scrambled out of it and leaped to his feet to make a run for safety.

Unfortunately for him, he rose just in time to catch one of Cavanaugh's slugs in his chest. His arms flung out to the sides as he flew off his feet in what amounted to a backward dive into the gully.

More of Cavanaugh's bullets kicked up dirt and gravel around the remaining two men. One of them swung around and returned his fire. None of those wild shots came close enough for Cavanaugh to hear them passing him, and before the ambusher could draw an accurate bead, he jolted forward and fell on his face. When he'd turned to face Cavanaugh, he must have raised up just enough to present the back of his head as a target for one of the defenders in the wagons.

That left just one man for Cavanaugh to deal with, but that hombre wasn't giving up. Powdersmoke gushed from his rifle as he sent several shots Cavanaugh's way. Cavanaugh's horse jumped wildly as a slug creased his shoulder. Cavanaugh had to stop shooting and grab the reins with his left hand to tighten them and bring his plunging mount under control.

Something sizzled past his ear. That hombre was getting the range, but the horse capering around made Cavanaugh a difficult target. That was probably the only thing that saved his life.

He kicked his feet free of the stirrups and dived out of the saddle to the left, landing on his shoulder and rolling a couple of times as the spooked horse danced away from him instead of stomping him. That was a bit of luck, and Cavanaugh didn't want to waste it. He came up on one knee and brought the rifle to his shoulder again.

From where he was, all he could see of the third man was his head and right shoulder. Cavanaugh took less than a second to aim and squeezed the trigger.

At the same time, flame spurted from the muzzle of the rifle the man was aiming at him. The bullets' paths must have almost crossed as they whipped through the air.

Cavanaugh felt a phantom hand pluck at his right sleeve. But the man in the gully toppled out of sight. Cavanaugh figured he must have hit the man, either in the head or shoulder—and no matter which, he ought to be out of the fight. A glance at his sleeve showed him where the enemy's bullet had ripped it, but the flesh underneath was untouched. You couldn't come any closer than that.

Cavanaugh leaped to his feet and debated for a second whether to go after his horse or run forward, to make sure the bushwhackers in the gully were done.

Movement spied from the corner of his eye made up his mind for him. He looked across the little valley and saw a man on horseback leaning forward in the saddle as he urged his mount on to greater speed. Cavanaugh recognized the barrel-chested, red-bearded figure fleeing the scene.

"Why, that's Billy J. Pike, his own self," Cavanaugh murmured.

He whirled around and ran toward his horse. Pike was behind this attack on the wagon train. Cavanaugh didn't want him to get away with that.

The horse had settled down some after being upset by the bullet graze. Cavanaugh slowed down and called softly to the animal as he approached. The horse lifted its head and regarded him warily, but they had been together for a while and the horse was used to him. Cavanaugh got close enough to take hold of the dangling reins. The horse didn't try to pull away from him, but instead settled down even more.

Cavanaugh thumbed some rounds through his rifle's loading gate to replace the ones he'd fired, then slipped the weapon back in its sheath and swung up into the saddle. He rode hard out into the valley and then swung to follow the frantically galloping Billy J. Pike, who disappeared over a little rise.

Smoke whistled for Drifter and mounted quickly when the big black stallion trotted up to him. He rode toward the wagons and spotted Sally standing next to the lead vehicle with Annabelle Wilkinson. The colonel leaned out of the wagon bed, over the back of the driver's seat.

Women holding rifles were climbing out of the other wagons. The battle seemed to be over, but they were still armed in case of more trouble.

Relief went through Smoke as he saw that Sally appeared to be unharmed. He reined in and dismounted, then asked her, "Are you all right?"

"Fine," she said. "None of those shots came anywhere close to me."

"You're lucky," he said. Turning to Annabelle, he asked, "What about the rest of you? Anybody hurt?"

"Two horses were killed," she said. "A couple of others were wounded, but I think they'll be all right. No one else was injured." A fierce expression appeared on her face. "What about the men who ambushed us?"

"A couple of them are dead," Smoke told her. "I suspect some of the others are, too. But at least one of them got away."

"I'm sorry to hear that, about the one who got away, I mean. Do you think they intended to rob us?"

"That's the only thing that makes sense. I'll go check on the ones on the other side of the valley. Might be a good idea to tell the ladies to stay on this side of the wagons until I get back, so they'll have some cover if any more gunplay breaks out."

Annabelle nodded in understanding. Sally started to reach for her horse's reins, evidently intending to accompany Smoke, but the stern look he gave her prompted her to say, "I'll stay here with the ladies."

"Good idea," he said. He mounted up and rode Drifter toward the long and relatively shallow gully—the spot where the other bushwhackers had been hidden.

When he got there, it took only a few moments to confirm that the three men who'd been hidden over here were dead. There was no way of telling who had drilled them, that stranger who had rushed down from the knoll and alerted the travelers to their danger, or the women from the wagons themselves. They had mounted a vigorous defense when they found themselves under attack. The important thing was that the outlaws no longer represented a threat.

Smoke rode back to the wagons and reported his findings. He told Annabelle, "The way you ladies reacted to that ambush was pretty impressive. You all did your jobs like well-drilled soldiers."

"Thank you, sir, thank you!" Colonel Wilkinson boomed from the driver's seat of the lead wagon, where he now sat. "I tried to pass along everything I know about such things to my daughter, and Annabelle did a splendid job of whipping this outfit into shape, if I do say so myself."

"We knew when we started west that we were likely to run

into trouble somewhere along the way," Annabelle added in a much less bombastic fashion. "We all figured it would be a good idea if we knew how to take care of ourselves. Before we left, we practiced what we would do in certain situations, and we've continued to do so as we traveled."

She paused and then said, "Today was the first time we've actually had to put all those plans into action, though."

"You did a fine job of it," Smoke told her. "I'd better get those dead horses unhitched. It's a good thing you brought along some extra draft animals."

"We wanted to be prepared," Annabelle said. She turned and called, "Roberta, can you give Mr. Jensen a hand?"

A tall woman, with broad shoulders, walked up from the second wagon. She looked strong enough to handle most tasks, and she pitched in with enthusiasm to help Smoke with the grim chore of unhitching the gunned-down horses.

Susie Beale came forward, too, and said, "If I can do anything to help, I'd be happy to, Mr. Jensen. I grew up on a farm."

Susie, like her friend Delia, was a mite on the delicate side, Smoke thought. He just smiled and said, "I'm obliged to you, Miss Beale, but I reckon Miss Roberta and I have this job under control."

"All right, but if you need help with anything, let me know. Delia and I want to earn our keep on this trip."

The brief conversation with Susie set the wheels of Smoke's brain in motion. He had halfway expected that hard case Gus Gerhardt and his bunch to follow them and try to cause more trouble. Gerhardt had seemed like the stubborn sort, unwilling to admit defeat.

But there had been no sign of them so far. None of the men involved in this ambush had been with Gerhardt in Big Rock. Smoke hoped they could dodge that particular problem the rest of the way to Brimstone Butte, even though they might run into other mishaps—such as being ambushed by outlaws.

Smoke and Roberta were getting the fresh horses into the

traces when a sudden flurry of gunfire in the distance made him look up.

More trouble, but it wasn't close, and it might not have anything to do with them.

Smoke wasn't going to bet on that, and out of habit, he reached down, grasped the butts of his Colts, and lifted the revolvers out of their holsters, just a little bit, before allowing them to slide back down into leather.

If gun trouble came their way, he was going to be ready for it.

CHAPTER 19

The wagons had fallen out of sight behind Hank Cavanaugh by the time he spotted Billy J. Pike again. The outlaw was still riding hard, putting as much distance as he could between himself and the site of the failed ambush—and also between himself and the bodies of his former comrades.

This attempted holdup had been a disaster for Pike, but if he got away, he could go somewhere else, then start over and assemble a new gang, and bring more violence and death into the world at the expense of other innocents.

It wasn't Cavanaugh's job to prevent that from happening, of course, but he knew he'd have a hard time living with himself if he just turned his back on this situation. Bringing Pike to justice wouldn't interfere with any of the plans he had for the future. At least, he hoped not.

There was the varmint! And then, suddenly, Pike was gone again. Cavanaugh stared for a second. It was as if Pike had vanished into thin air.

No, he had just charged down a crumbling bank into a dry wash, Cavanaugh realized as he caught sight of the empty creek bed cutting across the landscape. He heard the muffled sound of hoofbeats from Pike's horse on the wash's sandy bottom as he sent his own mount sliding and lunging down the slope.

He hoped the horse wouldn't fall out from under him and break a leg. That would be a catastrophe.

The horse reached the bottom of the wash safely, and Cavanaugh turned to follow Pike. He hoped the outlaw hadn't noticed that he was being followed; if he had, this twisting wash, with its blind bends, would be a good place to set a trap for the pursuer.

Cavanaugh drew his Colt as he rode, put the reins between his teeth again for a moment, and slipped a cartridge into the chamber that he usually kept empty so the gun's hammer could rest on it. He wanted to have a full wheel at his disposal when he caught up to Billy J. Pike.

Cavanaugh followed the wash for at least half a mile without catching sight of Pike. He could still hear the man's horse moving along ahead of him, though. But Cavanaugh knew Pike could have dismounted and sent the horse on, riderless, to make it seem as if he didn't know that he was being trailed.

That natural caution paid off when Cavanaugh rounded a bend and spotted a flicker of movement to his right. Instinctively, he dived left out of the saddle as a rifle cracked and a bullet screamed through the space where he had been, only a mere second earlier.

Cavanaugh's yell sent the startled horse plunging ahead, out of the line of fire. His gun was in his right hand as he scrambled up onto both knees and braced himself on his left hand. He had a clear line of sight to a spot about fifty feet away, where the wash's bank had crumbled, leaving a pile of sandstone rocks.

Billy J. Pike crouched behind those rocks, holding a rifle and lining up another shot at Cavanaugh.

Cavanaugh triggered a round that struck one of the rocks Pike was using for cover. The bullet kicked up a spray of grit that flew in Pike's face and caused him to jerk back. The rifle in his hands blasted again, but the shot went wild and high. He stumbled backward and straightened, so more of his body was visible as he pawed at his eyes with one hand. That grit must have half blinded him.

Cavanaugh aimed and fired twice, taking his time, since the range was a little long. The booming reports echoed back from the walls of the dry wash.

His shots were accurate. Both slugs pounded into Pike's chest and caused his stocky frame to shiver from the impact. He dropped the rifle and pressed both hands to his bloody chest. He reeled two steps to the side and collapsed.

Keeping his gun aimed at the fallen figure, Cavanaugh rose to his feet and advanced. As he came closer, he heard Pike's harsh breathing as it rasped in the outlaw's throat.

Pike lifted his head slightly and blinked pain-wracked eyes at Cavanaugh. "Y-you," he managed to get out past lips covered in bloody froth from a bullet-ventilated lung. "The kid . . . from Hidden Valley."

"That's right," Cavanaugh said. "You're not long for this world, Pike. Is there anything you need to say or a message you want me to pass on to anybody?"

"You . . . you . . ." Vile curses spilled from Pike's mouth, concluding with "You . . . can go to hell!"

Then his voice dropped to a whisper as he added, "D-don't leave me . . . out here . . . for the buzzards."

It would have been a fitting fate for him. More than likely, he had left plenty of victims for the buzzards in the past. But Cavanaugh didn't have enough of a cruel streak in him to point that out.

Instead, he said, "I'll see to it that you're laid to rest, proper-like. I'll even make sure they put Billy J. Pike on the marker."

Pike sighed as if in satisfaction when he heard that. His eyelids drooped and closed. His chest stopped rising and falling, and the harsh breathing faded to silence.

Cavanaugh reloaded two of the three chambers he had expended, eased the hammer down on the empty one, and went to catch his horse. He would need it to round up Pike's mount so he could load the dead outlaw onto it.

Then it would be time for him to pay a visit to that wagon train and find out how bad the situation was there.

The wagons were ready to roll again, but Annabelle Wilkinson insisted that burying the dead outlaws was the decent thing to do.

"Just because they were terrible men who were trying to kill us, that doesn't mean we can ignore the fact that they were human," she said. "It won't take that long to lay them to rest."

Smoke could have left the varmints for the scavengers, right where they had fallen, without ever losing a second's sleep over it, but most of the women looked like they agreed with Annabelle—and most importantly, so did Sally.

"We'll take turns digging," Helen Pryor said. "That way, we'll all share the work."

Smoke didn't argue, because he didn't mind waiting awhile before departing. For one thing, he was curious about the man who had warned them of the impending ambush and then had taken part in the battle on their side. The fella had disappeared, chasing after the outlaw who'd gotten away, and Smoke figured the shots they had heard earlier might have come from a fight between those two. He was curious to find out who had won—and who had given them a hand.

He hoped that if the man had survived the skirmish, he would return to the wagon train.

"Just one big grave," he told the women. "And it doesn't have to be as deep as you'd normally dig, either. And even that's probably more than these owlhoots deserve."

The women looked at Annabelle, who nodded in agreement

with Smoke. Roberta, Helen, and a couple of others fetched shovels from the wagons and started digging, marking out a plot big enough to contain the five bodies.

Six bodies, Smoke corrected himself a few minutes later when he spotted two horses heading toward them. The man riding in the lead trailed another animal behind him, with an unmoving burden draped over its saddle.

"Sally," Smoke called softly, "get your rifle."

She was watching the women work on the mass grave. Turning toward Smoke, she saw the approaching rider, too, and went over to the buckboard to pick up her carbine from where she had placed it on the seat. Then she and Smoke walked out a short distance away from the others and waited for the stranger.

He had his horse's reins in his left hand and kept his right well away from the gun on his hip, probably to make sure it was obvious he wasn't looking for trouble. As he came closer, Smoke could tell that he was relatively young, probably in his middle twenties. The sandy-brown hair under a darker brown hat was long enough to touch his shirt collar. He had a neatly trimmed mustache, the same color as his hair. The range clothes he wore were clean, but showed definite signs of age. However, his gun and holster appeared to be well cared for, as did his saddle and the horse he rode. Those were things in his favor.

Smoke had seen dozens, if not hundreds, of young, drifting cowhands just like him. The stranger reined his horse to a stop about twenty feet away and nodded to Smoke, then pinched the brim of his hat respectfully as he nodded to Sally.

"Ma'am," he said. He went on to Smoke, "I'm not hunting trouble, mister."

Smoke nodded toward the grim burden on the horse the young stranger was leading. "I reckon you found some already, by the looks of it."

Without looking around at the dead man, the stranger said, "He was an outlaw named Billy J. Pike. I had a run-in with him a few days ago at a place called Hidden Valley."

"I've heard of it," Smoke replied. "It's said that men who are on the dodge stop in there fairly often."

A smile tugged at the stranger's mouth under the mustache. "If you think that makes me an owlhoot, too, you're wrong. I was just passing through and needed some grub and a place to rest my horse for a spell. Turns out that the fella who runs the place, an old German called Augustus Rasmussen, fries up a mighty good buffalo steak."

Smoke couldn't help but return the smile. This young fella was likable, no doubt about that.

"I've heard that about Rasmussen, too," Smoke allowed. "Why don't you light down from that horse? Never did like talking for too long when I'm looking up at a man. My name's Smoke Jensen."

The young man swung down from the saddle and said, "My name's Cavanaugh. Front handle is Hank." He tipped his head slightly to the side. "I think I've heard of a man named Smoke Jensen. Supposed to be mighty fast with a gun."

"That would be me," Smoke admitted. "This is my wife, Sally."

Cavanaugh raised a hand to his hat brim again and said, "It's an honor to meet you, Mrs. Jensen."

"I'm pleased to make your acquaintance as well, Mr. Cavanaugh," Sally said. "Especially since it's thanks to you that we didn't ride unaware into that ambush."

"I just happened to top that rise over yonder"—Cavanaugh jerked a thumb toward the knoll—"and spotted some fellas lurking in a gully and pointing rifles at those wagons. Figured they had to be up to no good, so I thought it would be wise to sound a warning. Then they started shooting at me . . ."

The young man's voice trailed off as he shrugged eloquently.

"Did you know Pike was part of the gang?" Smoke asked.

"No, sir, not then. I caught a glimpse of him lighting a shuck out of here and recognized him then. He had five men with him at Hidden Valley, and he was the big skookum he-wolf of the bunch, so it seems likely to me he set up this ambush."

Smoke nodded and said, "There were five men with him today, all right. Bound to be the same ones." Smoke looked meaningfully at the corpse draped over the second horse's saddle. "And you caught up to Pike."

It wasn't really a question, but Cavanaugh said, "Yes, sir, I did. He didn't give me any choice, but to bring him back dead."

"You didn't have to go after him at all."

"I reckon not, but it wouldn't have set right with me to let a skunk like that get away and trouble more folks later. I don't hold with such things."

"Neither do I," Smoke said. He stuck out his hand. "Shake, Cavanaugh. You're all right."

The young man grinned. "Don't mind if I do." He clasped Smoke's hand firmly. "To tell the truth, I'm mighty proud to be shaking hands with the famous Smoke Jensen."

"You can lay off that talk," Smoke advised him. "I'm just plain Smoke to my friends." He glanced over his shoulder. The women had stopped working on the grave, and all of them were gathered together to watch as he and Sally met the stranger.

He told Cavanaugh, "Come on, I'll introduce you to the ladies and the colonel."

Cavanaugh looked puzzled. "Am I loco, or is everybody in this wagon train a woman, except for that old fellow? And, um, good-looking women, at that?"

"You're not loco," Smoke told him. "This is a wagon train unlike any you've ever seen before."

* * *

Hank Cavanaugh was a polite, well-spoken young man, and after being introduced to the women, he immediately volunteered to help dig the grave for Pike and the other outlaws.

"We're taking care of that," Lucy Dunning told him. "We like to . . . What's the expression I heard someone say once? We like to stomp our own snakes."

"I reckon I can see that," Cavanaugh said. "You ladies put up a pretty fierce fight when those varmints bushwhacked you."

"We've all dealt with adversity in our lives. Some of us more than others, of course, but we've all survived rough times. So don't worry about us being able to take care of ourselves."

"To be honest, the thought never entered my head, ma'am."

She smiled. "It's miss. But you can call me Lucy."

"Yes, ma—I mean, Lucy. I'll be mighty happy to do that."

Cavanaugh left the women to their task and walked over to the lead wagon to join Smoke and the elderly gentleman, who'd been introduced to him as Colonel Jasper Wilkinson.

"Smoke tells me you apprehended the leader of that band of scoundrels, young man," the colonel said.

"I don't know if *apprehended* is the right word, sir. I would have taken him alive if he'd surrendered, but he threw down on me and I didn't have any choice but to shoot back."

"No, of course not. I'd have done the same thing if I still had my sight. The fact that you're alive is a testament to your ability to handle trouble."

"I had some luck on my side," Cavanaugh said. "But I'm a decent hand with a gun, if I do say so myself. Nothing like Mr. Jensen here, of course. I mean, Smoke," he added before Smoke could remind him to call him by that name. "From what I've heard, there aren't many men out here who are anywhere near as good with a gun as him."

Cavanaugh looked at Smoke as if expecting him to confirm that, but Smoke just shrugged. Evidently, he wasn't one to brag on his own accomplishments and abilities.

Colonel Wilkinson was a lot more talkative. All it took to open a floodgate of talk from the old-timer was for Cavanaugh to express a mild interest in the unusual situation of a wagon train populated almost entirely by women. The colonel explained how all the ladies had been either widowed or orphaned by the war and were now on their way to Wyoming to make fresh starts in their lives on the ranch he'd inherited from his distant cousin.

"You're willing to share your good fortune with them like that, Colonel?" Cavanaugh said. "I'd say that's mighty generous of you, sir."

"Not at all, son, not at all," Wilkinson said with a dismissive wave of his hand. "I believe one of the reasons we're put on this earth is to give assistance to those who are less fortunate than us. It's the very least I can do to help my daughter's friends."

Cavanaugh looked at Smoke. "What about you, Smoke? What's your connection with this?" He added hastily, "If you don't mind my asking, that is. It's none of my business and I don't mean to pry. I'm just curious, that's all."

Smoke chuckled and said, "Don't worry about it, Hank. Sally and I got acquainted with the colonel and Annabelle and the others when they stopped for a couple of days in Big Rock, the town near our ranch. Sally took a liking to them and so did I, and we figured it might be a good idea to ride along with them and make sure they get where they're going."

"And today is a fine example of just how lucky we are you came to that decision," the colonel said. "Those road agents might well have wiped us out if you hadn't been with us, Smoke. And if you hadn't warned us, of course, Hank. I'd say we owe our continued survival to both of you fine gentlemen."

"I'm just glad I came along in time to give you folks a hand," Cavanaugh said.

Within a short time, the grave was finished and the bodies of the outlaws were placed in it. Now that he could get a good look at them, Cavanaugh recognized the other men. They were the ones who had been at Hidden Valley with Billy J. Pike.

He mentioned as much to Smoke while they were filling in the grave, following a rather long-winded prayer from the colonel, who didn't seem to be on even a nodding acquaintance with brevity. The two men insisted on doing the work of replacing the dirt, since the women had dug the grave.

"I never heard of Pike and his bunch," Smoke said, "but it's just as well they're not still running wild. Men like that spread death and misery everywhere they go." He paused and then added, "You shouldn't feel bad about the ones you killed."

"I don't," Cavanaugh said. He smiled, but his face was still serious. "You figured out that I hadn't ever shot anybody before, didn't you?"

"A fella gets a look in his eyes the first time he has to pull the trigger on another man, no matter how justified it may be. You strike me as the sort who can handle it, though, Hank."

"I hope so. I think that's going to be the case."

A short time later, the grim chore was concluded and the shovels had been replaced in the wagons. Cavanaugh fashioned a crude cross out of a couple of broken branches and shoved it into the ground at the head of the grave. He begged a piece of paper and a pencil from Annabelle and pressed the paper against the side of a wagon to print: BILLY J. PIKE.

Then he spiked the paper down on the jagged end of the makeshift cross and said to a curiously watching Smoke, "I promised Pike I'd see to it that his grave had a marker with his name on it." Cavanaugh grunted. "I never said how permanent that marker was going to be."

"You kept your word, though," Smoke said.

"Yes, sir, I did. Well enough that it won't keep me awake at night."

The women were getting ready to move on again. Cavanaugh walked over to the lead wagon, where Annabelle had just climbed to the seat and started untying the reins from the brake lever.

Taking off his hat, Cavanaugh said, "Ma'am, I'd like to ask you a question, if I might."

"Go ahead, Mr. Cavanaugh," Annabelle told him.

"Well, you see, there's nowhere I have to be at any particular time, so I was wondering if it would be all right, maybe, if I was to ride along a ways with your wagon train." He grinned. "I've never been to Wyoming, and if I'm being honest, I'm a mite curious about the place."

Annabelle gave him a stern look and said, "None of us are looking for beaus, Mr. Cavanaugh. If you see a wagon train full of women and think that you've blundered into some sort of romantic golden opportunity—"

Cavanaugh looked shocked as he interrupted her to say in a fervent tone, "No, ma'am! A fella would have to be blind not to realize you ladies are all good-looking, and my eyes work just fine, but I give you my solemn oath, I don't have any improper intentions. Or even proper intentions, if you're talking about actual courting. I promise not to make calf's eyes or suggest any moonlight strolls."

Annabelle looked intently at him for a moment and then laughed. "All right, I believe you," she said. "But I'm still not sure it would be a good idea—"

"Let the lad accompany us, Annabelle," the colonel said from his place beside her on the driver's seat. "I can tell by his voice that he's trustworthy. And he seems to be quite capable, too, if how he's conducted himself today is any example. If we encounter any more brigands, it might come in very handy to have him on our side."

Annabelle considered. She nodded and said, "All right, Colonel. I trust your judgment. You can come with us, at least for now, Mr. Cavanaugh, as long as you behave yourself."

"Thank you, ma'am," Cavanaugh said. "I won't give you cause to regret this."

He put his hat on and turned to head for his horse.

But as he walked away, Cavanaugh thought it was a shame that the last thing he'd said to Annabelle Wilkinson was such a bald-faced lie.

Chapter 20

Danny Murphy reined in as Gus Gerhardt raised his left hand in a signal for the group of riders to stop.

Only five men brought their mounts to a halt among the trees on the hilltop. J.D. Styles was no longer with them.

Instead, the former gambler lay in a lonely grave more than twenty miles back.

Gerhardt, in a surprising display of compassion, had suggested that Styles remain in Big Rock and continue recovering from the gunshot wound in his leg, while the others followed the wagon train. Styles had refused, insisting he wanted to do his share in earning the money Andrew Rickett was going to pay them for bringing back Susie Beale and Delia Tracy.

Gerhardt had shocked the others even more by declaring that Styles would receive his share of the payment whether he went along on the job or not.

That didn't sit well with Abner Farnum, but Farnum knew not to push his displeasure too far. Gerhardt would tolerate only so much defiance, especially with the others backing him up.

But in the end, it didn't matter, because Styles was bound and determined to go along. Gerhardt had shrugged and told him the decision was his to make. With his leg heavily bandaged, Styles was in the saddle when the bunch rode out on the trail of the Wilkinson wagon train.

Gerhardt wanted the wagons to be well away from Big Rock before they made their move to grab Susie and Delia—and settle the score with Smoke Jensen at the same time.

Danny had a hunch that Gerhardt intended to kidnap Annabelle Wilkinson, too, if he could manage it. In fact, that might well be Gerhardt's main goal in all of this.

Three days out of Big Rock, Styles had come down with a fever and his leg had swollen up. When they had made camp and Concho Warren unwrapped the bandages around Styles's leg, the sickening smell that came from the wound made it evident that gangrene had set in.

"Only chance you've got is for us to take that leg off, J.D.," Warren had told the former gambler.

Even with the bad shape he was in, Styles hadn't lost his deftness with a gun. His Colt had appeared in his hand as neatly as he'd ever palmed an ace, and he said, "Anybody comes near me with a knife, I'll blow a hole in him. A man with one leg's got no chance in this world."

A note of desperation entered his voice as he said, "There must be something else you can do, Concho."

A shrug was Warren's response. "There are some herbs I can try. I remember the old medicine men talking about them, down along the river. They might make the pain a little better, if nothing else."

So Warren had treated the festering leg with Comanche medicine, making a poultice for the wound and a potion for Styles to drink. For a day or two, the stuff actually did seem to help. Styles's fever went down, and he felt strong enough to ride.

But the improvement hadn't lasted. Inevitably, Styles's condition had worsened again, and he lay for several days under a tree in the camp the group had made and raved and thrashed. Whiskey was the only thing that eased him enough to let him rest.

"How long are we gonna wait here?" Abner Farnum demanded one night as the men gathered around the campfire. "J.D. ain't never gonna get better, and we all know it. Hell, he'd know it, too, if he wasn't out of his head all the time. And while we wait, them wagons are gettin' farther and farther ahead of us."

"We know where those wagons are going," Gerhardt snapped. "And moving as slow as they do, they can't get far enough ahead of us so that we can't catch them when the time comes. A few days of hard riding and we'll be right behind them again."

"Yeah, but it'll be that much longer before we get back to Big Rock and collect the money we've got comin' from that Rickett fella."

Coldly, Gerhardt said, "J.D.'s been a good partner to all of us. He deserves as much of a chance as we can give him."

Danny found that loyalty admirable, which wasn't something he would have predicted he'd ever be feeling about Gus Gerhardt. But everybody had some good qualities, he supposed, even ruthless outlaws. Gerhardt and Styles had ridden together a good long time, longer than any of the others.

But no matter how much of a chance they gave Styles, he wasn't going to make it. Danny hated to admit that Abner Farnum was right about anything, but the man had nailed that.

Styles was doomed.

Maybe the former gambler wasn't as out of it as they thought and had overheard that campfire conversation. Maybe he hadn't, but just knew, in his more coherent moments, where things stood. Two mornings later, at dawn, a single gunshot had roused the men. They jumped out of their bedrolls, grabbing for their irons, and looked around to see if they were under attack.

They didn't see anything unusual in the gray light until they looked under the tree where J.D. Styles lay and found him with his head tipped to the side, a good-sized chunk blown out of it.

The Colt that had done it was still gripped loosely in Styles's hand, where his arm had fallen to the side in death.

"I thought I told you to take his gun away from him," Gerhardt said to Warren.

"He told me if I tried, he'd shoot me," Warren replied with a shrug.

"You could have done it while he was unconscious."

"Maybe. And maybe he would have woken up and drilled me. Under the circumstances, it didn't seem worth the risk."

Gerhardt was displeased, but at the same time, though, Styles's death was a relief. They buried him near the same tree where he had died; instead of a marker, they left an ace of spades on the grave, weighted down with a rock. The card would stay there from now on, and somehow that seemed fitting.

Now, after days of that hard riding Gerhardt had talked about, they were close enough to see their quarry again. Earlier that day, they had heard a lot of gunfire in the distance to the north, and that had worried everyone in the bunch. This was rough, mostly empty country through which they were traveling. The Wilkinson party could have run into trouble from some other source. All the women might even be dead now, which meant there would be no payment waiting back in Big Rock.

Even more worrisome for Danny Murphy was the chance that something had happened to Susie. The beautiful redheaded young woman might not have survived.

Because of that concern, Danny blew out a big sigh of relief as he spied the wagons rolling slowly up the narrow valley that lay before them.

"Looks like a grave down yonder," Concho Warren commented as he studied the scene.

"Mighty big for a grave," Gerhardt said.

"I don't know what else a mound of freshly turned earth could be, do you?"

Danny asked anxiously, "Do you think some of the women

were killed?" He was still thinking about Susie, and about her friend Delia as well.

Abner Farnum snorted and said, "Not likely. If any of those gals were dead, it makes more sense the rest would have dug individual holes for them. They wouldn't just dig a mass grave and toss their friends into it."

"That's right," Gerhardt said. "But Concho is right, too. That has to be a grave. So somebody must have attacked the wagon train, and they're the ones who got tossed in." He scratched his jaw. "Indians, maybe. Or outlaws."

With a skeptical frown, Farnum responded, "So you're sayin' that bunch of women got jumped by Injuns or owlhoots, but managed to kill all of 'em without losin' a single one on their side? Because I don't see any graves other than that big one."

"Don't forget," Warren drawled, "they have Smoke Jensen with them."

Farnum snorted again. "I don't care how famous that damn Jensen is. He ain't bulletproof. And I'll bet most of those stories folks tell about him are nothin' but tall tales dreamed up by crazy hombres who got nothin' better to do."

"Maybe. But I've heard too much firsthand about what Jensen's capable of, to doubt too much about what he can do."

"That's enough talk," Gerhardt said heavily. "As soon as those wagons are out of sight, we'll follow them and start looking for a good place to make our move." He looked over at Warren. "When we do, it's going to be your job to take care of Jensen, Concho. Don't worry about anybody or anything else. Just find Jensen—and kill him."

"It'll be my pleasure, Gus," Concho Warren said with a smile.

The wagon train put several more miles behind it before making camp that evening. Everyone seemed happy to be well away from the site of the ambush and the ensuing battle.

The water in the water barrels was starting to run low, so the travelers were also pleased that Smoke had located a spring-fed pool at the base of a rocky bluff. He tasted the water carefully and declared it good. The horses would have plenty to drink, and they could refill all the barrels.

"If I'm remembering right," Smoke told Annabelle and the colonel that evening, "we've got a pretty dry stretch coming up, right there along the border between Colorado and Wyoming. There may be water in some of the washes, but there's just as good a chance there won't be. But what we take on here ought to be enough to get us through to a more hospitable region. From there, it won't be long before we reach Brimstone Butte. All the range north from there is pretty good, which is why cattlemen have moved in their herds."

"We can't get there soon enough to suit me," Annabelle said. "It's been a long trip from Mississippi."

Smoke heard weariness in her voice, and she looked tired, too. Her face was drawn, and her eyes were shadowed. The journey was taking a toll on her, as it was on all of the women.

Surprisingly, considering the colonel's age, he seemed to be the freshest one in the group. Of course, because of his blindness he didn't do any actual work, which probably accounted for that, Smoke thought.

Elsewhere in the camp, Hank Cavanaugh approached the fourth wagon, where Lucy Dunning was examining one of the wheels by the light of a burning brand she had brought from the campfire.

"Problem?" Cavanaugh asked as he walked up.

"This spoke has a crack in it," Lucy replied. She pointed at the damaged spoke. "I'm afraid it's going to give out before too much longer."

Cavanaugh bent to examine it more closely. After a moment, he straightened and said, "You should take a strip of rawhide a few inches wide, let it get good and wet, and then after it's soaked for a while, wrap it around there as tightly as you can and tack it in place. Once it dries, it'll shrink even tighter and reinforce that spoke. That ought to hold up well enough until you get where you're going."

"Are you an expert in wagon wheel repair, Mr. Cavanaugh?"

He grinned. "Not hardly. In fact, I've never actually tried that little trick I just told you about. I just heard old teamsters talking about it once. But I have a good memory for things I've overheard."

"We've had to work on more than one wagon wheel during this trip, and it just so happens that your advice is good. I'll see if I can find a piece of rawhide and do that very thing."

"I'm glad I could help—even though you didn't exactly need it, did you?"

Instead of answering his question, Lucy said, "We haven't been introduced officially, have we? I'm Lucy Dunning."

"Yes, ma'am. Earlier, you told me to call you Lucy, but I didn't catch your last name until now. I'm Hank Cavanaugh."

"I think all of us know who you are, Mr. Cavanaugh."

"Now, if I'm going to call you Lucy, you have to call me Hank. That's only fair, isn't it?"

She looked at him and said, "I believe Annabelle warned you that you can't go around trying to court any of us. She doesn't want any distractions, and trust me, neither do the rest of us. We have too much riding on this journey."

"Why, I'm not courting you, Lucy," Cavanaugh replied without hesitation. "I apologize if it seemed like I was. I'm just trying to be friendly and helpful."

"Of course," she said dryly. She cocked her head and went on, "How did it happen that you came along just in time to help us out of that ambush today?"

"Just pure luck, I guess. I sure wasn't heading anywhere in particular."

"Then it was a stroke of good fortune for all of us, wasn't it?"

"Yes, ma'am, I'd sure say so. Excuse me, I mean Lucy."

"You don't have to call me that if it's difficult for you."

"Oh, it's not," he assured her. "It's not hard at all."

"Well, in case it gets that way, you don't have to worry about it. You can just stay well away from me, and then it won't be a problem for you, will it?"

"I reckon not . . . Lucy."

He smiled, ticked a finger against his hat brim, and turned away, pausing to add over his shoulder, "If you have any more trouble with that wheel, let me know. I might have overheard something else that could come in handy."

She didn't have anything to say to that, so he walked back toward the campfire, smiling to himself. A cup of coffee sounded good right about now.

Chapter 21

Sheriff Monte Carson was strolling along the main street in Big Rock, trying to figure out where he wanted to have lunch, when he spotted the group of horsemen entering the settlement from the south.

The riders followed a trail that turned into one of the town's cross streets. It didn't occur to Monte until later that this trail was the same one the Wilkinson wagons were on when they reached Big Rock.

He did a quick head count as the men guided their horses into the main street. Fifteen strangers.

That was enough to make any lawman wary, especially when they had the tough look about them that these did.

Except the man who was in the lead. It wasn't a case of him not looking tough. But he was a definite cut above the others.

For one thing, his clothes were more expensive. Even covered with trail dust, their quality was obvious in contrast to the typical range garb worn by the other men. His trousers and coat were black, as were his boots and hat. He wore a vest over a white shirt and had a black string tie knotted around his neck.

The Colts he wore in a two-gun rig were nickel-plated and sported ivory handles. They probably cost more than Monte's wages amounted to in six months.

His saddle was flashy, too, black leather with silver trim; and the horse he rode was, of course, a tall, well-muscled black stallion.

Overall, he looked like he ought to be on the cover of one of those lurid novels published by Beadle & Adams. Monte Carson disliked him on sight.

But a peace officer couldn't allow such things to influence him, so he turned to follow the riders on foot. That impulse proved to be prophetic when the horsemen drew up in front of the sheriff's office and the leader swung down from his fancy saddle.

Monte stepped up onto the boardwalk in front of the office at the same time as the man in black. "Are you looking for me, mister?" he asked.

The stranger turned to face him. He had sleek, dark hair under the black hat and was clean-shaven and handsome. He smiled slightly and said, "You're the law here?"

"That's right. Sheriff Monte Carson. What can I do for you?"

Monte's name didn't appear to mean anything to the man. That didn't bother Monte. In his previous line of work, that of hired gun, he had achieved some notoriety, but that had faded after he settled down in Big Rock.

"My name is Mason Loomis," the stranger introduced himself. "I wonder if I might have a word with you, Sheriff Carson."

"Sure. Come on in the office, if you'd like. Probably still some coffee in the pot."

"I'll pass on the coffee, thank you, but I am in the market for information. Excuse me just a moment." Mason Loomis turned to the still-mounted men who had accompanied him into Big Rock and spoke to one of them. "Stable the horses, Tom, and take mine with you. Then see about getting hotel rooms for us, and after that, you and the boys can get something to eat or pay a visit to one of the local watering holes."

"Sure thing, Mr. Loomis," the man called Tom replied with a nod. The riders all turned away to carry out Loomis's orders.

"Sounds like you're going to be in Big Rock for a spell," Monte commented.

"Only overnight, more than likely. We've been on the trail for quite a while, though, and it wouldn't hurt to give the horses some extra rest." Loomis smiled again. "But if you tell me what I'm hoping to hear, I expect we'll be riding out first thing in the morning."

Monte opened the office door. "Well, come on in, then, and tell me just what it is you're looking to find out."

Loomis might have passed on the offer of coffee, but Monte decided he could use some. He hung his hat on one of the pegs just inside the door and went to the stove in the corner of the office. While Monte poured himself a cup from the pot, Loomis stood in front of the desk and looked around, appearing interested in his surroundings. Monte figured that wasn't actually the case. The room looked like dozens, if not hundreds, of other sheriffs' and marshals' offices out here on the frontier. There was nothing special about it to attract any attention.

Monte carried the cup over and set it down. He gestured toward the chair in front of the desk and said, "Make yourself comfortable, Mr. Loomis."

With a doubtful expression, the visitor glanced at the well-worn chair, but he sat down and looked across the desk as Monte settled into the old swivel chair behind it.

"I imagine you keep pretty close track of the people who pass through your town, Sheriff," he began. His voice had a crisp accent, but it wasn't very pronounced. He came from back East somewhere, Monte guessed, but had spent enough time elsewhere to soften his words just a bit.

Monte nodded and said, "It's my job to know what's going on in Big Rock, that's for sure."

"Then I'm certain you'd be aware of it if a small wagon train had come through here this past week."

Monte took a sip of the coffee to cover up the surprise he

felt. He hadn't forgotten about Annabelle Wilkinson and her friends, but thoughts of them had receded to the back of his mind. They'd been gone long enough that they ought to be pretty close to Wyoming by now—if, in fact, they hadn't crossed the state line already.

"Wagon trains still show up from time to time," he allowed, "but there aren't as many traveling through these parts as there used to be. The railroad is changing all that."

"Indeed, it is," Loomis said. "You'd remember these wagons, Sheriff. Not only is it uncommon to see such a thing these days, as you pointed out, but the group of travelers is composed entirely of young, beautiful women."

Loomis paused and then added, "With one exception, that is, an old gentleman who calls himself a colonel. He's the father of the woman who's leading the, ah, expedition."

"Calls himself a colonel, you say? You mean he really isn't?"

Loomis made a curt, dismissive gesture. "I suppose he held that rank at one time, but only in the Confederate Army. An undisciplined bunch of traitorous rabble hardly counts as an actual military force, does it? Ranks achieved there are hardly worth considering."

"That undisciplined rabble won quite a few battles, as I recall," Monte said, unable to restrain the annoyance he felt. "And Robert E. Lee and 'Stonewall' Jackson and plenty of others were considered fine officers when they were helping win the Mexican War a few years before that."

Loomis smiled and said, "My apologies, Sheriff. I didn't mean to bring up the war. It's well behind us now, and that's where it needs to stay." He grew more serious. "At any rate, it's vitally important that I locate those wagons and the women traveling with them. Can you confirm that they've been here and tell me if you know where they were going?"

The instinctive dislike Monte felt for Mason Loomis made him wary. Of course, as a lawman he was naturally cautious, anyway. He wasn't going to answer questions just because somebody asked them. He needed more than that.

"What's your interest in those ladies, Mr. Loomis?"

"You called them *ladies*." Loomis leaned forward in the chair. "Then you have seen them."

"You said they were women. I was raised to be chivalrous and consider any female a lady until she proves otherwise. So don't read too much into my words."

"They're *not* ladies." Loomis's voice was brittle with anger now. "They're thieves, pure and simple. Especially Annabelle Wilkinson."

"Now you really are going to have to explain that." Monte's brisk, no-nonsense tone was that of a lawman about to crack down on somebody.

Loomis drew in a deep breath. A faint, rueful smile appeared briefly on his lips. He said, "We're getting off on the wrong foot here, Sheriff, and that's entirely my fault. I'm a stranger. You don't know me, and you don't know what Annabelle has done to me."

"Suppose you tell me, then."

"Of course. I'm the current owner of Cypress Hill, the plantation in Mississippi that was once owned by Jasper Wilkinson."

That didn't clear everything up, but it explained Loomis's accent and told Monte who he was dealing with—a dirty Yankee carpetbagger.

Monte had long since put any feelings he had about the war itself far behind him, but the way things had played out in the South after Lee's surrender still rankled, as they would have in any fair-minded person. Greedy opportunists had swarmed down from the North like locusts, turning their ravenous appetites on the defeated country and gobbling up all the best land. With the Union Army and corrupt judges and politicians backing them, they had claimed everything, from vast plantations to hardscrabble farms not amounting to more than a vegetable patch and one field of cotton.

Southerners' bank accounts, in those cases where such things still existed, were looted. Men were beaten and women were raped. Anyone who stood up to a carpetbagger could be gunned down with impunity, and if the scalawag didn't want to dirty his hands and do the job himself, he could get the army to string up any alleged offender. It was a hellish nightmare, all in the name of Reconstruction.

Things were improving now in the South, Monte had heard, but plenty of the Yankees who had seized power were still in control. Evidently, Mason Loomis was one of them.

None of that outrage showed in Monte's face or was audible in his voice as he said, "Do you have anything to back up that claim, Mr. Loomis?"

"As a matter of fact, I do," Loomis answered smoothly. He reached into his coat and pulled out several folded pieces of paper. He unfolded them and removed the first document from the sheaf. "This is the deed for Cypress Hill. You can see that everything is properly stamped and endorsed and entered into the records of the county in which the plantation is located."

Monte was no expert on such things, but he had seen enough deeds to know that the document looked genuine. Loomis leaned forward and dropped another one onto the desk.

"That's an arrest warrant for Colonel Jasper Wilkinson. I have one for Miss Annabelle Wilkinson, too, as well as others for each member of their party. In the eyes of the law, all of them are equally guilty of the crime of stealing a great deal of money from me."

"An arrest warrant doesn't mean somebody's been found guilty," Monte pointed out. "It takes a trial to do that."

"Trials were held—in absentia—because the Wilkinson woman and her friends had already fled. I assure you, Sheriff, they've been found legally guilty and are considered fugitives under the law." Loomis added another piece of paper to the ones lying in front of Monte. "Here's a reward poster for Jasper Wilkinson issued by the court back in Mississippi."

Monte spread out the documents, studied them for a moment, then squared them up and pushed them back toward Loomis.

"You seem to have proof of what you say. Did you take it into your head to track down these fugitives yourself?"

Loomis smiled again. "I'm a firm believer in the idea that if you want something done right, you should do it yourself, Sheriff."

"So you hired a bunch of bounty hunters and set out on their trail?"

"The men with me aren't bounty hunters. They're duly sworn special officers."

"Uh-huh." Hired guns was what they were, Monte thought. He knew men of that stripe when he saw them.

He had been one himself. And no better than he'd had to be, too. Some of the things he had done still haunted him on the dark nights when sleep was elusive.

"As a lawman," Loomis said, "I believe it's your duty to assist in the apprehension of fugitives."

"Don't tell me what my duties are, mister," Monte snapped. "I know them better than you do."

"Then you'll provide me with the information I'm after," Loomis said coolly.

Monte rested his hands flat on the desk for a moment before saying, "The wagons were here. But I reckon you knew that already, since you followed them."

"It's nice to have confirmation that we haven't lost the trail. It would be even better if you could tell me where they're heading."

"They never told me while they were here." Strictly speaking, that was the truth. Smoke had mentioned to him that the women were headed for a place in Wyoming called Brimstone Butte, but he hadn't heard that from any of them. "All I can say for sure is that they were traveling north when they left here."

"How long ago was that?"

Monte thought for a second. "A week, I believe."

Loomis nodded and said, "I see. Well, they don't have as big a lead as they once did. I'm sure it's only a matter of time until we catch up and bring them to justice."

"And recover the money they stole from you, I expect."

Loomis's voice was chilly now. "That's the goal, yes."

Monte leaned back in his chair and couldn't resist saying, "You seem like a pretty smart man, Mr. Loomis. How in the world did a bunch of women manage to steal anything from you?"

"You saw Annabelle Wilkinson while she was here, I take it?"

"Yes, I did. Didn't really speak to her much."

"She's a very beautiful woman."

Monte nodded. "I can't argue with that."

"Beautiful women cause men to do foolish things, such as trust them. I certainly should have known better. But Annabelle seemed to have accepted the fact that I now own Cypress Hill and had me believing that she was interested in staying there—with me." He shrugged. "I should have known that she just wanted to get into the safe that used to belong to her father. I wasn't aware that she had a key to it until it was too late."

"I reckon I can see why you want to catch up to her. I hope you aren't planning to take the law into your own hands."

"Whatever I do, Sheriff, it won't be any concern of yours. I'll be a long way from Big Rock before that happens."

Loomis stood up.

"My men and I will rest our horses for the night, and then we'll take up the trail again. Thank you for your cooperation, Sheriff."

Monte narrowed his eyes and said, "I don't mind telling you, Loomis, I'll be happy to see the whole bunch of you ride out."

"That might offend me . . . if I gave a damn what you think of me. Trust me, I've long since stopped worrying about things like that."

The Yankee turned and walked out of the office. Monte watched him go and mulled over the fact that Smoke was traveling with those women. No matter what they had done, Smoke Jensen wouldn't stand by and let Loomis and his hired guns get away with mistreating women. That would set off a storm of gun-thunder—with Smoke outnumbered fifteen to one.

Mason Loomis and the rest of those varmints didn't know what they were letting themselves in for.

Chapter 22

Out here in the middle of nowhere, there was no boundary marker to indicate where the dividing line between Colorado and Wyoming lay. Gus Gerhardt claimed they had to be in Wyoming by now, though, and Danny Murphy wasn't going to argue the matter. Nor were any of the other men.

They didn't care where they were. Too much time had passed already since they left Big Rock to suit them. They were just anxious to carry out this job, grab the two saloon girls, and take them back to the Empire Saloon so they could collect the money Andrew Rickett had promised them.

Tonight would be the night, Gerhardt had decided. Danny knew the others thought it was damned well about time.

The wagons had stopped to make camp in an open area, so sneaking up on them was going to be difficult. A distraction would be necessary, and Concho Warren would supply that.

"Concho, you slip in from the north, cut those horses loose, and stampede them through the camp," Gerhardt said as he and the other men stood in the gathering darkness about half a mile east of the camp. It was already dark enough that the fire the women had built was clearly visible in the distance.

Gerhardt went on, "You can get close enough to do that without being spotted or spooking the horses too much, can't you?"

"When I'm doing something like that, nobody knows I'm around unless I want them to, and that goes for horses, too," Warren said confidently.

None of the others doubted the claim, since they figured he was at least half-Comanche. Such stealth was in his blood.

Gerhardt nodded and told him, "I hope so, because we'll be counting on you, Concho. We can't hit them until that stampede has shaken everybody up and put a few of those women out of the fight."

"I can't guarantee who might get caught in it," Warren cautioned. "When spooked horses are running, they don't pay attention to whoever's in front of them. They just trample right over anybody unlucky enough to be in their way."

"I know that. You can't wait all night, but you might hold off on the stampede until those two saloon floozies are safe in one of the wagons, if you spot them." Gerhardt added, "And the same goes for the Wilkinson woman. She's coming with us as well, if I can manage it."

"I'll do the best I can," Warren promised with a shrug.

"Once you've stampeded the horses, you charge into the camp right behind them. Jensen will be running around, trying to figure out what's going on. You ought to be able to get the drop on him and gun him down before he knows what's happening. Once he's dead, it'll be easy to handle the women. The rest of us will be rushing in from both sides to take care of them."

Gerhardt divided the others into two groups. Danny Murphy would go with him to the west of the camp, he declared; Abner Farnum, Stan Hamilton, and Al Townsend would wait on the east, staying out of sight until the stampede served as the signal for the raid to begin.

"Abner, you're in charge of the second bunch," Gerhardt said. "The three of you will corral two saloon girls. If any of the others get in your way, don't hesitate to deal with them. They're liable to be armed, and they'll be trying to shoot you. Danny, you and I will find Annabelle and grab her."

Danny didn't like this plan at all. He had hoped to be the one to grab Susie. The two of them could slip off in the confusion, assuming she would go with him without raising a ruckus. Surely, she would see right away that he didn't mean to harm her. As a matter of fact, he would be rescuing her from what the others had in mind.

He would never sell her back into a life of degradation dominated by Andrew Rickett. He wouldn't allow Gerhardt and the rest to do it, either.

But just because things started out with a plan didn't mean they would stay like that. Very few plans survived the chaos of real life. He would watch for his chance to grab Susie and get out of there, and when it came, he would seize it.

With that determination in mind, he just nodded and said, "Sure, Gus."

Gerhardt looked at the sky, which was uniformly black by now and littered with a breathtaking sweep of stars.

"It'll be a while before the moon comes up," he said. "Let's go ahead and get this done while it's good and dark."

Smoke knew they were in Wyoming now. Another three or four days and they ought to be able to spot Brimstone Butte—the geographic feature, not the town—ahead of them. A thick red sandstone tower, it rose a couple of hundred feet above a broad valley between two mountain ranges. It was visible for a long distance. Even after the pilgrims were able to see it, several more days' travel would be required to reach it.

There was no logical explanation for such a prominent feature being located where the butte was, but Smoke had come across many such unexplained mysteries of the terrain on the frontier. *El Señor Dios* had his own reasons for doing things, Smoke had always supposed, and Smoke didn't figure on changing that belief now.

Actually laying eyes on the butte would perk everybody up. The journey had been long and wearying, and having visible evidence that they were nearing their destination would give the women the strength they needed to carry on just a little while longer.

Of course, once they got where they were going, they would face a whole new set of challenges that might prove to be just as daunting as the journey had been.

Smoke talked about that with Colonel Wilkinson as they sat by the fire that night. It would be time to turn in soon, because the wagon train always got an early start in the morning. For now, though, Smoke and the colonel sipped the last of the brew in their coffee cups and enjoyed their conversation.

As they conversed, Smoke lifted his head and looked across the camp. Earlier, Sally had been over by the Wilkinson wagon talking to Annabelle. The two of them were still there, Smoke saw, and they had been joined by Lucy and the two girls from Big Rock, Susie and Delia.

Despite Annabelle's initial reservations about letting them join the group, Susie and Delia had managed to fit right in. As far as he could tell, they had made several friends among the other women, including Lucy.

They were all a hardworking bunch, Smoke mused. That was good. They would need to be, once they reached the Three Cross Ranch. Even if the ranch had a good crew, there would still be plenty of work that needed to be done.

A sound drifted to Smoke's ears on the night breeze and caused his interest to perk up. He recognized the soft, nickering whinny from his favorite saddle mount, Drifter. The big black stallion had keen senses. Something had disturbed and alerted him.

Several other horses echoed Drifter's response. Smoke heard the animals moving around where they were picketed a short distance north of the camp.

"Something has spooked the horses, Colonel," he said as he

came to his feet. "Reckon I'll go take a look around and see if I can figure out what it is."

The colonel remained perched on the crate he was using for a seat, but he stiffened and his grip tightened on his walking stick. "What do you think it could be?"

"Wolf, more than likely. Might even be a bear or a mountain lion that's wandered over from one of those ranges to either side of us."

"Indians?"

"Can't rule it out," Smoke allowed. "But not likely, I'd say. There hasn't been any trouble from hostiles in these parts for a while. The last big fight was the one up on the Little Bighorn. After that, most of the chiefs who are inclined to fight took their people and drifted north toward Canada. A lot of them crossed the border and are still up there."

"Be careful," the colonel said. "Perhaps you should ask a couple of the ladies to arm themselves and come with you. Most of them are good shots."

Along the way, Smoke had watched the women practicing occasionally with their rifles, and knew the colonel was right about their gun-handling abilities. But he didn't want to stir the group up and make everybody nervous if there was no legitimate reason to do so.

"I'll check it out by myself," he said. "The ladies are close by, if I need help."

Colonel Wilkinson still looked worried, but he didn't say anything else as Smoke walked away from the firelight and into the gloom. Smoke reached down and eased both revolvers in their holsters, just to make sure they were sliding easily in the leather. He knew they would be, but such caution was a long-ingrained habit.

The horses were picketed about thirty yards north of the wagons on that side of camp. Smoke heard Drifter nicker again as he approached. The stallion definitely seemed bothered about something.

Smoke listened intently, halfway expecting to hear the growl of a wolf or a bear or the chuff of a mountain lion. If one of those creatures had the horses worked up, a yell and a couple of shots fired into the air ought to run it off. Most wild animals didn't want anything to do with humans.

The picketed horses were a dark mass in front of Smoke as they shifted back and forth in the shadows. Their hooves striking the ground as they moved around created a faint rumble.

Smoke realized suddenly that they were moving too much. Their picket ropes allowed them enough range to graze, but they appeared to be scattering more than they should have been able to do.

Then without warning, two shots blasted and a shrill, yipping cry tore through the night air. The rumble of hoofbeats welled up into sudden thunder as the frightened horses lunged away from the unexpected racket.

The panic-stricken surge aimed them straight at Smoke, who had come to an abrupt stop only a few yards away.

CHAPTER 23

The way the horses were spread out already, Smoke knew he didn't have time to get out of the way of the stampede. If he tried to dash one way or the other, the runaways would knock him down and trample him. And he certainly couldn't turn around and outrun them.

But even in the bad light, he recognized the tall, powerfully rangy shape of Drifter as the stallion ran toward him. Not surprisingly, Drifter had pulled slightly ahead of the other horses. Smoke darted a couple of steps to his right. As Drifter reached him, he threw his arms around the stallion's neck, hung on, and jumped up with all the power he could summon from his powerful legs.

The desperate leap lifted Smoke high enough that he was able to throw his right leg over Drifter's back. Smoke clamped down with his thighs and clung to the stallion as Drifter's great, lunging strides carried them through the night.

Smoke pulled himself higher and settled his weight so that he was riding bareback in a normal position. He saw the camp just ahead of them. The women were running around and crying out in startled fear as the stampede bore down on them.

With his hands gripping Drifter's mane, Smoke banged his heels against the stallion's flanks and veered him to the left. Drifter wasn't stampeding blindly now. He was under Smoke's control, and as he responded and angled away from the camp, the other horses obeyed their natural instincts and followed.

Smoke's swift action worked. It was a close thing, but the charging horses swept past the wagons to the outside, away from the campfire and the women.

Harsh shouts came from in front of Smoke. Those were male voices, he realized, followed an instant later by spurts of muzzle flame that ripped orange rents in the darkness. He felt the hot breath of a slug as it whipped past his ear.

When somebody started shooting at him, Smoke Jensen's instincts allowed him to respond in only one way. He guided Drifter with his knees, drew both Colts, and returned fire. The revolvers roared and bucked in his hands as he targeted the muzzle flashes he had seen.

As if lightning ripped the sky overhead, the hellish flicker of gunflame revealed three men on foot trying to get out of the horses' way. One of them snapped another shot at Smoke. As the bullet whined high, Smoke slammed a shot back at him. The man stopped short and came up on his toes as he pawed at his bloody chest. He stumbled and fell.

A second man went down with a scream under Drifter's slashing hooves. The third man stopped shooting and devoted his efforts instead to avoiding the horses. Smoke lost sight of him in the darkness.

More shots crashed from the direction of the wagons. Smoke wheeled Drifter and let the other horses scatter and mill. The stampede had been a diversion, he realized, a tactic intended to wreak havoc in the camp and cover an attack from both flanks. With both hands still gripping the Colts, Smoke charged toward the wagons to meet this new threat.

Danny Murphy ran toward the wagons beside Gus Gerhardt. Gerhardt had his gun out, but Danny hadn't drawn his. He knew he couldn't shoot any of the women, and from what he knew of Smoke Jensen, swapping lead with that hombre was one of the surest and swiftest ways on the face of the earth to die. His best chance of surviving this raid was to not do any shooting.

Anyway, all he really wanted to do was find Susie and persuade her to leave with him. If he could get her back to where the gang's horses had been left, he would take one of the mounts for Susie and scatter the rest. They could ride away from here into the night and never look back.

Something was wrong, though. They had heard Concho Warren fire those shots and let out a Comanche war cry, but although the horse herd had stampeded according to plan, the animals weren't charging through the camp and upsetting everything.

Instead, they galloped past the wagons on the far side, leaving the camp untouched. Danny heard more shots and saw muzzle flashes over there. That was about where Farnum, Hamilton, and Townsend were supposed to be. They must have run right into the horses.

That couldn't be good.

"Come on!" Gerhardt yelled at Danny. "Find the Wilkinson woman!"

In his obsessive lust for Annabelle Wilkinson, Gerhardt had forgotten about Susie and Delia. The promise of payment for kidnapping them and returning them to Andrew Rickett had just been an excuse to get the rest of the men to come along with him. He'd never actually had his sights set on anybody but Annabelle.

Without really thinking about it, Danny had suspected that all along. Gerhardt had confirmed it now. He reached the wagons and dashed around the closest one, with Danny right behind him.

Annabelle Wilkinson stood next to the other end of the vehicle with a rifle in one hand. The old man was between her and Gerhardt. He swung around, yelling something, and swung the walking stick in his hand at Gerhardt's head.

Gerhardt ducked the awkward blow and lashed out with the revolver he held. The barrel raked the old man's head in a vicious blow that knocked his hat off. The old man groaned and went down, with blood staining his white hair red.

He had slowed Gerhardt down enough that Annabelle had time to raise the rifle to her shoulder. Flame licked from its muzzle as a shot cracked.

Gerhardt was already diving forward at her. The bullet went over his head and he tackled her around the waist a fraction of a second later, driving her off her feet.

Danny felt a hammerblow to his body and reeled backward. He was hot all over. At the same time, the blood in his veins seemed to be turning to ice. Then his legs didn't want to hold him up anymore and he fell.

He'd been shot, he realized. That wild round Annabelle Wilkinson had intended for Gerhardt had struck him.

Now he and Susie would never be together.

That was the last coherent thought in his head before darkness surrounded him and carried him away.

Smoke was most concerned for Sally's safety. His keen eyes searched the confusion around the wagons. The alarm clamoring inside him got even louder as he failed to catch sight of her.

He caught a glimpse of something else from the corner of his eye. A rider streaked toward him out of the night. The man was dressed in dark clothes and had a black hat pulled down tightly on his head. His lean face twisted with hate as he yelled, "Jensen!"

The man's right hand came up with a gun in it. Powdersmoke and flame geysered from the muzzle as he fired.

Smoke answered with shattering blasts from both Colts. In the brief second when the attacker's face was lit up, both by the firelight and the orange flash from the twin irons, Smoke recognized him as one of the hard cases who had been with Gus Gerhardt back in Big Rock.

So Gerhardt had followed the wagon train. He had taken his own sweet time about striking back, but he had to be behind this raid. Smoke had no doubt of it.

The dark stranger rocked back in his saddle as Smoke's slugs slammed into him. He didn't topple off his mount, nor did he drop his gun. He found the strength to fire again.

This time, the bullet passed close enough to Smoke for him to hear its high-pitched whine.

Then Drifter and the other man's horse flashed past each other, like chargers carrying knights in a joust at one of those old-time tournaments. Smoke and the black-garbed gunman were facing away from each other now. Smoke used his knees to turn Drifter and saw the other man hauling his mount around, too.

They were still close enough to be in handgun range. Instead of charging, both men opened fire again from where they were. Drifter jumped as the gunman's slug burned his shoulder.

Smoke triggered his Colts and both bullets, once again, crashed into his opponent's body. This time, it was impossible for the man to continue the fight. He dropped his gun, swayed in the saddle for a second, and fell backward. One foot was caught in the stirrup. As the horse dashed off into the night, it dragged the man's body with it. Smoke saw the limp way the body bounced and flailed and knew the man was dead.

He turned away. His guns were nearly empty and he ought to reload while he had the chance.

The next instant, that opportunity vanished as he heard a scream and recognized Sally's voice.

Sally had gone with Lucy back to Lucy's wagon after talking to Annabelle, Delia, and Susie. Lucy had said she needed Sally's opinion on something. Sally couldn't think what that might be, since Lucy struck her as an intelligent, resourceful young woman, but she went along, anyway, curious to know what was on Lucy's mind.

When they reached the wagon, Lucy said, "I heard some of the others talking about how you used to be a teacher, Mrs. Jensen. Is that right?"

"It is," Sally said. "I was teaching school up in Idaho when I met Smoke, in fact. And as long as we've been traveling together, you can call me Sally, you know. I'm not *that* much older than you."

Lucy laughed. "All right. I was wondering, Sally, if I could ask your opinion about something related to teaching."

"Of course. Are you thinking about going into it once we reach Brimstone Butte? For all we know, they might be in need of a good teacher."

"Well, that, um, wouldn't be me." Lucy looked down at the ground, as if in sudden embarrassment. "What I was wondering is if you think I'm too old to learn how to read?"

"What?" Sally said, then instantly wished she hadn't reacted with such surprise. "I mean, yes, of course, you could learn. A person is never too old to learn new things, and that includes reading."

"Maybe you could, um, teach me some, then."

"I'd be happy to," Sally assured the younger woman. "In fact, we could start tomorrow. I'll get someone else to drive the buckboard so I can ride on your wagon with you, and there's no reason we can't start going over some of the basics while we're on the trail."

Lucy looked up. A smile appeared on her face. "Thank you, Mrs. Jensen . . . Sally. I sure do appreciate—"

A sudden blast of gunfire, followed by a bloodcurdling cry, caused both women to jerk around in shock.

Sally heard the rumble of hoofbeats and realized the horses picketed north of the camp were stampeding in this direction. Anyone caught out in the open was in danger of being trampled.

"Get into the wagon!" she told Lucy. "We have to get out of the way."

Lucy ran to the back of the vehicle and pulled the pins that held the tailgate in its raised position. The gate fell, but before the women could climb in, the stampeding horses veered away from the camp. More shots rang out. Sally saw muzzle flashes to the east, not far away.

She wondered where Smoke was.

Probably where those guns were going off, she thought. When powder was being burned, Smoke Jensen was never far away.

Lucy clutched Sally's arm. "Are we under attack?"

"It looks and sounds that way," Sally replied. "You should get inside the wagon, anyway, and keep your head down."

Lucy reached over the lowered tailgate into the back of the vehicle and pulled out a rifle.

"I don't like to hide from trouble," she said as she worked the weapon's loading lever and threw a round into the firing chamber.

Sally couldn't help but smile. She was the same way. But she wasn't armed at the moment, so she asked, "Do you have another rifle?"

Before Lucy could answer, a running figure loomed out of the darkness. One of the ugliest men Sally had ever seen, wearing a pair of overalls like a farmer, charged out of the night and crashed into her, knocking her off her feet.

She let out an involuntary scream as she fell. When she landed, her head hit the ground hard. The impact stunned her into senselessness.

CHAPTER 24

Hank Cavanaugh had been loitering around most of the evening, mending some of the leatherwork on his saddle and keeping an eye on Lucy Dunning in the hope of finding an opportunity to talk to her again.

When he'd decided to throw in with this wagon train, he hadn't intended to let himself be distracted by any romantic entanglements, but such feelings sometimes cropped up whether a fella meant for them to happen or not.

Lucy was smart, mighty pretty, and downright appealing. There wasn't a thing in the world he could do to change that, or the way he reacted to her.

So he already knew that Lucy was talking to Sally Jensen over by Lucy's wagon when all hell broke loose. Cavanaugh leaped up from where he was sitting cross-legged on the ground and charged across the camp. He wanted to reach the two women in time to protect them, if need be.

He hadn't gotten there yet when he realized the stampede was going to miss the camp. That was good, but it didn't mean the danger was over. Somebody had started that stampede. Guns were going off. Muzzle flashes tore holes in the night.

Cavanaugh hesitated. If the group was under attack, he wanted to help them fight it off. For the moment, Lucy seemed relatively safe.

A shot sounded from somewhere behind him, over toward the area where Annabelle Wilkinson's wagon was parked. Cavanaugh started to swing around in that direction, but as he did so, he saw a strange man rush out of the darkness where Lucy and Sally were. The stranger slammed into Sally and knocked her to the ground.

Then the strange fella made up Cavanaugh's mind for him by grabbing Lucy and jerking her off her feet. She screamed and fought him, but he threw her over his shoulder like a sack of flour and turned to run off again.

"Hold it!" Cavanaugh shouted at him.

He drew his gun as the man stopped. Lucy pounded frantically with her fists at her captor's back, but he ignored the blows.

Cavanaugh lifted the gun, but grimaced as he realized he couldn't risk a shot. There was too much of a chance he'd hit Lucy if he fired.

The stranger didn't have to worry about that. He produced a revolver and blazed away at Cavanaugh. Cavanaugh had no choice but to throw himself flat on the ground as slugs sizzled through the space where he'd been standing a second earlier.

When the gun-thunder stopped a moment later, Cavanaugh looked up and saw that the stranger had vanished, taking Lucy with him.

With horror and anger welling up inside, Cavanaugh leaped to his feet and ran toward the wagon. Sally Jensen still lay on the ground near the vehicle, apparently stunned or even knocked unconscious.

Cavanaugh wanted to check on her, but first he ducked behind the wagon's rear corner to use it for cover in case the stranger who had grabbed Lucy opened fire on him again.

A quick look around the corner showed him nothing but blackness. Somewhere out there, horses were still moving around, but the hoofbeats had an aimless quality to them. That would be the stampeded horses, Cavanaugh reasoned. Their panic was receding now.

A swift drumming made him tense. That was a horse running hard, under a rider's control. Expecting another attacker, Cavanaugh raised his gun as the horse approached, but then a familiar voice shouted, "Sally!"

Smoke Jensen had returned.

Fear clutched at Smoke's guts like a frozen fist when he spotted Sally lying on the ground. He called out her name as he pulled back on Drifter's mane.

Anger burst through him as he spotted Hank Cavanaugh standing nearby with a gun in his hand. Smoke didn't know what had happened here, but instinct made him want to swing up the Colt he still held in his right hand.

Cavanaugh pouched his iron, shoving the revolver back into leather and hurriedly holding up both hands.

"Mr. Jensen!" he called. "Smoke! Over here!"

Cavanaugh wouldn't be doing that if he'd had anything to do with whatever happened to Sally. Smoke holstered his own gun and swung down from Drifter's back as the big stallion was still moving.

He dropped to a knee beside Sally. Relief flooded through him as he saw that she was moving around a little. Her eyelids fluttered. She opened her eyes all the way as Smoke slid his arm around her shoulders and eased her up into a sitting position.

"Smoke," she said. "I . . . I . . ."

"Don't talk," he told her. "Let me look at you. Are you wounded?"

She shook her head and winced. "No, I just hit my head when that man knocked me down." She looked at him. "I'm not sure, but I think it was one of the men who caused trouble back in Big Rock."

"Bound to be," Smoke agreed. "I tangled with another of them, and he was definitely one of Gerhardt's bunch. I expected Gerhardt to come after us, and he finally did."

Cavanaugh said, "I don't know who Gerhardt is, but the fella who hurt Mrs. Jensen grabbed Lucy and carried her off."

"Oh, no!" Sally said as she looked up at the young man.

"Did you see them, Smoke?" Cavanaugh asked.

Smoke shook his head. "The varmint must have slipped past me in the dark. Once I knew Sally was in danger, I didn't pay much attention to anything else."

She caught hold of his sleeve and said, "Smoke, you've got to go after them and help Lucy."

"As soon as I know you're all right."

"I'm fine! Just go."

Smoke looked at Cavanaugh. "Did you see which direction the fella headed?"

"No, I'm afraid not. They could be anywhere out there in the darkness."

Before they could say anything else, a reedy old voice pleaded, "Help! Please help me!"

"That's the colonel," Sally said. "I'm all right, Smoke, really. Go check on him."

He came to his feet and helped her to stand. She put a hand against the wagon and leaned on it for support.

"Go see what's wrong with Colonel Wilkinson," she urged again.

Smoke nodded and snapped at Cavanaugh, "Come on." The two men hurried around the fire and across the camp.

The rest of the women were beginning to realize that the attack seemed to be over. Most of them had dived underneath the wagons or climbed inside one of the vehicles. They emerged now and gathered at the Wilkinson wagon. The colonel stumbled back and forth, his hands held out in front of him, and continued calling for help.

Susie and Delia reached him before Smoke and Cavanaugh did. Delia took hold of his arm, causing him to gasp and stop lurching back and forth. She said, “You’re all right, Colonel, you’re all right.”

In point of fact, though, the old man didn’t appear to be all right. He was bareheaded and disheveled. Blood from a wound on his head smeared his tangled white hair.

“Where’s Annabelle?” he asked pitifully. “I can’t find her. Annabelle!”

Susie tried to comfort him, but then she looked past him, spotted a man lying motionless on the ground, and exclaimed, “Danny!”

Smoke put a hand on a gun butt as he recognized the man on the ground as another of Gus Gerhardt’s hard cases. A bloodstain that was dark in the firelight was visible on the man’s shirt. He appeared to be either unconscious or dead.

Susie fell to her knees beside him. As Susie gripped the fallen man’s shoulders, Smoke moved up and said, “You’d better back away from him, Miss Beale.”

“No, he’s hurt!” she said without looking up at Smoke. “You have to help him!”

Smoke wasn’t in much of a mood to help any of Gus Gerhardt’s men, but he knelt on the other side of this one and checked for a pulse. He found one. The man was wounded, but still alive.

Helen Pryor and Roberta Walling hurried up. “The other man took Annabelle,” Helen said. “We saw him dragging her away, but we couldn’t do anything to stop him. We couldn’t shoot when he had hold of her like that.”

“That’s the same thing that happened with Lucy and the other man,” Cavanaugh said. “I couldn’t risk a shot, and he got away with her.”

The torment the young man was feeling was obvious in his voice.

Smoke straightened and looked around. He had gotten to know all the women during the trip, but he didn't trust his judgment completely in the aftermath of a melee like this.

"Is anybody else missing?" he asked. "Look around. See if everybody else is here."

It didn't take long to establish that Annabelle and Lucy were the only ones unaccounted for. Witnesses had seen both of them carried off: Annabelle by a man who matched Gus Gerhardt's description, and Lucy by a big, ugly man in overalls.

"What are we going to do?" the colonel moaned.

"Don't worry, sir," Smoke said. "I'll be going after them. Some of the men who did this are already dead, and the ones who aren't won't get away with it."

"I'm coming with you," Hank Cavanaugh declared.

Smoke looked at the young man and said, "No, you're staying here to look after the women."

"We don't need any looking after," Roberta said. "We can take care of ourselves. You just go after those sons of—"

She stopped and drew in a deep breath. "Just go after those men and bring back Annabelle and Lucy."

Smoke nodded to Cavanaugh and then looked at the women gathered around them as he said, "You can count on it, ladies."

CHAPTER 25

Gus Gerhardt didn't want to hurt the beautiful blonde he had dragged away from the camp, but she was putting up such a fight that he didn't have much choice. He had to settle her down somehow. As she clawed and punched and kicked at him, he paused in the darkness and slugged her on the jaw.

He pulled his punch as much as he could. His fist landed solidly, anyway, and jerked her head to the side. She sagged in his grip as his left arm encircled her.

A low groan came from her. She wasn't knocked cold, only stunned. He didn't know how long that would last. Stooping, he got his right arm behind her knees and moved his left arm to her shoulders. He picked her up effortlessly and trotted through the thick shadows toward the spot where he and his men had picketed their horses.

For some reason, the stampeding livestock had gone around the camp, rather than through it. Clearly, Concho Warren had failed in his assignment. If he had botched that job, there was a good chance he hadn't killed Smoke Jensen, either.

That meant Jensen might be coming after him, Gerhardt thought.

A few more shots roared in the night behind him as he fled with his captive. He wondered briefly if any of the others were going to live through this raid. He had already seen Danny Murphy fall, gunned down by the woman who now lay limp and senseless in his arms.

It galled him that they wouldn't be able to take those two saloon girls back to Big Rock and collect on them from Andrew Rickett. Gerhardt could have used that money.

But he had what he really wanted to get. A man could always find a way to make more money, but you didn't come across a gal like this one very often. If he hadn't gone after her, the memory of how he felt when he first laid eyes on her would have haunted him for the rest of his days.

Large, dark shapes loomed up out of the gloom—the horses. If Gerhardt ran up to them, it would make them skittish, so he called to them softly and they calmed down some at the sound of a familiar voice.

Since everything had gone to hell back at the camp—and Danny Murphy, at least, wasn't going to be needing his horse anymore—Gerhardt lifted Annabelle Wilkinson onto the saddle of that mount.

She moaned again. She would be coming around before too much longer, he knew. No time to waste.

A lasso was hanging from the saddle. Gerhardt grabbed it, looped the rope around Annabelle's wrists, and lashed them to the saddle horn. He ran it under the horse's belly, secured her feet as well, and then finished by tying it again to the horn. Annabelle couldn't go anywhere now.

That didn't stop her from straining against the bonds and trying to writhe and kick her way free as awareness returned to her. She realized immediately that she was a prisoner, and she didn't like it.

Curses spilled from her mouth, the kind of obscenities that Gerhardt never would have expected from her. Evidently, she wasn't quite as much of a genteel Southern belle as he had taken her for at first glance.

Gerhardt didn't mind, though. She could call him whatever names she wanted, as long as she couldn't get away from him.

"You might as well take it easy, Annabelle," he told her. "You're not going anywhere except with me."

"You better not be planning on sleeping ever again, you—" She added a few more choice epithets. "I'll cut your throat as soon as I get the chance!"

"Well, then, I won't give you the chance."

Gerhardt moved over to his horse and was about to untie the animal's reins when the sound of harsh breathing and running footsteps made him turn sharply. He drew his gun and aimed at whoever was hurrying toward him in the darkness.

Before Gerhardt could pull the trigger, a familiar voice called, "Gus! Where are you? Are you there, Gus?"

"Abner! Over here!"

Abner Farnum stumbled up. He was carrying something. The moon still hadn't risen and the starlight was faint, but it was bright enough for Gerhardt to realize that Farnum had one of the women slung over his shoulder.

"Is that one of those saloon girls?" Gerhardt asked hopefully.

"Damn it, no," Farnum rasped. He was out of breath. "I don't know who she is. I just saw her and grabbed her. Figured she was better than nothing. If she's pretty enough, we can sell her and still get something out of this deal."

"Where are the others from our bunch?" Gerhardt asked tightly.

"I'm pretty sure Stan and Al are dead. Somebody on horseback, Smoke Jensen maybe, gunned Stan down, and Al got caught in that stampede. Those horses must've trampled him to hash. I don't know what happened to Concho. Never saw him again after we split up. Where's Murphy?"

"Dead," Gerhardt snapped. "Throw that girl over a saddle and let's get out of here while we can!"

* * *

Smoke's first impulse was to set out after the missing women and their captors right away, but he knew better than to give in to that inclination. The night was too dark. It would be just blind luck if he and Cavanaugh were to stumble over the ones they were looking for.

Going after them now also risked taking off in a completely wrong direction, which would allow Gerhardt and his partner to build up such a big lead that it would be all but impossible to catch them.

No matter how much it grated at Smoke's nerves, he knew the sensible thing to do was to wait until morning when he and Cavanaugh would be able to pick up an actual trail.

In addition, that allowed him to keep an eye on Sally tonight and make sure she was all right after being knocked unconscious. A hard hit to the head like that could have delayed effects. He had known men who seemed fine after such a wallop and then collapsed later.

The delay also allowed Smoke and Cavanaugh to check on the men who had been responsible for the raid on the wagon train. Cavanaugh brought along a bull's-eye lantern from one of the wagons as they began looking around.

Two corpses lay to the east of the wagons where the stampeding horses had passed. Both were fairly mangled, but one was still intact enough for Smoke to recognize the man he had gunned down.

The other, who had suffered the full force of the slashing hooves, was barely recognizable as human.

A short distance away, they found the body of the black-clad gunman who had started the stampede. He had been dragged off by his runaway horse, Smoke recalled, but his foot had finally slipped from the stirrup and he was left lying there. Being dragged like that had left him pretty battered, too, but the bullet holes in his chest from Smoke's .45s were still visible.

Counting Danny Murphy, wounded back at the wagons, that made four men. Gerhardt's group in Big Rock had numbered seven, Smoke recalled.

That left three men unaccounted for, Gerhardt himself and two others. And they had two prisoners in Annabelle and Lucy. Smoke was confident he could locate the trail of riders, as soon as it was light enough to see.

He and Cavanaugh left the corpses where they had fallen. They had buried Billy J. Pike and the other outlaws who had attacked the wagon train earlier, but as far as Smoke was concerned, the buzzards and coyotes could feast on these carcasses. He was fresh out of sympathy for hard cases and owlhoots.

Smoke and Cavanaugh returned to the wagons and found that Danny Murphy had regained consciousness. He was sitting up with his back propped against a wheel. Susie Beale knelt beside him, finishing up the job of wrapping bandages around his wounded torso.

Delia Tracy and Helen Pryor stood nearby, each woman holding a carbine with the barrel pointing in Murphy's general direction. Their expressions were grim and watchful. If Murphy tried anything funny, they were ready to shoot.

Smoke glanced around and didn't see Sally. He wanted to check on her first, but Murphy was right here, so he asked, "How's he doing?"

Susie looked up as she finished tying a bandage in place. "I think he'll be all right," she said. "The bullet put a deep graze in his side and he lost quite a bit of blood, but I don't believe it hit anything too vital."

"I'd say my blood is pretty vital," Murphy put in. His voice was slurred a little, telling Smoke that the women had given him enough whiskey to dull the pain of his injury while Susie was tending to it.

"Well, three of your friends didn't think you were important enough to wait around for," Smoke said. "They abandoned you, Murphy. Rode off and left you here, not caring whether you were dead or alive."

Smoke hoped that might spark enough resentment in Murphy to make him spill anything he knew about where Gerhardt and the others might have gone.

"That's not true!" Murphy insisted. "Gus and the boys wouldn't desert me if they believed I was alive. Gus saw me get shot. He must've figured I was a goner."

"No matter what he figured, he didn't stop to check," Smoke said. "He just grabbed Miss Wilkinson and carried her off. She's all he wanted. You didn't matter to him at all, mister."

Murphy swallowed hard and then muttered, "He figured I was dead. Had to."

However, he didn't sound completely convinced of that anymore.

Murphy went on, "What happened to the others?"

"They're dead. I killed the man who started the stampede and one other, and the third man got caught in it and trampled."

"You killed Concho. I don't believe it. He was slick with a gun. Real slick."

"Not slick enough," Smoke said flatly. "One of the other men who got away was a big, ugly galoot who wears overalls like a farmer. What's his name?"

Smoke wouldn't have been surprised if Murphy refused to answer, but the whiskey must have been making the young man less wary. He slurred, "Thas's Abner. Abner Farnum."

"What about the third man?"

Murphy shook his head. "There ain't any third man. There were just . . . just six of us. J.D. died a ways back. J.D. Styles. A good man." He glared at Smoke. "You killed him! He never did recover from that bullet you put in his leg."

"He shouldn't have pulled a gun on a woman. Especially not my wife. So only two got away, Gerhardt and this Farnum. Where would they go, Murphy?"

"Dunno. Wouldn't tell you if I did."

Susie leaned closer to him, put a hand on his shoulder, and said, "Please, Danny. Help Mr. Jensen if you can. They took two of our friends. Annabelle and Lucy have been good to Delia and me. I want them to come back safe and sound."

"I'm sorry," Murphy said. "Sorry Gus was so bound and determined to get that woman. I never wanted to take you and Delia back, Susie, I swear I didn't."

Delia had been listening. She said sharply, "Take us back? What do you mean?"

"That fella Rickett, the one at the saloon, he was gonna pay Gus and the rest of us to take you two away from the wagon and bring you back to Big Rock. It was gonna be a good payday. But I never wanted to do it. Never seemed right . . ."

His voice trailed off as his head tipped back against a wheel spoke. The blood loss, the whiskey, and the shock of being shot had caught up with him.

Susie looked alarmed for a moment, but then she must have realized that Murphy's chest was still rising and falling. He had just passed out.

She eased him down to the ground on his unwounded side, then glanced up at Smoke and said, "I'm sorry he wasn't more helpful, Mr. Jensen."

"I didn't figure we'd get much out of him," Smoke said. "And to be honest, he probably doesn't have any idea which direction Gerhardt would go with his prisoners. More than likely, Gerhardt's not the type to share his plans with the men who ride with him. But without the two of you, it's not very likely he'd turn around and head back to Big Rock."

Delia said, "If I ever get back to Big Rock, I'm going to have some words for Andrew Rickett. Imagine, paying to have us carried off like . . . like rustled cattle or something!"

"I plan to have a talk with Rickett myself, one of these days," Smoke said. "But right now, I want to see Sally. Does anybody know where she is?"

Helen Pryor replied, "She said she was sleepy, so she went to Lucy's wagon to lie down. You should be able to find her there, Mr. Jensen."

Smoke nodded his thanks and turned away. Hank Cavanaugh stopped him by saying, "What do you want me to do, Smoke?"

"Get some rest yourself," Smoke told him. "We'll be hitting the trail mighty early in the morning."

Chapter 26

Sally was all right. She woke when Smoke climbed into Lucy Dunning's wagon. As she sat up quickly, a stray beam of light from the campfire outside glinted off the barrel of the revolver in her hand.

"Rest easy," Smoke told her. "It's just me."

"Smoke." She lowered the gun and set it aside as he knelt to take her in his arms. She rested her head against his shoulder and asked, "Has there been any more trouble?"

"Not a bit. Hank Cavanaugh and I checked on the men from Gerhardt's bunch who were left behind. They're all dead. They won't hurt anybody ever again."

"What about that young man who's sweet on Susie?"

"Danny Murphy? Annabelle shot him, but he's still alive. She was trying to drill Gerhardt, but she got Murphy instead. The bullet knocked a chunk of meat out of his side and he lost some blood, but he ought to recover." Smoke paused. "Unfortunately, he claims not to have any idea which direction Gerhardt would have gone with those prisoners, and I believe him."

"Then Annabelle and Lucy are still missing?"

"I'm afraid so. According to Murphy, Gerhardt and a man named Farnum are still alive. They're bound to have Annabelle and Lucy. Cavanaugh and I are going after them first thing in the morning."

"You can't pick up the trail tonight?"

Smoke smiled in the shadowy interior of the wagon bed. "Preacher can see in the dark like a mountain lion, but I'm not Preacher. I don't like it, but it's smarter to wait until we can see before we go after them."

Sally nodded and said, "That makes sense, I suppose. I just hate to think about Annabelle and Lucy being defenseless in the hands of men like those two."

"I'm not sure I'd consider Annabelle and Lucy defenseless," Smoke said. "They strike me as pretty tough ladies who know how to take care of themselves."

"Yes, but sometimes that's not enough when you're dealing with evil men like Gerhardt and his friend."

She had a point there, Smoke had to admit. But he believed—or at least hoped—that Gerhardt would be more concerned about putting distance between himself and the wagon train, rather than anything else he and Farnum might do to occupy themselves with the prisoners.

"We'll track them down as quickly as we can," he promised. "Until then, it doesn't do any good to worry." He rested his hands on her shoulders. "Are you all right?"

"I told you earlier, I'm fine. My head aches a little, but that's all. Honestly, I'd be surprised if it didn't hurt after a knock like the one I got."

"That's just it. When you get walloped in the head like that, sometimes you don't realize just how bad you're really hurt."

"Injuries like that are known as concussions," Sally said. "I've read about them. But I really don't believe I'm suffering from one. My mind is clear, and so is my eyesight. And my head doesn't hurt any more than normal after being hit like that."

"Yeah, I can tell by the way you're talking that you're not having any trouble thinking," Smoke agreed. "I reckon you know how you're feeling, better than anybody else, so I'll take your word for it. But I'm going to be right here with you the rest of the night, so if you start feeling funny, you let me know right away."

She laughed and snuggled against him. "What if I start feeling like I require some thorough medical attention from my husband?"

"You just hold on to that thought until we're sure you're all right," Smoke told her as his arms tightened around her, "and then I'd be happy to oblige you."

Sally was fine the next morning, as Smoke had hoped and expected she would be. She had slept soundly in his arms during the rest of the night.

He had dozed, his slumber light in case he needed to react to any change in her condition. He wasn't fully rested when the eastern sky turned gray and he climbed out of the wagon, but his iron constitution and youthful resilience allowed him to feel fairly refreshed.

He smelled coffee before his feet even hit the ground. Roberta had stirred up the embers of the campfire, added wood, and had flames dancing brightly again. A coffeepot was already sitting on its blackened metal stand at the edge of the fire, giving off that wonderful aroma that perked up Smoke even more.

"Arbuckles' will be ready soon," Roberta told him as he walked up.

Smoke drew in a deep breath. "Smells like chuckwagon coffee," he commented.

"It ought to. My pa taught me how to make it, and he went up the trail from Texas to the railhead half-a-dozen times."

"You were raised on a ranch?"

"My family lived on one down in South Texas, but I wasn't raised there. I was full grown when Pa decided to head west after the war. We'd lost almost everything to the Union Army when the soldiers came through, and then the damn carpetbaggers took the rest."

Roberta's shoulders rose and fell as she went on, "Things were all right for a while after we got to Texas, but then five years ago lightning spooked a herd and the cattle stampeded and destroyed the chuck wagon. My pa was inside it. The cowboy I was fixing to get hitched to got caught in that stampede, too, and didn't make it out. So when my ma decided to move the whole family back to Mississippi, even though we'd be starting over again, I didn't see any reason not to go along with her and my little brothers."

"Those were tough breaks."

"Life's full of 'em," Roberta said.

Hank Cavanaugh ambled up to the fire, stretched, and yawned.

"I've been keeping an eye on that Murphy fella," he said. "We got him bedded down under one of the wagons, and the ladies have been taking turns guarding him." Cavanaugh paused, then went on, "Not Miss Beale, though. Miss Tracy said that wouldn't be a good idea."

"Probably not," Smoke agreed. "She's sweet on him. I don't think she'd turn him loose after what he did as part of Gerhardt's bunch, but you never know."

"We're still setting out after those varmints this morning?" Cavanaugh asked. His voice was tighter with tension and worry now.

Smoke glanced at the graying sky. "As soon as we get some coffee in us. We'll take along some biscuits and jerky and eat in the saddle instead of waiting for breakfast."

The two men were standing up drinking their coffee when Sally joined them and slipped an arm around Smoke's waist.

"Still feeling all right?" he asked her.

"Yes. I knew when you left the wagon, but I lay there and rested for a little while longer." She tipped her head back to look up at him. "How long do you think you'll be gone?"

"However long it takes to find those men and deal with them. I hope we can catch up to them today and make it back here by tonight, but it might be longer than that. We'll take supplies for a couple of days."

Roberta said, "I'll start gathering up some provisions for you."

"You'll be careful?" Sally said.

"Of course," Smoke replied with a smile.

She laughed softly and shook her head. "I don't know why I waste my breath. You'll do what has to be done, whether it allows you to be careful or not."

"That's generally the way of it," Smoke admitted.

"And I wouldn't have you any other way, I suppose. But is it too much to hope that someday we can have some peace and quiet?"

"A person can always hope," Smoke said.

He and Cavanaugh were in the saddle a quarter of an hour later. The sun wasn't up yet, but a reddish-gold arc had appeared in the eastern sky, providing enough light for Smoke to see the ground fairly well as they rode past the horse herd, which was once again picketed north of the camp.

Since Smoke didn't believe Gus Gerhardt would return to Big Rock, the opposite direction seemed to be as good a place to start as any.

They began by casting back and forth over an area several hundred yards wide as they worked their way in a generally northward direction. Smoke took the lead and kept his eyes on the ground as he rode slowly across the landscape. The light was still poor enough that he ran the risk of missing something if he wasn't careful.

That caution paid off a half hour later when he spotted several pairs of faint hoofprints angling off to the northeast. He reined in and called to Hank Cavanaugh to do likewise. After swinging down from the saddle, Smoke dropped to one knee to study the hoofprints more closely.

He might not be quite as skilled a tracker as the old mountain man called Preacher, but he was better at reading sign than most men. When he straightened from scrutinizing the tracks, he said confidently, "It must be them, all right. Four horses, two of them carrying less weight, and they came through here four or five hours ago."

"It'll be hard to make up that much ground," Cavanaugh said.

"Maybe, maybe not. Their horses can't keep going without resting any more than ours can, and our mounts are fresh right now. They'll have to stop to rest their mounts before we do. They'll probably do that when they figure they've put enough miles behind them to be safe."

"So we follow as fast as we can?"

"Without riding our horses into the ground or losing the trail, yeah," Smoke said. He climbed into the saddle and nudged Drifter into motion. The big stallion settled into a ground-eating lope and Cavanaugh's horse followed just behind.

Gus Gerhardt was frustrated to the point of distraction. His life had had its ups and downs, just like anybody else's, but here lately it seemed like everything that could go wrong—had.

First, his plan to kidnap those two saloon girls, along with Annabelle Wilkinson, hadn't even come close to working. He had gotten Annabelle, and Abner Farnum had grabbed that other girl, Lucy, but the two who were actually worth money were still a long ways back there somewhere.

So were the other four hombres who'd been riding with him. He hadn't been that fond of any of them, but even so, he didn't like losing them. They had been willing to back his play, whatever it might be, and now he was left with just Farnum, who wasn't all that reliable.

For example, it was Farnum who was supposed to untie the extra mount and bring it along after they had gotten Lucy Dunning tied into the saddle of the horse that had belonged to

Stan Hamilton. You never could tell when you might need a fresh horse.

But Farnum had fumbled the job and the horse, now loose, had spooked and run off. Gerhardt hadn't wanted to take the time to go chasing after it, while they were still that close to the wagons, so they had forgotten about that horse and lit a shuck out of there on the ones they had.

One horse, more or less, wouldn't make any difference, Gerhardt had told himself, but the loss was just one more reminder of how he couldn't count on Farnum not to foul up.

Now, after they had been riding for hours and the horses were worn-out—not to mention the riders—Annabelle had started in on him again as soon as Gerhardt called a halt.

She had cursed him, of course, being as colorful and inventive as ever, and then she demanded, "Untie us and get us down out of these saddles. You can't just leave us like this."

"I don't reckon you're giving the orders, little missy," Gerhardt snapped at her.

"Don't call me *little missy*, you damned, no-good—" More spewing of bad language followed until Annabelle finally ran out of steam.

Lucy took up the crusade, only in a lot less obscene manner.

"Please, mister," she said to Gerhardt. "We've been riding for hours. We have to stretch our legs and, um, tend to our other needs."

Farnum leered at her and said to Gerhardt, "That's right, Gus. We don't want these gals to stiffen up so bad they can't move around. We might need 'em to wiggle a little."

"We don't want them running off, either," Gerhardt said.

But he wasn't a cruel man. That wasn't exactly true, he mused. He did have a cruel streak running through him, and he knew it. Often, that cruelty was necessary to make a point. He didn't mind hurting people when there was a reason for it.

If he and Farnum were careful, they could get the women

dismounted and even allow them, one at a time, to go into a nearby thicket of brush to relieve themselves.

"All right," he said as he approached the blonde. "You first, Annabelle."

"You don't have the right to call me by that name," she told him with a sneer. "You shouldn't be so familiar."

Farnum let out a bray of laughter. "Lady, I'll bet a brand-new hat ol' Gus intends to be a lot more familiar than that with you before he's done."

"Shut up, Abner." Gerhardt untied the rope holding Annabelle in the saddle.

As soon as she was loose, she jerked her left leg up and kicked him in the chest.

The impact knocked Gerhardt back a step, but he was still close enough to reach out and grab her ankle before she could pull it away. He heaved up on her leg. She toppled off the horse on the other side with a frantic yell, which cut off when she landed on the ground.

Gerhardt was around the horse and beside her in an instant, reaching down to grab her and jerk her to her feet. He clamped one big hand around her wrists and held them with brutal force until he was able to dig a length of rawhide cord out of his saddlebag and whip it around her wrists.

He lashed them together in front of her and gave her a shove that sent her stumbling for several feet. She managed to retain her balance and stood there glaring at him as her chest heaved with rage.

"Try something like that again and you won't get out of that saddle until we get where we're going," he warned her.

"Don't you try anything, gal," Farnum told Lucy as he approached her horse. "I ain't anywhere near as nice as Gus is."

Lucy was cooperative. Once she was off the horse, she allowed Farnum to tie her hands without putting up any fuss.

Gerhardt escorted the women to the brush and laid out the

ground rules: They could go into the thicket, one at a time, and he wouldn't follow them—as long as they stayed where he could see their heads. If he lost sight of them, or if he heard them moving through the brush away from him, all bets were off.

The brief stop proceeded without incident. Gerhardt tended to the women, while Farnum led the horses to a nearby creek and let all four of them drink.

Gerhardt wanted to warn Farnum not to let the animals run off this time, but he knew Farnum would take offense if he did. He didn't need that bother right now.

A short time later, they were mounted again and riding northwest toward the rugged mountains once more. These peaks weren't high enough to have snow on their crests, like the main ranges of the Rockies visible in the far distance beyond them, but they loomed impressively despite that.

Annabelle and Lucy still had their hands tied in front of them, but they weren't roped into the saddles anymore.

"Where exactly are we goin', Gus?" Farnum asked. "Are there any settlements up there ahead of us?"

"There are bound to be," Gerhardt replied. "At least, a few trading posts. I've been hearing more and more about how cattlemen are moving into Wyoming and starting big spreads. They can't do that without having a few towns here and there to supply them. Where there are towns, there are bound to be saloons and cathouses."

They could dispose of Lucy Dunning in such a place, he knew. Any girl as young and pretty as she was would fetch a good price from a madam or a saloonkeeper.

He planned to keep Annabelle with him as long as he could, though. He was nowhere near ready to let go of her yet.

"Have you ever been through these parts before?" Farnum asked.

Gerhardt shook his head. "No, but I'm not worried."

"Not even about Smoke Jensen?"

Gerhardt frowned and said, "Jensen's not going to ride off and leave those other women just because we carried off these two. Sure, he'll probably put out the word about what happened, but look around, Abner. You really think we have to worry about the law out here in the middle of nowhere?"

"It ain't the law I'm worried that much about. I'm just not as convinced as you that Jensen won't come after us."

"If he does, he'll be sorry. The two of us can handle any one man who tries to give us trouble."

Annabelle stared over at Gerhardt as he said that. After a moment, she began to laugh. She kept on with it, sounding tremendously amused by his expression of confidence that they could handle Smoke Jensen.

Gerhardt almost wished she'd go back to cussing.

Chapter 27

Smoke and Hank Cavanaugh pushed on steadily all day. While Smoke could tell from the tracks they were following that they were whittling down the lead Gerhardt and Farnum had, they still hadn't closed in on the hard cases.

That frustrated Smoke, but they couldn't ask any more of their horses than they already were. Drifter might have been able to withstand a harder pace, but Cavanaugh's horse couldn't.

Being set afoot out here would not only doom them, it would probably do the same for Annabelle and Lucy. Smoke and Cavanaugh were their only hope for rescue.

They stopped occasionally to rest and water the horses. What food they ate, they gnawed on while in the saddle. By late afternoon, weariness began to settle over both men. They were young and strong, but everyone had their limits, even Smoke Jensen.

Any chance of rescuing the women and making it back to the wagon train today had vanished. Smoke heard discouragement in Cavanaugh's voice as the younger man said, "I thought we would have caught up to them by now."

"Most things take their own time," Smoke said. "You can hurry them along—maybe—but who's to say you won't just make things worse by doing that? The trick is knowing when to rush and when to proceed more deliberately."

"I suppose. I'm just worried about Lucy, that's all."

"She's a mighty sweet girl," Smoke allowed. "Mighty easy on the eyes, too." He smiled. "Are you thinking about maybe sticking around once the ladies get to Brimstone Butte, Hank?"

"I don't know," Cavanaugh replied, sounding a little annoyed. "It's not like I don't have plans for my life."

"And Lucy doesn't fit into those plans?"

"I don't know where Lucy fits. The thoughts just go around and around in my head so much, I feel like I'm on a bucking bronc most of the time."

Even though there was only a few years difference in their ages, Smoke felt considerably older than his companion at that moment. Just how many years did you have to have under your belt, he wondered, before it was all right to consider yourself an old married man?

That was pretty much the way he was feeling right now, along with being grateful that he had settled down with Sally and didn't have to worry about the sort of romantic confusion plaguing Hank Cavanaugh.

Once the sun dipped behind the western mountains, darkness dropped like a curtain over the Wyoming landscape. Cavanaugh sighed and said, "I reckon we should have been looking for a place to make camp."

"Not necessarily," Smoke said. "Take a look up there ahead of us, a little bit to the right, maybe four or five miles away."

Both men reined in while Cavanaugh studied the area Smoke had indicated. A few heartbeats of tense silence passed before Cavanaugh said, "That's a campfire, isn't it? Right against the base of those hills?"

"Looks like it to me," Smoke said. "I reckon we've found them."

Farnum had the fire blazing brightly before Gerhardt realized what he was doing.

"Blast it, there was no need to make it that big," Gerhardt complained.

"It gets cold up here," Farnum said. "I damn near froze last night while we were riding. I figured it wouldn't hurt anything to warm up tonight." He leered at the women, who sat on the other side of their fire with their heads down. "Those two can help with the warmin' up, too."

"Forget it. One of us will be standing guard all night, and whoever's not on duty will need to get some sleep. There'll be time for sporting when we get where we're going."

It wasn't easy for Gerhardt to make that decree. He wanted to get closer to Annabelle Wilkinson, wanted it so fierce that he hadn't been able to think about much else all day.

But there was a time and a place for such things, and out here on the trail, while they were still potentially in danger, didn't fit the bill.

Farnum wasn't in a mood to let it go, though.

"Damn it, Gus, you can do whatever you want with your gal—or *not do* whatever—but you got no right to tell me what I can't do!"

"I'm not going to argue with you, Abner. It doesn't make sense to let ourselves get distracted now. Let's just boil some coffee, rustle a little grub, and then get some rest. Tomorrow will probably be another long day in the saddle."

With a sneer distorting his ugly face even more, Farnum turned away.

"The hell with that," he muttered. "I ain't near as hungry for beans and bacon as I am for that little brown-haired gal."

He stalked around the fire toward the women. Lucy was the closest to him. With a look of horror on her face, she shrank back against Annabelle as Farnum approached. Annabelle put her arm around the younger woman's shoulders and glared defiantly at Farnum as he loomed over them.

Farnum's back was to Gerhardt. It would be easy for Gerhardt to pull his Colt and put a bullet in Farnum's back. Farnum was so focused on the lust he felt that he'd never see it coming.

But then there would be only one of him to handle two prisoners, Gerhardt realized, and that was a recipe for disaster. For now, he couldn't afford to kill Farnum.

Once they had found somebody willing to pay a decent price for Lucy, though, things would be different.

Farnum would be sorry then that he had been foolish enough to defy Gus Gerhardt.

Farnum held out a hand toward Lucy and said, "Come on, girlie. You and me are gonna take a little walk. It won't be so bad. You'll see. I'll treat you nice." He grinned. "Well, I reckon that depends on how nice you treat me."

Annabelle tightened her arm around Lucy's shoulders and looked across the fire at Gerhardt.

"Aren't you going to do something?" she asked. "Can't you put a stop to this?"

"Abner's right," Gerhardt said dully, with reluctant acceptance. "He's got a right to do what he wants."

Visibly fuming, Annabelle turned her gaze back to Farnum and said, "If you touch this girl, I'll kill you. I swear I will."

"Lady, I don't care how many threats you spout. I ain't scared of you, and I've waited long enough." Farnum reached down suddenly and clamped his hand around Lucy's left arm. He said, "Now come on!" as he tried to jerk her to her feet.

Lucy came up off the ground, but she wasn't cooperating. She lunged at Farnum and her hands shot out, fingers hooked like talons, as she clawed at his face.

He jerked his head back and bellowed a curse as she tried to get her nails into his eyes. His left arm swung up and around. The back of that hand cracked across Lucy's face and would have knocked her off her feet if he hadn't still been gripping her left arm.

Annabelle started to leap up, but before she could enter the fray, another shape lunged out of the shadows surrounding the camp and crashed into Abner Farnum.

Smoke and Cavanaugh rode toward the fire and didn't rein in until they were less than a mile away. Then, not wanting the sound of their horses' hoofbeats to alert their quarry, they dismounted and continued to approach on foot, leading Drifter and Cavanaugh's mount.

When they were about a quarter of a mile from the camp, Smoke called a halt.

"We'd better leave our horses here," he told Cavanaugh in a whisper. "Any closer and we run the risk of their horses scenting ours and making a fuss."

Cavanaugh just nodded. They tied the animals to a small, scrubby tree.

When they went ahead on foot, Smoke led the way, placing his steps carefully so as not to snap any dead branches or kick rocks that might rattle. He was impressed by Cavanaugh's ability to do likewise. The younger man made hardly any sound as he followed Smoke through the shadows.

Eventually, they were so close that Smoke went to hands and knees and motioned for Cavanaugh to do the same. They crawled to within a few yards of the campfire, just beyond the circle of its flickering light, and then stopped and stretched out on their bellies.

Smoke had been able to hear the men talking as he and Cavanaugh drew closer. Although he couldn't make out the words at first, Gerhardt and Farnum didn't sound happy with each other. Annabelle spoke up at one point, and she sounded upset, too.

The two men were arguing about something. Smoke could make a pretty good guess what it was. As he and Cavanaugh lay there, they were close enough to understand what Gerhardt and Farnum were saying.

Farnum wanted to have his way with Lucy, and although

Gerhardt didn't like it, he wasn't going to stop his companion from carrying out his vile intention. Farnum stepped up to Lucy and grabbed her. When he pulled her to her feet, she started putting up a fight.

Smoke heard the faint whisper of metal against leather and knew Cavanaugh had drawn his gun. He put out a hand and gripped the man's shoulder.

"You can't shoot with Lucy so close to him," Smoke breathed against Cavanaugh's ear.

He felt the tension in Cavanaugh's muscles from the urge to kill Farnum, and Smoke didn't know if Cavanaugh would be able to overcome it, but then he slid the revolver back in its holster.

A second later, Farnum backhanded Lucy and knocked her away from him, but he still had hold of her, so she didn't fall. Even so, there was enough separation between them now that Smoke might have risked a shot.

He didn't get the chance because Cavanaugh, unable to hold himself in check this time, leaped to his feet and threw himself at Farnum.

The tackle knocked Farnum away from Lucy, who fell to the ground. Across the fire, Gerhardt surged up with a yell. He clawed at the gun on his hip.

Smoke came to his feet and drew in the same swift, efficient movement. The Colt in his hand roared and bucked before Gerhardt could pull the trigger.

Gerhardt was moving to his right as Smoke fired. The bullet didn't take him in the chest as Smoke intended, but smashed into his upper left arm instead.

Gerhardt yelled in pain as the slug twisted him halfway around. He threw a wild shot at Smoke as he fell. Smoke ducked and heard the bullet whistle past his head, too close for comfort, but still a clean miss.

Gerhardt was rolling as he hit the ground. He moved fast

for a man of his bulky shape—and one who was wounded, to boot. The tactic carried him out of the firelight and into the thick shadows around the camp. Smoke snapped another shot at him, but saw the bullet kick up dirt where Gerhardt had been but a second earlier.

Near the fire, Farnum recovered his balance and roared like an angry grizzly bear as he grabbed the front of Cavanaugh's shirt. He swung the young man away from him. When Farnum let go, Cavanaugh flew backward, out of control, and landed at the edge of the flames. He yelled in pain and tried to scramble away from the fire on his hands and knees.

Farnum lifted a brutal kick, which caught Cavanaugh in the belly. It was a vicious blow, but it did Cavanaugh a favor, because it knocked him away from the flames.

Despite her hands being tied in front of her, Annabelle snatched a burning branch from the fire, leaped at Farnum, and thrust the blazing brand in his face. Farnum screamed and reeled backward.

Gerhardt's gun crashed again from the darkness. Smoke heard the wind-rip of the slug and returned fire. He caught a glimpse of Gerhardt as the man scrambled to his feet and staggered behind the horses. Another tongue of flame lashed from Gerhardt's gun as he fired past the animals.

Cavanaugh got a hand on the ground and shoved himself to his knees. A few yards away, Farnum was stumbling around, pawing at his burned face and blistered eyes.

Cavanaugh reached for his gun, but found only the empty holster. While he was being knocked around, his Colt must have fallen out somewhere. He looked around frantically, but didn't see it.

Annabelle had gotten behind Farnum. She lowered her shoulder and ran at him, ramming him so hard that he was thrown forward. Unable to catch himself this time, he fell face-first into the fire, which he had built up.

As the blaze ate mercilessly into his flesh, he shrieked and thrashed and tried to push himself up, but the flames burned his hands, too, and his arms went out from under him. Farnum continued screaming, causing Cavanaugh to feel a fleeting moment of sympathy for the man.

But then he remembered what Farnum had been about to do to Lucy.

"Burn in hell, mister," he said as he stumbled to his feet. He turned to Lucy and helped her up, pulling her into his embrace and folding his arms around her.

On the other side of the fire, Smoke warily circled the skittish horses. Gerhardt might have taken off, but the man was wounded and probably losing strength. More than likely, he was still lurking somewhere in the shadows, hoping for another shot at Smoke.

Gerhardt got that chance, rearing up suddenly and firing so close that Smoke seemed to feel the muzzle flame beating against his face. Gerhardt had rushed his shot, though, and it missed its mark.

Smoke triggered twice. His bullets smashed into Gerhardt's chest and drove him backward. He let out a strangled cry and dropped his gun as he fell. Smoke saw the weapon hit the ground and kicked it away to make sure Gerhardt wouldn't be able to grab it again.

Gerhardt wasn't even trying to recover his gun. His back arched and he dragged in a final rattling breath before he sagged to the dirt. His arms fell loosely to his sides.

Hearing a step behind him, Smoke whirled and was ready to fire again, but it wasn't Farnum coming up on him. He held off on the trigger.

Annabelle Wilkinson stood there holding another burning branch from the fire. The makeshift torch spilled light over Gerhardt's motionless form. Smoke saw the large bloodstain on Gerhardt's shirt. The flickering glare from the torch reflected on the man's sightlessly staring eyes.

The threat of Gus Gerhardt was over.

The sharp stench of burning human flesh made Smoke turn. He saw Farnum lying with the upper half of his body in the fire. The man was silent and unmoving now, which was enough to tell Smoke he was dead.

Not far away, Cavanaugh hugged Lucy. Both of them appeared to be all right, as far as Smoke could tell.

"Are you hurt?" he asked Annabelle as he began thumbing fresh rounds into the Colt to replace the ones he had fired.

"No, I'm all right," she said. "So is Lucy. Sore and exhausted from riding all day and most of last night, but they didn't hurt us. Farnum was about to molest her, but thank goodness you and Hank got here in time." She smiled slightly. "I had a feeling that you might. In fact, I was counting on it."

"Sorry we cut it as close as we did."

Smoke pouched the reloaded iron and strode over to the fire. He reached down and took hold of Farnum's ankles to drag the dead man out of the flames.

Farnum's head and upper body were grisly sights. The fire had burned off most of his clothing and blackened and blistered the flesh.

Probably wasn't any more than he had coming, Smoke thought, but it was still a hell of a thing to look at.

So he didn't, turning away instead and saying, "Let's get out of here. We'll camp somewhere else tonight and head back to the wagons first thing in the morning."

Chapter 28

Just as Smoke expected, they were able to spot Brimstone Butte, the geographic formation, several days before they actually reached it. The towering edifice served as a beacon of sorts, something inspiring for the women to fasten their eyes on and move toward as they put all the dangerous travails of the past behind them.

Sally was no worse for what had happened, her headache fading quickly and gone completely by the time Smoke and Hank Cavanaugh returned to the wagon train with Annabelle and Lucy. They brought the extra horses with them, since Gerhardt and Farnum didn't need the mounts anymore.

When Smoke came in sight of the settlement that also bore the name Brimstone Butte, he turned Drifter and rode back to the wagons. Annabelle was handling the team hitched to the lead wagon, with her father riding on the driver's seat beside her, as usual.

A bandage was still wrapped around Colonel Wilkinson's head, but his wound, which he had received when Gerhardt hit him with a pistol, was healing well.

Even though the colonel hadn't suffered a serious injury, he had been gloomy and withdrawn ever since the raid. Smoke suspected that the old-timer felt he had let his daughter down by not being able to stop Gerhardt from kidnapping her. Despite his handicap, he probably felt as if he should have been able to do something to keep that from happening.

Maybe knowing that they were near the end of their journey would cheer the colonel up, Smoke thought as he fell in alongside the wagon.

"We're nearly there," Smoke said. "If you look up yonder on the left, you can see a few roofs, a church steeple, and smoke from some chimneys."

He pointed to a large sweep of trees that ascended a gentle slope toward a rocky ridge to the west. That was where the settlement was located, built along the banks of a creek that emerged from a cleft in the ridge and flowed eastward across the broad basin between mountain ranges.

Half a mile beyond the town rose the butte that gave the place its name. The tower was roughly circular, its red sandstone face deeply riven with cracks. It was impressive, rising a couple of hundred feet to its flat top.

When Smoke looked past the butte, he saw a sprawling landscape, green with grass and other vegetation. The country behind the wagons hadn't been completely barren and arid, but it was a mixture of green and brown and tan and didn't hold nearly as much promise to the eye as the range extending all the way to the northern horizon.

Smoke's eye was that of a born cattleman, although he hadn't been aware of that as a youngster back in the Ozarks, and he knew he was looking at ranching country. Good ranching country that would provide a fine home for these pilgrims, who had traveled so far.

"I see the town," Annabelle said with excitement creeping into her voice. "I wish you could, Colonel."

"It's enough for me that you can, my dear," Wilkinson said. "We'll need to stop and let that lawyer know we've arrived, so we can officially take possession of the ranch."

"That'll be the first thing we do," Annabelle promised. "Smoke, do you think we'll have time to reach the ranch today, or will we need to spend the night in town and go out there tomorrow?"

"It's not the middle of the day yet," Smoke said. "Depending on how far it is, I'd say there's a good chance you can make it to the Three Cross. You'll probably know more after you talk to the lawyer."

"Yes, of course."

Annabelle slapped the lines against the horses' rumps, obviously eager to get there.

Smoke turned Drifter and rode back along the short line of wagons. Helen Pryor handled the reins of the second vehicle, Roberta Walling had charge of the third, and Lucy Dunning was back on the driver's seat of the fourth wagon, none the worse for her ordeal as a captive of Gus Gerhardt and Abner Farnum.

Hank Cavanaugh rode his horse beside Lucy's wagon. The two had hardly been out of each other's sight since they got back. Sally had declared to Smoke that there would be wedding bells once the party reached its destination, probably sooner rather than later.

From what he'd seen of the way Lucy and Cavanaugh looked at each other, he couldn't disagree with her.

"You can see the town up ahead," Smoke told the smitten couple. "We'll be there in a little while."

"And how much farther is it from there to the ranch?" Lucy asked.

"I don't know, exactly," Smoke said. "Judging by that map Annabelle has, we stand a good chance of reaching it today, though."

"It can't be soon enough for me. I'm ready to spend some time not rocking back and forth on this hard seat."

Smoke smiled and nudged Drifter on. Sally brought up the rear in the buckboard. She smiled, too, and greeted him by saying, "I heard what you told Lucy and Hank. Are we really almost there, Smoke?"

He nodded. "We are. It'll be good to have this journey finished, won't it?"

"It certainly will. Then Annabelle and the others can finally settle down peacefully on their new ranch."

Smoke's smile stayed in place on his face, but a feeling of unease stirred inside him. He wasn't a superstitious man by nature, didn't believe in jinxes or things like that, but somehow he sort of wished Sally hadn't said that.

He kept that feeling to himself as he rode toward the lead wagon again. On the way, as he reached the third wagon, the one Roberta was driving, he spotted Susie Beale and Delia Tracy inside the bed, sitting with Danny Murphy.

The young hard case still had to be considered a prisoner, Smoke supposed, but as the only survivor of Gus Gerhardt's bunch, he wasn't much of a threat anymore. Also, he was still recuperating from the wound he had received during the raid on the wagon train. He had lost some weight and his features were pale and drawn; however, barring anything unforeseen, he was going to recover from the injury.

Susie lifted a hand to catch Smoke's attention. He checked Drifter to ride beside the rear of the wagon as Susie leaned over the closed tailgate.

She said, "Mr. Jensen, I want to know if you've made up your mind what you're going to do about Danny when we get to the settlement?"

From behind her, Murphy said, "Blast it, Susie, I told you not to bother Mr. Jensen with that. Whatever he decides to do, I'll accept it. I'll take any punishment that's dealt out to me and not complain about it."

"It's not really my decision, Susie," Smoke told the redhead. "Annabelle is the leader of this wagon train. I'd say it's up to her."

"But you know she'll go along with whatever you suggest,"

Susie persisted. "Danny shouldn't have to go to prison or . . . or worse."

Murphy said flatly, "If a noose is my destiny, so be it. I deserve it for what I tried to do."

Smoke shook his head. "I don't reckon any judge or jury would sentence you to hang. Nothing you did resulted in anybody dying." He chuckled. "In fact—and I don't mean any offense by this—nothing you did accomplished anything except to get you shot, Danny."

"That's right!" Susie said. "So you see, Danny didn't really break any laws, if you think about it that way. He shouldn't be turned over to the sheriff or marshal or whatever they've got in Brimstone Butte."

"I never should've gotten mixed up with Gerhardt in the first place, and I'm sorry I did," Murphy said. "I'll take what I've got coming to me."

Susie turned to look at him and said sharply, "Oh, hush! We all know how sorry you are. And if it ever came right down to it, I don't believe you'd hurt me or anybody else."

Murphy looked solemn as he shook his head. "You don't know what-all we did."

"Did you ever kill anybody?"

"Well . . . no."

"Did you ever even shoot anybody?"

"I, uh, I don't think so. Shot in the air over a posse's heads a few times, that's all. You know, to, uh, scare 'em off."

Susie looked at Smoke again and asked, "Is that a crime, Mr. Jensen?"

"I'm sure a lot of lawmen would consider it to be one," Smoke said. "You didn't do any of those things in Wyoming, though, did you, Danny?"

Murphy shook his head. "No, sir. This is the first time I've ever been in Wyoming."

"Then it seems to me you haven't broken any laws in this jurisdiction."

"See?" Susie said excitedly. "I told you, Danny!" She turned back to Smoke. "Please, Mr. Jensen, do whatever you can to help us."

"I'll think about it," Smoke said, nodding. "I'll talk to Annabelle."

"Thank you!" Susie clutched Murphy's arm and beamed.

Behind her, Delia rolled her eyes and shook her head, but then she smiled, too, obviously happy for her friend.

"No promises, though," Smoke added.

He lifted a hand in farewell and nudged Drifter ahead. He didn't mention that he happened to know Annabelle had decided already not to press any charges against Danny Murphy. She figured he was harmless now, and not only that, he was clearly head over heels in love with Susie, and she with him. Neither of them cared about the other's checkered past.

Might be a second set of wedding bells in the future, Smoke mused as the wagon train rolled on toward its destination.

CHAPTER 29

The settlement of Brimstone Butte had a business district three blocks long, with the main street running north and south. The cross streets extended for a couple of blocks east and west, and were lined with residences that ranged from plain log cabins to nice, whitewashed houses built of lumber that must have come from the sawmill on the other side of the creek.

That creek ran along the northern edge of town. A sturdy bridge of thick beams spanned the stream as it bubbled and leaped along between its banks.

The settlement had been here for only a few years, but it already had a well-established look about it. A couple of churches, one at each end of town, and a building that was obviously a school testified to that. Smoke saw a bank, a couple of hotels, two large general mercantiles and a number of smaller shops, a lawyer's office and a doctor's practice, a pair of cafés, a blacksmith workshop, and a big livery barn with an attached corral.

He also saw a square stone building with a sign on the awning over its porch: BRIMSTONE BUTTE MARSHAL. There was some law here, although it remained to be seen how effective it might be.

The whine of the big saw at the mill could be heard before the wagons even reached the southern end of the street. More lumber meant more buildings, and more buildings meant growth. Folks had to have houses in which to live.

Smoke noticed one more thing about Brimstone Butte: There were half-a-dozen saloons scattered along the street.

That was proof positive there were ranches in the area. Cowboys needed places to drink and carouse and blow their forty-a-month-and-found.

Smoke was a few yards ahead of the lead wagon as the group entered the settlement. He had already spotted a sign on a frame building: HERBERT RADCLIFFE, ATTORNEY-AT-LAW. Smoke recognized the name from the documents Annabelle Wilkinson had shown him.

He angled Drifter toward the hitch rack in front of the lawyer's office, knowing that Annabelle and the other drivers would follow him.

As he reined in, he noticed that the next building up the street was the Thundercloud Saloon. At that moment, a couple of men in range clothes pushed through the batwings and sauntered out onto the walk.

They stopped short and stared at the wagons.

Smoke supposed big canvas-covered vehicles like these were an uncommon sight in Brimstone Butte these days. That shouldn't have been the case, he thought. The railroad hadn't come through these parts, and new settlers had to get here somehow. Wagons made the most sense.

Those two punchers seemed mighty interested, though. They turned and hurried off in the other direction while Smoke was dismounting.

The wagons and the buckboard moved over to the edge of the street and parked. Annabelle stopped the lead wagon in front of the lawyer's office.

"We're here, Colonel," she said. "Brimstone Butte, Wyoming. We made it at last."

"Only to the town, my dear," Colonel Wilkinson pointed out. "We still haven't reached the ranch."

"But we will soon. Very soon. Come on. Let's go see this attorney and get everything taken care of."

"You don't need me to do that," the colonel said. He lifted a hand from the head of his cane and made a self-deprecating gesture.

"Nonsense. You're the owner of the Three Cross now. You have to be there."

Colonel Wilkinson shrugged and nodded in acknowledgment of that point.

Smoke moved over to stand next to the front wheel on the side of the wagon where the colonel sat.

"Let me give you a hand, sir," he said.

"Thank you, son. Since my daughter insists that I take part in this meeting, I suppose I should do so."

Smoke helped the old-timer climb down from the wagon, steadying the colonel while Annabelle stepped to the street on the other side.

Sally had disembarked from the buckboard and tied the team to another hitch rack. She joined Smoke and the Wilkinsons on the front porch of Herbert Radcliffe's office.

The door swung open before Smoke could reach for the knob. Radcliffe must have seen through the front window that he was about to have visitors.

"Can I help you folks?" he asked. He was a tall, lean man, with curly brown hair that was graying. A pair of spectacles perched on his nose. He wore a brown tweed suit and looked like a lawyer.

"You're Mr. Radcliffe?" Annabelle asked.

"I am."

She held out her hand to him. "Miss Annabelle Wilkinson. This is my father, Colonel Jasper Wilkinson."

Radcliffe's eyes widened behind the spectacles. "My goodness," he said. Then he took Annabelle's hand. "When I saw the wagons, I thought for a moment that they might herald your arrival at last, Miss Wilkinson, but I still had my doubts."

"Why is that?" Annabelle asked as the handshake concluded.

"Well, I received your letter saying that you and your group were coming, but it's been so long . . ."

Annabelle smiled and said, "It's a long way from Mississippi, Mr. Radcliffe."

"Indeed, it is. I trust you didn't have too much trouble during the journey?"

"Some," Annabelle conceded, "but we made it. We're here and ready to claim the colonel's inheritance."

"Of course." Radcliffe swallowed and tugged for a second at the stiff collar of his shirt as if it suddenly had gotten too tight. "I suppose you had better come in."

Then he looked at Smoke and added, "And you are, sir?"

"Smoke Jensen," Smoke introduced himself. He shook Radcliffe's hand, too. "And I don't have any part in these legal proceedings. My wife and I are friends with the colonel and Miss Wilkinson and the other members of their party. We just came along to make sure they got here all right."

"Came along from where, if I may ask?"

"Big Rock, Colorado."

"My, that's a long way!"

Annabelle said, "I'd like for Mr. and Mrs. Jensen to come in, too, if that's all right, Mr. Radcliffe. I trust them if I need any advice on anything."

"Of course. That's fine. Please, all of you, come in—"

Radcliffe stopped short as he glanced along the street. The slightly nervous look on his face turned into one of outright worry. Smoke followed the direction of Radcliffe's glance and saw several men walking along the street toward the lawyer's office.

Two of them were the cowboys who had come out of the Thundercloud Saloon a few minutes earlier.

When Smoke saw that, he knew the men must have hurried off somewhere else to spread the word of the wagons' arrival in town. That was sort of understandable—any new arrivals usually drew considerable interest in frontier towns. Anything to break the routine of day-to-day life was welcome.

Something about these men stirred Smoke's warning instincts, though. Two of the other three fetched by the cowboys from the saloon also looked like regular punchers.

The fifth man wore range clothes, too, but they were higher quality and didn't sport as many signs of wear and tear. He might be the owner of a big spread, or he might be the foreman of the crew on such a ranch.

The confident, almost-arrogant way he strode along the street seemed to indicate that he was accustomed to being in charge.

Smoke was curious why such an hombre might be taking an interest in the new arrivals, as well as why Herbert Radcliffe had tensed up when he saw the fellow approaching. Those thoughts flashed through Smoke's mind in the moment when Radcliffe hesitated after issuing his invitation to come in.

The lawyer recovered quickly and said, "Right in here, folks. We'll get everything taken care of."

He stepped aside and held out his arm to usher the newcomers through the open door and into the office. Sally and Annabelle went first, the colonel and Smoke brought up the rear, except for Radcliffe himself, who followed them in.

"Please, ladies, have a seat there in front of the desk. Gentlemen, I'm afraid I have only one other chair—"

"That's fine," Smoke said. "I don't mind standing."

He had already seen a ladderback chair sitting against the wall. He picked it up and placed it next to the two cushioned chairs that were already in front of the desk.

"Here you go, Colonel," Smoke said as he took hold of the

old-timer's arm and guided him into the chair. Sally and Annabelle had already taken the other two seats.

"Thank you, my boy."

Smoke stepped back, crossed his arms, and leaned against the wall beside the door.

Radcliffe sat behind the desk and opened one of the drawers. He rummaged in it for a moment and then brought out a small sheaf of papers with a string tied around them. As he untied the string, he said, "Here are the original copies of the will and the deed to the Three Cross Ranch, as well as a paper officially transferring ownership of the property to Colonel Jasper Wilkinson. Colonel, once you've signed this document, I'll send it to the county seat so it can be filed in the proper office."

Radcliffe frowned and went on, "Wait. This paper will have to be signed, and you . . . I mean . . ."

"Don't worry, son," the colonel said. "I can still write my name. Annabelle will position my hand properly, and I assure you, the signature will be legible."

"Yes, but the legitimacy of a signature on an official document is contingent upon the signatory being capable of reading the document—"

"I'll read what it says to my father, Mr. Radcliffe," Annabelle said. "Surely, that will be sufficient to make the signature legally binding."

Sally added, "And my husband and I will be glad to witness that signature and attest to its legitimacy. Won't we, Smoke?"

"Sure," Smoke said.

Radcliffe nodded and said, "That does seem as if it would be sufficient—"

The door swung open and heavy footsteps sounded as a man entered the office. In an angry voice, he demanded, "What the hell do you think you're doing, Radcliffe?"

The way the door opened, the man hadn't seen Smoke standing there. Smoke could see him well enough, though, to recognize the arrogant-looking hombre who had been fetched by the cowboys from the Thundercloud.

Straightening away from his casual pose against the wall, Smoke said, "Maybe you shouldn't be sticking your nose into things that are none of your business, mister."

The man whipped around toward Smoke, his face twisting in an angry snarl as his hand dropped to the butt of the gun holstered on his hip.

He froze in mid-draw as he found himself looking down the barrel of the Colt that had appeared as if by magic in Smoke Jensen's hand.

CHAPTER 30

The man had wrapped his hand around the black butt of his revolver and started to pull it from the holster, but he let go of the weapon and allowed it to slide back into leather.

"Take it easy," he said harshly as he lifted his hand away from the gun.

"I reckon that would be good advice for you to take," Smoke said. "You're the one who busted in here and started bellowing like a bull."

The man glared hate at him. He didn't need to know who Smoke was, or what was going on here, in order to feel that way.

All he needed for hate to erupt was for somebody to stand up to him.

Smoke sensed that about this man right away. For that reason, he didn't lower his gun.

Herbert Radcliffe had come up out of his chair at the interruption. He said, "Please, Mr. Jensen, gunplay isn't necessary. I'm certain Mr. Farley means no harm."

"Don't be so sure about that," the man called Farley snapped. "What the hell are those pilgrim wagons doing outside, Radcliffe? You said you were going to put a stop to this before they ever got here."

"What does that mean?" Annabelle asked with a note of anger in her voice, too.

Radcliffe raised his hands and patted the air. "Please, everyone, let's just all settle down. There's been a misunderstanding—"

"Misunderstanding, my hind foot," Farley said. "The boss told you to get this straightened out, lawyer man, and by grab, you'd better do it."

"Mr. Jensen," Radcliffe said again. "Your gun . . ."

Smoke lowered the Colt and slid it back into its holster. He could get it out again quickly enough if he needed to.

He said, "It sounds to me like you've got some explaining to do, Mr. Radcliffe. But first, do you want me to throw this fella out of here?"

Farley sneered at him and said, "You're welcome to try, mister, anytime you feel like it. Just because you're slick on the draw doesn't mean you can handle me without some gun work being involved."

Smoke had to admit to himself that Farley looked like he could give him a pretty good tussle. The man was an inch taller and perhaps twenty pounds heavier, but there didn't appear to be any softness about him. He was all muscle. His raven-black hair was visible beneath a pulled-down black hat. His jaws were bristly with a close-cropped beard of the same shade. His face and hands had the deep tan of a man who spent most of his time working outside.

Smoke might have liked him if he hadn't had such a cruel, ruthless cast to his features.

"It's all right," Radcliffe said. "Mr. Farley can stay. With your permission, of course, Colonel Wilkinson. And yours, Miss Wilkinson."

"I don't even know who this man is," Annabelle said coolly.

"Cole Farley," the man introduced himself. "I'm the foreman of the Thundercloud spread." He paused. "Which includes what used to be the Three Cross."

Annabelle shot to her feet. "What!"

Radcliffe said, "That's a matter that's in some dispute—"

Annabelle was glaring at Cole Farley, but she turned her furious gaze on the lawyer when he said that.

"There's no dispute," she said. "My father inherited the Three Cross Ranch from his cousin Albert Lowe when Mr. Lowe passed away. It says so plain as day in the last will and testament he left." Annabelle pointed at the papers on the desk. "That will right there, in fact."

"No one is questioning that's what the will says," Radcliffe began, "but wills can be set aside—"

"Not unless there's something illegal about them!"

"Or unless some other controlling statute takes precedence," Radcliffe said.

"I don't think anything takes precedence over a legally executed last will and testament."

Radcliffe grimaced. "The crux of the matter is, as you say, Miss Wilkinson, the legal execution of the will. Added to that is the issue of the taxes outstanding on the property."

"Whatever the taxes are, we'll pay them," Annabelle snapped.

Smoke didn't know if she actually possessed the money to do that, but she sounded confident enough.

Cole Farley spoke up, the sneer as evident in his voice as it was on his face.

"You can't pay them, lady," he said, "because they've already been paid. My boss, Otto Blaylock, paid them. That means he legally owns the Three Cross now."

Annabelle looked sharply at Radcliffe again. "That can't be right. If there were delinquent taxes, as the new owner my father should have been given the opportunity to pay them."

"There was also the question of an abandoned claim," Radcliffe ventured.

"We didn't abandon anything! I wrote and told you we were coming to claim the inheritance!"

A whine edged into the lawyer's voice as he said, "Yes, but so much time had passed. I had no way of knowing if you actually intended to honor what you said in that letter, or, indeed, if you were even still capable of doing so. For all I knew, Colonel Wilkinson was dead and might have died intestate—"

Smoke broke in this time. This was none of his business, but his keen brain had cut through Radcliffe's blather and he thought he had a pretty good idea what had happened.

"You never filed that will, did you, Radcliffe?" Smoke asked in a flat, hard voice.

"I . . . I saw no harm in a brief delay. I thought I would hear from Miss Wilkinson again, confirming that she and her father were on their way."

The colonel blew out a breath that fluttered his drooping white mustache.

"We were a mite busy getting here, son," he said. "It seems to me that once my daughter notified you of our intentions, that should have been enough to seal the deal!"

"I just didn't know—"

Smoke said, "Did Blaylock slip you a little money to sit on that will until the taxes came due so he could swoop in and grab up the ranch?"

"You better be careful, Jensen," Cole Farley said. "Insulting a powerful man like Otto Blaylock isn't going to get you anything but trouble."

"Blaylock's not here," Smoke pointed out.

"No, but I am, and I ride for the man. I won't stand for anybody lying about him."

Smoke and Farley were looking at each other again as if they might reach for their guns at any second. Radcliffe came around the desk and got between them, although he looked uneasy about putting himself in that position.

"Mr. Jensen, I'll have you know I'm a reputable attorney, and I've never taken a bribe in my life." Radcliffe looked and sounded like he was trying to work up some justifiable outrage, but he wasn't having much luck at it. "I'm human and capable of oversights and mistakes, and if such a thing has happened in this case, that's all it is."

"Whatever you say, counselor," Smoke bit off.

It was possible that, technically, Radcliffe was telling the truth. He might not have taken a bribe to make it easier for Otto Blaylock to grab the Three Cross.

But if Blaylock was the big skookum he-wolf around these parts, as he appeared to be, it took no great stretch of the imagination to think that Radcliffe had known what the cattleman would want. He could have done what he did, simply to curry favor with Blaylock.

Coldly, Annabelle asked, "When were you going to tell us about this, Mr. Radcliffe? Before or after my father signed that paper transferring ownership of the Three Cross to him?"

Farley squinted at Radcliffe. "You were fixing to do that? Sounds to me like you're trying to play both sides, mister. That won't work."

Fine beads of sweat covered Radcliffe's face. He pulled a handkerchief from his pocket and blotted away some of them, but his features were still rather shiny as he said, "I was about to inform you that there were some matters that might require adjudication, Miss Wilkinson, but despite that, the deed transfer is still the first step in the process. If your father is still willing to sign it—"

The colonel thumped his walking stick on the floor and barked, "Damned right I'm willing to sign it. That ranch is mine, and no range hog is going to steal it from me!"

"Watch your mouth, old man," Farley said, his upper lip curling in contempt.

"Watch yours," Smoke told him.

Farley raised a hand and pointed a finger at the lawyer. "You know better than this, Radcliffe. You know what the smart thing to do is, and this isn't it."

"I have to do what the law requires, Cole."

Farley's disgusted snort eloquently conveyed what he thought of that, and of Herbert Radcliffe.

Colonel Wilkinson leaned forward in his chair and said, "Give that document to Annabelle, Mr. Radcliffe, and let her read it to me. I'll sign it, and then we'll go out to the ranch."

"Don't they say possession is nine-tenths of the law?" Farley asked. "We've been running Thundercloud cows on what used to be Three Cross range for months now."

"It's still Three Cross range, sir, and your cattle are interlopers!" the colonel said.

Farley ignored that and went on, "The boss has moved the spread's headquarters over there. It's closer to town and has better water. He's had his eye on that place for a long time."

Smoke said, "So that's why he wanted to steal it?"

"You took me by surprise the first time, Jensen. Maybe things won't go that way next time around."

"Why?" Smoke snapped back at Farley. "Because you intend to back-shoot me next time?"

Smoke wasn't trying to goad the man into a fight. On the other hand, he didn't particularly care if Farley took offense.

Cole Farley had taken all he was going to take. He called Smoke a vile name that would have justified a swift and violent response for saying it in front of ladies, even if he hadn't done anything else.

But he followed the curse with a swift punch that whipped toward Smoke's head, and the battle was on.

Chapter 31

Smoke was just as fast with his fists as he was with a gun. His left arm came up in a blur of speed and his forearm struck Farley's, blocking the punch the Thundercloud foreman threw.

At the same time, Smoke's right fist rocketed through the opening Farley had created with his wild punch and slammed into the man's jaw. Farley's head rocked back and his hat fell off. He took an involuntary step backward.

Smoke hit him again, this time with a left cross that slewed Farley's head to the side. A third blow crashed home as Smoke's right fist found Farley's chin.

Farley flew backward and hit the door hard. It opened inward, so it didn't pop open, but the men waiting outside must have heard the impact. As Farley bounced off and fell to his knees, someone flung the door open and a man yelled, "Fight! Fight! Come on, Thundercloud!"

"Stop, please stop!" Radcliffe cried as he ran back and forth in front of the desk, waving his hands, but no one paid any attention to him. The four ranch hands tried to rush through the door, all of them ready to throw themselves into battle for the brand.

Their eagerness worked against them. They got hung up in the doorway for a few seconds because they couldn't all get through at once.

That gave Smoke time to snap, “Sally, get Annabelle and the colonel out of the way.”

Sally was already on her feet. She took Wilkinson’s arm and urged him toward the area behind the desk. More than likely, that would be the safest place in the room. The desk would provide some protection, and a filing cabinet stood to either side on the rear wall, making a little nook back there.

Smoke could havc drawn his Colts and stopped the attacking cowboys in their tracks, but he wasn’t the sort to shoot down men who weren’t gunning for him.

No, he would meet them on their own terms—even though he was outnumbered four to one.

The first two men finally bulled their way into the office and rushed at Smoke. But once again, their enthusiasm proved to be a disadvantage, because one of them tripped over Cole Farley, who was trying to push himself up off the floor as he groggily shook his head.

The man fell on top of Farley and knocked him to the floor again, where the two of them promptly got their arms and legs tangled up.

The next man hurdled over them, but his leap carried him right into Smoke’s fist. Smoke felt the man’s nose break under the perfectly timed blow. Blood spurted hotly across his knuckles. Momentum carried the lower half of the man’s body forward, while the collision with Smoke’s fist drove the upper half backward. The man sprawled on top of Farley and the other Thundercloud hand.

The whole thing might have been comical, Smoke thought fleetingly, if he hadn’t known that these men would beat him badly if he gave them half a chance. Cole Farley might even urge them to stomp him to death.

As powerful as Farley seemed to believe Otto Blaylock was, he might figure they could get away with killing a stranger in a fight.

Depending on how diligent the law was in Brimstone Butte, he might well be right.

The other two cowboys were in the office by now, but they couldn't attack Smoke head-on because they couldn't get around the three men on the floor. They split up, obviously intending to circle Farley and the other two fallen men and come at Smoke from different directions.

Farley heaved up from the floor, throwing the other men aside in the process.

"Get him!" he yelled as he pointed at Smoke. He charged straight ahead as the other two closed in from the flanks.

Smoke always had confidence in his ability to handle himself in a fight, but the odds were a little steep here. Even so, he was ready to stand there and start slugging.

Those odds evened suddenly as Hank Cavanaugh and Danny Murphy appeared. Cavanaugh charged through the doorway first, with Murphy right behind him. Each of them tackled one of the men attacking from the sides.

That left Smoke free to deal with Cole Farley. The Thundercloud foreman's face was already bruised and swollen from the punishment Smoke had dished out, but that didn't hold him back. He lunged forward, not as out of control in his attack this time. His fists flashed—not in wild punches, but in carefully aimed and timed blows.

Despite Farley's more surgical attack, Smoke was able to block most of the strikes. A couple of them made it through his guard, however, and landed with enough force to rock Smoke back a step. He bumped against one of the chairs in front of the desk.

Farley must have believed Smoke was about to trip over the chair. He abandoned his strategy and bored in with a flurry of swift blows.

Smoke hunched his shoulders, absorbed the punishment, and, as soon as Farley was within reach, hooked a left and a right into the man's belly, each punch landing with so much force that Smoke's fists sank almost to the wrist.

Farley doubled over and, despite his tan, turned white. Smoke pivoted, clubbed both hands together, and brought them down on the back of Farley's neck like a man splitting a big chunk of wood.

Farley's face hit the floor with tooth-rattling force. He twitched once, moaned, and then didn't move again.

Smoke turned and saw that Hank Cavanaugh was holding his own with the man he had jumped. They surged back and forth across a short section of floor, trading punches.

Danny Murphy wasn't quite so fortunate. The man whose nose Smoke had broken had gotten up and managed to grab hold of Murphy from behind. He hung on to the Irishman's arms while another of the Thundercloud cowboys hammered punches to Murphy's midsection. Smoke knew that assault was liable to break open Murphy's healing wound and cause a considerable setback in the injured man's recovery.

Smoke acted fast. He drew his right-hand Colt, but reversed it, and slammed the butt against the skull of the man holding Murphy for the beating. The man's hat had flown off when Smoke hit him earlier, so there was nothing to blunt the blow's force.

The cowboy let go of Murphy as his knees buckled. He wound up on the floor again, senseless as well as bloody-nosed this time.

Without the man holding him, Murphy was able to duck underneath the next punch his tormentor aimed at him. He stepped in and threw a left and a right that drove the cowboy off his feet.

Not far away, at that same moment, Cavanaugh landed a perfectly aimed punch to the chin of his opponent. That man folded up as well, although he wasn't out cold. He still muttered and moved around a little, but Cavanaugh had knocked all the fight out of him.

"That's enough!" Smoke said in a loud, commanding voice. He drew his Colts and motioned Cavanaugh and Murphy back with them, then trained the weapons on the men huddling in defeat on the floor.

Two of them were still somewhat coherent and understood what was going on when they looked up and found themselves staring down the barrels of Smoke's guns. They swallowed hard and looked like they thought they were about to head for the last tally in the sky.

"Get up," Smoke told them. "Get your friend with the bloody nose on his feet, too. Among the three of you, you ought to be able to drag the other two out of here. Get started on that."

One of the men wiped the back of his hand across his split lips.

"Mister," he said, "you don't know what you've done. You're gonna be mighty sorry you ever laid eyes on Cole Farley."

"I already am," Smoke snapped. "I said to get busy."

Cavanaugh drew his gun and also covered the men as they cleared out of Radcliffe's office. Murphy stood to the side, one hand resting on the back of a chair as he leaned on it, the other arm pressed to his side.

"Did that bullet graze bust open?" Smoke asked him.

"I don't think so," Murphy replied. "I don't feel any blood seeping out." He managed a weak smile. "I sure hope it didn't do any damage. Susie told me to stay out of it. If I got hurt worse, she's liable to kick my behind from here to Denver and back." The youngster grew more serious. "But Hank and I could tell you were in trouble in here, Mr. Jensen, so we couldn't just stand by and do nothing."

Smoke nodded and said, "I'm obliged to you for your help. I might've been able to handle that bunch alone, but it was a lot easier with you fellas lending a hand."

Farley and the other Thundercloud riders were gone now. Susie rushed into the office and cried, "Danny! Are you hurt? I told you not to fight!"

"I'm fine," he assured her, although he looked like he was in some pain.

Lucy, Delia, and Helen followed Susie into the office. Each of the women carried a carbine.

It was getting a mite crowded in here, Smoke thought, so he said, "It's all right, ladies. The trouble's over. Why don't you take Hank and Danny back out to the wagons and tend to any bumps and bruises they might have?"

"That sounds like a good idea," Helen said. "Come on, everybody, let's let Annabelle and the colonel finish up their business here."

Smoke turned to Radcliffe when he and Sally, Annabelle and her father, were the only ones in the office with the attorney.

"I hate to agree with that varmint Farley about anything," Smoke said, "but I have a hunch he was right about you playing both ends against the middle, mister. You can start rectifying that situation by doing the right thing with that deed transfer document you were talking about."

"Of course," Radcliffe said. He still looked frightened and upset, but he was on firmer ground dealing with matters of the law. Turning to Annabelle and the colonel, he went on, "I assure you, I honestly believed there was a good chance you wouldn't appear to claim the inheritance, Colonel Wilkinson, in which case I was duty bound to look after the best interest of another client."

"Otto Blaylock, you mean," Annabelle said.

"I represent Mr. Blaylock in his legal affairs, yes. You can appreciate what a delicate position I was in—"

"What I would appreciate, sir," Colonel Wilkinson broke in, "is if you would let me sign that paper and then do your job."

"Yes, of course." Radcliffe bustled behind the desk again.

In five minutes, it was all done. The colonel had signed the ownership transfer document—and quite legibly, as he had promised—and Smoke and Sally had witnessed it.

Smoke asked Radcliffe, "Is there a post office in Brimstone Butte?"

The lawyer looked a little surprised and confused by the question.

"Why, ah, yes, there is. Just down the street in Trammell's General Store."

Smoke nodded. "You fix that paper up to mail to the county seat, then, and I'll see to it that it's turned over to the post office."

"I can do that later—"

"I reckon we'd all feel better about things if it was taken care of now," Smoke said.

With some reluctance and resentment, Radcliffe prepared the document. He folded it, wrote an address on the back, and sealed it with wax. When he handed it to Smoke, he said, "This isn't necessary, you know."

"Never hurts to be careful," Smoke said.

He left the lawyer's office, along with Sally, Annabelle, and the colonel. Annabelle said, "Thank you for your help, Smoke. Once again, I'm not sure how we would have handled that if you hadn't been along."

"That's why we came with you," Sally said. "No matter what you do, there are always unexpected things happening."

The colonel said, "That's one of the lessons of war, my dear. No battle plan escapes unscathed."

Smoke motioned for Cavanaugh to mount up. Danny Murphy was sitting on a lowered tailgate, with Susie clinging to his arm.

"Are you still all right?" Smoke asked him as he untied Drifter from the hitch rack.

Murphy nodded. "Yes, sir. I'll be fine. I'm sorry I wasn't more help than I was. Reckon I'm not fully recovered yet."

"Of course, you're not," Susie told him. "It hasn't been that long since you were shot!"

Smoke said, "You jumped right in without worrying about what kind of shape you were in. I appreciate that."

Murphy blushed. "You're, uh, you're mighty welcome, Mr. Jensen."

Smoke nodded to him and swung up into the saddle. He checked to see that Sally had resumed her place on the buckboard and then rode alongside the lead wagon, where Annabelle and her father had climbed to the driver's seat.

"I reckon you still want to head on out to the ranch today?" he said.

"More than ever," Annabelle replied with an emphatic nod. "I'm not sure what we're going to find waiting for us—"

"More trouble, I suspect," the colonel put in.

"But whatever it is," Annabelle went on, "I want to confront it and deal with it."

Smoke nodded and said, "That sounds good to me. We'll stop at the general store and mail this document, and then the wagons can roll on to the Three Cross."

Chapter 32

Regarding the map Annabelle had brought along, Smoke had studied it thoroughly enough that despite its lack of fine detail, he had no trouble determining their route out of the settlement. They passed the towering butte and headed north through the richly grassed basin.

Within a couple of hours, they began spotting cattle grazing on that grass.

Smoke told Annabelle to stop her wagon and wait for a few minutes while he took a closer look at those cattle. Waving for Hank Cavanaugh to join him, he rode out toward the nearest animals, most of which appeared to be Herefords, with a few Texas longhorns mixed in.

Smoke knew that a decade earlier when Texas cattlemen had begun to move north into Wyoming and Montana, they had driven herds of longhorns up here, but in the years since, other breeds had started to replace those tough, rangy critters better suited to the more arid regions of the Southwest. The Hereford had come to dominate, even as it had done the same on the Sugarloaf.

The big, placid red-and-white cattle didn't spook as Smoke and Cavanaugh approached. They were accustomed to having men on horseback around them. Smoke reined in when he was close enough to see the brand burned into the hip of one of the cows. He pointed it out to Cavanaugh.

"I'm afraid I don't know what I'm looking at," the young man said.

"That wavy line along the top could be a river, but in this case it's a cloud," Smoke explained. "The three lines slanting down from it represent rain. That's a thundercloud—the name of Otto Blaylock's ranch."

Cavanaugh nodded. "Yeah, I reckon I can see that. Pretty creative."

"Blaylock, or whoever came up with it, must have some imagination." Smoke smiled. "I'll give him credit for that."

"Coming up with a way to grab the colonel's ranch was pretty creative, too. Can't really give him credit for it, though."

Smoke grew more serious as he nodded.

"We don't actually know what happened yet. Could be that lawyer manipulated things and hoped they'd turn out so Blaylock benefited. Then he'd be in Radcliffe's debt."

"I don't guess how the situation came about is as important as what we're going to do about it."

"You're right about that," Smoke said. "This is the edge of what should be Three Cross range. The Thundercloud is farther north. If Blaylock's stock has drifted this far south, he's been running them on the Three Cross for a while."

Smoke rested both hands on the saddle horn and leaned forward.

"All this country used to be open range," he told Cavanaugh. "A lot of it still is. It's unusual for a ranch to have a legitimate claim on as much land as you'll find on the Three Cross and the Thundercloud. That's the way things are going, though. The more settled the West becomes, the more folks will start relying on deeds and fences—and lawyers."

"It sounds like you're not convinced that's a good thing," Cavanaugh commented.

Smoke shrugged and said, "I was lucky enough to see the last of the old days and the old ways, and the men who made them special." He gazed off into the distance. "Memories won't ever keep things from changing, though, no matter how much we cling to them. A friend of mine named Audie, who used to be a professor, knows all kinds of things, and he once quoted a Bible verse to me: *The sun also ariseth, and the sun goeth down, and hasteth to his place where he arose.*"

"Ecclesiastes 1:5," Cavanaugh murmured.

"You know your Good Book," Smoke said.

"Some," Cavanaugh allowed. "And it seems to me that's a mighty sad verse. Some of the good things ought to stay the same."

"It's a pretty thing to think about," Smoke agreed as he turned his horse away from the Thundercloud cattle, "but it'll never happen."

He heeled Drifter into motion and rode back to the wagons, with Cavanaugh following him.

"Those are Mr. Blaylock's cows, aren't they?" Annabelle asked as the two riders reached the lead wagon and reined in.

"They are," Smoke confirmed.

Colonel Wilkinson asked, "Did you see any wearing the Three Cross brand?"

"Not yet, Colonel, but we didn't really take a good look around. Do you have any idea how much stock you inherited from your cousin?"

Annabelle answered Smoke's question. "Not really. Mr. Radcliffe's letter didn't go into detail about that. But given the size of the ranch, there must be hundreds of cows on it. Maybe even thousands."

Smoke nodded and said, "If any of the old crew are still around, we might be able to get a reasonably accurate tally. You'll need to have a roundup so you can cut out all the Thundercloud stock and drive it back to Blaylock's home range. Once you've done that, you'll have a lot better idea what you're dealing with."

"Do you think Mr. Blaylock will allow us to do that?"

"Now, that's another question all by itself," Smoke admitted. "We'll have to wait and see. Shouldn't be too much longer, though. I figure we'll be at Three Cross headquarters in another hour."

"We can't get there soon enough to suit me," Annabelle said with a grim, determined note in her voice.

The wagons rolled on. Smoke saw more and more cattle grazing. He checked the brands on some of them and found that they were all in Thundercloud iron.

He toyed with the idea that somebody had worked over the Three Cross brand with a running iron to turn it into a Thundercloud, but decided that was unlikely. Besides, he didn't know if the original brand was actually three crosses, like the one old Hernán Cortés had used a few hundred years earlier when he arrived in the New World, or the number 3 followed by a cross. Either was possible.

Smoke was a hundred yards ahead of the wagons when he spotted several men on horseback emerging from a line of trees ahead of him. They rode in his direction. He reined in to wait for them and did a quick count.

Eight men. Mighty bad odds if it came to a fight.

Then he recognized one of the riders as Cole Farley and decided that trouble was a definite possibility.

Farley knew the Wilkinsons had intended to head for the Three Cross when they finished their business at Herbert Radcliffe's office. He must have returned to the ranch with the other Thundercloud men and put together this "welcome party." As they rode closer, Smoke could see that they were a pretty salty-looking bunch.

The sound of hoofbeats behind him made him look over his shoulder. Hank Cavanaugh and Danny Murphy were riding quickly toward him, obviously intent on improving the odds as they had done earlier in the settlement.

Unfortunately, even with them siding Smoke, those odds would still be better than two to one. Cavanaugh seemed to be a pretty good hand with a gun, but Smoke didn't know how well Murphy would do. He couldn't count on a lot of help from either man.

Farley and his companions stopped about fifty feet away as Cavanaugh and Murphy came up alongside Smoke, one on either side. Farley nudged his horse forward a couple of extra steps and called, "I told you, you wouldn't take me by surprise next time, Jensen!"

"You didn't have to come out and greet us," Smoke said. "We would have found the Three Cross without any trouble. Of course, if you want to show us the way, we'll be obliged to you."

"We'll show you the way to hell if you don't turn around and go back where you came from!"

"Does Otto Blaylock know you're out here trying to start a fight, Farley?"

It was a blind shot, a question uttered on a whim, but Smoke saw from the reactions of some of the other men that the thrust had gone home. They suddenly looked nervous, as if they had been willing to follow the orders Cole Farley gave them as their foreman, but were uncertain whether this was the right course of action.

"Mr. Blaylock trusts me to take care of the ranch. That's all you need to be concerned about, Jensen. That and the likelihood you're going to be filled with lead in about a minute if you don't light a shuck and take those damn wagons with you."

The riders with Farley appeared to be capable of carrying out that threat. Smoke could tell by looking at them that they weren't professional gun-wolves. They were cowboys and could handle the regular chores around a ranch.

But each man had a gun rig buckled around his hips, and Winchesters were sheathed on every saddle as well. They could burn plenty of powder in a hurry if they needed to.

In a calm, level voice, Smoke said, "You boys had better listen to me. There are more than a dozen women back there with those wagons, and every one of them is looking this way. If you gun down me and my friends here, what are you going to do next? Kill all those women, since they're witnesses? Is that what you came out here to do today?"

"Don't listen to him!" Farley yelled. "You're trespassing, Jensen. We're fully within our rights to shoot you. Nothing illegal about it, so we don't have anything to fear from anybody who sees it."

Hank Cavanaugh spoke up, sounding just as icy-nerved as Smoke. "I'd be willing to bet that some of those women are doing more than watching, mister. They have rifles, and they're lining up their shots. If any guns start going off, they'll blow you right out of your saddles."

Smoke tried not to grin. He had a hunch Cavanaugh was right. He didn't doubt for a second that Sally had her cheek nestled against her carbine's stock, and the sights were probably smack-dab on Cole Farley's chest. He wouldn't be surprised if Annabelle, Lucy, Helen, and Roberta were ready to get in on the fight, too. Delia and Susie as well.

"I'll say it plain, Farley," Smoke said. "I'm a man who's used to stomping his own snakes. It goes against the grain for me to say that we need to rely on the law to sort this out. But every now and then, that's the best way to handle a problem. Why not let it go to court? If your boss can make a strong enough case that the Three Cross belongs to him now, I'm sure he'll wind up with it."

Farley let out a bark of laughter. "Otto Blaylock came up here when there weren't a dozen other cattlemen in the state.

He battled Indians, rustlers, and blue northers that would strip the hide off a man or a cow. You really think a man like that is going to sit back and let the law tell him what he can or can't do?"

"If he's smart, he will," Smoke said. "Otherwise, all the changes in the world will come along sooner or later and roll right over him. Maybe none of us like it, but that's the way it is."

One of the other Thundercloud riders edged forward and spoke to Farley in a voice low enough that Smoke couldn't make out the words. Farley snapped back angrily at him, but the other puncher stood his ground.

After a moment, Farley said something else to the man, then turned back to Smoke and blustered, "This isn't over, Jensen. Not by a long shot!"

He jerked his horse around and spurred it cruelly. The animal leaped ahead, through an opening in the line of riders as some of the cowboys got out of his way in a hurry. Farley galloped off and disappeared into the trees where the men had come from.

The man who had spoken to him rode forward. He was older, the spare, leathery sort of hombre who had probably been a ranch hand for many years. He stopped about twenty feet away from Smoke, Cavanaugh, and Murphy and nodded to them.

"Obliged to you for not lettin' Cole stampede you into slappin' leather, Jensen," he said. "Some good men would've died today if the guns had come out, no matter who won the fight."

"I was thinking the same thing," Smoke said.

"Name's Bick Tuttle. *Segundo* on the Thundercloud."

"Smoke Jensen. But you seem to know that already."

Tuttle nodded. "Cole told us your name. He didn't recognize it. Some of us did. That's why we weren't lookin' for a fight."

The cowboy lifted his reins. "Me and these other boys will escort you to the ranch headquarters."

"You mean the Three Cross?"

Tuttle chuckled and said, "I reckon that's what's got to be sorted out, ain't it? But it's where you'll find Otto Blaylock these days, and he's the fella you're gonna have to deal with."

He started to turn his horse, then paused and added, "I wouldn't be lookin' forward to it, if I was you."

Chapter 33

The former Three Cross ranch house, currently the headquarters of the Thundercloud spread, looked to Smoke as if it had been added onto recently.

Otto Blaylock must have done that after he moved in, Smoke mused, since the original owner, Albert Lowe, had been dead for a while.

The house was a sprawling structure built of logs, with a second story over part of it and wings extending to the sides. A big porch stuck out in front of it. A pole fence enclosed a yard. The fence had an arched opening in it, and mounted on that arch was a slab of wood with the Thundercloud brand burned into it.

Yeah, Otto Blaylock had put his mark on the place, all right, Smoke thought. He probably wouldn't be inclined to give it up easily.

When the wagons rolled up in front of the house, led by Smoke, Cavanaugh, Bick Tuttle, and the small group of Thundercloud hands, a white-haired man, with his hands tucked into the back pockets of his denim trousers, stepped out onto the porch and stood watching them.

Despite the rumpled thatch of snowy hair, the man had an air of vitality about him. The hair contrasted sharply with his seamed, deeply tanned face.

Smoke knew without having to be told that he was looking at Otto Blaylock.

As Smoke dismounted, the cattleman descended the porch steps and approached the gate along a stone path. He gave Smoke a curt nod and said, "I reckon your name's Wilkinson."

"No, sir," Smoke said. He looped Drifter's reins around an iron hitching post. "I'm Smoke Jensen." He nodded toward the lead wagon. "That's Colonel Jasper Wilkinson and his daughter, Miss Annabelle Wilkinson."

Blaylock's pale blue eyes flicked to the two people in the seat of the lead wagon, looked away, and then went back again with increased interest. He wasn't wearing a hat, but his hand raised a little, anyway, as if, out of habit, he was about to pinch the brim of a Stetson.

"Ma'am," he said respectfully. "Colonel."

To Smoke's surprise, he found himself not immediately disliking this man. He didn't know what Otto Blaylock was capable of, certainly, but his first impression was of a tough, capable, but not cruel, frontiersman.

He needed to reserve judgment, though, until he found out what Blaylock was going to do next.

"I suppose I ought to introduce myself," Blaylock went on. "I'm Otto Blaylock. This is—"

He stopped short and laughed.

"I was about to say this is my place, but I reckon that's what we're gonna have to hash out, isn't it?"

"Among other things," Annabelle replied coolly.

"Please, ma'am, get down from that wagon and come on inside. My housekeeper has a pot of coffee on, and I expect you'll all stay for supper." Blaylock looked along the line of wagons. "Your friends are welcome to make themselves at home. My men can help with your teams—"

"That won't be necessary," Annabelle broke in. "We've been taking care of ourselves for months now, ever since we left Mississippi. I assure you, we can continue to do so."

"Yes, ma'am, whatever you say." Blaylock glanced at Smoke. "I've heard of you, Jensen. What's your part in this?"

"I don't really have one, other than befriending Colonel Wilkinson and his daughter and the other ladies. My wife and I came along with them to make sure they got here all right."

"All the way from Mississippi? From what I heard, you have a spread in Colorado these days."

"That's where we made their acquaintance," Smoke explained.

"What about those other two gents on horseback?"

"More friends we picked up along the way," Smoke said, knowing that Blaylock referred to Hank Cavanaugh and Danny Murphy.

"You're all welcome here," Blaylock said.

He ushered them onto the porch and into the house, which was plainly but comfortably furnished. The rooms had high ceilings, and Indian rugs were spread on the wooden floors. Several sets of antlers were mounted on the walls.

Once they were inside, the colonel extended his hand and said, "I'd like to shake hands with you, sir. Friend or enemy, there's no reason we can't respect one another."

"I couldn't agree more, Colonel," Blaylock said as he firmly clasped the old-timer's hand. He turned to Annabelle. Although she hesitated for a second, she took Blaylock's hand as well, but dropped it quickly.

Smoke said, "I'm curious how you knew we were coming, Mr. Blaylock. It seemed almost like you expected us today."

"I did. I knew when my foreman, Cole Farley, came back from town in a lather, rounded up a few more men, and rode off again, like he was heading out to meet trouble. So I went to the bunkhouse and asked some of the men who didn't go with him what it was all about." Blaylock's voice hardened slightly. "My men know they're better off answering when I ask them a question."

"They told you there was trouble in Brimstone Butte?"

"I know about the ruckus in lawyer Radcliffe's office, if that's what you mean. It's not like that's the first brawl Cole's been mixed up in."

"A bit of a hothead, is he?" Colonel Wilkinson said.

"Don't get me wrong, Colonel," Blaylock said sharply. "Cole's a good man and I rely on him. He's devoted to the Thundercloud spread. Just because he has a temper doesn't mean I won't side with him against anybody else."

"Nor would I expect you to, sir. A commander must always be loyal to his troops if he expects their loyalty in return."

Blaylock regarded him intently for a moment and then nodded. "I see we think alike on some things."

A handsome, middle-aged Mexican woman entered the room then, carrying a tray with cups and saucers and a coffeepot on it. She placed the tray on a low table made of heavy beams and poured the coffee, then passed out the cups.

Sally had come inside with Smoke and the Wilkinsons. Smoke introduced her to Blaylock, who again looked as if he wanted to tip the hat he wasn't wearing. They all sat down in heavy, overstuffed chairs, except for Smoke and Sally, who settled down on the short divan beside the table.

"Gracias, Juanita," Blaylock told the housekeeper. Then he said, "Colonel, if I can ask, how did you lose your sight? I could tell from the way your daughter was helping you that you can't see."

"It was during the war, as you might expect. An exploding shell during a bombardment."

"A tragedy," Blaylock murmured.

"Not as much of one as the lives of all the fine Southern boys who were lost."

"I was down in Texas then," Blaylock said. "Other than over in East Texas, the war never had much of an effect on folks' lives. On the frontier in those days, we still had our hands full with the Comanche."

Annabelle said, "I think we should talk about the reason my

father and I—and our friends—are here, Mr. Blaylock. This is our ranch, and you've stolen it from us."

Blaylock took a sip of his coffee and regarded her over the rim of the cup. When he set it down, he said with a hard edge in his voice, "You like to get right down to business, don't you, Miss Wilkinson?"

"I don't see any point in wasting time on niceties. What do you intend to do about this?"

"I've done what I intend to do. I paid the overdue taxes on this spread and took possession of it. It's part of my Thundercloud ranch now, and that's all there is to it."

"My father inherited the Three Cross Ranch from his cousin, and a legal transfer of ownership to him has been filed. *That's* all there is to it. This is our ranch, not yours, and you'll need to get off it and take all your cattle with you."

Annabelle's bold statement contained one element that was a bit of a stretch, Smoke thought. The document transferring ownership to the colonel had been mailed, but not filed. That probably wouldn't take place for several days. However, that shouldn't change anything in the long run.

"You believe in speaking your mind, don't you?" Blaylock said to Annabelle, sounding as if he didn't quite know whether to be angry or amused.

"I don't see any reason not to."

He nodded curtly. "I like it when a man is plainspoken. I'm not as accustomed to it coming from a woman, but I have to say I admire you for it, Miss Wilkinson."

"I don't give a fig about your admiration. You're a thief."

Blaylock's rugged jaw clenched for a moment. A little muscle twitched in it. He was angry now, no doubt about it.

Then he reined in his temper with a visible effort and said, "I'm not a thief. My attorney informed me that the legal claim to this ranch appeared to have been abandoned, and anyone who paid the taxes on it could claim ownership. I followed Radcliffe's advice, that's all. If he lied to me, that's his responsibility. I've taken possession of the Three Cross in good faith, improved it, and moved some of my stock onto it. In my opinion, that establishes a legitimate claim."

"Your opinion is wrong, sir. I wrote to Mr. Radcliffe on behalf of my father and informed him we were on our way to claim the inheritance. That claim was never abandoned."

Blaylock shrugged. "Time and tide wait for no man, as the old saying goes. And no woman, or bunch of women. You took too long getting here, Miss Wilkinson. It's too late. The whole thing's over and done with."

Annabelle leaned forward. "We'll take you to court—"

"Go ahead," Blaylock interrupted, waving a hand in dismissal of the threat of legal action. "It won't do you any good."

Colonel Wilkinson said, "Because you control the judges in this region, just as the Yankee carpetbaggers took over the legal system in the South?"

"I don't like being compared to Yankees," Blaylock snapped. "But I repeat, if you want to sue me, go right ahead."

A tense silence settled over the room. Smoke wasn't surprised at how this confrontation had played out so far. He could tell that Otto Blaylock was a stubborn man. Nobody carved a cattle ranch out of the wilderness without being bullheaded.

But Annabelle and the colonel were equally stubborn. At least, they were talking about lawsuits, not a range war.

Not yet.

"Or there's another way we can proceed," Blaylock said abruptly into that silence.

"What do you suggest?" Annabelle asked, sounding skeptical.

"There's plenty of room here, and the weather will be good for several months yet," Blaylock said. "Your party can park the wagons and set up camp. And there's plenty of room here in the house, too. I'd be pleased and honored if you and your father would agree to be my guests, Miss Wilkinson. Maybe if we all get to know each other better, we can reach an agreement that'll satisfy everybody."

Annabelle stared at him, as if in amazement. Colonel Wilkinson looked surprised, too.

Smoke and Sally traded a glance. Neither of them had expected Otto Blaylock to make an offer like that.

After a moment, Annabelle said, "I don't see what good that's going to do. It's not going to change the facts of the case."

"Facts can look a mite different when you're better acquainted with somebody. You might be more inclined to see things from the other person's point of view."

Annabelle shook her head. "I don't think that's very likely."

"Consider it from a practical standpoint, then," Blaylock argued. "What are you going to do, turn around and go all the way back to Brimstone Butte? You won't make it before nightfall. In fact, I don't reckon you can get those wagons off Thundercloud range before it gets dark."

Annabelle opened her mouth to object, but Blaylock held up a hand to forestall her protest.

"Sorry, that was just habit. You can't get off this ranch, whatever it's called, before night. So you might as well stay here and be comfortable."

Annabelle still looked opposed to the idea, but she said, "What do you think, Colonel?"

"It's been a long, tiring journey, my dear. I don't see how accepting Mr. Blaylock's offer will compromise the position we've taken regarding the ranch."

"Unless he plans to make us sign some sort of contract to stay overnight," she said with a quick scowl directed at Blaylock.

"You're not a Westerner, ma'am," he said. "When we extend our hospitality, it doesn't come with any strings attached."

Their gazes met squarely for a few heartbeats, and then

Annabelle said, "My apologies, Mr. Blaylock. I didn't mean to insult you."

"Not a bit, ma'am. We're beginning to understand each other now." He smiled. "Just like I said."

Blaylock turned to Smoke and Sally and went on, "What about you, Mr. and Mrs. Jensen? The invitation extends to you as well. Plenty of room for you here in the house."

"And we gratefully accept," Sally replied. "I have to say, it'll be nice to sleep in an actual bed again."

Blaylock rested his hands on his knees. "It's settled, then. I'll have my men unload whatever you need from the wagons, and we'll see to it that your livestock is cared for and your people are all settled down comfortably."

"Thank you," Annabelle said, although she didn't sound all that gracious about it.

The housekeeper had withdrawn to one side of the room after pouring the coffee. She still stood there with her hands clasped in front of her. Blaylock turned to her and said, "Juanita, we'll have four guests for supper. That won't be any problem, will it?"

"Of course not, Señor Blaylock," she said. "I will begin preparations right away."

"Gracias," he told her. Turning back to the others with a smile, he continued, "Now, let's put all the disagreements aside for the time being. I want to hear about your journey up here. I imagine it was quite a trip. I remember that when I drove a herd of longhorns from Texas more than ten years ago, it took forever and seemed like we had to fight something every step of the way!"

Colonel Wilkinson said, "It wasn't an easy journey, I can tell you that, sir. It would have been even more difficult if not for the help we received from Smoke and Sally and the other friends we made along the way."

"Tell me about it," Blaylock said as he sat back with a smile on his face.

Juanita hurried through the big kitchen at the rear of the house and left through a back door. She went to a smaller building, not much more than a cottage, that stood a short distance from the ranch house. This was the foreman's cabin, where Cole Farley lived apart from the rest of the cowboys who resided in the long bunkhouse on the other side of the ranch headquarters, next to the barn and corrals.

She opened the door and stepped into the house with the easy familiarity of a regular visitor.

Cole Farley looked up from the table where he was sitting with a whiskey bottle and an empty glass in front of him. For a second, his sullen face changed expression as if he were glad to see her, but then his features settled back into a look of surly resentment.

"What is it?" he growled.

"Señor Blaylock has guests in the big house," Juanita said.

"Hell, I know that. I heard the wagons roll up."

"No, I mean they are *in* the house. The blond woman and her father, and the man and woman called Jensen. They have been talking with Señor Blaylock, and he has asked them to have supper with him."

Farley leaned back in his chair and stared at her. "You mean he's being friendly with them?"

"They have argued over who owns the ranch," Juanita replied with a shrug, "but then he invited them to stay. The rest of the party will camp outside. But the blond woman and her father and the Jensens are going to be the señor's guests in the house."

"Damn it!" Farley clenched a fist and slammed it down on the table so hard the bottle and glass jumped a little. "What the hell does the old man have in mind?"

Juanita smiled, but it was a chilly expression that didn't reach her dark eyes.

"I will tell you what he has in mind," she said. "He is smitten with the blond woman. He wishes to make her his. I saw it in his eyes when he looked at her."

"Why, the old goat!"

Juanita shrugged again. "He has been a widower for a long time. He misses the touch of a woman. The sound of a woman's laugh. The smell of her hair when he plunges his face into it. No man ever forgets those things or desires them any less, no matter how much time goes by without them."

Farley's eyes narrowed. "He hasn't been bothering you, has he?"

"He values my services as housekeeper and cook too much to risk losing them by angering me," she replied with a laugh. "No, Cole, put your mind at ease about that. I am yours, and yours alone."

"And it damned well better stay that way," Farley said. He frowned. "What are we going to do about this?"

"About Señor Blaylock and the woman? What can we do?"

"I don't know, but if he up and married her, then she'd get her hands on the Thundercloud, anyway, wouldn't she? She might figure that was easier than fighting the boss for it. Then I'd be left out in the cold, and chances are you would be, too."

"You are certain he plans to leave the ranch to you?"

Farley scraped his chair back and stood up. He began to pace back and forth as agitation grew on his face.

"He's hinted at it often enough. He doesn't have any other family. There's nobody else for him to leave it to—except the fella who's been right beside him, helping him run the spread all these years."

"You should find out if he has prepared a will," Juanita suggested. "That lawyer in town, Radcliffe, he would know. He handles all of the señor's legal affairs."

Farley stopped pacing and thought about what she had said. Slowly, he nodded.

"I'll have to have a talk with Radcliffe. That sniveling little weasel will spill anything if you put some pressure on him. He'll go along with anything, too, if he believes there's a chance he'll make money out of the deal."

"You are thinking that if there is no will, one could be prepared? And someone who is familiar with the señor's signature—you, let us say—could affix his name to it well enough that a court would accept it, especially with his attorney's testimony to support its validity?"

A grin spread over Farley's face. "I knew there was a good reason I fell for you, Juanita."

She snorted and said, "I have given you many good reasons. This is just one more."

"Yeah, but this one will make us rich, providing that we can act before the boss succeeds in mending fences with that blonde. There's already bad blood between them. It could get worse. And if it was to get worse, it might break out into a full-fledged range war."

He reached for Juanita, took hold of her, and pulled her tightly against him. Her arms went around his neck.

"You know what happens in range wars, don't you?" he asked in a husky whisper. "Folks get killed. Even stubborn old ranchers."

His mouth came down hard on hers.

Chapter 34

During Smoke's life, he had spent many nights wrapped up in a bedroll under the stars, but over the past few years, since he and Sally had established the Sugarloaf, he had gotten used to sleeping in an actual bed.

So after weeks on the trail, he had to agree with her that it was nice to experience sheets and a mattress again.

Even so, there was nothing that could quite replace being able to look up and drink in the spectacular sight of millions of stars scattered across an ebony sky. Smoke was half asleep and thinking of that in his drowsy state when he heard the frightened yell from somewhere outside.

"Fire!"

No cry was more terrifying to Westerners, especially in towns where the dry wood of buildings could go up in a flash. Even a small blaze could spread beyond containment in a matter of minutes and race from building to building until it had destroyed an entire settlement.

Forests and grasslands were also prime targets for flames. Luckily, it had been a wet enough year that most of the vegetation in the basin was green, which would make it more difficult for a wildfire to spread.

Smoke was wide-awake instantly. He rolled out of bed and

had reached the window before Sally sat up groggily. He thrust the curtain aside and peered out.

Earlier, after supper, Otto Blaylock's housekeeper, Juanita, had shown them to a room on the second floor. From there, Smoke had a good view of the ranch headquarters. The horses from the wagon teams had been herded into a corral separate from the ranch's remuda. The wagons themselves were parked about fifty yards away from the cluster of buildings.

It was one of them that was on fire.

Flames shot up from the canvas cover over the back. From here, Smoke couldn't tell which wagon it was; there wasn't much to distinguish between them.

He also didn't know if anyone had been sleeping inside it. On pleasant nights like this, most of the women spread their bedrolls underneath the vehicles or sometimes out in the open.

Tonight, for example, he saw several of them in their nightclothes, standing under some trees beyond the wagons. The flickering light from the blazing vehicle revealed looks of horror on their faces as they watched the fire.

Sally had made it out of bed by now. She rushed to his side and asked, "Smoke, what is it?"

"One of the wagons is burning," he said. "I need to get down there."

The wagons were parked close enough together that it was possible the flames might spread from one to another. Smoke knew he needed to get the burning one away from the others, if he could, and as quickly as possible, too.

He wore only the bottom half of a pair of long underwear. He yanked on his denim trousers, jammed bare feet in boots, and rushed out of the room, bare-chested.

"Stay here!" he flung over his shoulder at Sally, but he knew the likelihood of her actually doing that was slim.

Otto Blaylock was already at the head of the stairs, wearing a nightshirt crammed into a pair of pants.

"What the hell's all the commotion?" the rancher demanded.

"One of our wagons is on fire," Smoke told him. He grabbed a newel post and swung himself onto the stairs. He took them three at a time going down and heard Blaylock following, at not quite so reckless a pace.

No lamps burned downstairs, but enough light from the burning wagon spilled through the windows for Smoke to see where he was going and avoid the furniture. He ran to the front door and threw it open. The crackling of the flames was clearly audible on the night air. The acrid smell of smoke carried to him as well.

Some of the ranch hands were running out of the bunkhouse. On the frontier, everybody turned out when someone yelled, "Fire!" Along with Smoke, they raced toward the burning wagon.

The wagon tongue was angled down to the ground in front of the vehicle. Smoke didn't think about what he was doing. He just assumed command naturally as he hurried toward the front of the wagon. He waved his arm and shouted to the cowboys, "Get behind it and push!"

He reached the wagon tongue, got his hands under it, and lifted. Someone stepped up beside him and took hold of it as well. He glanced over and recognized Bick Tuttle, the second-in-command of the Thundercloud crew. They raised the long wooden beam with its attached harness fittings and leaned it against the driver's box. Smoke reached up and disengaged the brake lever.

Both men had to jump back as the wagon lurched into motion. Half-a-dozen cowhands, as well as Hank Cavanaugh and Danny Murphy, were behind it, pushing as hard as they could with their shoulders wedged against the wagon body. With the canvas cover blazing the way it was, the heat from the flames had to be beating uncomfortably against the faces of those men.

The wagon's sideboards were beginning to burn by the time

the men had shoved it far enough away from the others, to be safe. They staggered back, holding up their arms to shield themselves from the heat.

Otto Blaylock ran up, carrying a bucket with water sloshing out of it. He threw the water onto the flames. It didn't do much good, but Sally, wearing a robe over her nightdress, arrived then with a second bucket and emptied it onto the fire as well. Blaylock ran back to the well to pump his bucket full again.

Smoke took the empty bucket from Sally and ran to the well, too. As soon as he got there, he saw that Bick Tuttle had filled a bucket.

"Give me that," Smoke said as he took the full bucket from Tuttle and handed him the empty one. "Fill this!"

He dashed back to the fire, where Blaylock was throwing water on the flames.

Over the next few minutes, more men joined the small bucket brigade and established a rhythm, but the water they threw on the fire wasn't enough to save the wagon. The flames completely consumed the canvas cover, ate deeply at the sideboards, and left holes charred into the wagon bed. The vehicle's iron frame stood out like a skeleton from what was left.

At least, the fire hadn't spread to the other wagons or anywhere else other than a scorched patch on the grass where the burning vehicle had stood. This wasn't as big a disaster as it might have been.

But the women were upset, anyway. Smoke couldn't blame them for that. Annabelle was so angry she was stalking back and forth near the burned wagon. The other women formed a group and looked on. Danny Murphy had his arm around Susie's shoulders, and Hank Cavanaugh stood with Lucy, but didn't touch her.

The cowboys had gathered in a group of their own and were standing a short distance away with wary expressions on their faces.

They had good reason to be worried. Annabelle swung sharply toward Blaylock, pointed a finger at him, and said, "You! You're responsible for this."

Blaylock leaned back slightly, his eyes narrowing in surprise and anger at Annabelle's furious, accusatory tone.

"How in the world do you figure that?" he asked her.

"There's no way that wagon caught fire on its own. One of your men started it. That's the only explanation. And you probably ordered him to do it!"

"You're wrong," Blaylock said coldly, "and I don't appreciate you saying that. I've extended my hospitality to you and your people—"

"So you could trick us and take us unaware when you tried to destroy our wagons."

"That doesn't make a lick of sense! Why would I want to destroy your wagons? Then you and the other ladies would be stuck here. If I wanted you to leave, that's the last thing I'd do."

What Blaylock said made sense, Smoke thought. Nothing he had seen or heard from the cattleman made him believe that Blaylock would stoop to doing something like this.

Smoke might have said as much to Annabelle, but he knew she was too angry to listen to him right now. She might need to cool off first before she would be able to see reason.

Blaylock went on, "It's more likely one of the ladies knocked over a lamp or a candle—"

"That didn't happen," Roberta Walling said. "No one was in that wagon when it caught on fire. And thank goodness for that, because it means nobody was hurt."

"Roberta's right," Helen Pryor added. "None of us stayed in the wagons tonight. The weather's pleasant enough we all spread our bedrolls under the trees."

Smoke had thought that was the case. He cast his eyes over the group of women and did a quick head count. They were all there, all right.

He walked up to Annabelle, who was still glaring at Blaylock, and said, "Maybe we ought to find out if anybody saw anything suspicious." He turned to the assembled women. "Did any of you ladies happen to notice somebody around the wagons earlier tonight?"

"I think we were all asleep," Helen said. She looked at the others. "Did any of you see anything?"

Some of the women shook their heads, others murmured negative responses.

Smoke said, "Hank, Danny, how about you fellas? Did you notice anything unusual?"

"I sure didn't, Mr. Jensen," Danny Murphy replied. "I was asleep, too."

"I was awake," Cavanaugh said, "but I didn't see anything. We didn't post a guard tonight, since we're staying here at the ranch, but since I was awake, I sort of wandered around, anyway. You know, just taking a look. But I was on the other side of the ranch house when I smelled smoke. I ran around here and saw that one of the wagons was on fire."

"So you're the one who raised the alarm?" Smoke asked.

"That's right."

That jibed with Smoke's memory. He'd been half asleep when the shout roused him, but he recalled that it had been a man's voice yelling "Fire!"

"Maybe that fella's the one who started it," one of the ranch hands called.

Cavanaugh's head jerked toward the man angrily.

"Why would I do that?" he demanded.

It was a good question, Smoke mused. Cavanaugh had opened himself to suspicion by admitting that he had been up and roaming around when the fire broke out. Would he have done that if he'd actually been guilty?

For the life of him, thinking back over the time he had known Hank Cavanaugh, Smoke couldn't think of any reason why he would do such a thing, either.

No, he didn't suspect Cavanaugh, but that didn't stop a few

of the women from casting dubious glances toward him. Not Lucy Dunning, who had grown closer to Cavanaugh during the journey, but some of the others.

Smoke looked around. He didn't see Cole Farley anywhere. It seemed like the ranch foreman would have responded like everyone else when the cries of "Fire!" started. After all, the blaze had been a threat to the Thundercloud headquarters, including the place where Farley lived.

The fact that Farley was nowhere around made the skin on the back of Smoke's neck prickle a bit.

Annabelle said to Blaylock, "All this talking doesn't change the fact that you asked us to camp here, and one of our wagons is destroyed a few hours later. You didn't want us here in the first place. Maybe you thought that if we lost all our belongings, we'd have to go somewhere else and start over."

Blaylock shook his head solemnly and said, "I might fight you in court over this, Miss Wilkinson, but I'd never attack a bunch of women this way. And I'd never try to hurt somebody I'd invited into my home as a guest, either."

"It's our home," Annabelle said through clenched teeth. "Mine and my father's."

The colonel came up beside her and put a hand on her shoulder.

"I don't think you're going to get anywhere arguing with Mr. Blaylock, my dear," he said. "Let's just be thankful Smoke and the others acted quickly enough that only one wagon was lost."

Blaylock said, "The men who pushed that wagon away from the others were my hands, miss. I'd remind you of that, too. If burning you out was my idea, don't you reckon I would have given them orders to let the flames go?"

That was a good point, too. For the first time, a flicker of doubt appeared in Annabelle's eyes, Smoke thought.

"All right," she said grudgingly. "The damage is done, and

there's nothing we can do about it tonight. Sure, we lost some supplies and furnishings in the wagon that burned, but nothing we can't replace as soon as everything is settled."

"You'll come back in and try to get some rest, then?" Blaylock asked.

Annabelle pulled her robe more tightly around her and lifted her chin defiantly.

"No, I'm going to get my bedroll and stay out here with the other ladies." She turned to her father. "Colonel, you should go on back in and be comfortable. Sally, you'll see that my father gets back to his room all right, won't you?"

"Of course," Sally answered without hesitation. She linked arms with Wilkinson. "Come along, Colonel."

Blaylock turned to Tuttle and said, "Bick, see to it that what's left of that wagon gets wet down really good. We don't want any sparks kindling a new fire."

"Sure, boss," the old cowboy drawled. He called orders to several of the ranch hands to continue dousing the burned-out wagon until they were sure that every last ember had been extinguished.

"Say, where's Cole?" Blaylock asked with a frown. He had finally noticed the foreman's absence.

Tuttle shook his head. "Don't have any idea. I haven't seen him since earlier today."

"He should have turned out like everybody else. Go around to his cabin and make sure he's all right."

"Sure, boss," Tuttle said again. His legs, permanently bowed from riding, carried him swiftly off into the shadows.

Sally and Colonel Wilkinson had reached the porch steps. Smoke watched them go up the steps and into the ranch house. The women were slowly returning to the campsite they had made under the trees. Smoke caught the attention of Hank Cavanaugh and Danny Murphy and gestured for them to come over and join him.

"Since we don't know exactly what happened, it would be a good idea to keep our eyes open the rest of the night," he told them. "We can switch out standing guard."

"That sounds like a good idea to me," Murphy said. "I don't want anything happening to Susie or any of those other ladies."

"I agree," Cavanaugh said. "Smoke, you don't think I had anything to do with that fire, do you?"

"Honestly, I don't," Smoke replied. "You've been a good friend to all of the ladies." He chuckled. "Not just Lucy."

"Well, I, uh . . ." Cavanaugh sounded embarrassed. "Lucy and I are sort of . . ."

"You don't have to go on," Smoke told him. "She seems like a mighty fine young woman."

"She is. The finest I've ever met."

Murphy said, "None of those cowboys acted like they knew anything about the fire, either. Who do you reckon could be to blame for it, Smoke?"

An idea was beginning to form in Smoke's mind, but before he could give voice to it, something else happened that caused the three men to whirl around.

A gun blasted somewhere in the night, not far away.

CHAPTER 35

Smoke hadn't buckled on his gunbelts when he rushed downstairs to help with the burning wagon. None of the other men appeared to be armed, either, except for Hank Cavanaugh, who had a Colt holstered on his hip.

"Come on, Hank," Smoke told the young man as he broke into a run toward the sound of the shot.

Armed or not, he wasn't going to stand by and do nothing while trouble broke out.

Only one shot had crashed through the night. It came from the other side of the ranch house. That was the way Bick Tuttle had gone, Smoke recalled, when Blaylock sent him to check on Cole Farley.

When Smoke came in sight of the cabin where the foreman lived, he immediately saw that the door was open and light spilled out on the ground in front of it. A man sprawled there, unmoving.

As Smoke ran closer, he recognized the motionless figure—Bick Tuttle.

That didn't really surprise him, since he had known that Tuttle had come around here. But he didn't know for sure who had shot Tuttle, or why.

He could make what he thought was a pretty good guess, though.

"Hank, cover that door in case somebody else is inside," Smoke told Cavanaugh. He dropped to a knee beside Tuttle. The second-in-command's chest rose and fell in the light from the cabin. He wasn't dead, but the large bloodstain on his shirt indicated that he was wounded pretty badly.

Smoke got his arm under the middle-aged cowboy's shoulders and carefully raised him into a sitting position. Tuttle's eyelids flickered a few times and then stayed open as he tried to focus on Smoke. He finally managed to do so.

"J-Jensen," he said.

"How bad are you hurt?" Smoke asked.

Tuttle struggled to get the words out. "Dunno. Shot through the body. The damn varmint. Never expected him to . . . to . . ."

"Farley's the one who shot you?"

"Yeah. Saw the lamp was burnin' in the cabin. Opened the door. He was sittin' . . . sittin' at the table. Juanita was tendin' to him. Had what looked like a bad burn on his arm."

"I expect he got that injury when he set the wagon on fire," Smoke said. "It probably caught faster and bigger than he expected it to."

"Dunno," Tuttle said. "Never got the chance to ask him. When he saw me lookin' at him and realized what I'd seen, he grabbed up a gun from the table. I never figured he'd shoot me . . ."

Tuttle let out a long sigh and closed his eyes. For a second, Smoke thought he was gone, but then he saw that the *segundo* was still breathing.

Cavanaugh was in the cabin doorway, his gun up and ready. He said over his shoulder, "There's nobody in here, Smoke. I can see the whole place from here. Farley's gone."

"Blaylock's housekeeper isn't in there?"

"Nope. The cabin's empty."

Smoke nodded. If Juanita was gone, chances were that she was with Farley. Whether she had gone with him voluntarily or he had forced her to accompany him, Smoke had no way of knowing right now.

It was possible, too, although unlikely, that she had run back into the house after Farley shot Tuttle. There had been time enough for her to do that, Smoke supposed, but just barely.

Otto Blaylock trotted up and knelt on Tuttle's other side. He asked, "Is he dead?" His voice was rough, but Smoke heard genuine worry in it.

"He's still breathing," Smoke told the rancher. "Some of your men need to lift him carefully and take him into the ranch house. Lay him down on a table and then find Sally." Smoke's voice was grim as he added, "She's had plenty of experience dealing with bullet wounds."

Blaylock called orders to four of his men who had followed him from the front of the house. He and Smoke straightened to their feet as the cowboys took hold of Tuttle and gingerly lifted him. They carried him toward the ranch house.

Blaylock asked, "Who shot him?"

"Your foreman, Cole Farley."

"You're jumping to conclusions, Jensen. Just because this is Cole's cabin—"

"Tuttle's the one who said Farley shot him," Smoke broke in, not wanting to waste any time listening to Blaylock's protestations of disbelief. "I heard it plain as day and so did Cavanaugh."

"That's right, Mr. Blaylock," Cavanaugh put in.

Blaylock stared at them. "But why? Why would Cole do such a thing?"

"Because Tuttle saw that Farley had a bad burn on his arm. I reckon he got it while he was setting fire to that wagon, and he knew Tuttle realized that. So he acted without thinking and tried to shut him up."

Smoke paused and then went on, "If he'd just stopped to think for a minute, he might have been able to lie his way out of it. He could have said that he saw the wagon burning and tried to put it out. He might have gotten the injury that way. But he was too hotheaded to do that."

"Cole's the impulsive sort, all right," Blaylock said with a certain degree of reluctant acceptance in his voice. "I have a hard time believing he'd shoot Bick, though. The two of them were friends."

"Maybe not as much as you thought. What about Juanita?"

Blaylock looked at him sharply. "What *about* Juanita? What's she got to do with this, Jensen?"

"She was doctoring Farley's arm when Tuttle saw them. Are she and Farley friends, too? Or more than that?"

Blaylock scowled and said, "Sure, they're friends. I reckon I've seen them together at church socials and the like, and hoped that maybe someday it'd be more than that. I thought they were both fine folks and it would be nice if they wound up together."

"Maybe they're not as fine as you thought." The wheels of Smoke's brain were turning over rapidly. "Juanita was there all the times you were talking to Annabelle and her father, earlier today. She knew that you're willing to fight it out in court, but also that you want to work out some kind of arrangement with the Wilkinsons. That's why you asked them to stay here. She could have told Farley about that, and he set the wagon on fire, hoping to cause trouble between you and them."

"Why the hell would he do that?"

"You tell me," Smoke said.

"It's none of his business what deals I make. The man just works for me. If he thinks he has any say . . ."

Blaylock's voice trailed off. He closed his eyes, lifted a hand, and rested it on his face.

"Oh, hell," he murmured.

"You've thought of something?" Smoke asked.

"I mentioned several times while Cole was around that I

don't have any heirs. All my relatives are dead. So I figured to leave all my holdings—the Thundercloud, the businesses I own in Brimstone Butte, like the saloon and the hotel and one of the stores—to the ones who helped make them successful. I was going to leave the businesses to the fellas who run them, and the ranch"—Blaylock took a deep breath—"was going to the half-dozen members of the crew who have been with me the longest. Cole and Bick and a few of the other men."

"But since you were leaving the businesses in the settlement to the men who run them, Farley could have thought you intended on him having the Thundercloud all to himself."

"Damn it!" Blaylock burst out. "I never told him that, not once, but I guess he could've gotten it into his head that was what was going to happen." The rancher shook his head in bafflement. "I don't understand. Even if I lost what used to be the Three Cross, there's no doubt the original Thundercloud spread is mine. If Cole thought he was going to inherit my estate, he'd have gotten that, no matter what happened."

"Maybe he wanted all of it," Smoke suggested. "If he stirred up an outright war between you and the Wilkinsons, maybe you and the colonel and Annabelle would all wind up dead and then Farley could grab the whole thing."

A look of horror came over Blaylock's rugged face. "I suppose it could have played out that way," he admitted, "but I've known Cole Farley for years. I hate to think he could have turned out to be so ruthless."

Hank Cavanaugh said, "Greed does funny things to men, Mr. Blaylock. It can turn an honorable man bad and make him do things you'd never expect from him."

Smoke frowned slightly as he glanced at Cavanaugh. That statement was a little more than he would have expected from a young, drifting cowhand. But he supposed that like many men on the frontier, Cavanaugh might be well-read and self-educated beyond his appearance.

Blaylock said, "If it's true that Cole shot Bick, and if you're on the right trail about why he did it, Jensen, where is he now?"

"There's no telling," Smoke replied with a shake of his head. "He could have realized that he'd made a mistake by shooting Tuttle and took off for the tall and uncut as fast as he could. His plans were ruined, and he couldn't stay here. He must have taken your housekeeper with him, too, unless she's in the ranch house."

"Let's go take a look," Blaylock said curtly. "I want to see how Bick is doing."

When they reached the house, they found that Bick Tuttle was laid out on a table with a blanket underneath him. He had a thick bandage tied in place on his right side and was unconscious, but he was breathing with a steady rhythm.

Sally stood beside the table, wiping her bloody hands on a rag. Smoke saw red stains on her bare arms almost up to the elbow.

"I think Mr. Tuttle is going to be all right," she said before Blaylock could ask about him. "I was able to get the bullet out, and I don't believe it hit anything too major. He lost a great deal of blood, of course, and I can't be certain exactly how much damage the bullet did, but at least he has a chance to recover."

"Thank you, Mrs. Jensen," Blaylock said. "I can't tell you how obliged I am to you for helping him."

"He'll need medical attention from an actual doctor," Sally said. "You should fix up a wagon so it'll be comfortable in the back and not jostle him around too much. You ought to go ahead and take him in to Brimstone Butte tonight. I think I saw a doctor's office there, didn't I?"

Blaylock nodded. "There's a doc, all right, a pretty good one. I'll see to it that the men get ol' Bick there safe and sound. A wagon can't go too fast in the dark, but they ought to be there by morning."

"I think that's a good idea."

"You, uh, you haven't seen Juanita, have you?"

Sally frowned. "Your housekeeper? No, now that I think about it, I haven't. I would have thought she'd come out to see what was going on."

Smoke said, "You can take a look around, Mr. Blaylock, but I'd be willing to bet a hat that she's gone. She went with Farley, either willingly or unwillingly."

"Farley?" Sally said. "Smoke, what's going on?"

Smoke explained the theory he and Blaylock had come up with, while the cattleman stood there wearily scrubbing a hand over his face and looking disgusted by the whole thing.

Smoke didn't blame him. It had to be a terrible feeling when someone you'd depended on let you down unexpectedly like that. He almost felt sorry for Otto Blaylock.

But mostly, he wanted to find Cole Farley before the treacherous foreman tried something else to strike at the Wilkinsons and prevent any sort of settlement from being arranged between the two parties.

Farley would be desperate now, and Smoke wasn't convinced for a second that the man would give up his ambitions just because one hand in the game had gone against him.

"You didn't have to shoot him," Juanita said for what seemed like the twentieth time since she and Cole Farley had ridden away from the Thundercloud headquarters.

Anger welled up inside Farley. "Damn it, what do you think I should have done?" he demanded. "The old coot saw I had a burned arm. Bick's not a fool. He would have figured out I'm the one who set that wagon on fire."

"And now everybody knows it was you, because you shot him. What else could they think?"

Farley had been pondering that very question, even though it was hard to force his brain to work. The pain from his scorched and blistered left arm was a terrible distraction. Juanita had daubed some grease on it and wrapped a bandage around the arm, but it still hurt like a son of a gun.

He had never expected the flames to shoot up so quickly and fiercely. He should have anticipated that, since he'd poured a bottle of coal oil over the wagon's tailgate before dropping a lit lucifer in there, but the swiftness of it had taken him by surprise, anyway.

Despite the pain, he had hammered and prodded his thoughts into an idea that might work. As he and Juanita rode through the night on the horses they had grabbed from his string in the corral, after he'd gunned down Tuttle, he said, "All right, listen. We'll ride back to the ranch in the morning, and this is what we'll tell them. You and I were in my cabin when some fella neither of us had ever seen before showed up and threw a gun on us. He intended to rob the place. Tuttle showed up, and this varmint shot him down. Then he grabbed you and ran off, taking you with him as a hostage. I went after you, and I finally caught up, killed the stranger, and rescued you. Nobody can claim that's not what happened. Right?"

For a moment, Juanita didn't respond. Farley assumed she was considering the plan he'd just laid out.

Finally, she said, "Señor Blaylock and the others will want to know who this so-called stranger was. They will ask where the man's body is."

"I can tell 'em I was in a hurry to get you back to the ranch, so I didn't take the time to fetch his body. We'll even find a spot where we can say I caught up and had the fight with the hombre. Then I can take them back to the spot, but his body won't be there because the wolves dragged it off. Or a bear."

"What about your arm? How will you explain that injury?"

Farley thought about that and replied, "I'll say that when I jumped the fella, we had a fight and I rolled into his campfire. That's reasonable enough, don't you think?"

"I don't know," Juanita said slowly. "Señor Blaylock is a smart man. He may not believe your story about the wolves. There would be no tracks to support it."

"Blaylock likes me," Farley argued. "He's going to leave the Thundercloud to me, isn't he? He'll want to believe my story, so he'll be willing to overlook a few little things. You wait and see."

"Maybe. But there is one thing you have failed to consider, Cole. What if Señor Bick is alive? He will know it was you who shot him, not some mysterious stranger."

Farley scoffed at that idea. "I drilled that old mossback dead center," he said. "There's no way Tuttle survived being shot like that. He was dead by the time he hit the ground, so he wouldn't have had the chance to talk to anybody."

"You had better hope that is true. You are betting everything on it."

Farley grimaced in the darkness. Even though he didn't want to admit it even to himself, what Juanita said was troubling to him. There was a slim chance that Tuttle had lived long enough to tell somebody who shot him. If he and Juanita rode openly up to the ranch tomorrow morning, he might be riding right up to a hang rope.

"We'll have to do some scouting first," he said. "Maybe you ought to ride back by yourself first. You can say that I was still fighting with the kidnapper when you lit out. If everything's all right, you can beg Blaylock to put together a search party and then they can come looking for me. I won't be far off, of course. I'll be heading back to the ranch when they find me."

Farley grinned in triumph.

"There, that'll work just fine, won't it? All you have to do is play your part. If you do that, nothing can go wrong."

"Maybe," Juanita admitted with some reluctance in her voice.

"No maybes about it. I guarantee that idea is foolproof. I've told you all along, Juanita, you just string along with me and you'll wind up getting everything you want. I'm going to be the boss of the whole Thundercloud range, including the Three Cross! Nothing can stop us—"

Farley bit back a curse and hauled his horse to an abrupt stop as large shapes suddenly loomed out of the shadows around them. He recognized the grotesque shapes as men on horseback, and that realization was followed immediately by the familiar menacing sound of gun hammers being cocked. That metallic ratcheting struck icy fear into Cole Farley's belly as he and Juanita were surrounded.

"Hold it right there, my friend," a cool, unruffled voice said. "I just heard you mention the Three Cross Ranch. I want very much to hear whatever you can tell me about what's going on there."

Chapter 36

There was still no sign of Cole Farley or Juanita by the next morning. A grizzled old cowboy named Mackey, who had been a cook on a chuck wagon, came into the house and rustled breakfast not only for Otto Blaylock and his guests, but for the rest of the crew as well. Everyone gathered around the big dining table in the ranch house.

"Those boys I sent with Bick to Brimstone Butte ought to just about be there by now, if they're not already," Blaylock commented after a sip of the strong black Arbuckles' in his cup. "I told 'em to send a man back on a fast horse to let us know they got there all right and how Bick was doing. The others can take their time coming back with the wagon."

Sally said, "If Mr. Tuttle survived the trip to town, he ought to recover. I think there's a good chance he made it."

"If he does, it's because of what you did, ma'am," Blaylock said. "And I'm mighty obliged to you for it."

"I just did what anyone would have done."

"Anyone with experience patching up bullet wounds." Blaylock cocked a bushy white eyebrow in Smoke's direction. "From what I've heard, being married to this fella, you've probably had plenty of experience along those lines."

"Don't believe everything you hear," Smoke responded with a smile.

"How about what we read?" one of the cowboys asked. "We've got some o' them yellowback novels out in the bunkhouse that are about you, Mr. Jensen."

Smoke waved a hand dismissively. "Pipe dreams, most of them, I expect. Or maybe I should say *bottle dreams*, since I'd bet my hat most of the scribblers who turn out those books are drunk at least half of the time. You'd have to be, to sit down and make up a pack of lies for a living."

That comment drew laughs of agreement from the crew, and Sally smiled as well. Colonel Wilkinson chuckled, but Annabelle remained as sober and concerned as ever.

Sally had invited the two of them for breakfast, as well as the rest of their party. The other women, along with Hank Cavanaugh and Danny Murphy, had decided to stay outside in their camp under the trees and prepare their own meal.

Annabelle had a good reason for accepting the invitation. She had explained to Sally, and Sally had mentioned it to Smoke, that she wanted to conclude negotiations with Otto Blaylock as quickly as possible.

Annabelle didn't hold out much hope of coming to an agreement that would satisfy everyone, but she was still willing to try. She had come around to believing that Cole Farley had acted on his own the night before—instead of setting the wagon afire on Blaylock's orders.

Since most of the people at the table seemed to be in a good mood, Smoke ventured to say, "I've been wondering about something. Did any of you fellas ride for the Three Cross when Albert Lowe was still alive?"

"I did, Mr. Jensen," one of the men replied, "and so did these four fellas." He pointed them out. "When Mr. Blaylock moved the Thundercloud headquarters down here, he told us Three Cross boys that we could stay on if we wanted. I've ridden a grub line before, and I didn't want to go back to it, if I didn't have to."

"Same here," one of the other men said, and the remaining members of the former Three Cross crew nodded.

"Maybe one of you can tell me how many head were under Three Cross iron when Mr. Lowe passed," Smoke said.

All of the former Three Cross punchers looked toward Blaylock, who said, "I can tell you that. When I came down here, I had a roundup and tally done. There were eight hundred fifty-seven head of stock. They're all still wearing Three Cross brands, too. I didn't change them. I wanted to keep things straight, just in case there were ever any questions."

He cast a meaningful glance toward Annabelle, who returned the look impassively.

"Where are they?"

"Up on my north range. The northern part of the original Thundercloud spread. I had them moved up there when I brought some of my herd down here." Blaylock looked at Annabelle. "Don't worry, it's good graze where they are. I just thought it might be a good idea to shift things around a little."

She nodded and said, "I'm glad you have all this information, Mr. Blaylock." She paused. "It'll make things easier when the case comes to trial."

A look of frustration crossed Blaylock's face. Smoke had studied the way the man looked at Annabelle Wilkinson, the tone of his voice when he talked to her, and he knew Blaylock already had feelings for her, despite having known her for less than twenty-four hours.

Just like Gus Gerhardt, Otto Blaylock had taken one look at Annabelle and wanted her. Wanted her bad. Smoke found that a mite baffling. Annabelle was a very good-looking woman, no doubt about that; and more than just beauty, she possessed an intangible appeal that said she would be a passionate, fulfilling partner.

Smoke recognized that, but his feelings for Sally made him immune to it.

Come to think of it, he had experienced something of the same sort when he first laid eyes on Sally, and the sensation had never diminished.

Not for the first time, he thought about what a lucky man he was.

Blaylock might have had some comment to make in response to what Annabelle had said, but he didn't have a chance to voice it. The ranch house's front door opened and Hank Cavanaugh hurried in, almost at a run.

"Smoke, there's a rider coming," he said. "Fast enough that it might mean trouble."

Out here on the frontier, nobody galloped a horse unless there was a good reason for it. Smoke knew that and so did the other men. He stood up and headed for the door. Blaylock and the Thundercloud crew were close behind him.

They went into the ranch yard and looked south along the trail that led from Brimstone Butte. The swift rataplan of hoofbeats originated in that direction. A moment later, the rider came into view.

"That's Orrie Prewitt," Blaylock said. "I recognize that shirt of his."

"He's one of the men you sent to town with Tuttle, isn't he?" Smoke asked.

"Yeah. I guess Orrie was the one who got picked to hurry back and let us know how Bick's doing—" Blaylock broke off what he was saying and stiffened. "What's wrong with him?"

Now that the rider was closer, Smoke could tell that he was hunched over in the saddle and swaying slightly from side to side. He looked like a man who was hurt, but was determined to get where he was going.

Several punchers hurried forward to meet the rider. By now, Prewitt was slumped so far forward in the saddle that he was no longer controlling the horse. The cowboys yanked off their hats, waved them in the air, and yelled to get the horse's attention. It swerved and slowed sharply and then reared up. Prewitt fell, but two men were there to catch him and lower him to the ground.

Another man grabbed the spooked horse's reins and led the animal away. Everyone else gathered around the newcomer, including the women from the camp. They formed a good-sized group.

Smoke, Sally, and Blaylock were in the forefront. Blaylock asked sharply, "What's wrong with him?"

One of the men who had caught Prewitt looked up from where he knelt and said, "Looks like he's been shot, boss."

Danny Murphy said, "I thought I heard a gun go off a little while ago, but I wasn't sure."

Smoke hunkered on his heels next to Prewitt. "That's a bloodstain on his shirt, all right. Looks like he's been drilled through the shoulder."

"There's blood on his back, too," the cowboy said. "The bullet must've gone right through him."

Sally said, "We had better take him inside. I'll get the wound cleaned and bandaged."

Prewitt had been lying there motionless, his face pale and drawn, apparently unconscious. But as the men took hold of him to lift him, his eyes opened and he said, "Wait! Where . . . where's the boss?"

Blaylock leaned over him. "I'm right here, Orrie. You have something to say to me?"

"Gunmen out there . . . closin' in on the ranch . . . I rode right into 'em . . . without seein' 'em first. One of 'em . . . took a shot at me . . . I was hit . . . but I had to warn you . . ." Prewitt's lips drew back from his teeth in a grimace or a grin, or a little of both, as he went on, "Ol' Bick made it to town . . . all right . . . Doc says he's gonna . . . be okay."

Blaylock reached down to squeeze Prewitt's uninjured shoulder. "Good man," he said. "You brought word just like you were supposed to. But who were the men who shot you?"

"Dunno . . . but there were a bunch of 'em . . . fifteen, twenty, maybe more . . . and if I didn't know better . . . I'd swear I saw Cole with 'em."

"Farley!"

"Yeah. I think maybe he was the one . . . who shot me . . ."

Prewitt's eyes closed again and his head slumped back. He had passed out.

"Get him inside," Sally ordered briskly. "I'll tend to him."

As several of the Thundercloud riders lifted the wounded cowboy and carried him toward the house, Smoke and Blaylock traded looks.

Smoke said, "Sounds like Farley was quick on the trigger again."

"Yeah, but who in blazes are the rest of the bunch Orrie saw? He made it sound like they're getting ready to attack the ranch."

"Could be Farley's thrown in with a bunch of outlaws, since he figures he can't come back and be welcomed."

Blaylock nodded and looked around at Annabelle. "Miss Wilkinson, I reckon I'm going to have to insist that you and all the other ladies get into the ranch house as quick as you can. If there's trouble, you need to be somewhere bullets can't reach."

"For once, we're in agreement, Mr. Blaylock. But we're not going to just run and hide." Annabelle turned to the women and said, "Lucy, Helen, Roberta, see to it that everybody gets their rifle and as much ammunition as they can carry, and then we'll all assemble in the ranch house." She looked back at Blaylock. "If there's going to be a fight, we'll do our part."

Even under the strained circumstances, Blaylock grinned and said, "Ma'am, if I wasn't mighty impressed with you already, I sure am now. Me and my boys will be glad to fight alongside you and your ladies."

Smoke said to Cavanaugh and Murphy, "Go with the ladies and give them a hand if they need it."

The two younger men nodded and hurried with the women toward the campsite.

"Get your rifles, boys," Blaylock told his crew. "There's no telling how much time we've got—"

Not enough time to prepare adequately, Smoke realized as hoofbeats suddenly pounded close by and a peal of gun-thunder rolled out to shatter the peaceful early-morning air.

Chapter 37

Sally had followed the men carrying the wounded Orrie Prewitt into the house, so she was already out of the line of fire. Smoke was grateful for that.

Too many people were still out in the open, though. The women had to abandon the idea of arming themselves. Smoke shouted, "Into the house now, everybody!"

"Come on, ma'am," Blaylock said as he grabbed Annabelle's arm and urged her toward the house. With his other hand, he took Colonel Wilkinson's arm and added, "You, too, Colonel!"

Smoke had buckled on his gunbelts before going down to breakfast this morning. Both Colts fairly leaped into his hands as he pivoted, searching for the source of the attack.

A few feet away from him, one of the Thundercloud hands suddenly grunted in pain and took a lurching step sideways. He managed to lift a hand to his bloody chest before he collapsed.

Men on horseback burst into view, charging toward the ranch headquarters from both sides. Puffs of powdersmoke came from the guns they wielded as they continued firing at the group in front of the house.

Smoke's Colts came up and began to roar and buck as he returned the fire. One of the attackers pitched from his saddle and landed in a rolling sprawl.

Hank Cavanaugh and Danny Murphy had their guns out as well. Smoke had returned Murphy's gun to him a couple of days earlier, willing to accept that the young man was no longer a threat just because he had been part of Gus Gerhardt's gang, and now he was glad that he had come to that decision. Murphy stood shoulder to shoulder with Cavanaugh, both of them blazing away to cover the women's retreat to the house.

The Thundercloud punchers who were armed were putting up a fight, too. The attackers peeled off, having lost a couple of men and evidently figuring that was enough—for now.

Smoke knew they wouldn't be giving up, though.

In fact, even as they broke off the assault, several of them threw more shots over their shoulders. One of those bullets ripped through Otto Blaylock's left thigh as he hustled Annabelle and her father up the steps to the porch. Blaylock cried out in pain and let go of the Wilkinsons as his wounded leg buckled underneath him.

Annabelle shoved her father toward the door and told him, "Keep going, Colonel!" Without hesitation, she turned back and reached down to clutch Blaylock's arm. Her grip kept him from falling. Gritting her teeth with the effort, she hauled him upright and they stumbled through the door into the house.

In the brief lull, Smoke, Cavanaugh, Murphy, the rest of the women, and the remaining ranch hands made it into the house as well. As Annabelle helped Blaylock into a chair, the cattleman bellowed, "Break out all the guns you can find and cover the windows, boys!"

"If there are any extra rifles, pass them out to some of the women," Annabelle added with the same tone of command.

She glared at Blaylock for a second and he added, "Do what the lady says!"

But then he grinned up at her, and Smoke, who happened to be looking that way, saw Annabelle's expression soften for a second.

Danger had a way of cutting through the differences between folks, especially when the scent of powdersmoke was in the air.

Sally ran up and said, "Smoke, are you all right?"

"I'm fine," he assured her. "How's that fella who was shot?"

"I think he'll be all right," she said. "I've got a man keeping pressure on the wound. When the bleeding stops, I'll take a better look, but the wound appears to be a clean one."

"You've got more work waiting for you." Smoke gestured toward the chair where Otto Blaylock sat. "Mr. Blaylock caught a slug through the leg."

"I'm all right, damn it!" Blaylock responded, having heard Smoke's comment. "I was hurt worse than this plenty of times back in my Indian-fighting days. I just need something to tie around this bullet hole and a rifle to put holes in those varmints outside!"

Annabelle pulled up the skirt of her dress and reached underneath it to tear off a strip of petticoat. She showed it to Blaylock and said, "Will this do?"

"For a start!" he responded, still grinning.

He tried to take the makeshift bandage from her, but she knelt in front of him and tied it around his leg.

The gunfire had died away, but Smoke had a hunch the battle was far from over. Some of the cowboys had armed themselves with rifles from the supply of guns kept in Blaylock's office and study, but there weren't enough of the weapons to go around. A few of them had been wearing handguns at breakfast. The men spread out, stationing themselves at windows to try to repel any further attacks.

Blaylock's grin vanished as his face took on an angry expression. "Who in blazes are those fellas, anyway?" he demanded. "I know Orrie said that Cole Farley was one of 'em, but where did Farley come up with an army like that?"

"From what I saw, they looked like hired guns," Smoke said. "But from what I figured, Farley didn't have the kind of money to put together a crew like that."

Blaylock shook his head. "No, he didn't. I pay good wages, but not enough to hire a dozen or more gunfighters."

Some of the windows were raised; in others, the panes had been broken out by rifle barrels. Enough were open so that the voice shouting from outside could be heard clearly by everyone in the front room of the ranch house.

"Inside the house!" a man called. "Do you hear me?"

Colonel Wilkinson cursed bitterly. "Annabelle," he said, "do you hear that?"

Annabelle's face had drained of color. Her voice was bleak as she replied, "Yes, I do. It's Mason, all right. We should have known . . . but I never dreamed he'd follow us all the way up here."

"That Yankee snake would go to any lengths if he thought there was money waiting at the end of it." The colonel came over to Annabelle and patted her on the back. "I'm sorry, my dear, I truly am. I was hoping we'd seen the last of that scoundrel."

Smoke said, "You know the man who's behind this attack?"

From outside, the man called Mason shouted, "If you come out and give me those plates, there's no need for anyone else to be hurt, Annabelle. All I want is what's rightfully mine."

"Plates?" Smoke repeated, baffled by this unexpected turn of events.

"Printing plates, Mr. Jensen." The words came from beside him as Hank Cavanaugh walked over. "For printing money, to be precise. Counterfeit bills."

Annabelle caught her breath sharply and turned to stare at the young man, whose demeanor had changed. He was still young, but he no longer looked like a carefree, drifting cowboy. A stern purpose had come over him.

"Who are you?" Annabelle asked in a hushed whisper.

"Henry Cavanaugh, ma'am. I work for the United States Secret Service. I was sent out here to pick up your trail when you were spotted in Colorado."

Smoke thought he was a fairly smart fellow, but a lot was going on here that he clearly didn't know about. He said to Annabelle, "That man outside—Mason—is an old enemy of yours, ma'am?"

She took a deep breath. "Worse than that," she said. "He's a former partner who believes that I double-crossed him." A faint, humorless smile tugged at her lips. "And he's right. I did."

"The man's a carpetbagging scalawag!" Colonel Wilkinson blustered.

"His name is Mason Loomis," Annabelle went on. "The colonel is right. Mason is a carpetbagger who came to Mississippi after the war. He gained a great deal of political power and seized a considerable amount of property, including Cypress Hill, our plantation. But we were able to make an arrangement with him." She smiled, but the expression didn't appear a bit happy. "We became business partners."

"And the business was counterfeiting money," Cavanaugh said.

From outside, Mason Loomis called, "I'm getting impatient, Annabelle. Give me what I want, or I'll wipe you out!"

Ignoring the threat, Colonel Wilkinson took up the story. "Despite what I may have led you to believe, I was not a field commander during the war. I was one of the officers in charge of printing currency for the Confederacy. Using the knowledge I gained in that endeavor, it wasn't that much of a stretch to turn my efforts to duplicating American bills."

"How could a blind man do that?" Smoke asked.

"That was, ah, another deception on my part. Actually, I didn't lose my sight during the hostilities. Annabelle and I decided to claim that I had, in the hope that it might throw off any pursuers who came after us. They wouldn't be looking for a blind man."

Remembering some of the things he had noticed about Colonel Wilkinson's behavior, Smoke wasn't all that surprised by this admission.

Wilkinson's voice choked with emotion as he went on, "But ever since I was clubbed in the head by that lout Gerhardt, I . . . I truly haven't been able to see. Poetic justice, I suppose, for all the lying I've done in my life."

Annabelle put a hand on his shoulder and squeezed. "Don't talk like that, Colonel. I still hope your sight comes back—"

"It doesn't matter, my dear. Mason has caught up to us, and I have no doubt he'll carry through on his threat and put an end to us." Wilkinson sighed. "My only regret is that so many decent, innocent folks will suffer for our sins as well."

Smoke said, "Nobody's giving up. This fella Loomis may have a bunch of hired guns with him, but we have a sturdy house to defend and some good fighting men of our own."

"Damned right we do," Blaylock growled. "Nobody is surrendering."

Annabelle said, "But if you turn me and my father over to him, he might let the rest of you live."

"Not a chance in hell," Blaylock declared. "I'm not going to let any harm come to you, Annabelle."

She stared at him and asked, "Why in the world would you feel that way when we came in here and tried to take the Three Cross away from you?"

"Maybe I knew all along my claim to it was kind of shaky," Blaylock admitted. "But I'm a stubborn old coot, and I don't like to let go of something once I've got my hands on it." He smiled. "Might not be so bad, though, to have the Three Cross for a neighbor again. And you."

Before Annabelle could respond to that, a cowboy at one of the windows yelled, "Here they come again!"

Gunfire crashed outside and all but drowned out the last of his words.

Chapter 38

A couple of swift strides took Smoke to one of the undefended windows. The glass was already knocked out. It crunched on the floor underneath his boots.

As he knelt there, carefully avoiding the broken glass, he saw several gunmen rushing toward the house. Others hidden behind the cover of the bunkhouse and the barn covered their advance with a steady volley of rifle fire. Bullets sang through the window near Smoke's head. Coolly, he lined up a shot, anyway, and squeezed the Colt's trigger.

One of the attackers rocked back as the slug from Smoke's gun drove into his body. Momentum carried him on for a few stumbling steps before he pitched forward on his face and didn't move again.

Smoke had already shifted his aim by that time. He fired again and saw a man's arm jerk as the bullet shattered his elbow. The attacker fell to his knees and screamed as he clutched his wounded arm. He managed to get back to his feet and try to retreat, but he had made it only a short distance before a shot fired from one of the other windows crashed into his back and knocked him down.

One of the cowboys cried out and toppled backward, hit by a shot from a hidden rifleman. Blood fountained from his bullet-ripped throat. His bootheels drummed on the floor for a moment as death throes gripped him. Then he was still.

Lucy Dunning fired a rifle from one of the windows. Hank Cavanaugh knelt at the other side of that window and joined in the battle from there. Lucy paused to reload and looked over at Cavanaugh as a lull in the firing allowed her to say, "I can't believe you lied to me!"

"I had a job to do," Cavanaugh said. "And you lied to me, too. You never said anything about being part of a bunch of counterfeiters!"

"You already knew, so it didn't matter, did it?"

Lucy lifted the rifle and started shooting again.

On the other side of the doorway, Susie Beale and Delia Tracy were firing from a window there. Danny Murphy came up behind them, keeping low because of the lead flying around in the air.

"Susie, get back," Murphy urged. "I'll take over here."

"Go find somewhere else to defend," Susie said. "Delia and I are part of this group now, and we're going to fight for it!"

"But you heard what Hank said! They're criminals!"

"And you and the rest of Gerhardt's gang never broke the law? You were a bunch of owlhoots!" Susie laughed wildly. "Besides, we're criminals, too. We're prostitutes, and there are plenty of places where that's against the law."

Delia paused in her shooting to turn her head and say, "Annabelle and the others are, too. I used to work in the same house as her, a few years after the war. I reminded her of that, and that's the only reason she agreed to let us come along. The whole bunch were in the business at one time or another, that's how they all got to be friends. The counterfeiting got them out of it."

Susie stared across at her. "You knew all of this?"

Delia shrugged. "Helen and Roberta and I talked a lot, after they got used to us being around. It didn't mean anything. We're all the same, when you come right down to it."

"Not anymore," Susie insisted. "I'll never go back to that life!"

"You won't have to," Danny told her. "I'll see to that."

"Neither will I," Delia said. "I won't—"

She stopped short and looked down at her chest, where a deep red stain was spreading across the front of her dress. Her eyes rolled up in their sockets and she collapsed, falling over sideways.

"Delia!" Susie screamed. She started to stand up to go to her friend's aid, but Murphy grabbed her and pulled her down. Susie crawled across the glass-littered floor toward Delia, while Murphy thrust his revolver over the windowsill and thumbed off shots until the cylinder was empty.

Smoke heard heavy footsteps on the porch and knew that some of the attackers had reached the house. Suddenly, a lit lantern sailed through one of the shot-out windows and crashed to the floor, shattering and spraying burning coal oil across the planks.

Otto Blaylock grabbed a blanket off the back of a chair, where it was draped, and lurched toward the blaze on his wounded leg. He threw the blanket over the flames, smothering them.

But as he did so, he was hit again, this time in the body. The bullet's impact twisted him around. Once again, he would have fallen if Annabelle hadn't leaped to catch hold of him and brace him up.

Another lantern was thrown into the house and this time the spreading flames caught the floor on fire. Shouts from the rear of the house warned Smoke that they were under assault from that direction, too. He turned and saw Sally backing through a doorway, firing a pistol back in the direction she came from.

He sprang to her side, got his arm around her waist, and swept her aside, off her feet, as bullets stormed past them. He let go of her and drew his left-hand Colt. Gun-wolves swarmed into the big room, smoke and flame spewing from their gun muzzles.

Two men charged toward Annabelle and Blaylock. Colonel Wilkinson leaped forward. Whether he was acting on instinct or his sight had started to come back to him at this perilous moment, there was no way of knowing. But he swung the walking stick in his hand with desperate strength. It landed with bone-crunching force on the skull of one of the attackers.

The second man slammed two shots into the colonel's chest, driving him back against Annabelle and Blaylock. All three of them went down in a heap.

Blaylock, although wounded, was able to reach out and snag the gun dropped by the man Colonel Wilkinson had struck down. He tilted the barrel up and pulled the trigger. The bullet caught the second gunman under the chin and bored up through his brain at an angle. The man fell backward, dead when he hit the floor.

But someone else was right behind him. Cole Farley roared, "Blaylock!" as he leveled a gun at the cattleman.

Blaylock got his left hand on the floor and pushed himself up as he swung the Colt toward Farley. The two revolvers blasted at the same time. Blaylock was already so stunned by the shock of being shot that he couldn't tell if he was hit again.

But his eyesight, though blurry, was clear enough for him to see Farley stumbling back and doubling over, pressing his left arm to his belly where Blaylock's shot had ripped through his guts. The gun in his hand went off again as he jerked the trigger, but his arm had sagged and the bullet went harmlessly into the floor. Farley folded up in a heap.

Smoke moved so fast, it was almost impossible for the eye to follow him, darting and whirling and making incredible shots, sometimes firing in different directions at the same time as if he had more than one set of eyes.

And each time he pulled the trigger, another hired killer fell, cut down by bullets aimed with almost supernatural instinct and precision.

The ranch house's front door was kicked open and several

men crowded through. Hank Cavanaugh and Danny Murphy met them with a fierce exchange of bullets that saw the attackers fall, but the young defenders were hit, too, staggered but resolutely staying on their feet.

The last one through the door was a sleekly handsome, well-dressed man who shouted, "Annabelle!" as he searched for her. Spotting her kneeling next to her fallen father and Otto Blaylock, his face contorted in evil triumph and the gun in his hand came up.

Then Smoke was in front of him, Colts booming, and Mason Loomis was thrown backward by the two slugs that pounded into his chest. His arm jerked higher as he fell; so when he fired, the bullet flew harmlessly into the ceiling. Loomis crashed down on his back with his arms and legs splayed out. He twitched a few times before death claimed him.

Smoke's guns were empty now, but he no longer needed them. As the echoes of gun-thunder faded away, an eerie silence replaced them. The battle was over.

When Smoke looked around, he knew that, but old habits were hard to break. He pouched the left-hand iron and briskly began reloading the gun in his right hand. Sally came up to him, and without stopping what he was doing, he asked her, "Are you hurt?"

"No, except for my ears ringing from all that gunfire, and my eyes burning from the powdersmoke." She hugged his arm. "What about you?"

"I'm fine," he said. His voice sobered as he added, "Not everybody made it, though."

Unfortunately, that was true. Annabelle was on her knees next to her father's body, bent over him, crying. On the other side of the room, Susie sobbed as she cradled Delia's limp form. Danny Murphy, bloodied but still on his feet, rested a hand on her shoulder and squeezed, letting her know he was there for her.

Hank Cavanaugh limped over to Lucy Dunning, who appeared to be unharmed. She started to resist when he took her in his arms, but then she returned the embrace and pressed her head to his chest in obvious relief that he had come through the battle alive, if not unscathed.

With both guns reloaded now, Smoke checked the bodies of Mason Loomis and Cole Farley. The men were dead. Loomis would no longer pursue Annabelle and her friends. Farley would no longer scheme to take over the ranch for which he had ridden. It was good riddance to both of them, as far as Smoke was concerned.

He just wished that ending their plans hadn't come with such a high price.

Two members of the Thundercloud crew had been killed in the fighting and five more were wounded to varying degrees. Colonel Wilkinson and Delia Tracy were the only fatalities among the members of Annabelle's group, although Roberta Walling and two other women were wounded. The injuries suffered by Hank Cavanaugh and Danny Murphy were not life-threatening, although it would be a while before Cavanaugh, with a bullet through his leg, would be riding a horse.

Otto Blaylock, who also had a wounded leg, would be laid up for even longer, since he'd been shot through the body as well. But as he assured anyone who would listen, he was too blasted old and stubborn to die from being shot only twice.

Colonel Jasper Wilkinson had died defending his daughter. Smoke had gotten to know the colonel well enough to believe he would have been satisfied to know he had met his end that way.

The members of Loomis's hardcase crew who survived the fight—four in all—were turned loose with a warning to leave Wyoming and never come back—and not to stop in Colorado, either. As Smoke told them, if he ever laid eyes on any of them again, he would kill them on sight himself.

They never saw Juanita again, and based on what Loomis's

men told them, Smoke assumed she had taken off for somewhere else when the attackers never came back from the ranch.

It was not the most satisfying conclusion, but for an affair with so many messy layers, it might well be the best that anybody could do.

They all gathered that night at the campsite near the wagons. The fire inside the ranch house hadn't destroyed the building, but it was going to need work before it was livable again. The wounded men were in the bunkhouse—except for Blaylock, who had insisted on being helped out here for the discussion that was now going on. He sat in a chair that had been brought from the house.

"It's true," Annabelle said as she stood beside Blaylock and looked at the circle of those gathered near the campfire: Smoke, Sally, Lucy Dunning, Hank Cavanaugh, Susie Beale, Danny Murphy, Helen Pryor, Roberta Walling, with her arm in a sling, and Bick Tuttle, pale and heavily bandaged, but up and around, plus a couple of the other women from Annabelle's group.

She went on, "Lucy and Helen and Roberta and the others know this, of course, but we were indeed counterfeiters. They didn't actually take part in it, mind you. Just my father and I, in partnership with Mason Loomis. With his connections in politics and banking, he had no trouble distributing the false bills the colonel and I provided. But he was cheating us, and I hated him, anyway, because he'd forced me to move back into Cypress Hill with him." Her chin lifted with a touch of defiance. "I don't mind admitting what I was when things were so bad, right after the war, but I was damned if I was going to stay a Yankee carpetbagger's mistress.

"So I got in touch with Helen and Roberta and some of the other girls I knew from those hard times, and we agreed to head west and make a new start."

Smoke said, "But you took the counterfeit printing plates with you, and that caused Loomis to come after you."

Annabelle smiled wearily. "That and the cache of authentic money I took, too. I didn't believe he had earned it. I still don't."

Hank Cavanaugh spoke up, saying, "Did you have any idea that the Secret Service was about to uncover your operation in Mississippi?"

"I'd heard rumors," Annabelle admitted, "and I wasn't going to allow that to happen. I didn't think the government would send anyone after us."

"As long as you had those plates, you could have started printing money again," Cavanaugh pointed out.

"And we might have if we'd had to resort to it. But we honestly intended to try to make a go of running the ranch." She looked at Blaylock. "That's why I was prepared to fight as hard as I had to, in order to claim it."

"Well, that's all finished," Blaylock said gruffly. "As soon as I'm up to it, I'm going into Brimstone Butte, grab Herbert Radcliffe by the scruff of his neck, and shake some sense into that weasel. Things will be put right, I give you my word on that, Miss Wilkinson. The Three Cross is the Three Cross again, and it's yours. I won't clear out, though, until the house is rebuilt and put back to rights."

"I appreciate that, Mr. Blaylock."

"All I ask is that you give me the chance to be a good neighbor to you . . . Annabelle."

Annabelle's smile was genuine as she said, "I think I'd like to have a good neighbor, Otto."

"Wait just a minute," Cavanaugh said. "You're still a counterfeiter, Miss Wilkinson, and I'm still an agent of the United States Secret Service. My superiors would say that it's my duty to arrest you."

"If you do, you won't have any evidence against me. Those printing plates were in the wagon that Cole Farley burned. They're nothing but pieces of slag now. No one would ever be able to identify them."

Cavanaugh stared at her for a moment, opening his mouth and then closing it again. Then a smile spread slowly across his face.

"I guess I'll have to send a wire to Washington, DC, explaining that the case will have to be closed, due to lack of evidence, and tendering my resignation at the same time."

"You're quitting?" Lucy asked quickly.

"I kind of like it out here," Cavanaugh told her, "and I'd already figured out that I don't like working in DC. The air smells a lot better here in the high country, a long way from any politicians."

She slipped both her arms around one of his and rested her head against his shoulder.

Danny Murphy said to Annabelle, "I thought I might stay on, too, if you'll have me as one of your crew, ma'am. I've cowboyed some, and I think I've got a hankering to do it again."

He had a hankering for Susie, too, Smoke thought with a smile. That young man would help the girl get over the loss of her friend.

Sally leaned closer to him and said quietly, "It looks like they have everything worked out, Smoke. What are you and I going to do?"

"I figured we'd stay here for a while and make sure nothing else goes wrong, but after that, there's only one thing left for us to do."

"And what's that?"

"Go home," Smoke said.

At first glance, everything looked the same in Big Rock when Smoke and Sally entered the settlement four weeks later—Smoke riding on Drifter, Sally handling the team hitched to the buckboard. It had been a leisurely, enjoyable journey back from Wyoming.

But then Smoke noticed that the front door of the Empire Saloon was closed and the place appeared to be deserted.

He frowned. He had been planning to have a word with Andrew Rickett about the way the saloonkeeper had hired Gus Gerhardt and his hard cases to steal Susie and Delia and bring them back. That conversation was going to be accompanied by a suggestion that it might be wise for Rickett to depart from Big Rock and never come back.

Monte Carson spotted them and hailed them with a grin on his face. As the sheriff walked up to meet them, he said, "Howdy, Smoke, Sally. Mighty good to see you again. How'd your trip up to Wyoming go?"

"Oh, there were a few little bumps along the way," Smoke said. "Maybe we'll stop at Louis's for a cup of coffee before we head on out to the Sugarloaf. Come along and we'll tell you the whole story."

"I'll sure do that," Monte replied with an emphatic nod.

"Before we do, though," Smoke said, "how come the Empire Saloon is closed?"

"Because that fella Rickett is dead. He got caught palming an ace one night and tried to gun down the man who caught him. He wasn't quite fast enough with the derringer up his sleeve, though."

"Well, that's a shame," Smoke said.

"Really?" Monte looked confused. "I'm not sure why you'd think so."

Smoke grinned. "Let's go get that cup of coffee, Monte, and I'll tell you all about it."

TURN THE PAGE FOR AN EXCITING PREVIEW!

THE STORM OF THE CENTURY HITS TEXAS— WITH A VENGEANCE.

A stranger on a mission of revenge. A hurricane on a path of destruction. An epic stand-alone adventure from the bestselling masters of the Great American Western . . .

At the height of the Civil War, a Confederate soldier was captured and held in New York's infamous Elmira prison camp. He managed to escape during a snowstorm—after killing a sadistic guard—and make his way to Texas. There, he started a new life in the small lumber town of Pine Lick, where he served as sheriff until he retired. Today, his son wears the badge; his nightmares of the war are long forgotten. But tonight, his past will return with a vengeance . . . when nature unleashes its fury.

Sheriff Mack Armstrong is as fine a lawman as his father, dedicated to protecting the townspeople of Pine Lick—especially when trouble shows up. But when he hears that a mysterious newcomer is armed, angry, and looking to kill a man named Armstrong, he barely has a chance to react. Another force of nature arrives—even deadlier than the stranger. It's a once-in-a-lifetime hurricane, the worst he's ever seen. The windstorm tears apart the sawmill, the church, the homes. The torrential rains destroy the dam, then flood the streets.

And all Sheriff Armstrong can do is save as many people as he can—before the stranger gets revenge. . . .

Chapter 1

Pine Lick, East Texas
Late Summer, 1888

Whiskey pulled the wet bandana from his back pocket and patted his sweaty face. He leaned back in the wooden chair as far as he could go without toppling over, hoping to catch a stray breeze wafting through the open door.

The humidity set his joints to hurting something fierce. He considered grabbing the bottle in the sheriff's bottom drawer just to take the edge off. Instead, he got up and walked over to a table just big enough to hold the washbasin. He dipped his head in the lukewarm water, using his cupped hand to pour some of it across the back of his neck.

"Why don't you bring some of that water over here, *boy*."

The man in the cell looked like a hundred pounds of melting lard wearing filthy clothes.

"I ain't your boy, and if you wanna keep talking like that, I'm happy to open that cell door and make you forget all about the heat." Whiskey dunked his bandana in the water and draped it around his neck. Whatever bit of cooling it brought couldn't compare to the heat of his anger.

"I'm happy to take my chances," the man said with a lopsided grin on his bearded face. His fingers gripped the iron bars, twisting them as if he could pull them apart. He was a scoundrel Whiskey had caught in Maxel's General Store the night before. The man, a stranger to the town, had first beat up Pap Maxel's teenage daughter as she was closing shop, before helping himself to three burlap sacks' worth of goods. Luckily, Whiskey had been making his rounds and heard the commotion. When he spied Miss Lana through the window, on the floor and doubled over in pain, with the top of her dress nearly torn right off, he kicked in the door and had a go at the would-be thief. His knuckles still hurt, but it was a good kind of hurt. The kind that meant a job well done.

Quicker than a jackrabbit, Whiskey grabbed the shovel handle he kept by his desk and cracked it against the man's fingers. The prisoner flew back from the bars, howling like a whipped dog. He jammed his hands under his armpits.

"You broke my fingers, you no-good varmint!"

Whiskey settled back in the creaking chair and leaned the shovel handle against his desk. "Well then, if you're a praying man, you might want to get down on your knees and give a little thanks to the Lord that your fingers is all I broke. Now sit down and shut your mouth before I really get angry."

Moaning in agony, the man said, "I need a doctor."

"How about I get a seamstress to sew that mouth of yours up? After what you did to Miss Lana, there's plenty women in town who would volunteer for the privilege. And some of them aren't as nice as me."

The prisoner shut up for a while, but more so because he set to whimpering in pain rather than from Whiskey's threat.

Whiskey heard the ring of familiar spurs as he was popping his knuckles, hoping it would relieve some of the pain.

"Morning, boss," he said as the sheriff strolled in.

"Whiskey."

The sheriff removed his tan Stetson and wiped his brow

with the sleeve of his shirt. He spotted their prisoner and turned to his deputy.

"He broke into Maxel's and put a beating to Miss Lana."

"She okay?"

"She'll be hurting some the next couple of days." Whiskey tapped the side of his head. "How long this will take to heal is anyone's guess."

The prisoner, sitting on the unpadded bunk, lifted his swollen and bleeding fingers so the sheriff could see.

"Your boy did this to me!" A trail of snot went from his nose to the fibers of his overgrown mustache and into his mouth. "I want a doctor and to press charges!"

The sheriff pulled up a chair beside Whiskey. "What'd he do?"

"Called me *boy.*"

"Like he did just now?"

Whiskey made it a point not to look into the cell, lest his ire get the better of him again.

"Mmm-hmm."

The sheriff addressed the prisoner. "You say that again to my deputy and I'll come in there and finish what he started." He sauntered to the cell and stared hard at the man's hands. "Claws like that won't be much good for stealing . . . or hitting on defenseless women. Might be, in the end, that ol' Whiskey did you a favor. He just might have saved your neck from a future hanging."

They eyed one another for a while, before the prisoner broke first and went back to his suffering.

"What's your name?" the sheriff asked him.

"That's none of your business," the man said with his back to him.

"I'm about to make it mine in five seconds." The sheriff took the key to the cell out of his pocket and brandished his pistol. When the man turned around, his eyes went wide.

"All right! Fine! Name's Kelly."

"Kelly what?"

"Kelly Marsden."

The sheriff grinned. "Your momma named you Kelly? No wonder you have a hair up your hind end." His laughter clearly irritated the man, who once again turned away from him to nurse his hand.

"You look tired," the sheriff said to Whiskey. "Go on home. I've got it from here. I'll see if there are any warrants for ol' Kelly."

Whiskey slowly extracted himself from the uncomfortable chair and tucked the wet bandana in his back pocket. "I'll make a round first before hitting the hay."

It was going on eight o'clock and the town was just coming alive, seeing as it was a Sunday. Pretty soon the sounds of church bells would fill the air.

"You had to babysit this plug-ugly fella all night. I've got morning rounds. Get some sleep. You earned it."

The sheriff was a quarter of a century younger than Whiskey, but the deputy always deferred to him, and for very good reason. He'd known the man since he was knee high to a grasshopper and respected the hell out of his father.

"Thank you, boss. Much appreciated."

Whiskey had gotten no more than one foot out the door when the sound of beating hooves stopped him in his tracks. He spied a young man on a blood bay headed straight for the sheriff's office.

"Company's coming."

The sheriff was beside Whiskey just as the rider dismounted, holding tight on to the reins. The boy was covered in sweat and out of breath.

"You the sheriff?" he asked. The towheaded rider looked to be no more than ten or eleven.

"Pretty sure I am," the sheriff said as he tapped the star on his vest.

"You need to come to the reservoir quick! There's been a murder!"

"Just slow down, son."

The boy's chest heaved mightily, and his mouth opened and closed like a catfish on land. It looked as if tears had carved a path through the dirt on his face.

"Now, what's your name?" the sheriff asked calmly.

"Arch . . . Archibald Gibbons."

"Okay, Archibald. Who's been murdered?"

The boy's upper lip trembled. "My pa."

Sheriff Armstrong's spine stiffened.

"Did you see who did it?" In a way, he hoped the child was not a witness to his father's murder, having found the body after the fact. It would make his job more difficult finding the murderer, but it would be less of a blight on the child's mind.

"I don't know. A man. He came to the edge of the lake and started yelling his head off. My pa yelled back, and they started fighting, us in the water, and him on land. Then out of nowhere, he shot my pa dead!"

Whiskey looked at the sheriff. "My bed can wait."

"All right then." He asked the kid, "You in shape to take us there?"

"Yes, sir."

"Then lead the way."

Whiskey and the sheriff mounted their horses, a pair of paints from the same breeder, and put the spurs to them as they followed the boy to the scene of the crime. Whiskey knew that even though the Lord took the seventh day off to rest, misguided men were always busy at their dirty work.

The hard run to Lake Stanton just a few miles away cooled the sweat on Sheriff Mack Armstrong's face and neck. Sure, there were better reasons to get out of that stifling office, but murder wasn't a new or rare occurrence in Pine Lick. Ever since the lumber boom, folks from every point on the compass had been coming to the growing town in search of the almighty dollar.

Situated just south of the more than thirty million acres of Piney Woods, Pine Lick was a perfect location to take advantage of the country's increasing need for lumber. The railroad hadn't made it there yet, so the cut trees traveled by way of river to the sawmill in town, where they were processed before heading further south along the Angelina River.

With the economic boom came a never-ending stream of bad actors. One of the previous sheriffs had been shot down while having his supper at the Sawdust Saloon. He never had a chance to see who hated him enough to take his life. After him was another short-lived sheriff who went by the name of Bushwhack Bill. Old Bill had had his horse shot out from under him by a gang of bank thieves. They took off with the loot while Bill suffocated under his horse's deadweight.

Then came Mack's father, who had maintained law and order while keeping this side of the grass. He'd retired his tin star to fill his time building the modest family farm. He saw what Pine Lick was itching to become, and decided he'd rather live out the rest of his life in relative peace and hard work while his body could still stand it. The last thing he'd wanted Mack to become was anything even remotely related to law enforcement.

Mack figured he wasn't the first son to go against his father's wishes, and he was damn sure he wouldn't be the last.

"Gettin' close," he said to Whiskey. His deputy slipped his Colt revolver from its holster.

Riding alongside the worried kid, he said, "Fall back behind us and stay there."

The kid did as he was told.

The paints dug into the grass and soil, hugging up the rise to the lip of the lake. Sheriff Armstrong gave the dam a quick look, as he always did, just to make sure there were no signs of leakage. Hastily constructed years ago, the dam's worsening condition kept him up plenty of nights.

For the moment, that wasn't his top concern.

The man lying in the grass beside a canoe with his arms stretched above his head was front and center. A large man wearing worn overalls standing beside the body saw them and waved them over. He was dripping wet and holding his moth-eaten hat in his thick, callused hands.

"I seen what happened and swam across. Thought maybe I could help, but he was already gone."

Armstrong and Whiskey's heads were on a swivel.

"Good man, Bear. Did you see who shot him?"

Michael "Bear" O'Hanlon nodded his head. His wiry black beard brushed against his chest. "My eyes may not be what they once were, but I swear it was that fancy fella who's building the lodge over yonder."

"Cheever?" Whiskey asked.

"Yep. That'd be him."

Armstrong dismounted and checked the man's pulse. He saw the neat hole in his throat and motioned with his head to Whiskey to make sure the boy didn't come any closer.

"You see Cheever shoot this man?"

"I sure enough did. What with all the shouting going back and forth, it was hard not to."

The sheriff nodded at his deputy. "Stay here with the boy and Bear. I'll find Cheever."

"Maybe it'd be wiser if I went with you. He did just shoot a man."

Armstrong's stomach coiled with disgust. "Yes, an unarmed man in a boat with a young boy. Cheever's a gutless coward. I'll be fine."

Buzzards had already started circling in the leaden sky. "Bear, make sure that body isn't touched."

The big man looked up and said, "Can do, Sheriff."

The Arcadia Men's Retreat was just a hundred yards from the scene of the crime. The main house had been completed, the fresh smell of wood from Pine Lick's own sawmills riding whatever warm, moist breeze was about. Half a dozen smaller bungalows were in various states of construction, most of them complete. Being a Sunday, the working crew had the day off. The sheriff had heard that there were plans to build a dozen more, at least if the opening was a success.

Armstrong tied up his horse at the hitching post and pushed his way inside the main house. The heat of anger burned red on the back of his neck. He flexed his fingers and balled them into fists.

"Cheever! Where the hell are you?"

After a slight pause came a reply. "In the study, Sheriff."

Striding through the vestibule, Armstrong opened a door to an empty room. He'd yet to pay a visit to the lodge house and had no idea where the study was located.

"I'm not in the mood for hide-and-seek," he said. "Why don't you just come to me with your hands over your head?"

"If you insist."

Cheever sounded as if Armstrong's presence was an inconvenience. Armstrong pulled his Colt out of its holster, ready to see the wealthy snob catch a bullet if needed.

Tony Cheever had arrived at Pine Lick a year prior, leaving his home in Chicago to, as he'd been overheard saying by many within earshot, tame the south and add whatever level of sophistication was possible. His goal was to build a men's retreat catering exclusively to the wealthy. Hunting, fishing, a chance to get away from the hustle and bustle in the fledgling cities of the Midwest and Northeast, were the advertised main attractions, though anyone with half a brain knew there would be a lot of power-brokering going on over expensive scotch and cigars. Cheever was going to charge astronomical fees to enjoy the very things the citizens of Pine Lick did every day of their lives.

But to do so, he had to make the lake and neighboring land a rare and exclusive commodity. To that end, he'd been buying up what he could and making a general nuisance of himself to anyone who dared trespass. One thing Cheever did not do was share. Not for free, anyway.

Cheever emerged from an open doorway on the left side of the oak-paneled hall. He wore a white three-piece suit, his jet-black hair slicked back on his head, a pencil-thin mustache plastered above upper his lip. His hands were half-raised in clear defiance of Armstrong's order.

"To what do I owe the honor?"

"I'm taking you in, so if you'll oblige, I'd like you to turn around and put your hands at your back."

He arched an eyebrow. "Taking me in. What for? Is it a crime to read a book on a Sunday morning? I admit it wasn't the Bible, but that shouldn't be an offense to anyone but the local preachers around these parts."

Armstrong stepped closer. "I'm happy to do this the hard way."

Cheever did not turn around or put his hands at his back. "I'd like to know what I'm being arrested for, if that's not too much to ask."

Not punching Cheever in the face was just about too much for Armstrong to ask of himself. Instead, he grabbed the man by his upper arms, wheeled him around, and pushed him against the wall.

"You're too smart to play this dumb. I'm taking you in for murdering a man at the lake."

Cheever grunted as Armstrong slapped the cuffs on him, driving his knee into his back, but managed to keep his composure.

"Murdering a man at the lake? That's patently ridiculous."

Armstrong turned him around so they could see eye to eye.

"I have two witnesses. You care to change your statement?"

Cheever's eyes went dead and cold. "I've never murdered anyone in my life. You sure you want to go through with this? My lawyers can make your life very unpleasant."

Armstrong had heard that Cheever had amassed his fortune from being a card sharp who bounced from city to city, adding to his coffers at every stop. Looking at the man's blank, unreadable face, he understood all the stories told about him. His was a poker face that told no tales.

"I'll take my chances," Armstrong said, roughly leading him out of the lodge house.

Armstrong was hot and angry and in need of some kind of release. When Cheever stopped at the doorstep and was about to open his mouth, the sheriff walked past him as if he were cigar smoke hanging in the air. Cheever went down like a sack of flour. With his hands cuffed behind his back, his face smacked off the wooden porch with a satisfying crunch, followed by a spate of yowling that would bring the chickens on home.

For the first time that day, Sheriff Armstrong smiled.